The Rise and Fall of Radiation Canary

Geonn Cannon

Supposed Crimes LLC • Falls Church, Virginia

Published in the United States.
Supposed Crimes LLC
Falls Church, Virginia

First Print Edition

ISBN: 978-1-938108-42-6

www.supposedcrimes.com

This book is typeset in Goudy Old Style,
licensed by Ascender Corporation.

Dedicated to Erin Rinehart, for not letting me forget about it

OVERTURE

(2014)

I think each time is going to be the last time, so I try to appreciate it every time it happens. So I can look back when I'm old and gray and smile and tell my friends at the nursing home, "Oh, yeah, girls. I was famous."

This time it happens at SeaTac. I'm waiting for a plane, trying to read but continuously distracted by people-watching, when I notice someone is watching me. She's trying to be subtle about it, but the way her head suddenly snaps down or how she's trying to whisper to her friend without moving her lips gives her away. I don't mind it, but it's fun to see if they'll get up the nerve to actually say something or if they just want to gawk like I'm a display at the zoo.

Finally she stands up and makes her way over. I have enough time to pretend I'm done reading, to bookmark where I am and lean forward as if I'm looking for a distraction. My elbows are on my knees and I affect a bored attitude to give her confidence to finish her trek. When she finally does reach me, I try to look surprised by her appearance. She smiles bashfully.

"I'm sorry. I'm so sorry."

I hate it when they start with apologies, so I just smile and sit up straighter. "It's all right. Hi."

"Are you Karen Everett?"

"For my whole life."

She laughs nervously and reaches into her bag. She pulls out an actual digipak CD case and hands it over to me. I recognize it by the color; a burnt-orange with a sepia-toned filter. It's the next-to-last album we released as a band. I turn it over and look at the cover with nostalgia that's too keen for being just two years old. *Vagabonds & Ragamuffins* is written across the bottom of the cover in scrolled script, and the four of us are posed above it in our costumes.

Lana is crouching in front of us all, elbow on bent knee so she could hold her chin in the palm of her hand. She's holding a cigarette and wearing a string of pearls, her bangs feathered down over her forehead. I'm standing behind her in a three-piece suit, my blonde hair covered by a bowler cap. I have a thick black mustache that covers my top lip, and my eyes are shadowed to make them stand out.

Vagabonds was our vanity album, I guess. Each song on the album is dedicated to the memory of some unsung hero. On the cover, Lana is supposed to be

Dorothy Parker, and I'm Nikola Tesla. Behind us, Nessa's hair is up in a pompadour and she's wearing a high-necked checkered dress with a carpetbag in her right hand (she's Nellie Bly, intrepid world-traveling reporter). Codie is seated on a stool wearing a purple flight suit with a pair of goggles over her eyes, leaning forward as if into the wind (Harriet Quimby, the first woman pilot whose historic flight across the English channel was overshadowed by the *Titanic*).

I have an ink pen, but the girl offers me a Sharpie before I can retrieve it. "What's your name?"

"Michelle."

"Hi, Michelle." I point with my Sharpie. She looks like a deer caught in the headlights. "Is your friend not a fan?"

"Oh! No, she loves you. It's just that she doesn't have your CD. I mean, it's on her iPod. I have the CD because I listen to it in the car all the time."

"Well, tell her I said hi to her, too."

"You could sign it to both of us. Her name is Erin."

"Okay." I sign in the same spot I usually do on this album cover, just above my head but below the band name. *To Michelle and Erin, However you listen, as long as you listen. Karen Everett.* I hand it back to her with her pen, and she exhales sharply and nods her head in gratitude. "You were my favorite band. It sucks that you had to break up."

I never know what to say to that. Them's the breaks? Tough titty? And breaking up sounds so final. It's not exactly what happened to us, but why worry about semantics? I just nod and shrug like it's one of those things.

"Thank you. And thanks for coming over."

"Yeah. Thank you so much. Whatever you do next, Erin and I will be right there to buy it on release date."

I put my hand in the center of my chest and dip my head in a seated attempt at a bow. "I'm honored."

She goes back to her seat and shows the cover to Erin. The way they lean into each other, and the way they respond to each other, makes me realize that they aren't just traveling companions. Erin sees me watching and waves, and I lift my fingers in response.

I stuff my book into my satchel, sling the strap over my shoulder, and twist around to scan the shops behind me. I don't mind fans, I don't mind autographs, but the post-signing moment is always awkward. Once we've acknowledged each other's presence - fan and be-fanned - there's a tension between the two of us. We're not friends, we're not acquaintances, but there seems to be an expectation of kinship. It's just easier if I pretend to want a slice of pizza before the plane takes off.

I get up and walk away, giving it enough time so the ladies won't think it's in response to Michelle coming over. I'm glad the CD they offered was *V&R*. I'm proud of that one, how it turned out. "Minding Doves," the song I wrote for Tesla, is one of my favorites. I have a soft spot for all our albums, but that one holds a special place. I'm glad that now it'll be special to Michelle and Erin, too.

Seeing the cover again makes me remember the photo shoot. Making sure my hair had the appropriate curls to emulate the famous Tesla portrait, letting Nessa smooth down my mustache so that it sat right, watching as Lana got into her part as Mrs. Parker… I can't help but think back to those days. The end is way too recent for me to be waxing nostalgic already, but ten years is a long time. A third of my life was wholly dedicated to those three other girls. Now that it was over, it seemed like so long ago when I sat on a stone retaining wall and listened to music played by people I'd never seen.

That's how it all started, at least for me. Just a shy girl with a notebook, sitting on a stone wall. I never would have dreamed what was being born when I chose to start sitting there, just like the others had never imagined how important their choice of practice space would play in their fate.

Back then, we were just four girls who liked to play music. Between then and now, though, we were something more.

We were Radiation Canary.

Album One
ACTION AFTER WARNINGS
(2004-2005)

Track One

I could hear them from a block away. Someone else probably would have heard them sooner, someone not so focused how to tie together all the ideas they'd been scribbling in a notebook all week. I had the ideas, they just needed structure. So I was walking with the bare minimum of attention paid to the cracks and varying elevation of the pavement to avoid tripping, my conscious efforts imagining a frame I could hang the words from, when I realized there was music in the air.

It was coming from a little Lego block of a building, a brick and stone square separated into three office spaces. The front of the building had three entrances, each one with a number and letter displayed over the door. It looked like a boulder left over after the area was developed, right next to a retaining wall that held back the sloping forest floor. Evergreens towered over the building and created a nifty little acoustic shell. The music was coming from the space on the far right, 564/C, and nature caught the sounds and projected them back down the street to where I was standing.

I had been walking long enough to justify taking a little rest. The retaining wall was just high enough for me to hop up onto it so that my legs dangled when I sat. I put my messenger bag on the flat stone next to me, took out my notebook, and uncapped my pen with my teeth. I bobbed my head unconsciously to the music as I flipped pages to find an empty space.

The music was hard to categorize. Maybe someone would call it rock, while someone else would classify it as country but I had never really been into labels. If it sounded good, I would listen to it, and whoever was playing had talent. I tapped the heels of my shoes against the wall in time with the beat as I stared at the words I'd written during my lunch break.

Basically I just had a few ideas that sounded good in my head. The challenge was turning the scrawls into an actual, coherent poem. I chewed my bottom lip and began to write.

"It's so comforting to hear 'nine times out of ten'
Nothing goes wrong and everybody wins
But it's never brought to your attention
That someone's bound to be the exception."

I realized I was using the rhythm of the band's music to frame my poem, but

I didn't care. It was like drafting in the wake of a semi. It made things marginally easier, and I was able to write three whole stanzas before I checked my watch and realized how late it had gotten. I jumped off the wall, brushed a hand over the seat of my skirt, and stuffed my things back into my messenger bag. The band was still playing as I hurried off, and their music quickly faded away into the background music of the neighborhood.

At first I didn't plan to take breaks from walking, but when the music was there I couldn't pass up the opportunity. Soon I started planning my walks around the fifteen or twenty minutes I would spend on the retaining wall with pen in hand. The first poem had turned out really well and I felt like I owed it to the music. The band I liked seemed to share the space with other people and at first I used their cars to differentiate. After two or three days that wasn't necessary. Whoever the band was, they didn't sound like any of the other bands that used the same rehearsal space.

It felt vaguely like something out of a myth. The songwriter wandering through the woods hears music coming from a stone in the ground and has to write words to go along with it. It was my muse, and I couldn't stay away now that I'd found a way to organize and vocalize my thoughts. I didn't know what I would do when and if the band moved somewhere new, or if they broke up to go their separate ways.

One random day about five months after I discovered the space, I was deep into a new poem when the music suddenly stopped. The silence was startling, like sudden deafness, since there'd been nothing to signal the song was nearing an end. I jumped as if I had been jolted from a nightmare and looked around. Now that the spell had been broken the neighborhood seemed utterly still and quiet. I waited to see if they were going to start again, but silence dragged on. I tapped my pen against the page of my journal, but the momentum was lost. I had already been there for twelve minutes, so I began packing my things to go back home.

I had just hopped off the wall and capped my pen when the door to 564/C opened. The girl who came out was around my age, college-age or so, and looked nothing like I had pictured from the music. She was Indian, her hair pulled tight against her head and pinned back in a ponytail of wild waves. Her T-shirt was pale-purple and tucked into a pair of bleached jeans. She stopped and leaned against the wall next to the door, patting her pockets as she finally noticed me staring at her.

She took me in for a moment and then lifted her chin as a greeting. She withdrew a pack of cigarettes and reached into her back pocket. "Hey."

I nodded. "Hi."

She grimaced, hand coming back empty from her pocket. "You would happen to have a light, would you?"

I actually did. A girl I once had a crush on smoked and wore skirts without pockets. I started carrying the lighter and figured out how to light other people's cigarettes as a way to lean close to her. We stopped hanging out after I made a clumsy pass at her, but I kept it in my pocket like a totem. I rummaged through my bag, wondering what confluence of events led me to carry around Kim's lighter all this time just so I would have it for this stranger. Kismet or karma or both had teamed up for this moment, I was sure. I walked over, holding the little silver lighter up like a trophy before I tossed it to her. "I don't know if it has any fuel or whatever. It's kind of old."

She caught it one handed and flicked it open with a deft move I was sure had been born from long practice. A little flame popped up, and I felt pleased to help her out. She lit her cigarette, then offered the Bic back to me.

"No, keep it. It was for someone I don't talk to anymore."

"Thanks. Codie Renton."

"Uh, Karen Everett. Nice to meet you."

She slipped the lighter into her pocket with one hand and crossed her fingers around the cigarette as she took a drag. Her bottom lip stuck out slightly as she exhaled a flume. I wasn't sure of the etiquette. Should I just walk away, or was I under some social obligation to hang out with her for a few minutes? It wasn't like we were at a party, but I would feel awkward if I had to walk away with her staring at me.

She looked at me and then broke the silence. "You can hear us play, right? Sitting out here?"

"A little, yeah."

"What do you think?"

I shrugged. "It's good."

She nodded as if the question had been a test that I passed. Her cheeks hollowed as she inhaled and then she blew smoke out her nose.

"We're Little Cat Feet."

"Huh?"

She gestured at the door with her cigarette. "The band."

"Oh. That's a..."

She smiled. "It's amateurish."

I wasn't sure how, but I wasn't going to ask for clarification. I didn't like the name, but I wasn't about to badmouth it. The Beatles sounded like a stupid name out of context.

"It's a nice name."

"It's what we got," she said.

"Do you sing?" She had a beautifully lilting accent, the kind that always gets mocked by turning it into Apu from *The Simpsons*, but I could listen to her all day. She was shaking her head.

"Drummer."

"Oh." What's the response to that? "Cool."

She laughed and exhaled through pursed lips. "Yeah. It's cool." She finally looked at me. For half a second, I thought her eyes were purple, but the blue was just reflecting the color of her blouse. It was a crazy effect, and I was so mesmerized that it took me a second to realize she'd asked me if I played anything.

"Ah, I... yes. Sort of. I play, but not..." I gestured vaguely with my hand. "I play violin and cello. Not like a rock band musician or anything."

"You can have strings in a rock band."

I shrugged. "I'm not really a musician. I just take the lessons because the music clears my head so I can write."

"You're a writer?"

My answer was interrupted by the door opening again. A brunette stepped outside and stood between us like she'd simply manifested out of thin air. Her appearance was so sudden that I was stricken dumb. She was absolutely gorgeous. Thick black hair and green eyes, and thin lips that were slightly parted as she stopped herself from speaking as she tried to figure out who I was. Her white dress shirt was unbuttoned over a tank top. Her eyes locked with mine and, for a half-second, I felt brutally judged. Even worse, I figured I was probably found wanting. I resisted the urge to back away as she turned to face Codie.

"We're ordering pizza. Do you eat meat this week?"

"Yep, sure." She scuffed her foot on the pavement.

The new arrival looked at me again. "And who are you?"

"Karen." After a pause, I added, "Everett."

Codie said, "She's my parole officer. She showed up to make sure I was behaving myself."

The newcomer rolled her eyes. "Are you one of the neighbors? If we're being too loud, we apologize, but we've talked to that building manager five times already--"

I shook my head quickly. "No! No, I'm not complaining, I just..." I tried to point at Codie while simultaneously gesturing at the retaining wall. "I was just walking. And resting. Then listening. And she needed a lighter, and I had one, but I gave it... to her. I'll go."

"No, you don't have to." She turned back toward Codie, ignoring me again now that my existence had been explained. "Pepperoni and sausage okay with you?"

"Yep."

The brunette nodded and went back inside. The door swung shut before Codie said, "That's Lana, our lead singer. Or will be, if we ever come up with any lyrics."

I thought about my journal but pushed it out of my mind. "Well, at least you guys sound great."

"Sometimes that's enough. Sometimes it isn't." She took another drag and dropped the cigarette, using her heel to snuff it. "Better go back in. Thanks for the lighter. Maybe we'll see you around."

"Sure."

She went back inside, and I walked back to my satchel. I shoved my things back inside and slung it over my shoulder. As I walked off, a guitar began to play with a drum beat backing it up. I decided I was going to stay away from the wall for a couple of days, just until I got over the self-consciousness of meeting the people on whom I was eavesdropping. I hadn't just been trying to be nice, though. The music really was fantastic.

Lana Kent lay on her back and stared at the water-stained acoustic tile of the ceiling. Her arms were stretched out to either side, her palms flat on the carpet. Nessa was idly playing the keyboard with her left hand, holding a half-eaten slice of pizza with the right. Codie had left an hour earlier, calling it a night after paying her part of dinner and taking the slices to go. Nessa suggested practicing without her, but Lana didn't feel like it. They needed songs, not just music. Any fifth grader could play music; a band needed songs.

Finally she decided inspiration wasn't going to hit. She sat up and crossed her legs in front of her, resting her elbows on her knees. "You should go home."

Nessa stopped playing. "You sure?"

"Yeah. We're not getting anything done." She tried to disguise the irritation she felt with levity. "Go home, get some rest. Do you have to work tomorrow?"

Nessa nodded and finish her pizza. "I should be off around six, though." She unplugged her keyboard to put it in the small closet in the hallway. They shared the space with three other bands, so rather than lugging everything back and forth to every rehearsal they locked their instruments so they would be out of the way of whoever used the space next. Her guitar went home with her, however. She loved the Telecaster, and she hated to let it out of her sight.

"Codie's got a late shift. We'd only be able to get an hour in, if that. Plus I have a dance class Friday morning and I want to get to bed early." She pushed her hand through her hair, her frustration coming back up. "So we'll meet up again on Friday afternoon."

"Friday works."

Lana nodded and looked at her guitar. She didn't know why she bothered to schedule so many rehearsals. All they did was play melodies that went nowhere. It would be different if she could actually write a song to go with the music, but she always ended up with nursery rhyme nonsense. She had a cat, and it was fat, how about that, fat cat rat-a-tat. Nessa had put away her keyboard, and Lana stood up to put her guitar in the cabinet where they kept their instruments between sessions.

Nessa tossed the remnants of their pizza in the trash. "We sounded good today."

"Yeah."

Nessa started to say something else, but then she let it drop. She and Codie both knew Lana's moods well enough that they avoided pushing when she was in a dour state.

Lana felt guilty, so she met Nessa halfway. "You both sounded amazing."

"We know," Nessa said. She winked and playfully punched Lana's arm. "Okay, I'm out. See you Friday."

Lana waved goodbye. She threw away the paper plates and napkins from their pizza and got the wires out of the way so no one would trip over them. The other bands rarely bothered to leave the rehearsal space as neat as they found it, but Lana couldn't stop herself. She locked the door behind her and walked to the car. She remembered the girl she'd seen with Codie that afternoon, the one who apparently listened to them play. Their first fan. She smiled at the thought and looked toward the retaining wall. The girl - Carol? - wasn't there, but some paper was being picked up by the breeze.

She wasn't the sort who had to pick up every piece of litter she saw, but every now and then she felt a compulsion. She changed direction and, when she got closer, she saw that the paper was still in a notebook. The wind had opened the cover so it lay flat, and the pages were lightly flapping like flags.

It wasn't a cheap notebook, either. The cover was fake leather, and it could be held closed with a strip of rawhide long enough to wrap twice around the book's width. She opened it and looked at the first page to see if there was any kind of contact information, but whoever it belonged to hadn't written anything in the obvious places. She thumbed through and then began to notice that the writing was arranged in stanzas. She slowed down and leaned against the wall to focus on one page at random.

"I don't have any of the answers you want
Only the same questions no one asks
We all put on a decent front
But we're wearing the same masks."

Lana's heart was racing as she read on, occasionally looking up to see if anyone had appeared. It had to belong to the blonde girl she'd seen Codie talking to during the smoke break. Maybe Codie knew how to get in contact with her. What had she said her name was? Not Carol. Karen something. Lana held the book open and read it as she walked to her car. She could hear the music wrapping around the words in her head and her breath quickened. After months of trying to tackle the problem of lyrics, it seemed as if the answer had just dropped into her lap.

Track Two

I was in my attic room sawing away at the violin when I realized what had happened. I stopped mid-chord and looked at my satchel, willing myself to be wrong before I even began my futile search. I dropped to my knees and pulled the bag to me. I yanked the top open and dug through the junk on the surface before I gave up and just dumped everything on the floor. I ran my hands through the stuff and cried out in frustration when it became undeniable.

My journal was gone.

I had a vivid memory of emptying it on the retaining wall when I got out the lighter, but I'd been in such a hurry to stuff everything back in that I'd forgotten it. There was a narrow little ditch between the wall and the ground; that had to be where it was. I felt a sudden panic about losing all my poems from the past year. All the times the words had fallen right, all the phrases and beautiful couplets that I'd stressed out over, gone forever. Maybe someone had stolen it, or maybe there was a sprinkler system that went off and drenched it. All my beautiful words were dripping down a page that had been turned into mulch.

I refused to cry, and I refused to give up until I had a destroyed journal to mourn over. I shoved my shoes back into my sneakers and flew out of my room, skimming down the stairs toward the front door. I collided with Ted at the landing, startling us both. He grabbed my shoulders to keep me from falling backward and he smiled in surprise.

"Easy, kid. It's just stew."

I blinked at him in complete confusion. "What?"

He nodded at the kitchen. "Dinner. Soup's on."

I shook my head. "No, I can't. I have to go. There's something I have to do."

His smile faded slightly. "You know how your Dad feels about family dinners."

My cheeks were red, but not from any emotion I could really name. Ted calling us family was a guilt trip. Dad had gone through a lot of hell before he admitted why he and Mom got divorced. Even though he was with Ted now, it seemed like any small fracture could send him back to therapy or, God forbid, that camp where he tried to "fix" himself. I squirmed away from Ted with an apologetic look.

"I'm sorry. I have to go. It'll only take me a few minutes and then I'll be back."

"Let her go."

I looked past Ted and saw Dad standing at the kitchen door. His glasses were fogged around the edges by steam from cooking, and he was wiping his hands on a towel. I'm no Amazon, but I've been taller than him since the seventh grade. Yet somehow he could still make me feel like I was six-years-old with just a glance. He smiled reassuringly.

"It's important, right? You wouldn't risk breaking your neck like that unless it was dire."

"I wouldn't. It is. I swear, I'll be right back, but I have to go now."

"Go on," he said. "The food will still be here when you get back. And I do like family dinners... but part of being a family is knowing when something else comes first."

"Thank you, Dad." I gave Ted a look that I hoped conveyed my appreciation for what he'd tried to do, but I didn't have time to express it completely. We would talk about it later, I was sure, but for now I could only think about my journal being tossed out by some well-meaning groundskeeper. I stepped around him and left the house.

I covered the half mile between our house and the offices in a dead run. It had been five hours. So many horrible things could happen in five hours. I was panting by the time I finally arrived. It was dark enough that the tall security lights at the corner were on, bathing the entire area with an unreal white glow. A pair of stray cats, startled by my sudden appearance, darted for cover behind a garage.

My shadow clung to my feet as I jumped up onto the retaining wall like a tightrope walker and walked to the spot where I usually sat.

Nothing. I even ran my hand through the ditch, but I only got dirt under my fingernails for the trouble. I scanned the pavement, looked up into the trees, then finally dropped onto my ass on the stone. Gone. I don't even know how many finished poems were in the journal, let alone how many snippets and ideas I'd just lost. It was like losing a part of my soul, just gone into the ether. Vanished without a trace. I put my face in my hands, not caring about the dirt on the fingers of one hand until I realized Dad would have a fit about it. But for the moment, I could only mourn the loss of my work.

When I got home, I was in tears. Dad gave me a hug and asked what was wrong, but I couldn't even articulate the enormity of what I had lost. He stroked my hair and told me that everything happened for a reason, and I nodded to placate him. At the moment the thought of starting over from scratch was so daunting that all I wanted to do was curl into a ball and weep.

Lana spent the night in her living room with the book open in front of her, a guitar balanced on her folded legs. She leaned forward to see the handwritten words and strummed music that seemed to go along with them. She sang quietly until she found the right tempo for a song, nodding her head as she found something that fit. "The points of the crescent moon are wickedly sharp tonight," she sang softly, "and without you here the stars just don't look right."

Someone pounded on the wall but she just muttered, "That's not the right rhythm..." and kept on. She had a composition book open on the floor, unwilling to mark the stranger's notebook but also reluctant to lose the progress she had made. She copied lyrics and annotated them with chords, tapping her fingers on the page to get an idea of how Codie might play it.

The knocking moved from the wall to the door and she finally had to acknowledge it. She reluctantly put away her guitar and went to shower, humming the music as she shampooed her hair. By the time she finally went to bed she was smiling, certain that this was a milestone in the band's progression. She stared at the ceiling for a long time before she fell asleep, and she knew what she had to do.

She had to teach a dance class at noon, but then her afternoon was completely free. She drove to the rehearsal space and parked facing the street. The notebook was sitting on her passenger seat and she kept reaching over to touch it like a holy relic. The words in the book had haunted her all day. Memorization hadn't been her intention, but now she could hear the words clearly without even trying. She composed in her head, thinking of how Codie and Nessa would make the songs come to life.

Lana didn't know what she planned to say or do when the blonde returned, but she had to get permission to use the poems. She would do whatever it took to get permission, and all she could do was hope the price wouldn't be too high.

It was a dead-end road, so she figured Karen Whatever could only arrive from one direction. There was a chance she might come barreling through the forest, but that seemed unlikely. She slid down in her seat and prepared herself for a long wait.

After an hour, she was ready to go inside and play a little just to get her fingers limber. She was bored, frustrated, and hot. The longer she waited, the less likely it seemed this stranger would let them do anything with her writing. Why would she? It was ludicrous. Of course, she had been listening in to their band practice. Maybe she liked them enough that she would be willing to be a part of their work.

She was so distracted by her own self-defeating thoughts that the girl was halfway across the parking lot before Lana realized it was her. There was a defeated slump to her posture, her gaze focused on the ground in front of her as she shuffled along with her hands in her pockets. Her long hair hung down from underneath a pink cap. The strap of her messenger bag hung across her chest, the bag itself banging against the side of her oversized jacket.

Lana opened the door when Karen was directly in front of the car, but the other girl didn't look up.

"Hey. Karen, right?"

She slowed and lifted her head, suspicious. The cap was pulled down to her eyebrows, making her look a little like a mushroom. She relaxed when recognition dawned.

"Oh, hey. You're Lana, right?"

"Right. Hang on." She leaned into the car and grabbed the book. She straightened and held it up. "Is this yours?"

Someone might have thought it was a winning lottery ticket the way Karen's face lit up. It was a complete and utter change, her eyes widening as her back straightened.

"You found it!"

Lana smiled proudly. "Yeah, it was lying over there." She gestured with her chin. "I looked for an address or something, but there wasn't anything in it."

"Yeah. Stupid of me." She thumbed through the book as if confirming it was real, and then looked up with a palatable look of relief. "Thank you. Thank you so much."

"No problem. I read some of the poems, too. I hope you don't mind. I think they were really good."

"Oh." She looked back down and smoothed her hand over the pages. "That's fine."

Lana cleared her throat and looked at the front door. "Listen, uh. We're not having practice today. Want to go grab something to eat? I have an idea I want to run by you."

Karen didn't look up from her perusal of the book, as if she was trying to commit it all to memory in case she lost it again. "You want to run something by me? Why? You don't even know me."

"Maybe we could change that. C'mon, I'm buying."

That was the tipping point. Karen shrugged and finally closed the book. She held it against her chest with one arm as she walked to the passenger door. Lana had to lean in and reach across the seats to open the door for her, since that side didn't work right, and then tossed the garbage from the front seat into the back.

When Karen was finally settled in, Lana pulled out onto the main road. Karen smoothed the tails of her coat over her thighs and said, "I guess we're sort of even. I listened in on your practice, and you looked at my poems."

Lana smiled. "Yeah, guess so. That's kind of what I wanted to talk to you about. Maybe we could find a way to make it work out for both of us."

"What do you mean?"

"Have you ever thought about putting your poems to music?"

Track Three

Codie Renton was reformed. Ish.

She kept telling herself that as she walked through the parking lot, past the rows and rows of shining Detroit-born temptation. She was a boring citizen now, on the straight and narrow, but she'd spent the ages between fifteen and twenty-three being exceedingly good at one thing, and she couldn't just turn off the skill. She fought the itch in every grocery store parking lot, passing each and every prime target with a look of longing most people reserved for potential sexual partners. She scoped the parking lot and clocked the security cameras while simultaneously looking for witnesses.

Totally clear. It was a crying shame.

She walked past, moving a little faster than before just to put the car out of sight. Once she would have already been behind the wheel, her groceries either in the backseat or left behind. Within two minutes she would be on the road, and twenty minutes after that she would be safely at the garage. Alonso would do his magic and by dawn the car would basically no longer exist. She got into her own car and left the parking lot while her better angels were still winning the battle.

The chop shop was in her past. She was a legit grease monkey now, and while there was always the urge to take an engine apart instead of just troubleshooting it, she'd been clean for almost six months now. Occasionally she would break into a car and drive through a neighborhood, then return it to where she'd found it with a full tank of gas. It was like a nicotine patch; giving her the thrill without the actual crime. Well, petty crime. Still, it kept her out of trouble, which is what Lana wanted. Even if she was caught in the act, it was hard for the owner to get too upset when they saw the tank was full. They were usually more confused than anything.

Codie put away the groceries when she got home and saw she had a voicemail from Lana. She put it on speaker and left the phone on the bathroom counter as she undressed for a shower. She only had forty minutes before she had to get to work. Even if her boss let her be late because she worked faster than anyone else, she didn't like to set a precedent. She was being a good girl.

"Hey. I talked to a girl today about maybe having her write songs for us. She has some really good ones in a journal that I literally almost tripped over. Could be a really good thing for the band. What do you think? Call me back."

They needed songs, Codie thought. They sounded fine, but no one bought instrumental albums. They could do soundtracks for movies, but that wasn't the kind of band they were. And it wasn't fair to Lana. She was more than just a guitarist; the girl could sing. She just needed someone to put words in her mouth. And none of them liked the idea of being a band who farmed out their songwriting to rhyme mills. Pay a fee, get a verse. It would be like paying someone else to design your tattoo. It was done, but the result said nothing about you.

Having a songwriting machine in the band was exactly what they needed. She finished her shower and sent Lana a text.

"Sounds good. Bring her to practice tomorrow. Let's hear what she sounds like."

Nessa was skeptical about adding a fourth person to the group. She thought they were doing just fine on their own, and the lyrics would come when they were ready. Right now they had a few good tracks that she called soundscapes. She and Lana had a really good rhythm, and Codie brought it all together with a drum that lurked like a heartbeat. Steady, solid, strong. Adding someone else could throw off the whole mix. And she only played the cello and violin? What kind of classical crap was that?

"Lots of bands have strings," Codie told her as they set up on Friday. They were the first ones to arrive, and that meant they were in charge of unlocking the closet and getting everything ready for practice.

"Like who? The Corrs? I don't want to be the damn Corrs."

Codie grinned. "Just give her a chance, okay? Adding a fourth could be just what we need. And lyrics... we do need lyrics."

Nessa sighed. "The lyrics will come when we're ready."

"Maybe we're ready now. You keep saying it'll come, it'll come. But now that opportunity is knocking, you want to just keep waiting?"

Nessa conceded she had a point and, rather than admitting defeat, gestured at the marks on the walls. "Who was in here this morning?"

"Dowager."

"I think their lead singer spits crap onto the walls."

Codie nodded. "You know Liam? Their drummer? He told me that their lead singer is trying to spit fire. He drinks this shitty homebrew moonshine and then tries to light it."

"Asshole. This isn't just his rehearsal space. He could have burnt the whole place down."

"Who could've burned what place down?" Lana came in and shrugged out of her jacket. Her hair was done up in a ponytail. She was wearing two tank tops and a pair of low-riding jeans that showed off her stomach.

"The lead singer of Dowager," Nessa said. "He wants to be a fire-breathing dragon."

Lana rolled her eyes. "I'll talk to him." She stopped and turned to the girl who had followed her into the space and stopped at the threshold. Nessa had barely even noticed her. She was pink-faced and blonde, a little baby fat on her jaw keeping her from making the leap from cute to sexy. The sweater that obscured the shape of her body wasn't doing her any favors, either. She had a large instrument case in each hand, her shoulders hunched from holding them both.

"Karen, meet Little Cat Feet. Codie, I think you met her yesterday, but Nessa... this is Karen Everett. Karen, this is Codie Renton, and Vanessa Grace. You can call her Nessa."

Nessa smiled. "Hey."

Karen nodded shyly, and Lana nodded for her to set up in front of the drums. Karen put down the smaller case, then opened the other one to reveal a gorgeous cello. Nessa was impressed. A cello was a beautiful instrument with an equally beautiful sound, but it didn't belong in Little Cat Feet, or whatever they were going to end up calling themselves. It wasn't their sound.

"I thought I'd sort of, um, try out. See how you guys felt about how I play before we commit to anything."

Nessa nodded and went behind her keyboard. She sat on her stool and felt like a judge waiting to pass down a verdict. "So what are you going to play? Bach? A little Rachmaninoff?"

Karen hesitated. "That... wouldn't really fit your sound would it? I mean, I've heard a little bit of what you play and I came prepared to fit in. I suppose I could give you some Bach..."

Lana said, "No. Play what you prepared."

Karen looked at Nessa and Codie. "Do you know 'Lose Yourself'?"

Codie leaned back. "The Eminem song? Uh, yeah." She glanced at Nessa, who nodded.

"Okay. Nessa... you start with the intro and I'll join in."

Nessa took a moment to remember how the song sounded, then began to play a reasonable facsimile. It was good enough for an impromptu session, and as close as she could get to the real thing without sheet music. Karen tapped her heel against the edge of her seat, set the bow against the strings. She nodded her head along and then began to play. Nessa was so surprised that she almost stopped playing, but she kept up with only a minor fumble.

Codie picked up her sticks and gave them a beat, and Lana smiled as she strapped on her guitar. Nessa and Karen seemed to be creating a wave in the middle of the studio, and Lana gave it form with her guitar.

Karen sawed at the cello, producing a throaty bellow from the strings that made the song sound more like a growl. She nodded to Lana, who took over the bass while Karen paused just long enough to switch from a full-throated moan to a plaintive wail. Codie's drum pounded, and this time it was Nessa's melody that tied them all together. She realized she was smiling, moving her shoulders to the music, and Codie looked like she was having more fun than she'd had in ages. Lana only knew the words to the chorus so she began to sing it at the appropriate time.

Nessa knew that she would have applauded if her hands had been free. She was grinning like a fool as Lana sang. This was it. Their sound, their band, their music. This was what they had spent so many hours trying to achieve.

The song trailed to an end, and Karen tucked her hair behind her ears. "I could play you something a little more standard on the violin, if you–"

"You don't have to do that," Nessa said. Everyone looked at her, and she shrugged. "I was the only one who wasn't sure about you, but I don't need to hear anything else." She looked at Lana, who nodded at Codie. Nessa grinned. "Welcome to the band."

Lana let her guitar hang from the shoulder strap. "We usually practice between four and seven, or whenever our schedules allow. Sometimes just two of us show up, but usually we skip it if the whole band can't get together. Any questions?"

Karen looked anxious about whatever she was thinking, but she spoke up anyway. "Are you guys in love with the name Little Cat Feet?"

Codie laughed out loud and lay her drumsticks down. "Why?"

"We're a band of women, and if we have a cat reference in our name, the critics won't have to be geniuses to come up with something rude and crude."

Nessa chuckled. "Well, do you have any other suggestions?"

Karen looked bashful. "I've come up with a few... but I do have a favorite."

Track Four

"You're late, kid."

"I know," Lana said. She was almost ready, though. She'd been stunned when Lockstep's drummer had started tapping on the window, pointing at his watch that it was their turn for the rehearsal space. It not only meant they'd completely lost track of the time, it also meant she was minutes away from being late for her shift at her real job. Teaching dance class was great, but this job actually paid her bills. Despite her distraction, she had made it in the nick of time and was dressed, she was just cutting it closer than she liked. Not to mention she had to put up with everyone else's glee that Miss Punctual was actually running late.

They had spent most of the session just playing, but then Karen suggested throwing in some lyrics. Lana hadn't been prepared and ended up off-key more often than not, but there was a frisson of energy that came with actually filling in the blanks. Despite the rough edges, for the first time she felt like they were a band.

She swung open her locker door as she tied her hair back, using the mirror inside the door to make sure the collar of her uniform blouse was straight. Her badge caught the light and she licked her thumb to polish off some smudge of unknown origin. Her makeup was minimally applied, the best she could do quickly, but it would suffice. She remembered her mirrored sunglasses at the last second and slipped them on just as the last song came to an end out in the main room.

Finally ready, she shut her locker door and brushed past someone else who made a pointed reference to her watch. "I know, I know," Lana muttered, ducking her head to put on her peaked cap. She pulled the brim low over her eyes as she climbed the two steps that led behind the curtain to her mark.

"And now, the star of tonight's program... Officerrrrrrr Jill!"

Lana put her hands together and slipped them into the break in the curtain. She swept up and out, throwing the curtains open just wide enough for her to pass through. The crowd whistled and applauded as she strutted down the long, wide catwalk toward what she and the other dancers jokingly called the workspace. She ran her hand down her uniform tie and stroked it from neck to tip, touching her tongue to the corner of her mouth as she reached the pole. She hooked her elbow around it and spun herself around, tilting out toward the audience as she tugged on the tie's knot.

She pulled the blouse open while her back was to the audience, and then used the pole as a fulcrum to spin back around. Her bra was shockingly white against her tan chest, and the hooting grew louder. She plucked off her cap and tossed it toward the curtains as she began undulating to draw attention to her hips.

When Lana was eleven, her best friend Minnie said she'd overheard her mother say that their dance teacher, Miss Deakins, was a former stripper and showgirl. Lana hadn't believed it, even though she didn't really know what those words meant at the time, but soon discovered that there was a whole other world of dance that paid much better than the ballet. The same people who cursed the idea of their "hard-earned tax dollars" supporting the arts would blow forty-five bucks on a lap dance. Once Lana was eighteen, she had no doubt where she was going to moonlight to earn extra cash. Now she was the dance teacher her students whispered about.

The dance was rote, and she dutifully removed an article of clothing for each section of the song. Blouse off. Tie still around her neck. Sway and swing her hips. Chorus. Bend forward, head down, release hair. Shake head to make it wild. Strut. She scanned the crowd and noticed that there was a woman seated near the stage. Lana began playing to her, much to the woman's surprise. The woman didn't seem uncomfortable, so when it came time to take off her boot, she extended her foot toward her unexpected partner.

The woman stood up and pulled the boot off. Lana wiggled her toes and the woman brushed her finger over the arch. Lana shuddered and closed her eyes, then extended her other foot. The procedure was repeated and, once Lana was barefoot, she retrieved her boots and blew her new friend a kiss.

She thought back to the band practice. In between bursts of music, they discussed the idea of names. "I want something that can be iconic," Lana said. "I don't really care what it is as long as we have a logo. The Rolling Stones' tongue, Grateful Dead's dancing bears, even Wu-Tang Clan has that W thing. I want some kind of animal."

Codie said, "I don't want anything to do with dogs. Same reason Karen said cats wouldn't work. Four women calling themselves dogs would be way too tempting. Someone somewhere is going to make fun of us, and I don't want to make it easy."

Lana agreed. They had gone through the list of band names Karen had come up with, and Lana had a handful of her own choices. Karen refused to reveal her favorite until they'd gone through the list objectively.

Back in the present Lana bent forward at the waist to push her pants down her legs. She wore a thin g-string underneath and stayed down a moment longer than necessary, shaking her ass at the audience before she straightened. She took off her sunglasses, a pair of five-buck cheapos that she got six at a time, and tossed them to her lady in the audience.

She'd asked Karen what her favorite name was, and Karen had almost sheepishly admitted it was Radiation Canary.

Codie shook her head. "I don't even get that one. What does it mean?"

Karen shrugged. "They used to send canaries into coal mines to see if the air was safe. Well, this is for... like nuclear attacks. You go into the bomb shelter and send up a canary to see if the air is too poisonous."

Nessa grinned. "That logo could be real simple... just a canary silhouette inside a circle."

"But green," Lana said. "It would have to be very bright green, like it's been irradiated."

Karen had grinned and nodded, and then they began playing a song they were currently calling Untitled Number Four.

Lana reached back and unhooked her bra, letting it fall down her arms to bare her breasts before tossing it to the back of the stage. The lady she'd been playing to was perched on the edge of her seat, so Lana walked over and crouched down, turning to one side to display her hip. She smiled seductively over her shoulder, knowing the rest of the crowd had a lovely view of her ass when the girl tucked the bill under the waistband of her underwear. She straightened and spun, and made sure everyone got a good look at her tits and ass, toying with the elastic of the only clothes she still had on.

By the time the song ended, her skin was shining with sweat. Her underwear bristled with bills, and she scooped up a few more that had been draped over the chain that protected the dancers from toppling into the audience into anyone who would be all-too-eager to catch them. She slipped back through the curtain as the DJ asked for another round of applause, and she was gratified by how much louder it seemed than her first round.

"Guess they liked what they saw," she said to the dancer waiting to go on next.

"You're a hard act to follow, baby girl."

Lana's clothes had been gathered by someone else and placed on a chair. She gathered them up and went to her locker, stuffing the discarded clothes inside before she began counting her money. Most of it had been folded length-wise, and it stood out on either side of her underwear like some bizarre fringe. *Maybe in Paris, but it'll never fly in the Bible Belt,* she thought.

She found the ten dollar bill from her female admirer and discovered a note written in lipstick across the back. "Private dance? Tammy." A phone number was written under the signature, smudged from an attempt to write quickly but still legible.

Lana put the rest of the money in an envelope she kept at the back of her locker, but she kept Tammy's ten in her hand. She toweled off and looked at the clock. She had eighty-five minutes until she had to dance again - she would go with All American Girl, probably - but she could kill time by playing waitress. It would plump up her paycheck, and it would give her a chance to talk to Tammy a little more.

She put on a short black skirt and a black vest that opened in such a wide V that it really only covered her nipples. She toweled off her sweat and pinched her nipples to make sure they were nice and perky before she headed out of the dressing area. Shaun was behind the bar, and she smiled when she saw him. Six foot tall, former Army, biceps she could crack bricks on, and the gayest man she had ever met. He handed her a tray and an order slip.

"Nice moves up there."

"It's always good to get an objective viewpoint."

Shaun winked as she headed out onto the floor. Her first stop was, of course, Tammy's table. Tammy's eyes widened when she recognized her server, and Lana winked at her. "Hey, sweetie. What can I get for you?"

"Oh..." The sigh said it all. She settled back against her chair and let her eyes dip into Lana's cleavage. "I can think of a couple things."

Lana smiled. All in a day's work.

Track Five

Sometimes I repeat words until they lose their meaning and become an odd jumble of consonants and vowels. Simple words like 'swim' or 'racquet' can be rendered meaningless with enough repetition. Sometimes it helps with rhymes, deconstructing it into the bare components so that sound-alike words are easy to find. The night after my surprise audition, after I actually played my cello with the women I'd been listening to for so long, I lay under the blankets and listened to Dad and Ted watch TV downstairs and kept repeating the same two words in my head.

Radiation Canary... Radiation Canary.

No matter how many times I said it, the phrase seemed epic. I kept hearing Lana's voice, speaking my words while Codie and Nessa tied it together. And for once my playing seemed like more than just practice. I was doing more than just following staves. I was making music.

My phone rang, and I glanced at the display. Penny. I'd been so excited about what happened that afternoon I'd completely forgotten to call and cancel our date. I answered and winced, the apology ready, but she started talking first.

"I'm so sorry. Have you been waiting long? I'm fifteen minutes away, I swear."

"Uh." I pushed myself up on my elbow and smoothed my hand over the sheets. "No, I'm at home. I kind of forgot we had a date tonight."

There was a pause and I could tell I'd thrown her for a loop. She felt like she should be annoyed, but she had no ground to stand on. "Oh. Well, I guess that's good then." She laughed awkwardly. "Do you still want to get together? We could hang out, have some dinner..."

"I sort of already ate. And I'm kind of beat. I had a big day."

"Oh."

I waited for her to elaborate, but the dead air stretched on. "I think I joined a band today."

"A what?"

"A band. I rehearsed with a band today. We sound pretty good."

Penny said, "Oh. But, for... what? I mean, what do you do? You can't sing."

I rolled my eyes. *Thanks, dear.* "I play the cello and the violin."

"Oh, so not a *band*. I thought you meant like Queens of the Stone Age or something. So it's like a classical quartet or something?"

I closed my eyes. How could I love Penny when she always gave me a headache? "No, it's a real band. I write the lyrics for them, too. We played a couple songs and it sounded pretty good. Nessa, our piano player, thinks she knows a few people who will let us play on open mic nights once we're good enough to, you know, play in public. What do you think?"

"Sounds good." I could tell from her tone that she had lost interest. "So listen, I'll just head on home then? I'll talk to you tomorrow if you're not too busy with your 'band.'"

I hated that I could hear the air quotes. "Sure."

"Okay. See you then. Love ya."

"Love~" I looked at the phone and saw she'd hung up. "~you, too."

I closed the phone and put it on the night table. My book, miraculously rescued, was lying next to the lamp. I flipped through it and found one of the poems Lana had brought to life as a song that afternoon. I smiled as I remembered her sultry sigh of a voice inhabiting what I'd written, giving it form in a way I never would have believed. I turned the pages until I found a blank one. My pen was on the desk next to the blank composition book I'd bought that morning as a replacement, smiling since I didn't need it now. I uncapped the pen and began writing.

"I think you mean it when you end calls with 'love'
But lying in bed alone and staring at my clock
I don't think it matters to you when push comes to shove
Now I think you say it just to hear yourself talk."

I reread the verse and realized I was imagining it in Lana's voice. I wanted to my cello and build a foundation tune for it, but I didn't want to disturb Dad and Ted. I hummed a little under my breath, but then stopped before I could get very far. Already I needed the others or it didn't sound right. I moved my pen to the top of the page and hesitated before writing anything.

I didn't like leaving our songs untitled, but I had never bothered to give titles to two-thirds of my poems. I always figured that would come later. Now that later had arrived, I was a little stumped. I thought about the band name and decided that maybe our songs should be themed, at least on the first album. Radiation, nuclear bombs... I looked at the lyrics again and the title occurred to me. I wrote it across the top of the page in large letters, drawing over the lines to make them thicker.

DUCK AND COVER.

I smiled. I had just started the first song officially written for Radiation Canary.

Dad gave me an odd look when I asked if I could possibly rearrange my schedule at his hardware store around band practice, but he was willing. I think he was just happy to see me enjoying something again. I'd been in a rut for a long time waiting for something to happen. Now I was coming home happy, I was laughing again... I even enjoyed helping the customers at what I was now considering my day job.

We tried to meet at least three times a week, playing at night and on the weekends. Practice was more than just figuring out how to play together, it was figuring out how we fit together as a group. Lana had two jobs. She taught dance to girls between five and twelve, and she had another nighttime job that she was secretive about to the point where I didn't pry. Codie was a mechanic at a nearby garage where Dad had gotten treated really well after his car broke down on the freeway.

"Customer service is my middle name," Codie said when I told her.

Lana said, "What did it used to be?"

Codie grinned. "Gone in sixty seconds." She looked at me and shrugged. "I used to steal cars for a chop shop. But I'm reformed."

"Good to know."

"Codie was just a misguided youth," Lana assured me, strumming her guitar to the tune of Untitled Number Three. "I told her there were better ways and she saw the light."

"Hallelujah," Codie said.

Nessa cleared her throat. "I've been thinking about getting us some gigs." We looked over at her and she shrugged. "We keep calling these get-togethers practice and rehearsal. It's been three months since Karen joined us, and I think we have a good base to work from. We need to start playing for audiences to figure out how to perform."

Lana nodded. "You're right. You're absolutely right. Does anyone have--"

Nessa raised her hand. "Uh. I know some people. Or rather I knew them, through one of my foster brothers. I could ask around and see if anyone is willing to take a chance on us."

"Oh, they'll take a chance," Lana said. "We're completely unknown, so they can pay us with beer if they want, and even if the music sucks people will be too busy drinking to care." She nodded to Nessa. "Ask around. We may have to do some creative scheduling with work and all, but I'm in."

Codie and I both agreed, and Nessa gave us a relieved smile. I could tell she had been holding back, waiting for the right moment to speak up, and I smiled at her.

"Thanks, Nessa."

"Sure." She self-consciously adjusted her pages. "How about we do Untitled Nine?"

I said, "Oh. I've been giving them titles. Number nine is... uh. The Day After."

Lana grinned. "Perfect. Okay, let's go..."

She counted us in and I poised my bow against the strings. I closed my eyes and listened to the music, waiting for my cue. When it came up, I began to play.

"Hell, yeah."

I opened my eyes and saw Lana watching me with a smile on her face. I smiled back and Lana began to sing.

I was willing to play shows, to actually go out and play in front of people, but I knew that I would be content with the band even if we never left this room.

Nessa had been eyeing the stage since she got to the bar, trying not to be obvious about it. It was like buying a new car. She couldn't let the manager see how eager she was or they might make things more difficult. The manager was a friendly enough guy named Victor, but he seemed reluctant to hire an unknown band to play on one of his busiest nights. The trick was to not look desperate. Don't beg, don't lowball the offer of what they were willing to be paid, and let him think he was getting in on the ground floor of something big.

It was a very subtle con. She thought pretty Lana or sly Codie would have been much better suited for this mission, but she knew a lot of bar owners. The foster family she had lived with for most of her teens had also given her an older brother for the first time. She'd idolized him, following him down to the bars by the waterfront. He would go inside for a drink or to play a little pool, and Nessa would stay on the sidewalk to let him know if she saw their father coming down the street so he could slip out the back way. The bartenders started to see her as a mascot and, though she'd never officially been a patron, most of them treated her like she was a long lost friend.

Victor wasn't one of her old pals from the neighborhood. He was relatively new, had no connection to her foster family, and had no reason to agree just to make her happy. She'd purposely chosen him so that the victory would be sweeter. She'd also chosen him for logistics. The bar's biggest concern would be a customer disliking the music and deciding to take his beer money elsewhere. But Victor's bar was nine-tenths of a mile from the closest bar. Nessa figured that was too far to walk for a drink, but not far enough to drive. People wouldn't abandon the bar just because of the music, and she figured Victor would know that.

He scratched his chin, where a ribbon-thin black beard marked his jaw line.

"I guess maybe you could play for a couple hours on Sunday night. We're busy, but not too busy."

"I guarantee we won't send your customers running out into the street."

"If you do, I'll hold you responsible for the lost income," he said with a smile. They stood, and he held out a hand. "You look familiar. What did you say your name was?"

Nessa shook his hand. "Nessa Grace. You're probably thinking of Lincoln Grace. He was my foster brother. I didn't think you knew him."

Recognition lit in his eyes. "Link. Right. He used to drop by. How is he doing?"

"Still dead." She let go of his hand, keeping her face neutral. Before the end she thought he'd been getting better. Apparently he'd just been better at finding places she didn't know about. " He died three years ago. Car accident. He was drunk.quot;

"Damn. That's too bad."

"We thought so." Nessa shrugged and tried to disguise her anger; she didn't want to screw up the offer now that they were so close. She nodded at the stage. "So Sunday, right? What time should we show up?"

"Get here around eight, and you'll go on at nine. We shut down around midnight, but don't expect to play the whole time. I may have to trade you for the jukebox if enough people ask me to."

"I understand." She let him walk her to the door. "If you want to advertise, you can use the name Radiation Canary."

He nodded. "You mentioned that. What the hell is a radiation canary?"

She grinned as she stepped outside. "It's the best damn band you'll hear all year. See you Sunday."

Track Six

Lana stepped back and looked down at her guitar, a purple Fender Telecaster with black accents, glinting like a Gothic artifact in the lights of the rehearsal room. She loved the guitar, a gift from an uncle who insisted she had enough talent to justify the extravagance. She had only been seven, but she was old enough to know what was being bestowed upon her. From the Christmas morning when he showed her where her fingers were supposed to rest, she had felt naked without the guitar in her hands. She treated it with the proper reverence, polishing it until the face shone in the lights of the rehearsal space. It was her shield and her grail, and as long as she had it, she was untouchable.

She wore a white T-shirt under a black vest, houndstooth pants, and two-toned shoes. Her hair was tucked up underneath a pageboy cap, but a few tendrils had fallen out to either side of her head. She was trying out looks for when they finally took the stage, but it was more difficult than she'd expected. She didn't want to be too obvious, but she also wanted to make a statement.

As she played, Nessa and Karen improvised to keep up with her, and Codie dutifully kept the beat. Lana didn't have a microphone, so she had to raise her voice to be heard over the music.

"I don't say I love you just to hear it back
Love is something declared like a statement of fact
But if you're only saying it to feel like a lover
Baby, I got news... you better duck and cover."

She felt sweat under her shirt, even though there weren't any lights on her. It was the feel of playing, singing, of actually working a song. It felt like a third date, when things were actually starting to come together into something like a relationship. The band was on the threshold of actually being something, and she could feel it on the horizon.

Lana played through the interlude, aware she was smiling through an angry song but not caring. She would save the scowl for the real performance. And there would be performances, oh yes. The gig Nessa had gotten for them at Victor's pub was paying them in free drinks instead of cash, but payment was a payment. It was a start.

She looked at Karen, who was concentrating on her playing. She was on the violin for this song, standing between Codie and Nessa's stations. Lana nodded to her, and Karen smiled. They made it through the lyrics and Lana nodded to Nessa. The music trailed off, and the song ended with a flourish from Karen.

Nessa leaned back on her stool and shook her head. " Karen, I've said it before but I can never say it enough. I'm sorry I doubted you. You're exactly what this band needed. You and Lana have to be the face of the band."

Karen's eyes widened. "No. I haven't done anything. You guys--"

Codie said, "She's right, K. Nessa and I are vital, but we're not the band. Lana is the one who put us together, and you're the last piece that finished the puzzle. You named the band, you gave us our voice. Without you, we're still sitting in a room making noise. You and Lana are Radiation Canary." She pointed with her drumsticks. "Plus, I don't know if you've noticed, but the two of you are extremely pleasant to look at."

Karen's face was red. "Uh. Thank you. I'm honored." She bent down and picked up her journal off the floor. Karen opened it and flipped through until she found the page she was looking for. "I was thinking we could do this one."

Lana took the book. "I remember this. It used to be Untitled Number Eighteen, right?" She smiled and flipped through the other pages. "You titled them all."

"Uh. Yeah. I figured with our name, we should theme our debut album a little bit. Nuclear-type titles."

Lana's smile widened. "I love these titles. Listen... The Exclusion Zone, All Clear, Fallout, Mutually Assured."

"The songs don't always have anything to do with the title, but we can work on that if you think we should."

Lana nodded absently and went back to the page Karen had indicated, a song called "The Importance of Your Radio." She read a few of the lyrics and began to nod, then took off her guitar. "We're going to do this one. I'm going to go copy the page... be right back."

"Okay," Karen said.

As she left, she heard Codie asking Karen for a melody, and the three of them started working on the beat. The rehearsal space had a small manager's office with a photocopier, fax machine, and a telephone the landlord had told her she wasn't allowed to use. She had picked the lock after the third rehearsal and had been using it ever since. She turned on the copier and ran off four copies of the appropriate page. She gathered the pages, still warm from the tray, and then decided to save time by copying some of the other songs as well.

She waited for the songs to pop out of the machine, four pages and one song at a time, and looked at each one as they came out. The pages were covered with oddly-streaked whiteness, the clean lines of handwriting that had become sharp shadows thanks to the ink and the curve of the page on the flat glass. As she watched the pages stack up, she looked at the lock she had jimmied and the book in her hands, and guilt washed over her.

When she had a stack of songs, she carried the sheaf of copies back to the rehearsal space. She handed the book to Karen and cleared her throat to stop the music.

"We have to talk about something serious." She held up the pages and faced Karen. "You just met us a few months ago, and now I'm holding seven of your poems. Your name isn't anywhere on these."

Karen looked at the pages, oblivious. "Well, you know who wrote them."

"The people in this room do, yeah. But if we end up going our separate ways, you don't have any proof the songs are yours."

Nessa sat up straighter, her brow furrowed. "We're not going to steal her songs, Lana."

"No, we're not. But just to insure against future calamity involving... hell, I don't even know. And that's why she needs to be careful. These songs are property of Karen Everett. I'd like that to be official, so she doesn't ever have to worry about the future. I want her to be able to trust us with her best work when she comes up with it."

Karen was fully blushing now. "I don't know what to say. Besides, I think you've got my best work right there in your hand."

Lana shook her head. "Nope. You're years away from it." She picked up a pen and held it out to her. "Make sure you get the credit for it. You're our voice, Karen."

Karen hesitated and then took the pen. She wrote her name across the top of each page before she handed them out to the rest of the band. She hesitated and then added something underneath her signature. Lana craned her neck to see what the second line said and then smiled.

"Okay. I think that's a good compromise."

I folded the page so it would fit on the metal stand. At the top of the page was written a simple header: "THE IMPORTANCE OF YOUR RADIO, written by Karen Everett, property of Radiation Canary." My reasoning was sound. Yes, the words were mine, but they were just words without Codie's beat, Nessa's melody, and Lana's searing voice. Without all of us together, they weren't worth stealing. And without the four of us together, there was no Radiation Canary.

Codie counted us in and we began to play. The atmosphere in the rehearsal space had changed since Nessa told us we had a scheduled performance at a real, honest-to-God club. Now we had a goal, something we had to work toward. We weren't just finding the music. We were trying to find ourselves. And part of that was figuring out how we wanted to look onstage. I wore a long floral skirt and a black blouse, my long hair tucked behind my ears.

Lana had taken off her cap and was letting her hair hang loose over her shoulders. She looked like a goddess, and I knew people would fall in lust with her the moment she stepped out into the lights. Lust... not love. She only had a few minutes to get their attention, and lust was the best she could hope for. Love would come with time.

She stepped forward and lifted her chin, and I swear she could see a crowd somewhere. She wet her lips, eyed Codie, and then began to sing.

"Reaching out for you, trying to be heard
Gonna raise my voice, no one hears a word
I'm out here shouting into space, sound in a vacuum
Flip a switch, turn the dial, bring me into your room
Gonna make it something simple, easy to follow
I'm going to tell you the importance of your radio."

I smiled. The phrase was the title of an old UK program that was meant to prepare people for what to do if the bomb dropped. I found it online, and the connection was obvious. Codie kept the drum pounding, following the lyrics with a staccato beat that left spaces to be filled by me and Nessa.

The sound of Lana's guitar was nearly lost underneath the other instruments, but her voice was impossible to ignore. She sang with her chin up, her lips pulled back in a surly grin. She looked like someone losing a fight but carrying an ace up her sleeve. She had sweat on her upper lip and her neck and she glanced at me. She held eye contact as she reached the chorus.

I wanted her. Right there in the middle of the rehearsal space, with Nessa and Codie watching. Hell, they could keep playing. Lana smiled as if she could read my thoughts and I looked away, hunching my shoulders as I focused on my fingers and the movement of my bow.

When the song ended, Lana took a drink from her water bottle and flipped through the other pages. She was breathing hard, but she looked like she could go for hours. I tried not to let my mind run with that thought.

She wiped her thumb over her bottom lip as she examined the lyrics. "I think we need to alternate."

"What do you mean?"

"Well, the Beatles went back and forth with John singing one song and Paul singing the next. George sang a few songs, and even Ringo got in on the action. We all should have a chance to be heard, right? Karen?"

My eyes widened. "I'm not a singer."

Nessa smiled. "Last year you weren't the founder and songwriter of a band, either. Shit changes."

"We're still doing baby steps here. I figure we'll be more rounded as a group if we can take turns being in the spotlight. And hey, it will take some of the pressure off me if I get laryngitis or something. We can figure out the details as we go along. We might as well figure out what works and what doesn't early on." Lana held out the pages to me. "So which one do you want to sing?"

I could only stare and wonder how I'd gotten myself into this. Finally I took the pages from her and began shuffling through them. My voice wasn't strong enough for "Exclusion Zone." "Mushroom Cloud" and "All Clear" were out, too. I stopped on 'Fallout,' considering the words for a moment. It wasn't a song that required strong vocals, and there weren't any tricky verses. The lines were nice and compact so I would be able to breathe, and it wasn't so complicated I would neglect my playing.

"I guess I could sing this one."

Lana took the sheets back and gave copies to Nessa and Codie. She rearranged her guitar across her chest and ran her thumb under the strap so it didn't cut into her shoulder. "Okay. From the top." She looked at me, nodded, and suddenly I felt like maybe I could do this. I wet my lips, kept my eyes on Lana, and waited for the cue.

Track Seven

"It could be our thing. We wear blindfolds... on stage..." Lana glared over her shoulder from the passenger seat, and Nessa sank away from her. "Okay, okay. It was just a suggestion."

Lana's face relaxed, and she smiled. "We're not going to be the blindfold girls."

"Is it too late to change our name to Blind Justice?" Codie said.

"Yes," Lana said. "Sorry, Nessa. You'll just have to see the audience watching us." She smiled and looked out the window at the passing scenery.

Codie was driving them to the concert in her van, which was the only vehicle the band had access to that would fit all their instruments. Nessa and Karen were in the back, making sure nothing got jostled too much on turns. Karen had been silent since leaving the rehearsal space, and Nessa reached out and lightly pinched her forearm. Karen jerked back into focus and blinked at her.

Nessa smiled. "It's okay to be nervous."

"For you, maybe. I'm not... a musician. I'm just a writer who plays an instrument."

Nessa nodded. "But you do both so great. Listen, you write all the songs. If they reject the rest of us, we're just being rejected once. But you feel like they're going to reject you twice over. You're worried they'll reject you both as a poet and a musician. But you don't have to worry. I've played with a couple of other bands. I know what crap sounds like, and you don't have it in you. They may not love us yet, but they won't hate us. Trust me."

Karen took a deep breath and nodded. "Okay."

When they arrived, Nessa climbed out and walked to the edge of the parking lot. She put her hands on her thighs, bent at the waist, and threw up in the grass. When she walked back and took the water bottle Lana offered, she saw Karen staring at her.

"What? Did I get some on me?"

"No... what was that all about?"

"I have butterflies."

"But you just calmed me down. I thought you had it all together."

Lana grinned and put her hand on Nessa's shoulder. "She wasn't kidding about us performing blindfolded. Tell her what your other idea was, the gimmick you came up with before she joined the band."

Nessa shuffled her feet, and Karen was sure that she would see her blushing if her skin was lighter. She coughed and rolled her shoulders before she gave in. "Puppets."

"Puppets?"

Lana chuckled as she unloaded her guitar and Karen's cello. "Her plan is that we would play behind a scrim, and we'd hire people to hold up puppets. You know, like Gorillaz does with cartoons, or that guy in Limp Bizkit who wears a mask."

Nessa shrugged. "I have stage fright. It's nothing major, and I get over it quickly enough once I start playing." She moved to help Codie unload the drum set. "Don't let my throwing up overshadow what I said. It's still true. They're going to love us."

Karen took a trembling breath. "I wish I had your confidence."

Nessa pointed over at the grassy area beside the parking lot. "Want to throw up, too?"

It had been a joke, but Karen tensed slightly, nodded, and walked over to the edge of the pavement.

Lana watched her go and chuckled. "Better here than on stage."

"Don't be so sure," Codie said. "We want people to remember us. I think that would have been pretty memorable."

Lana pointed at Nessa. "That settles it. You and Karen don't get to eat before we go on. And you're not getting your free beers until after the show."

A couple of friends from Codie's garage had been press-ganged into acting as roadies. She said they were experts at quickly putting things together and then taking them apart, but she assured us they weren't criminals. I was too nervous to care. I'd invited Dad and Ted. And because I'm an optimistic moron, I invited Penny, too. I wanted her to see it was a real band. We'd had a few dates since I met the other girls, made out on the couch a few times on the couch, but she still didn't really believe Radiation Canary was anything worth getting excited about. Her eyes glazed over when I talked about them, like it was the plot of a movie I'd seen and she could care less about.

Dad and Ted were at a table near the stage. I could see them from where I was lurking in the doorway of a hall leading to the bar's back room. Boxes of liquor formed a bulwark against the wall to my right. I was shaking. Throwing up had helped a little, but I was still queasy. A handful of people were there to see us. Friends, family, bosses. I noticed that everyone in Lana's cheering section was inhumanly gorgeous and felt a twinge of nervousness.

Now I get to humiliate myself in front of Dad, Ted, and anonymous goddesses.

But at least I wouldn't be humiliating myself in front of Penny. The third seat at my table was empty and a quick glance of my phone told me she hadn't called or sent a text. Lana came to make sure I was ready to go on and I tried to hide my disappointment.

"Hey. You ready?"

"Yeah, but I don't want to sing for an hour or so. Can we hold off on 'Fallout'–"

"Sure, as long as you need." She touched my arm. "Are you okay?"

"I'm fine. I'll be fine." I managed a smile and followed her to where Codie and Nessa were waiting. We all debated about costumes, uniforms, some sort of matching theme that would identify us as a band, but finally decided anything special would be too formal for the venue. So I was dressed in my usual night-out clothes, a blouse with the sleeves rolled up, a denim skirt and knee-length boots. Lana's hair was back in a braid, and she wore a fedora low over her eyes. She wore two tank tops again, and her pinstriped pants were held up by a pair of thick suspenders. Nessa wore jeans and a white blouse, open at the collar to show off a navy blue T-shirt.

Codie, though, was representing the band. She'd stenciled the bright green canary silhouette onto the front of her T-shirt. She figured she was the only one of us who would always be facing the crowd, so it fell to her to be our billboard. Lana suggested putting the logo on the drums, and I asked her to wait until we had a few successful gigs under our belt before we did anything drastic. After tonight, having an instrument branded with a canary might be more like an albatross around our necks.

We moved toward the stage, but Lana said, "Hold up." We stopped and gathered in a circle in front of her. "Codie, we know each other because we happened to sit next to each other in high school. Nessa, you had the rehearsal room we wanted, so we offered to share. And Karen, we got damn lucky the walls are thin. I've wanted to make music my whole life, and because of you three, I get to do it tonight. We get to do it. I just wanted to say thank you before we go out because if we do well, it'll be too late and if we suck... well, it'll sound sarcastic."

Codie grinned. "Okay. We're sticking with the set list?"

"Karen wants to move 'Fallout' back by an hour, so we'll swap it with 'My Weak Hand.' Just remember this is a first gig. No one expects brilliance. We're going to hit a wrong chord, we're going to sing wrong notes. But we're going to hit them together, and we'll come back stronger for it. You guys ready?" She put her hand out.

Nessa covered it with hers. "Let's go."

I covered Nessa's hand moments before Codie covered mine. "Radiation Canary on three?" Codie suggested.

"How about..." Lana moved her hand to the top of the pile. She pushed our hands down and let them rise back up and counted down. "T-minus three, two one... ka-boom." She turned her hand upside down, moving her fingers like flames.

We stared at her.

She rolled her eyes and shoved me toward the stage. "We can work on it. The important part happens out there."

It was spring when I first heard music coming from a nondescript little rental space on a dead-end street. It was October when Radiation Canary took the stage for the first time.

Lana slung the strap of her guitar over her head and stepped toward the microphone. Feedback rang out as she introduced us, and then we went straight into a so-so rendition of "The Exclusion Zone." The sound system left a lot to be desired, but we didn't exactly give it a lot to work with. Nerves overcame us all at one point or another. My voice wavered far too much during "Fallout," which Lana had moved to the end of the second hour, and the power to Nessa's keyboard cut out for fourteen minutes during one of her heavy songs.

When we finally hurried off stage, soaked with sweat from lights and the nerves, Lana slumped against the wall and Nessa leaned next to her. Codie and I were too wired to do anything but pace as we waited for our well-wishers to make their way back. The bar was mostly empty except for the people who'd come specifically for us.

Lana was smiling, laughing. "God, that was terrible."

Nessa, also chuckling, slugged her on the arm. "Then why are you laughing?"

"Because it *happened*. It was terrible, but it happened. Guess which part matters more." She winked at me, and pushed away from the wall. She made it two steps before her legs went rubber and she collapsed forward. Codie caught her and gently lowered her to the floor, stretching her legs out and checking to make sure she was still breathing.

"Damn."

I was just the right side of panic. "Is she okay?"

"Oh, yeah. Just overwhelmed, adrenaline rush, hit a wall. She's going to be fine in a minute or two."

"Then what was the 'damn' about?" Nessa said, kicking Codie's boot.

"It's just... our lead singer passing out at the end of the last song? It would have been a hell of a way to end our first show."

I couldn't help smiling at the thought, and joined Codie and Nessa on either side of Lana to wait for her to wake up.

Track Eight

We finally left the bar around one, and we helped Codie unload her drums back into the rehearsal space. Lana had recovered as expected and, though embarrassed about fainting, headed out with her gorgeous friends. Codie offered to drop me off at home and left me with a complex handshake that I couldn't begin to describe or replicate. "We weren't perfect yet, but we weren't half bad tonight, K."

"No, we weren't." I looked in the back of the van where Nessa was sleeping with her arms around her keyboard, and I smiled. "You'll get her home?"

"Yep. See you at rehearsal Tuesday."

I wished them a goodnight and watched the van until it went around the corner. There went my band. I chuckled as I walked up the driveway, and it sounded incredibly loud. The silence of the neighborhood was daunting after the clamor of the bar. I felt like my footsteps were echoing off every house. I tried to sneak into the house quietly, which is a feat even when not carrying a violin case in one hand and a cello in the other.

I thought the lamp in the living room had been left on to help me see, but Dad was sitting on the couch with his arms splayed and his chin on his chest, fast asleep. I smiled and put down my instruments, then bent down and kissed the top of his bald head. He inhaled sharply, then sat up quickly and straightened his shoulders.

"Har."

I chuckled and whispered, "Hi. You didn't have to wait up for me."

"I didn't. Ted did." He looked around the living room and then at his watch. "Or I guess he decided I was the default waiter-upper." He cleared his throat and stood up. I was a lot taller than him under ordinary circumstances, but my shoes had heels and he was barefoot. It was awkward to look down so far at him. I was anxious and kept filling in the silence with horrible things he could say. *You think that's why we paid for your lessons?* or *Just what kind of girls have you been hanging out with?*

Finally he chucked my chin and said, "You were outstanding. I didn't much care for the venue, but ah... the music. The music was really good. You should keep practicing with those girls. They were phenomenal. The energy from the lead one, uh–?"

"Lana."

"Yeah. You're gonna get half your album sales from pictures of her alone. But keep working on it. You've got a good sound, and it needs to be nourished. If you need some extra time off from the store to practice, we can work something out."

I felt like the air had been sucked out of the room, so I just hugged him. "Thanks, Daddy. You really liked the music?"

"Oh, you know me. I think there hasn't been a decent musical act since Neil Diamond. But yeah. If I heard you on the speakers in the supermarket, I'd start to, you know..." He jerked his shoulders back, bobbed his head, and began to move his hips.

"Dad, don't, don't, Dad, don't."

He stuck his arms out and moved them in what I think he hoped was a dance move. I pushed his arms down and held them against his sides. He smiled, and I kissed his forehead.

"Thanks, Daddy. I'm going to take a shower and then go to bed."

"Okay. Sleep well."

I laughed in horror as he proceeded to dance up the stairs, waiting until he was out of sight before following. I undressed in the bathroom and took off my makeup, watching my real face reveal itself in the mirror. Dad liked my music, and he liked the band. As first reviews went, it could have been a lot worse.

Lana was well trained for long nights. She usually worked at the club from ten until six, then went to teach a before-school dance class. She slept during the day, five or six hours, fooled around on the guitar, taught an after-school dance class, and then either practiced with the band or went back to the club for her shift. Regardless, she was a bit reluctant to barhop with her friends who had come to the show. Eventually she gave in to their insistence and let them drag her out for celebratory drinks.

They toasted to Radiation Canary, praised Lana's voice, and forced her to autograph their napkins "for future eBaying." Lana eventually hit the wall and powered through it, following her entourage from bar to bar until they arrived at one where she recognized the bartender.

"Shaun! What are you doing here? Moonlighting?"

He smiled and pushed a glass of water in front of her. "I only work here, hon. You know you're at work, right?"

She frowned and looked around. Sure enough, it was Club Nightside. "Huh, look at that. They all start to look alike after seven or eight shots." She drank the water to rehydrate, thanked Shaun, and went to find her fellow dancers. It was strange to be at work without working. She fought the urge to note empty glasses and offer refills as she went back to the locker area.

One of the other girls, a statuesque blonde named Princess, peered around the open door of her locker and smiled.

"Hey, it's the rock star!"

"You brought me to work? Bitch." She slapped Princess on the ass.

Princess squealed. "I had to take my shift, and you needed a designated driver. Stick around. I'll give you a free dance in the private room."

Lana blushed. As far as the other dancers were concerned Lana was straight. But with this group, straight didn't seem to matter. Sometimes sex was just sex, and gender was a detail. As fun as it might have been to take advantage of Princess' tease, Lana needed to stay in the closet. Especially if she wanted to be famous. She opened her locker and began digging through the debris at the bottom for her Tylenol.

"Hey, did you see Bar-E out there?"

Lana shook her head and dry-swallowed two tablets. "Why? What did he want?"

"I don't know. I was telling him about your show, and he said he wanted to talk to you."

Lana grunted and shut her locker door. Princess was dressed in a French maid outfit, complete with a frilly apron and a little white cap. She put her foot up on the bench to carefully ease on her fishnet stockings. Lana felt warmth in her chest and forced herself to look away. She was too drunk to be tempted like this. But she peeked again, eyeing Princess' cleavage and the way the uniform hugged her curves, and her drunken mind betrayed her.

"Be careful. I might take you up on that private dance if you keep dressing that way." She hurried out before she could get herself into any more trouble.

Bar-E was really Barry Segel, the club's MC. He was a Nigerian-born, Jewish on his father's side Rastafarian who dressed like a Wall Street banker. He wasn't hard to spot in his little niche of stereo equipment in the back of the room. He spotted her approaching and waved her up. Lana waited until Princess was onstage and dancing before she leaned close.

"You wanted to see me?"

"I did! Princess told me you had a gig tonight. You got a band?" She nodded. "You have a CD? I could play it, get a little bit of marketing in."

Lana winced. "No, not yet. We're still looking for a recording studio in our price bracket." The truth was they hadn't been looking. They were a few songs short of a full album, but the real stumbling block was rental fees. Even if they pooled their resources, she didn't think they could afford the studio time.

Bar-E said, "My uncle's got a place where he lets me mix shit for work. You want to come in sometime when it's not busy, he usually has a couple of hours free in the mornings."

She thought she could hear her heart beating over the music. "What? How much is the studio per hour?"

"He don't charge that way. Look, if no one's gonna be using it, he doesn't mind if good bands use it. Princess said you girls were good tonight, so I think he'd be fine with it."

"Are you serious?"

He laughed and slapped her arm. "Get outta here. I'll slip some info in your locker. You'll have to be quick, probably. You may have to settle for only recording one song per weekend, and that could take a long time, but-"

"Hell, for free I'll take my sweet time." She stepped closer and kissed him hard on the cheek. "You're a god, Bar-E."

He put his hand over his heart and mimed it beating as he turned back to his board. He waved her off and Lana descended the steps. The maid costume was gone, leaving Princess bare-breasted. She turned her back to the crowd, presenting her rear end to a man so he could put money in the G-string. Lana waved and Princess winked. God, she was tempted. She watched for a moment, committing certain images to memory for later use, and then slipped out the door into the night.

The air felt frozen, and she hunched her shoulders against it. Her car was back at the bar where the night had started, and she didn't feel like walking, but being outside was sobering her up. She breathed deeply and walked toward the street. Cars were few and far between, and the wind picked up her hair. She looked for the mountains, but they were rendered invisible by clouds. She breathed in, tilted her head back to the sky, and shouted joyfully at the clouds until she didn't have any air left in her.

Finally she fell silent again. They were a band, with a name and songs, and they had played a gig. And they were good. And now they could possibly have an album. She started jogging along the side of the road, deciding the energy needed to be burned off if she was going to sleep before class in the morning, and it would hopefully burn off enough alcohol that she wouldn't have a hangover.

Track Nine

Two weeks later, the janitor unlocked the studio to let Radiation Canary in at four-thirty in the morning. They had arranged their sleep schedule accordingly the three days preceding so they would be mostly awake, but Lana seemed to have energy to spare. They rehearsed a few of the songs they'd been working on before committing to record anything, and Lana let Karen choose which one would be their inaugural song.

She chose a song called "Emerald (Seattle Song)," since she figured only locals would care about it. The lyrics were pretty harsh toward other cities in favor of their hometown. She felt guilty about it, but New York and Vegas had their own songs. If she was going to write about a city, she was going to write about Seattle. She had a printout of the lyrics, but Lana shook her head when she tried to hand it over.

"No, this one's yours."

"What?"

"We said we'd alternate. This one is you all over it."

Karen swallowed, looked at the lyrics, and then at Nessa and Codie. "Then I don't want to go first. Honestly, our first recorded song should have your voice on it."

Nessa said, "Without you, the band wouldn't have a voice at all. If we're going to record anyone first, you deserve the honor."

Lana said, "If you don't like the result, I'll do a version and we can make it a duet in post. Just relax. You can do this." She stepped away from the microphone that was positioned in front of the glass, leaving the lead spot open for Karen. Karen could only stare, and Lana squeezed her shoulder. Karen wet her lips and stood in front of the microphone. She felt naked without her cello or violin between her and the microphone. The producer had said they would do the strings later so she could focus on her vocals now, but she really wanted the security blanket to hide behind. She looked into the production booth and decided it was just an experiment. And if it was an experiment, it could be declared a failure without costing them too much time.

Nessa started to play a melody in the key of C major, a riff on "Somewhere over the Rainbow" that quickly turned into something deeper. Karen closed her eyes and listened for the right moment, when the music transitioned to A Minor. Then she took a breath and began to sing.

"Auntie Em said it was just a dream
Oz wasn't magic as it seemed
It wasn't really real, they all... say
Well sorry, Dorothy, Auntie lied
Come and sit here by my side
I'll take you to the Emerald City by the bay."

Codie and Lana came in together and the song seemed to sweep into life. In her head, she saw the first verse as sepia, and the added instruments turned it into full Technicolor. She raised her voice in response to it, her fingers tapping silently on her thigh in time with Codie's drums.

"There's no Tin Man in these woods
But we've got something just as good
You can see it all from the streetcar
The Space Needle's as high as you can go
And the Underground shows the secrets below
The monorail cuts through a giant smashed guitar."

For the chorus, the other three joined in with her. Lana had moved forward to share her microphone, and Karen gratefully allowed her the extra space. They sang together:

"New York's an apple that quickly gets rotten
Philly's Brotherly Love is too often forgotten
Chicago's got wind, Vegas is full of sin
These cities are gorgeous for a day or so
But their glory fades, and I'll always know
I only have one true home in this wide world
Because my city's an emerald."

Next was a musical interlude she would fill in later. She closed her eyes and imagined the melody of her strings, rocking her head slightly with the rhythm of the song. Hearing Lana's voice had spurred her onward, and she waited for the cue from Nessa to pick up the lyrics again.

"My sky may be gray but the grass is green
Safest harbors that I've ever seen
Cradled by mountains and kissed by sea spray
Glinda, don't take my ruby slippers away
I don't want to go back to the gray
Over the rainbow is where I'm meant to stay."

She got chills when Nessa and Codie joined in with her on two of the lines, adding an extra punch to the lyrics. But this verse was just hers, and she sang it over a simple melody from Nessa.

"I want to trade rainmakers for wizards
It's not just some story I heard
Once in a lullaby your auntie used to tell
The Emerald City is real, and I call it home
It's the greatest city I've ever known
Keep your Kansas, we'll take Seattle."

Lana joined her for the chorus again, and the guitar seemed to growl the words along with them. Codie was attacking the drums, and Nessa made a soft base for it all to settle upon when the cacophony dropped back down.

The silence seemed to drag on until Karen stepped away from the mic so it wouldn't pick up her sigh of relief. She pushed her hair out of her face and turned toward the others. Codie and Nessa were both beaming, but Lana looked radiant. She moved her guitar to one side so she could hug Karen. "Toldja you could do it," she whispered before pulling away.

"Right." Karen was trembling when she pulled away and poked both index fingers into Lana's chest. "Next song is going to be one of *yours*, bitch."

Lana laughed and traded places with her. "Gladly. Speaking of which, I think that was a great take." She looked through the glass at the producer. "What's the next step?"

We'd all tried, but I couldn't get used to the idea of waking up at three in the morning, so I dozed in the van on the way back home. I woke up when we got onto the freeway, and was vaguely aware of Lana humming from the front seat. I opened an eye and watched her, then recognized she was humming "Emerald." I shifted in my seat and said, "See? You could have sung it if you wanted to."

I saw her smile in the reflection in the side mirror. "If nothing else, we've given local businesses something to play on their commercials."

"Or to parody," Codie said with a grin.

I stretched in my seat. "Maybe we should offer it to the Chamber of Commerce. Radiation Canary, jingle writers. I can write eighteen different songs about soap."

We managed to get "Emerald" done, but we had to abandon the studio for actual paying customers before we could get started on any others. I didn't particularly mind. We had some more gigs lined up, courtesy of Nessa and surprisingly strong word of mouth from the first show. We were working on a CD, which meant it couldn't be a failure yet. As long as we were playing shows and putting together an album, we were still a band. I wanted to hold onto that feeling for as long as possible, because nothing was certain.

I closed my eyes and rested my head against the window. *Hold onto this moment, don't let it go, nothing is certain, what's next I don't know. Don't look back at the disaster, try to see what happens the day after.* I reached into my pocket for a pen. It wasn't complete, but I needed to be sure I remembered it. I wrote it on the back of the van's user manual.

In the front seat, Lana started humming "Emerald" again.

Track Ten

Nessa tried to fade into the background as much as possible. She sang a few harmony vocals on the tracks, but she mostly aimed at getting her part of each song done quickly. Lana and Karen seemed to be pulled in seven directions at once regarding every section of each song. Vocals and instrumental tracks, redoing each verse over and over again until they were confident it was just right. Nessa knew that trying to follow along would drive her crazy, so she just pulled out the pens she'd bought and doodled on whatever scrap paper she had available.

Codie, who also wanted to avoid the serious part of music creation, sometimes sat next to her and watched her draw. They were currently on their third weekend of recording, quietly sick of hearing themselves play but willing to push through for the sake of the songs. Today Nessa was working on concept art for the cover of their album. She looked over to make sure Codie was awake before she held up the sheet for judgment.

"What do you think?"

The canary's body was facing to the left, but its head was twisted to look at the right, as if something had caught its attention. The bird's foot, tail and head broke the ring that surrounded it. The whole thing was colored bright green, and she was in the middle of trying to add a subtle glow around the body so it looked radioactive.

Codie nodded, and took out her wallet. She pulled out a much-folded piece of paper and said, "It's good. What do you think of this?"

Radiation Canary was written in the center of the page in large typed letters. But they hadn't been printed off a computer. Nessa ran her fingers over the letters and felt where they had been pressed into the page. "Wow. A typewriter?"

"Yeah. I found one in a pawn shop for ten bucks. It's kind of ratty, but-"

"That helps," Nessa said at the same time. Each letter was slightly blurred. A defect with the 'I' key left the letters with an echo, and the top curve of the Rs were faded almost to obscurity. Nessa folded her drawing and held it up under the typewritten words, smiling at the way the two looked together. "I'd say that looks like a logo, huh?"

Lana came back from the control room, her hair tucked behind her ears.

"We have to go through the bridge of 'Mushroom Cloud' again." She spotted the drawing. "What's that?"

Nessa handed it over. "Maybe the album cover."

"Oh, yeah. I like this a lot." She handed it to Karen, who nodded. She gave it back to Nessa. "Keep that. I want it when we're ready to lock something in."

"Will do."

Nessa stepped back into place behind the keyboard and saw a roll of Scotch tape sitting on a stool. She reached over to pick it up and taped the logo to the front of the keyboard. Lana watched her with a smile and, when she was in position, faced forward. " One-a, two, three four..."

When they weren't sneaking studio time, they were rehearsing songs Karen had already written while she quickly tried to write more. Her journal was filled with poems, and each one only required a bit of fine-tuning to transform them into songs. An extra verse here, a chorus added to this jumble of lines. It was like adding on to a framework, building from a kit rather than starting from scratch. Lana, who had never been able to write songs of her own, managed to build a few of Karen's poems into beautiful verses.

So far they had managed to keep the band from interfering with real life. Codie took whatever odd hours she could get at the garage rather than being scheduled for a certain time. Nessa was the front-desk clerk at a local hotel, and their busiest hours were nights and weekends. She was able to work out a way to make sure she was free whenever the band had shows. Since she was the one scouting for and securing shows, it was easy for her to find the right balance.

Lana seemed to be spread thinner than the rest of them. Her night job, which she'd asked Nessa and Codie not to mention to Karen, had her working all night, and then she had dance classes before and after school hours. The rest of her time was spent with the band. She slept when most people worked or went to school, but it couldn't possibly be enough. More than once Nessa had shown up at the rehearsal space to find Lana outside sleeping in the backseat of her car. On top of that, she was taking on responsibility of being a go-between with the band and the man producing their album.

As exhausted as she was, she never let it transfer into the recording sessions. Her voice was as powerful as ever, and her playing was stronger than she could remember it being. It was as if she stored up reserves of energy that she only spent when the tapes were rolling. Nessa kept an eye on her though, the vision of her collapsing backstage replaying in her mind like a loop. She would intervene long before that happened again.

Somewhere around recording the eighth track, a bluesy number called

"Carry On," they found their voice. Nessa and Karen seemed to realize it at the same time, and their eyes met across the studio. This was what Radiation Canary sounded like, a combination of the sum of their parts, and this was when the band became an entity.

"Walking into the wind makes you strong
And I'm going to fight when I think you're wrong
I'm not going to miss you when you're gone
Baby, I'm going to carry on, carry on,
I'm going to carry on."

They used the studio for eight Saturdays, sometimes only getting one song done in a session and sometimes getting up to three. On one of the fast days, when they finished up the backing harmony on "The Question," Karen picked up her book while Lana went to listen to the finished product. Nessa was on the edge of her stool, toying with the effects button, the only person still in the studio with Karen.

She looked up and saw Karen staring at her. "Everything okay?"

"Yeah. But I think that's it."

Lana had just come back in, trailed by Codie. "What's what?"

"We have fourteen songs, including Emerald. I'm not sure of the exact time, but I think it's about forty-three minutes in total."

"Forty-six eighteen," Codie said.

Karen smiled and shrugged. "I think that's a good length for a debut CD, don't you?"

Codie whooped and banged the cymbals, and Nessa played a shattering-glass sound on the keyboard. Lana crossed the room and hugged Karen, almost knocking her over with the force of their impact. Nessa and Codie joined them, appreciating the moment of being done before they stepped back.

"Did we ever decide on a title for it?" Codie asked.

Karen said, "I thought *Action After Warnings* sounded good."

"Oh, yeah. Definitely." Lana chuckled and squeezed Karen's bicep. "We're done. I'm going to check out the control room. Come on. You guys deserve to be there, too."

The first CD of their music was a normal CD-R with the band name laser-burned across the top. Lana took out a Sharpie and held it out like a queen preparing to knight them. "Everyone, our first official band autographs... right there."

It took some creative spacing, but all four of them got their names on the disc. Lana convinced the man who had donated his time to produce it to sign his name as well, and she kissed the back of his hand when he offered it for her to shake. Bar-E's uncle had agreed to burn five hundred copies of the CD for a small fee, and they got a master which could be used to make more if needed. They also had MP3 copies of all the songs that they could put on the website Codie was going to make for them.

When they left, the storm clouds that had been threatening all morning finally opened up. They piled into the van and sat in the parking lot, the engine running so the CD player would work. Rain cascaded down the windows as Lana pressed play with a shaking finger, holding her breath until the music began.

The disc opened with a two minute instrumental called "Mutually Assured," which faded into "One in Ten." Lana's voice filled the van, and her real voice uttered a nearly-inaudible, "Hoh, fuck," as the chorus started.

In "Carry On," all four of them sang on the chorus. Codie's drum seemed to match the beat of the rain on the van, following along with Lana's blues riff. Under it all, Karen's strings were a constant presence. The violin started out "Mushroom Cloud," and Karen pictured it as a string that led to the center of the stage where Lana's voice took over.

"The Importance of Your Radio" started slowly, Lana's voice plaintive under Nessa's piano before it built into a sweeping orchestral explosion with the entire band playing loud and shouting the bridge into their microphones.

Lana was back on lead vocals for "My Weak Hand," and Codie laughed when she saw Lana mouthing along with her own lyrics. Lana, unashamed, began singing aloud and playing air guitar.

In rehearsal and during our first few gigs, Lana sang "The Exclusion Zone," but for the album she gave it up to Nessa. She utterly transformed the song, leaving the whole band dumbstruck as her voice filled the van. Karen looked over and saw her trying to hide in the collar of her coat, so she reached over and held her hand until the song was finished.

During "Duck and Cover," Lana leaned forward and pounded her hands on the glove compartment, laughing wildly as the others sang along with themselves. She leaned back and pressed the display button until it showed how much time was left on the disc. Suddenly serious, she nudged Codie. "Drive. We don't have much time."

"You think I'm going to pay attention to the road when I'm listening to our first album?"

"Just don't wreck. We only have about fifteen minutes. I want it to be organic."

Codie started the engine and the windshield wipers swept across the glass. "You want what to be organic?"

"Just go! And don't wreck."

Codie rolled her eyes and pulled out onto the main road.

They drove through "Survivors" and "Fallout," applauding themselves since there was no one else to do it yet. When they got onto the highway, the sun broke through as "All Clear" started. The juxtaposition of the song and rays breaking through the cloud cover made Nessa cry, though she was embarrassed enough by it that no one said anything. Lana pointed out something they could have done better on "The Day After" and, though they agreed, none of them particularly cared.

"The Question" was a soft, pleading ballad that was Karen singing almost a cappella with occasional assistance from Codie and Nessa. As the song neared its end, Karen realized why Lana had been so intent on driving while the CD played. She was shaking as Lana rolled down the window, leaning so that the rain-wet air hit her face as they drove.

As the Seattle skyline came into view, the silence after "The Question" was broken by Nessa's piano playing the first few chords of "Somewhere Over the Rainbow." The others rolled down their windows as well and started singing along.

They drove back into Seattle singing "My city's an emerald" as loud as they could.

Track Eleven

I did extra shifts in Dad's shop to make up for all the time I'd been taking off for the album. I made it upstairs, barely, and dropped into bed with all my clothes on, staring at the ceiling for a full minute before I realized it was still light outside. I didn't care. I was exhausted. The weeks of recording had finally caught up to me, and I was as mentally weary as I was physically. I was just going to take a quick nap before dinner. Just recharge the batteries.

My phone rang, and somehow the sound turned off the sun. I realized I must have fallen asleep, but I had absolutely no idea what time it was. Late? Early? I fumbled for the phone on my suddenly dark nightstand, my mind foggy and addled as I flipped the phone open and pressed it to my ear. "H'lo?"

"So you *do* answer your phone."

"Whosthis."

There was a disbelieving laugh. "It's Penny."

I was suddenly awake. I sat up with a groan. "Penny. Shit. I forgot about our date."

"You'll have to be more specific. You forgot about four of our dates. Which one are you upset about forgetting?"

I scratched my head. Could I really have forgotten four dates? Thinking back over the craziness of producing the album, I thought it was highly likely that she'd just slipped my mind. "I don't know. I'm sorry."

"I'm still downtown if you want to come join me for a late dinner."

I didn't know how I would be able to get downstairs for food, let alone to a restaurant. "I'm still just so exhausted from making the album and making up the work I missed... can we do it another day?"

Penny sighed heavily and said, "You know..." Another sigh. "Fine. Whatever. What day can you make it?"

I sat up and crossed my legs under the blanket. I heard "Duck and Cover" in my head, and I realized it was all about Penny. "You know what, I don't think any day is good for me."

"What?"

"You don't want me. You're happy just to have a girlfriend. You just want someone there at the end of the day. I don't want to play that role anymore. You're a great person, Penny, but you're a shitty girlfriend. We didn't have fun together. We didn't click, but we kept trying to make it work. We were just too scared to let it go. But now it's time, okay? We need..." I realized what had happened a few seconds too late. "Penny?" Nothing but an empty line buzzing in my ear.

I hung up and put the phone down. I hoped she got enough to know I was serious and not just venting. I was calm about it, rational, realistic. No yelling or screaming or tears... just stating the facts. Even if those facts were pretty brutal. Still, I cried. Not for what had just ended, but for finally giving up the hopes I had when Penny first took me dancing. We could have been something special.

The tears dried, and I found the strength to head downstairs. The lights were out, but the tree in the corner of the living room was still shining brightly. Even though I had seen it, must have seen it, during the past few days, it didn't really hit me until right then that it was a Christmas tree. It was mid-December, almost the new year. On Christmas 2003, I had been working at Dad's store and filling a journal with poetry I would never have the nerve to publish. Now they were songs on the debut album of my band. My chest swelled with self-pride, or self-worth, or something good with "self-" in front of it.

I went to my bag and took out my copy of *Action After Warnings*. God, I loved that title. I loved the simple cover art, Nessa's drawing that fit us so perfectly. Lana got what she wanted; people would know who this was when they saw it on a T-shirt. I put it in the CD player, turned the volume down low so it wouldn't disturb Dad and Ted, then went to scrounge for food.

I found evidence that Ted had prepared his famous fried chicken, and there was a plate waiting on the top shelf. A bent postcard sat on top of a thigh with a message in Dad's handwriting: "Reserved for Rock Stars: David Bowie, Elvis Costello, or our daughter. Whoever stops by first. Love you."

More tears, but better ones this time. I took the plate to the dining room table, peeling off the skin and looking out the window as I ate. I didn't want to be Elvis and, although it would be fun to borrow his body for an hour or six, I didn't want to be David Bowie, either. I wanted to be one of the four. I wanted to be part of the band.

As I ate, I listened to our music. I'd been playing the CD at the store, waiting to get tired of it, but I wasn't. Lana brought my words to beautiful life, and I couldn't get enough of hearing her. Nessa and Codie were amazing musicians. I wasn't merely lucky to find them, but I don't know a word big enough to encompass how fortunate I was.

Codie had designed the poster on her computer, printing it out only when it looked right. The logo Nessa had drawn was in the center, with the typewriter text running across the center of the image. The poster was an advertisement for their show on the tenth of January at a club called Cayj. She had her Bluetooth on, talking to Lana about the play list. "I get what you're saying, but the audience won't *know* they're not new songs. They'll want to buy what they just heard. Playing songs that aren't on the album is a bait-and-switch."

"Yeah, but they've already heard the songs at the show. If they want to hear something new, they're out of luck until the next album comes out."

Codie sighed. "I know. But imagine it's you. You hear a song you like, you go buy it. People don't buy new artists, they buy the song they like. Everything else is a gamble."

"I guess." She did sound convinced, and slightly defeated.

"Let them fall in love with the music first, and then they'll fall in love with Radiation Canary. We'll–"

Her computer chimed, and then a disembodied voice shouted, "Incoming!"

"What was that?" Lana laughed.

"I have an email from the website. I set it up to alert me." She pulled the chair out and sat down, clicking off the screensaver. The website was concrete gray, with the logo standing out in the middle of the page. There was a shadow against the background, as if the canary was hovering a few inches above it. She went to the email section and saw what had triggered the alert. The MP3s were available for a dollar each, and one of the zeroes in the sales table had changed into a number one. She grinned.

"Hey. Someone just downloaded 'Emerald'."

"What? We haven't even done a show to say it's available."

"Google is being not-evil. I think someone must have searched for songs about Seattle and stumbled over it. We got lucky." She waited, but whoever their first buyer was didn't buy anything else.

"So we had a sale?" Lana sounded excited.

Codie grinned and slumped in her chair, fingers laced over her stomach. "We just made twenty-five cents each. Congratulations, Lana. We just became professional musicians."

Track Twelve

Our play list was set up so I didn't constantly have to switch from the violin to the cello. We made minor adjustments every gig, but we made sure that there wasn't too much back and forth. Tonight we were playing a club called Diametric. They had a real stage, with wings and a dressing room. The stage was hidden behind a curtain which opened at show time, and we got honest-to-god applause when we started playing. I knew it was just a Pavlovian response to a show beginning, but I felt like it was actually for us.

Lana was in a sleeveless blouse and a vest, having decided that she wanted bare arms whenever she was on stage. In addition to looking sexy, she said it helped her to stand under the lights for the duration. Codie started us off with "Mushroom Cloud." She and Nessa had figured out an arrangement so that songs flowed from one to the next. There was room for applause, of course, but we didn't give ourselves any breathing room. We didn't want to give the audience a chance to stop listening even for a second.

"I've built up my strength like building a wall
And I get right back up every time I fall
But when I'm with you, I have no idea where I stand
Talking to you is like fighting with my weak hand."

Lana turned to face me during the interlude, one side of her colored blue from the spotlight. Her hair was down for this show, and she'd let it grow out so it draped her shoulders. I had gotten a haircut, prompted by Lana to cut it much shorter than I otherwise would have. The stylist then added waves upon waves and, when she turned me to face the mirror, I was stunned by how beautiful it looked. I actually looked sexy, and Lana had winked at my reflection and declared I was "definitely rock star material."

Now, my neck feeling naked as curls of hair stuck to the sweat on my brow, Lana turned to look at me. She smiled, flashing her teeth, and I realized that the three of us were just following in her wake. She was the only rock star on stage, and we were her support. I returned her smile, and she winked before looking back out at the audience. Completely bathed in blue, she was ethereal. She wasn't a rock star, she was a rock goddess.

She backed away from the microphone and let me, Codie and Nessa carry the vocals as she played. When the song ended, the crowd applauded enough to satisfy me as we transitioned into the next song, "Survivors." It was one of Nessa's songs, and Lana retreated back toward the drums to let the focus settle on her. The club had an actual piano, so she used it rather than her instruments. It changed the sound of the song completely, but for the better. I got chills and met Lana's eye. She was thinking the same thing: we had to get this girl a proper piano.

"I'll rise up, I won't let you keep me down
I won't keep my face to this shattered ground
While the hot wind keeps blowing debris around
When everything else in this world gets unsure
I'll get back on my feet with the other survivors."

Lana returned to the microphone as the song ended and said, "Ms. Vanessa Grace, give it up for her!" The audience complied with gusto, and Nessa seemed to sink down behind her piano already playing the intro to "The Day After."

When we finally let the music fade at the end of the show, the applause seemed louder and longer than people just being polite. Lana stayed in place at the microphone and introduced us all by name - I blushed when she said I was as talented as I was beautiful - and we joined her at the front of the stage. "I'm Lana Kent, and we are Radiation Canary. CDs are available backstage, autographs on request." She winked and then gripped my hand with her right, Codie's with her left. Codie took Nessa's hand, and the four of us took a bow before heading off-stage as the curtains closed.

A tall gray-haired woman with tortoise-shell glasses was waiting. She was underdressed for the club, but she seemed to be waiting for us nevertheless. She straightened when we approached and put on a smile.

"Great show, ladies."

"Thanks." Lana swept a towel over her face and kept walking. The woman fell into step with us. "We'll start the autograph session as soon as we get a drink and get washed up a little--"

"Oh, no. I'm not here for that. My name is Helen Lambert. I work with Cracked Pavement Records." She held out a card. "I was wondering if you ladies had representation."

"Nope."

Even I could see the predatory gleam in the Lambert lady's eye. "Oh! Well, then--"

"The no was to your offer," Lana said. "We're not interested."

Helen tried to laugh it off. "Surely you're joking."

Lana took the card from Helen's hand, then draped her sweaty towel over it before Helen could withdraw. She looked down at it in horror as Lana tossed the card to the floor.

"We're not interested. I'm not joking. Sorry you wasted your time, but I hope you enjoyed the show." She went into the dressing room and the rest of us, showing a united front, filed past Helen Lambert without a second glance. Once the door was closed, though, Lana accepted that we would want an explanation. "Sorry. I'm not playing hard to get, I just think we need to hold out for a decent offer. Anything we get now would be better for the record company than for us."

Codie smiled. "Don't worry, Lana. We get it. You made the right choice."

Nessa slapped Lana's arm and nodded to show she agreed. The dressing room had two shower stalls and two changing booths that closed with curtains. Lana wanted the gap between the show's end and the CDs going on sale to be as short as possible, so we'd flipped a coin to see who got to shower and who had to scrub up in the booths. Codie and Nessa won the showers, so Lana and I wet some towels in the sink and went behind the curtains.

"So," she said from the other side of the thin particle-board wall, "they're okay with it. What about you? Are you pissed I turned the lady down?"

"No. Makes a lot of sense not to jump on the first offer. I'm not even sure we're ready for a deal yet. We need more time to figure ourselves out. I mean, we didn't even know how great Nessa sounded on a real piano."

"Oh, God, I know. We should start a fund to buy her something worthy of her talent."

I chuckled as I undressed. My arm was sore from all the playing, but it was a good burn. It felt like I'd just spent three hours in the gym. I rolled my shoulders and wiped the sweat off.

"I'm just glad you knew to say no. My first instinct was to just go along with it."

Lana laughed. "That's why I'm the leader, I guess. It's like losing your virginity. You didn't just do it with the first person who asks, right?"

"Uh, right."

I guess I paused too long, because Lana said, "That sounded weird. I..." She let her voice drift off. "Oh, shit. Look, if you... I didn't mean anything by it. You're a smart girl. If you chose to have sex with someone, even if they *were* the first one to ask, it doesn't mean anything."

"No, I didn't. It's..." I winced, glad we were in separate booths. "No. I did not have sex with the first person who asked."

Lana was silent and, when she spoke again, her voice was quiet. "You... have, though. Right?"

"Is that a prerequisite for being a musician?"

"No! Of course not. But I mean, you're twenty-four years old. You said you have a steady girlfriend, so I just assumed."

I shrugged and pulled a T-shirt over my head. "It's tough when you live at home. I just never gave it that much importance. My first relationship imploded when I was fifteen, and I didn't want to risk having sex with someone I'd end up hating, so I've held off just to be safe. And I guess a couple of years have gone by and–"

Lana interrupted from the other side of the curtain. "Hey, I'm not... are you dressed?"

"Yeah."

She slipped into the booth. There was hardly room for both of us, but we managed without touching each other. She lowered her voice so it wouldn't carry. "I shouldn't have said anything. It's admirable. I practically gave mine away when I was sixteen in exchange for a nice dinner. I knew girls who assumed it was included in the price of their date's prom ticket. Prom, party, punch, and pussy." She touched my hand. "I'm impressed with you."

"Thanks. Uh, don't tell Codie and Nessa, huh? It's not something I really want broadcast."

"Of course. And, uh, Karen? When I asked if you were dressed, I meant pants, too." She grinned and slipped back out, and I realized I had dropped the skirt I'd worn on stage without putting on my street skirt. I sighed and finished getting dressed. At least I'd been wearing underwear.

Track Thirteen

Lana hesitated before she closed the van doors. Codie was taking the remainder of their CDs back to her loft, since she had more storage space than any of the others. It looked like there were still a lot left, but they had sold twenty-five in the hour between the end of their show and the club closing. Her wrist was sore from signing them, and Codie looked dead on her feet. Lana put her hand on the spot where Codie's neck and shoulder met, squeezed. "Sure you're okay to get home?"

"Yeah. It's my superpower. I stay awake while I'm vertical, and then turn narcoleptic when I'm horizontal." She winked. "I'll be fine. See you tomorrow."

Lana stepped back and let the van back out, waving when it turned out of the parking lot. Nessa had taken Karen home, so Lana walked alone to her lime green Pacer Wagon. She slipped her hand into the pocket of her jeans for her keys as the club door opened behind her. She twisted and saw the bartender come outside with a garbage bag hanging from one hand.

The bartender spotted Lana and smiled. "Hey. I thought Radiation Canary flew the coop. Are you the last bird standing?"

Lana laughed. "Something like that, I guess."

The bartender stopped, the bag of bottles clinking against her thigh. "I wasn't able to go over and check out your table, but you were really great. Do you have any CDs with you?"

Lana unlocked her car. "Sorry, they went on the van. But uh... I may have one. Let me check." The woman put down the bag and started over, and Lana bent into the car. She had to manually turn on the dome light as she pushed the seat forward to dig through the backseat. She thought she had one or two CDs lying around just in case someone asked, but with all the junk cluttering the backseat... She heard the bartender approach, and the car sagged slightly as she rested a hand on the open door.

"If I can't find it, all the songs are on the website. I could write down the address if–"

The bartender's hand slipped over the curve of Lana's ass. "I thought you were really great." Her tone had changed, and there was little doubt that she wasn't after a CD.

Lana cautiously withdrew from the car and stood up straight. The bartender was a little taller than her, with thick red lips and black eyes. She had killer curves, breasts and hips and ass, the body of a pin-up girl wrapped in denim and a club tee. One eyebrow arched, and she kept her hand on Lana's hip.

"So this sort of thing happens in real life?" Lana asked, a little breathless. She was surprised by how nervous she was. She was no stranger to come-ons, but for some reason this felt like something different. "Band members really hook up with random admirers?"

The bartender shrugged and flicked her head, tossing her hair so that the wind carried it away from her face. "It's happening now. My name's Alia."

"Lana."

The name was barely past her lips before Alia was kissing her. Lana was pushed into the wedge formed by the open door and the body of the car, and Alia pressed tight against her with an appreciative moan. Her hand moved over the curve of Lana's breast, wrinkling her shirt as she moved lower. Lana gripped Alia's studded belt, and Alia reached back with her free hand to guide Lana's hand to her ass. Lana dug in, and Alia growled.

"There you go..."

Lana pursed her lips and cooed, which prompted Alia to growl and manhandle her into the car. Lana sat sideways in the driver's seat and then lifted herself onto the console as Alia tried to follow her in. Lana dropped roughly into the passenger seat, pulling Alia to her for another kiss. Alia knelt in the driver's seat and Lana kept her leg tense so her knee wouldn't rest on the horn. They grappled awkwardly, and Lana broke the kiss with a sigh.

"I need a bigger car."

Alia reached back and pull the door shut. "I don't know. I think we can make this work." She reached up to turn off the dome light, and Lana sighed in submission as she was pushed back against the passenger side door. Alia seemed to know what she was talking about, and she wasn't going to argue with an expert. Part of her felt bad that it wasn't Karen getting this experience, but the guilt faded very quickly once her pants were off.

The living room light was on when Nessa got home, but the room was empty. She assumed her roommate had just left without bothering, which she was too tired to get irritated about.

She turned on the TV and went into the kitchen for a midnight snack. Nothing felt real after a show. She felt like she was doing everything wrong. *Would Patti Scialfa eat a bologna sandwich after a gig? Would Chrissie Hynde be caught dead going home to watch sitcom reruns?* It took a while before the buzz wore off and she felt comfortable doing things as Nessa Grace again. She went into the living room and stretched out on the couch, channel surfing to find something to watch.

She found a late-night talk show on basic cable and dropped the remote onto her stomach. Her sandwich was bologna and lettuce with mayonnaise. Maybe one day when she was famous, it would be her version of Elvis Presley's peanut butter and banana. Or, God forbid, Mama Cass and her ham sandwich.

The talk show was semi-famous for some controversy a few years back. It had originated as a Pacific Northwest show and it aired on local over-the-air channels. Then they lost their time slot, which created an uproar with their fans, and the host began a series of public appearances with the same format. The national media picked up on the story, calling it a true grassroots resurrection, and a contract was negotiated to bring the show to a national audience. It retained the host and everything that made it so beloved, including the locally-focused name: *Settle In, Seattle!* The show slowly gained a devoted following, and in recent years it had shown signs of possibly overtaking Jay and Dave.

The host, Nick Young, was tall and lanky enough to have earned the fan nickname "Scarecrow." He started the show with nicely coiffed hair but, by the end, it was usually spiked up in the front from repeatedly raking his fingers through it. He wore three-piece suits that were in similar shambles when the end credits ran. He had a frequent smile that seemed to widen his face, and small dark eyes that sparkled with mischief whenever he ran up to "confide" with the camera.

Nessa liked him. He worked hard to make his show interactive, even when it turned national, and he frequently had local talent on the show. At the moment he was in the midst of some skit with his sidekick Hank, but Nessa wasn't focused on that. She was thinking about something else he did, week in and week out, and an idea started to form.

She finished her sandwich and went to the computer. She loaded up the show's site and clicked the link for information about the show's Friday Night Auditions.

Every Friday night, a band performed during the last segment. The home audience was urged to vote - via website, phone, or text - about whether the band should come back or not. If the majority of votes were yes, then the band was brought back to do a week's worth of shows. That meant five appearances on a national show, and Nick usually used the bands for skits and house music in their episodes.

The website didn't say the acts had to be Seattle-based, but it probably helped. She knew she should talk it over with Lana and the others first, but what harm was there in just signing up? She pressed her hands together in front of her face to give herself a moment to think it over, then began to type.

"What's your band's name?" She typed in Radiation Canary. She filled in the other slots with information about their type of music, contact information, the minutiae of signing up for something... she attached the MP3s of what she thought were their best tracks - "The Day After," "The Importance of Your Radio," "Duck and Cover," and of course "Emerald." She hesitated with her hand over the mouse, and then clicked "Send."

The page went to a "Please Wait" graphic, and then an image of Nick Young appeared. He had one eyebrow up, his hands behind his back, his upper body tilted as if he was leaning out of the monitor to look at her.

"Good luck!" was written in the white space to one side of his head, with "Hope to hear you soon!" on the other side.

Nessa whispered a prayer and clicked away from the website. There was a chance it wouldn't lead to anything. But there was also a chance of Radiation Canary being on television six times in a single week.

"No risk, no reward," she murmured. She would tell Lana about the registration in the morning and hope she wasn't too annoyed by the idea.

Track Fourteen

Alia was good in the front seat, better in bed, and absolutely phenomenal in the shower. Lana woke up the next morning by herself, with a folded note tucked under the waistband of her panties. "Hope you play Diametric again *real* soon." A small winking happy face and an "A" was signed at the bottom, and Lana smiled as she placed it on the nightstand. Her first one-night stand, casual sex, and stranger sex, all rolled into one. She made a point to check her wallet and made a circuit of her apartment to make sure everything was where it was supposed to be before she relaxed too much. The only thing missing was a can of soda from the fridge, and she figured Alia had definitely earned that much.

She took a shower and let her mind wander to practical things. Where the next show was, what class was scheduled that morning... crap. After the aerobics with Alia, dancing was going to be a pain. She rested her hand against the tile, took off the detachable shower head, and aimed the spray at the spot where her shoulders met her neck. The muscles relaxed somewhat, enough that she was able to get out of the shower and dress.

When she got to the kitchen she saw that Codie was seated at the dinner table with a bowl of cereal, reading a magazine.

"Did you break in again?"

"Your girlfriend is hot," Codie said, ignoring the question. "She was leaving the building when I showed up."

"How do you know she came from here?"

"Well, I didn't get a good look at her this morning, but I seem to remember she was working the bar last night. Curvy as a dangerous road, lips red like chili peppers and just as hot..."

Lana shook her head. "I don't know what you're talking about. If you finished off my Cocoa Pebbles, you're out of the band."

Codie stuck her tongue out as Lana went into the kitchen. "We have to talk about image."

"No, we don't."

"Image is important."

Lana poured herself a bowl of Cocoa Pebbles and added milk. "No, it isn't.

Talent is important. The Beatles appeared on Ed Sullivan in suits and ties. By the end of their career, they were wearing cartoon military uniforms and calling themselves Sergeant Pepper. David Bowie was Ziggy Stardust and the Thin White Duke. Now we have Christina Aguilera getting famous with bubblegum, until the bubble pops, then changing into Xtina to have orgies in her videos. We don't worry about image and making ourselves a product. Otherwise we might as well put plastic boxes on our heads and call ourselves Devo: The Next Generation. Nothing against Bowie or the Beatles or even Aguilera. I love Bowie. But it's just damn depressing when someone lets their production overshadow what they're creating."

Codie looked up. "Did you say something? I wasn't paying attention."

Lana slapped the back of her head as she put her breakfast on the table and sat down. "We'll just wear what we like without worrying about what label they'll slap on us. That way if I decide to start wearing a jumpsuit on stage, or if Karen dyes her hair, we're not accused of trying to re-imagine ourselves."

"All right. But I had some good ideas."

"I'll bet you did." She swallowed a spoonful of her cereal. "What were your ideas?"

Codie held up her hands as if framing the scene. "Okay, the show starts with you and Karen in canary costumes–"

Lana rolled up Codie's magazine and hit her with it.

I held the phone between my ear and shoulder, writing on a scrap piece of paper. "Yeah, I got it. Curves like a dangerous road, chili peppers. I'll see what I can do with it."

"Thanks. Codie said it this morning and I couldn't get it out of my head."

I smiled and tried not to think of the conversation that had prompted phrases like the ones she'd just dictated. "Well, anything to save me the trouble of coming up with my own lyrics. Nice to have you guys picking up some of the slack."

"Me-ow," Lana said. "You at work?"

"Yeah." I glanced up to see if there were any customers. Dad's hardware store was usually dead this time of day. I had my journal open on the counter in front of me to use the free time for writing. I had flipped to a new page to take notes when Lana said she had the bones of a new song for me, and I was already trying to arrange them into rhymes. "So who is this curvaceous lady?"

"She's, ah, a friend."

I smiled. Lana had never expressly told me she was gay, but I wasn't blind. "So the song should be innocent?"

Lana made a dismissive sound. "I wouldn't necessarily say that. I'll let you know more details if you need them."

"Okay. Are we still on for practice this afternoon?"

"We'll see how much sleep I get between classes. If nothing else, you can get together with Codie and Nessa and just work on your songs."

We could do that, and we'd done it several times. Sometimes it was me and Lana, other times it was Lana and Codie, but the rehearsals never felt right unless all four of us were there. But I agreed, and Lana had to go because her first students were showing up. We exchanged goodbyes and I went back to the lyrics. Lana didn't seem like the kind of woman who would brag on stage about a conquest, but this was obviously relating to a real person. So maybe...

"Her curves take you by surprise, like a dangerous road
She'll make your heart beat faster, you just gotta... grab hold."

I could almost hear Lana's sharp intake of breath on the pause, a sultry sound that would convey more than I could put into words.

"Her lips shine like peppers but they burn hotter
She's slippery when wet, she's Aphrodite's daughter
You're her willing accomplice
You go along every time
Then she leaves you
Standing helpless
At the scene of the crime."

I tapped my pen on the page and chewed the nail of my pinkie finger. I imagined Lana singing it, her voice dropping to an almost plaintive sigh at the end of the last line. It would work, and it would be good. I noticed one of the customers making his way to the front of the store and I put the journal aside, putting on a customer-service smile by the time he reached the cash register.

Codie kept a solid, steady drumbeat as she recited the lyrics she wrote. "Why won't Willy win Wanda? We wanna know-whoa-whoa... Well, wet me teww you why-eye-eye. Wanda's... my... Walla Walla sweetheart, my Walla Walla sweetheart. Wanda went aww da way wit' me in Walla Walla, Washington."

It was just the three of us, since Nessa was a no-show and hadn't bothered to answer her phone. Codie suggested premiering a song she'd written, if I didn't mind. The song was crazy, and Lana was almost laughing too hard to keep playing along, but somehow she managed to keep it flowing. I had given up on the first verse, and now I was just tapping my foot to keep the beat. Codie gave the song a nice finish by sliding her brush over the cymbal, and took a bow when Lana and I gave her a standing ovation.

"Number one hit single," Lana predicted.

Codie grinned. "I figure we can play it in concert if one of us needs a break. It'll be a nice little breather between the real songs. You want to help me polish it, K?"

I shook my head. "It's yours, Codie. Let me know if you want some help when it's closer to done, but..."

"She just doesn't want to be associated with it. She has an *image* to uphold."

Judging from the way Codie laughed, I assumed it was an inside joke between them that I didn't quite get. I was about to suggest rehearsing "Scene of the Crime" when we heard a car pull up outside. Lana stood on a chair to look out the window next to the ceiling. "Nessa's here. About time." She jumped down. "Okay, once she's ready we'll go through the new stuff Karen's got for us. Are any of those piano-heavy?"

"Well–"

I was interrupted by Nessa's arrival. She was sweating, breathing hard, and her eyes were wider than I'd ever seen. Lana tensed.

"What's wrong?"

"You might be pissed."

Lana narrowed her eyes. "What did you do?" Nessa handed her a sheet of paper and then looked at me. I shrugged at her, and she shook her head. I left it to Lana to explain once she'd read whatever the paper was. Lana's eyebrows moved closer together as she read, and then she held it up like evidence in a trial. "Is this real?"

"Yeah."

"When did you do this?"

"Three weeks ago after the Diametric show. I didn't think anything was going to come from it. I mean, it was just something to do online, why not give it a shot?"

Codie said, "Uh-oh. Nigerian prince in trouble?"

I couldn't take the suspense. Nessa was literally trembling. "Come on, guys. What's going on?"

Lana didn't look angry, as Nessa had apparently feared; she looked shell-shocked. "According to this, we've been selected to appear on *Settle In, Seattle!* two weeks from Friday. We're going to be the Friday Night Audition." A smile started to spread across her face, and she was actually flushed. She laughed and handed the print-out to Codie, then looked at me. "We're going to be on TV."

Album Two
ROME BURNING
(2005-2006)

Track One

Lana decided to call off practice to take Nessa out to dinner, a way to thank her for taking the initiative and getting our first potential break. After we ordered, Lana got down to business. "We need to decide right now what song we'll do. I don't want to waste any time we could use on rehearsal. We can't just be good, we have to be good enough to get a majority of yes votes. We have to blow them away."

Codie said, "And we have to decide if we want to do a song from the CD or a new song."

Lana shook her head. "We're not going to have that discussion again. You were right; it has to be from the CD. First of all, I don't want to put the pressure on Karen to deliver a brand-new song and then pin all our hopes on it. Besides, the song we play on the show will be the only exposure the audience has to us. If they go looking and it's not available, they might not bother to buy anything else. The song will be an advertisement for the band."

Nessa had her arms crossed on the table. "Well, it is *Settle In, Seattle!* We should do 'Emerald.'"

Lana vetoed again. "It's a national show. We'd get votes from Seattle, maybe a few elsewhere, but it's everyone across the country who will be voting. I don't want to offend anyone in New York who might have otherwise voted for us. So we need something accessible to a wider audience. I'm thinking 'One in Ten' or one of the nuclear-related songs. 'Fallout' or 'Mushroom Cloud.' I mean, we're branding ourselves as Radiation Canary and half the songs on the album have titles relating to that."

I said, "How about 'The Importance of Your Radio'? Reaching out, trying to be heard..."

Nessa grinned. "It's perfect."

Codie nodded at Lana. "I know you hate the whole image thing, but we need to discuss it just this once. We're going to be on television. We need to make a visual impact as well as an audio one. We can use music videos and other appearances to establish our non-image image. Like you said, the Beatles wore suits on Ed Sullivan because it was the sixties. People expected clean-cut boys in suits. We need to figure out what we want people to picture when they visit our website and listen to our music."

The waitress had appeared a moment earlier with our food and began handing it out. "Couldn't help overhearing. You're musicians?"

Nessa grinned. "We're a band. Radiation Canary."

The waitress raised an eyebrow. "Nice name."

Lana smiled at me and winked. "Yeah. We're actually going to be on *Settle In, Seattle!* on the eighteenth. Be sure to watch."

"Wow, the Friday Night Audition? I love that. I don't know if you want my vote, though. The ones I vote for never seem to stick around. I'll be sure to watch, though."

Lana nodded her thanks. When the waitress left the table, she said, "Good luck!"

Nessa waved. "Say a prayer, if you know any."

I looked up from my food and then reached into my pocket for the pen I was always carrying these days. Lana watched me as I wrote on a napkin, holding it carefully so it wouldn't tear. She rested her elbow on the table, her hand against her throat like she was putting herself in a half-nelson as she twisted to read what I'd written. I took pity and turned the napkin around, and she read it to the others.

"Say a prayer if you've got one, say a prayer if you have one."

"Just trying it on for size."

Lana smiled. "I like it."

"Now I just need the song to go with it."

"I'm not worried. You're a machine."

I folded the napkin and put it in my pocket with the pen. Lana said, "Okay, Codie. What kind of image are you thinking about?"

"We can't just get up on stage and sing. Not this time. We have to be memorable."

Nessa said, "I'm suddenly very afraid."

Codie chuckled and popped a green bean into her mouth, smiling like a Cheshire cat as she chewed.

We became avid viewers of *Settle In, Seattle!*, gathering at Nessa's place to watch every night. The previous Friday's band hadn't gotten enough votes to come back so the last slot every night was used for either established acts or stand-up comics. We watched to see what the host responded to, who he seemed to enjoy, and to get a feel for the way the show was presented. We'd all seen it before, but now it was different. Lana approached viewing like a general surveying the battlefield.

Codie was working on a way to make the live performance of "Radio" spectacular. "We have the quiet first verse, and then it takes off during the first chorus. I'm thinking low light, just Nessa playing while Lana sings, and then we bring the lights up when Karen and I kick in. Lana, you can start playing then, too. It'll be this..." She waved her hands searching for the right word. "It'll be a benediction that turns into an anthem."

Lana nodded slowly. "We'll make it raise the hairs on the back of their necks."

After a week, Nessa had a list of guidelines for our image. "No matching outfits if we can avoid it. It's corny and it screams boy-band. Nothing military. No suits. We'll dress like women, because damn it, we're not trying to be men."

"Rah," Lana said.

The Friday Night Audition rolled around and we watched the band like we'd have to compete against them. They were called Fairy Tale Dream. The lead singer wore a top hat and tails over a Nirvana T-shirt and kept his eyes frighteningly wide the entire time he was singing. The drummer was manic enough that Nessa started calling him Animal from The Muppets.

When the cacophony ended, Lana said simply, "Boo."

Nick Young approached the band to thank them, then turned to the camera. He ran a hand through his wild hair again and said, "You know what to do! Text, email, call the number at the bottom of your screen, visit the website, or whatever you have to do to cast your vote for Fairy Tale Dream. The next week of their lives depends on you, so go on! Vote! I'm Nick Young, this is *Settle In, Seattle!* and I don't know about them, but I will definitely be here next week. Goodnight!"

Lana looked at me. "What do you think?"

"Well, we're better than them."

Nessa put down her vote. "One thumbs-down. Now we just need a few thousand more of those."

Codie said, "I'll be surprised if they come back. You could tell, Nick Young was *not* impressed with them."

"You think any bands make it onto Friday Night Auditions without his approval?" Lana said. "He likes them all. He likes *us*, or else he wouldn't have made the decision to let us come on."

"We don't know what he heard to make the decision. Could be they used one sample to get the appearance and this..." Lana waved her hand. "This was a bait-and-switch."

"Kind of like we're planning to do?" I asked.

Nessa shook her head. "We're not baiting or switching anything. I sent 'Radio' to him, so he knows what it sounds like. We're just embellishing it a little to make it more representative of our sound."

I shrugged. I was over-thinking everything, trying to think of everything that could go wrong. If we blew this, who knew how long we would have to wait for another chance to make it big. Of course, we already had record companies sniffing around. Maybe the show was an unnecessary boost. Just another gig. She saw me watching her and matched my shrug. We wouldn't get anywhere second-guessing our every move. "Radio" might as well have been our only song at the moment; we'd work it until it was perfect. If we got a no vote, we'd just go back to what we'd been doing before.

I felt the pressure lift slightly, but I didn't leave without confirming the rehearsal times for the next day. I started home on foot, singing "Radio" under my breath. Lana pulled up in front of me in her lime green Pacer and tapped the horn. She motioned for me to get in and, after a short hesitation, I did.

"You don't have to drive me home. I just live up the block."

She shrugged. "It's fine. Point it out to me?" I nodded and she drove on.

"You know, your car is kind of perfect for the band. It looks radioactive."

Lana laughed. "It does, doesn't it? Guess we got lucky." I pointed at the next corner and she turned me toward home. "So are you nervous?"

"Hell yeah. I almost begged to use one of your songs instead so I can lurk in the shadows behind you and let you be the face of the band."

"Now *that* would be a bait-and-switch. We all might take turns singing, but you're the lead. You'll have the majority of the songs on the album, so it deserves to be you up there." I looked and pointed at the house, porch light on as always. "That's me."

"Looks like a nice place."

I grinned. "I like it. Do you want to come in and meet my Dads?"

"Not tonight. I'm too nervous about the show. Tell 'em hi."

"I will. Thanks for the lift." She lifted her hand off the steering wheel to wave goodbye, waiting until I was mostly up the driveway before driving off. I stood on the porch and fumbled with my keys, turning slightly when I heard another car pull up. I expected Lana, but instead it was Penny's car. "Oh great." I kept my voice low and didn't move my lips to speak, sighing as I slipped the key into the lock. I heard her get out of the car and start across the sloped lawn.

"Excuse me. I'm looking for my girlfriend. It's been so long since I've seen her that I'm not even really sure what she looks like."

"Hi, Penny," I muttered. I left the door unlocked but went down to the yard. I didn't want to have this conversation in front of whoever was waiting up for me. "I wasn't sure where we left things. I mean, last time we talked you hung up on me in the middle of what I was trying to say."

"Right. I just wanted to stop by and tell you not to bother making any others.

Consider all our future dates retroactively cancelled."

I was stunned. "Wait. You hang up on me when I'm trying to end things, then you wait a few weeks, and now you're trying to break up with me instead? Is that honestly what you're doing?"

She held her hands out to either side. "It doesn't matter who breaks up with whom. The important thing is that we admit to ourselves this isn't working. And what is there to break up with, that's what I say. You've obviously moved on."

"What do you mean?"

"Whoever that was in the puke green Gremlin."

My ears burned, and I was too flustered to correct her. "I'm not dating anyone."

"Damn right you're not." She turned to walk back to her car.

"Else!" It sounded lame, and my voice withered. "I-I meant I'm... not dating anyone else."

Penny didn't acknowledge me. She got into her car and slammed the door. She didn't squeal the tires or burn rubber, but there was still something angry about how her car surged back onto the street and idled at the stop sign. I didn't watch her go.

Ted was up and on his computer when I finally went in. "Hey. I thought I heard you out there. You– everything okay?"

"Yeah. I'm just tired. Going to bed. Thanks for waiting up."

"Sure," he said. He sounded concerned, but he didn't follow me upstairs. I left the lights off and fell onto my bed, arms crossed over my face. I wasn't going to sob like some teenage drama queen. What happened wasn't the death of a relationship, it was pulling the plug. It had been kept alive on machines for too long, artificial life with no hope of recovery.

But still.

Still, still, still.

Track Two

To Lana's surprise, the one-night stand with Alia turned into something a little longer. They met for dinner, slept together again, and went out the next morning for breakfast. Lana told her about doing *Settle In*, which Alia thought was brilliant. She offered her services if they needed a cheering section in the studio audience, and she said that Diametric's manager would let her post signs imploring people to vote yes.

On Monday night, the band reconvened to watch the show and was horrified to discover Fairy Tale Dream had made it through. Nessa made a gagging noise and shook her head. "By the end of the week, no one will remember what good music sounds like."

Karen said, "On the bright side, after a week of these guys, we'll sound great even if we all get laryngitis."

Lana and Nessa both lurched forward and knocked on the wooden coffee table, and Lana playfully flicked Karen's ear. "Don't even joke about that."

"Ow," Karen said, then apologized for potentially jinxing them. They made it through Fairy Tale Dream's second performance, which was marginally better than their first. It would almost have to have been better than their first, actually. Nick Young didn't seem wholly pleased with their presence. He was more aloof and standoffish than normal, and said his goodnight from the desk rather than going over to join the band.

"He hates them," Codie said.

"It's his show," Nessa said. "He could veto the results."

"But he lets America vote. He has principles. I'd rather know he stood behind what the voting says than his own personal preferences."

They were watching the show on a portable television in the rehearsal space. When the show ended, they ran through "Radio" twice in the new arrangement. Nessa played a soft, gentle lullaby that wrapped around Lana's vocals. When they reached the chorus, Codie introduced herself by softly tapping the cymbals and then starting a steady heartbeat. I joined in, and Lana picked up the melody.

She stepped toward the microphone and started to sing, but she immediately shook her head and waved them off. "I can't do it."

"What?" from Nessa.

"It doesn't sound right. Yes, the benediction is fine by myself. But once it picks up, it has to be all of us. If we put that much power in the music, the voice has to match it, and I can't do that by myself. All four of us do the chorus."

Karen said, "And then we drop back for the last line. Back to you alone."

Lana smiled. "Yeah."

They tried it that way once. When the song finished, Codie whooped. "Hell, I'd vote yes for that song in a heartbeat. I already want to hear it again."

Lana's smile faded. "People are going to want this version. It's not on the website or the album. Shit..."

"It's okay," Nessa said. "The version on the album is just fine. People know there's a difference between live and studio recordings. It'll just make them get the live album when we release it."

"You're sure it won't screw up our chances?"

Codie said, "Who would you rather hear, the band who plays everything safe or the one who takes risks?"

Lana took a deep breath and nodded. "All right. One more, then I swear I'll let you all go to bed."

Codie scoffed. "Who here is sleepy?"

Friday arrived much faster than any of us expected. I didn't sleep at all Thursday night, and I got the feeling no one else did, either. We met at the rehearsal space late Friday morning so we could carpool to the studio. Lana was dropped off by a drop-dead gorgeous Amazon, and their departing kiss made me blush a little. Codie drove us in her van, our instruments safely stowed behind us. Nessa kept drumming her hands on her thighs, staring out the window.

We stopped for brunch, though none of us were very hungry, and Lana checked to make sure our outfits were loaded in the back of the van. She didn't want to leave anything up to chance. Finally, we were back on the road and arrived at the studio with time to spare.

The studio guard checked us off a list after checking the van, making sure we weren't smuggling in... actually, I'm not sure what he was checking for. What was the point of a security checkpoint when a tour group goes through the studio every ten minutes? He pointed us to the appropriate studio and Codie got us there without any wrong turns, which I took as a sign. I was taking everything as a sign. We passed four Starbucks, that's a sign. We were all wearing white, that was a sign. A song I liked came on the radio...

We followed a printed sign with the show's logo printed on it, through a cavernously high backstage area with golf carts and stacks of equipment. Then we rounded a corner and, after passing through a wall of blue serge, we were in the studio. It was like driving to a warehouse, walking through a garage, and then arriving in Wonderland. We were stage right, an angle they rarely showed on TV, and I was stunned at how small it looked.

"It's so much more... momentous on TV," Lana said.

"That's what they all say."

We turned toward the voice, both familiar and strange, and gawked as Nick Young approached us. His smile was exactly what we expected, but his hair wasn't done and stood up in wild chunks. He had a thin salt and pepper beard and, instead of his standard suit, wore an extremely faded T-shirt and blue jeans.

"You must be Radiation Canary. Jimmy at the gate told me you'd arrived. I wanted to welcome you in person."

"Hi," Lana said, taking the lead because the rest of us were incapable. She shook his hand and introduced us around. "We really like the show."

"Well who in your position wouldn't?" He winked at Nessa and motioned for us to keep walking. He fell in beside us. "Usually I only listen to one or two of the tracks people send us just to get a feel for the band so I can give them a yay or nay. But you girls... uh, ladies... womenfolk." He smiled, and he was charming enough that we smiled back. We reached the stage and he stepped in front of us and turned around. "I listened to all the songs you emailed. Just really great stuff. Do you have an album?"

Nessa said, "Yeah, yes." She pulled it out of her bag and held it out to him. "That's... you can keep that."

"Excellent, excellent." He turned it over and scanned the tracks. His smile faded slightly. "There was a song on the website called 'Emerald'–"

Lana said, "It's a bonus track. We figured we didn't want to put off people who aren't from Seattle."

"Oh! I see. So I assume you're not performing that tonight."

"Well, we have to play to the whole country, right?"

He laughed. "That you do."

"We're doing 'The Importance of Your Radio,'" Nessa said.

"Good choice. A very strong choice. Okay, uh..." He turned and gestured at the performance area. "That's where you'll rehearse, and you can do that whenever you get set up. We film at four, so be ready by then." He clapped his hands together. "There will be a woman around named Jane. She's evil, but she's on our side while the show is being put together. Listen to her, but don't be intimidated. Don't feed her after midnight. Don't get her wet. And if you claim to be too young to remember what a Mogwai is I'll deduct points from your performance. Good luck, ladies!"

He turned and hopped off the stage, disappearing behind the curtain before any of us had really registered the fact he was there.

"Did that really happen?" Lana asked.

"Seems like it did," Codie said.

Lana stepped off the stage and went over to the performance area. We followed and stood behind her in our relative positions: I was to Lana's right, Nessa to her left, and Codie at the back. I watched Lana, then looked out at the sea of empty chairs. I noticed that her right hand was trembling, and I stepped closer to her.

"Hey." She turned to look at me. "You won't be alone out here. None of us will be. If you get nervous, just focus on a few people in the audience. Focus on the sound of Nessa's playing. You'll be back at the rehearsal space, in the studio. Don't worry about them." I waved vaguely at the empty seats. "We'll be here for you."

She took a deep breath and nodded. "Okay. Thanks, K."

A woman appeared from backstage. "Are you the band?" She held up a hand and motioned for us to follow her with all four fingers. Then she turned and walked away without a second glance. Assuming this was the evil Jane, we hurried to catch up with her.

Track Three

The TV in the green room was mounted in one corner of the ceiling, and Lana couldn't help thinking of a hospital waiting room. She'd been in a few, and she'd been just as nervous. They spent the afternoon rehearsing, getting a feel for the room's acoustics. Codie pointed out that they were too static, with her and Nessa stuck behind their instruments. They came up with a move that they hoped would provide enough movement to keep people interested. They ran through it a couple of times, since it required Lana to know where Karen was without looking. Eventually their rehearsal time ended and they had to hope they were ready.

The show began, and the band watched on a closed-circuit television in the green room. Even though it wasn't the official and nicely edited version that would air later that night, it still felt close enough to real for them to get excited. Nick did the opening skit, which led into the theme song with him looking into the camera and, with an exasperated sigh, declare, "Looks like you better settle in, Seattle. It's going to be a long night."

The theme music played, and Lana tensed. The rest of the band gathered around her, breathless as the other guests were listed. Then: "And performing on this week's Friday Night Audition... Radiation Canary!"

They applauded themselves, and Lana couldn't help but smile. It was official. Her mouth was dry, but she resisted the urge to drink this early. She didn't want the urge to pee hitting in the middle of the song. She focused on the monologue.

"Who is the governor now? Does anyone know?" He turned to his sidekick for help. "Is it still Gregoire? Okay, okay. Just making sure. You can never be too sure these days. Have you been following this vote fiasco? Dead people voting, felons casting ballots. I don't know how I feel. I mean, we've seen how well living people vote. Why not give the corpses a chance?" Nick smiled, his left hand in his pocket while he gestured with his right. He looked like someone holding court at a society gathering. "I just like hearing people say the word 'gubernatorial.'"

She was already in her outfit for the show: jeans tucked into brown knee-length boots with buckles up the sides, a long billowing blouse - sleeveless of course - and a scarf. She plucked at the ends of the scarf, finding loose threads and teasing them until they came loose. She stopped when she realized she might pull the wrong thread. *Good, Lana. Show up on television in a moth-eaten scarf.* She focused on the others.

Karen was in a long blue dress that draped her shoes, topped with a light-weight tan jacket. Codie looked absolutely gorgeous, her tomboy rough edges smoothed over by hair and makeup to make her look devastatingly intense. Nessa had resisted the well-meaning sprites that occupied the cosmetics room but still came out looking even more elegant than usual. She wore a white tuxedo shirt with the sleeves rolled up and a pair of black trousers. It was her intention to fade into the background as much as possible.

Lana resisted the urge to chew her fingernails. Wouldn't look good on camera. She didn't eat anything for fear of indigestion or, God forbid, belching on camera. She was just going to sit on the couch, watch the show, and put all her energy into the song. Karen sat next to her during a segment where Geena Davis showed Nick how to properly shoot an arrow.

"You doing okay?"

"Yeah. Just another show, right? Not even a whole show... just one song. We can make it through one song."

Karen smiled. "Yep."

The night's second guest was a blur, a survivalist who had tried to survive in the wilderness with only the clothes on his back. A production assistant came to get them toward the end of the interview, and Lana drained a glass of water with one swallow. Then she put on a pageboy cap, tucking all the strands of her hair up underneath it until it was all contained. She was about to leave when Nessa stepped in front of her and put both hands on her shoulders.

"You won't be alone, even when the spotlight's just on you. You'll have me. You'll hear me. All right?"

Lana smiled, relieved, and hugged her. "Thanks, Ness."

"We'll knock 'em dead."

Lana knocked on the wooden doorframe as she passed, following the rest of the band down the strangely narrow corridor to the area immediately backstage.

Nick unfastened the top button of his shirt as the camera zoomed in on him, and he smiled through the lens to the audience at home. Lana watched from a bizarre angle, seeing him address the camera from a sidelong viewpoint, and she looked away. The crowd was draped in shadows, and much closer than the crowds at other venues. She hated the way the band was on the floor and the audience rose up. It was the opposite of what she was used to. Intimidating. The exit signs glowed red at the periphery of her vision.

"It's Friday, and you all know what's coming next. It's Friday Night Auditions, and the choice is up to you, so pay close attention." He held up their CD. "Tonight's band is local from here in Seattle; their first CD is called *Action After Warnings*, here they are, give it up for... Radiation Canary!"

The light came up on Lana, leaving the other three in shadow. The polite applause faded as Nessa began the soft melody that opened the song. Lana felt a fist clenching in her stomach but ignored it. The butterflies had turned to concrete and couldn't fly, so she used their weight as strength as she looked up. Above the camera, below the lights, to the top row of the auditorium.

"Reaching out for you, trying to be heard

Gonna raise my voice, no one hears a word"

She closed her eyes and focused on the melody. Her voice was more plaintive than on the album version, more of a plea, and she thought it worked beautifully.

"Gonna make it something simple, easy to follow

I'm going to tell you the importance of your radio.

I'm out here shouting into space, sound in a vacuum

Flip a switch, turn the dial, bring me into your room

Gonna make it something simple, easy to follow

I'm going to tell you the importance of your radio."

As she said "radio," Karen used the bow of her violin to knock off Lana's hat. They had practiced the move almost as much as the rest of the song, making it perfect so that Karen could flip the hat away and immediately start playing. Lana's hair collapsed around her face, and she backed away from the microphone as the rest of the lights came up to illuminate the rest of the band. Lana kicked her foot against the ground in time to the beat as she rolled her head to the side, hair flipping as she suddenly assaulted her guitar. The song had gone from a prayer to a shout in the space of a heartbeat.

Codie brought in the drums right before Lana's hair fell. As the drums reverberated through the studio, Lana focused on creating a driving rhythm. She closed her eyes and envisioned it as a tree, with Karen's strings wrapping around it like a vine. She thought she heard something off, then realized the audience was responding with applause. Goosebumps rose on her arms as she stepped forward again. This time Karen, Nessa and Codie joined in with her, and their voices joined the music.

"The worst things happen in silence

Quiet makes you think you're just alone

Drown out the absence

You've always known

We'll stay up with you until dawn's glow

Never forget the importance of your radio."

Lana turned to Karen, playing to her for a moment. She glanced toward

Nessa and Codie, both of whom were tearing up their instruments with almost religious fervor, sweat gleaming on their foreheads. Lana felt sweat in the small of her back, but she ignored it. She winked at Karen and turned back to her microphone. The next verse was hers, and she focused on random audience members who seemed to be responding.

They hit the last verse, and Lana swept her hand out to one side, letting the note die as Codie, Nessa, and Karen all stopped playing. The music seemed to evaporate as she sang the last line a cappella.

"That's the importance of your radio."

When she rocked back on her heel away from the microphone, the crowd applauded. There were a few whoops, which made her feel good, and she turned to offer her own applause to the other members of the band. To her surprise, Nick had crossed the stage and was standing between her and Karen. He was shaking Karen's hand, then turned to Lana and took hers. He squeezed it as he gestured with his other arm. He snapped his heels together and stood ramrod straight, as if he was announcing royalty.

"Radiation Canary, ladies and gentleman! Get on your internet devices and vote yes! Vote *yes*, I'm not even acknowledging there's a 'no' option this week. I'll be very disappointed in all of you if you don't bring these ladies back. That's it for tonight and for this week. I am Nicholas Young wishing you a goodnight." He blew a kiss to the camera and spun on his heel.

"Un-fucking-believable."

Lana's ears were burning, and she hoped the makeup covered the fact she was turning beet red. "Sorry. We changed the song a little–"

"A little? You turned it into a, into a..." His eyes were wide, and he shook his head as he gave up on finding the right word. "Remarkable. Absolutely remarkable. I don't fiddle with the results, but if these little ingrates vote no, I want you back here next Friday to give them a chance to do the right thing. Deal?"

Lana laughed breathlessly. "Yes, sir."

Nessa put an arm around Lana's waist, and Lana leaned against her. She had felt that twinge, that warning that she may be close to passing out again, and she nodded her thanks as Nick continued heaping praise on them. She didn't focus on what he was saying until she heard him mention an MP3 as "available on the website."

"What MP3?"

He looked at her. "This one. The live performance of your song. We generally offer it as a free download on our site. Of course, you're free to use it however you see fit."

"Looks like the fans won't have to wait for the live album after all," Lana said to Nessa.

Lana moved in a daze. The cameras were shut off, and people swarmed the stage. Lana just wanted to get out of their way, picking up her hat from the spot it had landed. She spotted Karen and hugged her. "Perfect. The hat flip... it was just perfect."

"I kept worrying about scraping your neck."

Lana had to reach back to make sure she wasn't cut, but even if she had been... "No, it was... you heard them. The cheers."

Codie launched herself at them, wrapping both in a wide hug that threatened to knock them all over. Nessa joined the pile, and soon all four of them were laughing. Codie stepped back and pointed to the retreating audience. "You know where they're going right now? To their computers, to look us up. Probably not all of them, but... a lot. A lot." She laughed and squeezed Karen's arm.

Lana exhaled and finally noticed how hot she was. She wiped her face with the end of her scarf. "Finally. Hard part's over."

Karen's eyes widened. "Are you kidding? All we've done is perform. Now comes the waiting for results, the long wait for the downloads and the CD orders... the hard part is just beginning."

"Maybe for you," Lana said. "I can wait with the best of them. I've been waiting for years." She looked around the stage, at their set-up that now looked abandoned and lonely. She laughed and shook her head. "I was waiting for this, and now... the hard part is definitely over. Now's the fun part. Also hard, but... oh, so fun." She put her arm around Karen's neck and walked her toward backstage. "Come on. Let's get our stuff and go celebrate. We've only got about five hours before the whole world knows who we are. Let's not waste it."

Track Four

We were surprised to see it was still light out when we finally left the studio. We'd gotten so wrapped up in the show that it felt like it should have been bedtime. We piled into the van and made calls to various relatives, telling them where to meet us for dinner. It was going to be a huge dip in the band's coffers, but we felt it was necessary. It didn't matter what the vote results were; we knew we'd done a great job and the band decided without discussion that it was a worthy expenditure.

"Geena Davis said she thought we were awesome," Lana said from the front seat. "I shook hands with Geena freaking Davis!"

Nessa was more impressed with Nick Young. "We'd have to wait a month or two to start our mad love affair, maybe even longer, just so it wouldn't look like favoritism. But I'm willing to wait for him."

We stopped to pick up the Amazon who had planted the good-luck kiss on Lana that morning, a bartender named Alia, and headed for the Space Needle. We had made reservations early, so we were shown to our tables as soon as we arrived. The best thing about a revolving restaurant is there's no such thing as a table with the best view; every table had the best view at some point. Alia sat on Lana's lap, which looked odd considering Alia was taller and built larger than Lana.

By the time our drinks arrived, the rest of our guests started trickling in: Dad and Ted, Nessa's roommate Clark, a few of Codie's friends from the garage, and a bevy of supermodel Amazons that I knew could only be Lana's mysteriously beauteous coworkers. Lana whispered in Alia's ear, and Alia shifted to a different seat. We were a large and boisterous group but we did our best to be unobtrusive to the other diners. We told the waitress who we were and why we were celebrating, and she promised to watch the show when she got off.

Everyone carpooled back to Codie's loft to watch the show. We arrived well before the show began, and Codie turned on the radio so it would feel more like a real party. Lana introduced us to a dapper man with short dreadlocks and told us his name was Bar-E, and he was the one who arranged studio-time for us. Codie, Nessa, and I all agreed to wait on him hand and foot the rest of the night out of gratitude. I think he was more embarrassed by the attention than anything, but pretty soon I saw him and Nessa getting cozy in the kitchen.

The morning and afternoon was starting to feel like a dream. I got hold of Nessa when she separated from Bar-E. "Are you waiting to see the show just to make sure it really happened?"

She grinned. "That's exactly why I'm eager to see the show." She patted my hand. "You want something from the kitchen? I'm heading that way."

"I'll come with you." I followed her through the crowd that had somehow doubled since leaving the restaurant, passing by two women in backless blouses. I eyed them, and then tapped the back of Nessa's arm. "How does Lana know all these gorgeous women?"

Nessa hesitated. "I don't think it's my place to tell you."

Intriguing. Cryptic. But whatever. I shrugged and helped her with the drinks. We carried them back to the entertainment area, which had a beautiful rug and copious seating arranged around a big credenza that held the TV, stereo, and more DVDs and CDs than most Borders stores. I gave Dad and Ted their drinks, then tracked down Lana and Alia on a strip of concrete outside the window that Codie swore was a balcony.

I leaned out, but stayed safely in the window frame. "Hey. You two want anything to drink?"

Alia pulled her arm free from Lana's. "Uh-uh. You two are the guests of honor. I'll get the drinks. Besides, I remember what Lana drinks." She kissed Lana soundly before she squeezed through the window past me. I watched her go, then cautiously stepped out onto the alleged balcony. I kept my back to the wall. "Don't do it. You have your whole life ahead of you."

She snickered. "Enjoying the party?"

"Yeah. You?"

"Still a little frazzled from this afternoon. It's a really good dream, I'm just waiting to wake up and find out it's really happening tomorrow." She hissed and rubbed her arms. "Ooh, I'm on edge. Your Dads are awesome."

"Thanks. Your friends are, um..." She laughed. "How do you know so many women like that? And where do I sign up?"

Lana twisted to look through the window, gauging Alia's location before she spoke. "They work with me."

"They're dance instructors? I might have taken lessons if I'd known that."

"No, my other job. At Club Nightside."

Well, that didn't make sense. "Club Nightside is a strip club."

Lana stared at me.

"What do you do at a strip club?"

Lana laughed and looked out at the city.

"Like... waitressing?"

"Yeah. I waitress, too. Keep it down, okay? I don't want Alia to know."

I nodded. I couldn't even picture it. Not that I really wanted to picture Lana naked and... I cleared my throat. "Why didn't you tell me?"

"It's not what every little girl dreams of doing to pay the bills, right?" She grinned and lifted a shoulder. "Besides, I'm going to quit soon. Once my face is on TV, there's a bigger chance people at the club will recognize me. And if those two worlds collide, it'll destroy my dance class. No one wants little Blakely and Madison learning how to grind a pole."

"Oh. That's too bad."

She grinned and nudged me. "Were you planning to come by and check out a show?"

I blushed. "No. 'Course not." I stuck my hand in my pockets and we looked at the city together. Alia returned and held out a drink to Lana. "Speaking of shows, I think ours is about to start. People are gravitating toward the TV."

"Okay. Get us a good seat."

She retreated and Lana took a deep breath. She toasted the city with her drink. "Our public awaits. They just don't know it yet. C'mon."

I went back in with her. Dad and Ted had saved me a spot on an armchair big enough for two, so I shared it with Nessa. Lana sat on the floor in front of the couch with Alia behind her. Codie, ever the hostess, was never in one place too long. Picking up discarded cups, getting more drinks or bags of chips. She was orbiting when the opening skit came on, and the room got surreally silent as the theme music started.

"Tonight, Nick's guests are actress, activist, and archer Geena Davis! Survivalist Marcus Luden! And performing on this week's Friday Night Audition... Radiation Canary!"

The room erupted in applause. Lana twisted and pressed her face against Alia's thigh, and Alia chuckled as she stroked Lana's hair. The show was bizarre, since we'd seen it all that afternoon. The survivalist tried to show Nick how to start a fire with kindling, which nearly resulted in setting the desk on fire, a good conclusion to any interview. Nick smiled into the camera. "We'll be right back with this week's Friday Night Audition. Stay tuned!"

Dad rubbed my shoulder. "Hey, you okay?"

"Nervous. Which is weird, since we've already done it, right?"

"Not weird at all, honey. You're just taking the nervousness you were too busy to feel then and moving it to now."

I saw Lana watching me, and I winked at her. Nessa found my hand and squeezed it, and Codie perched on the arm of the chair not occupied by my father. The show came back, and I would have sworn I forgot how to breathe. Nick introduced us, and it was like my ears popped right before he said the band's name. Time sped up a little. The camera angle shifted and there we were. The light faded up on Lana and she looked up into it, her eyes shining and so so green. Even I felt a chill when she began to sing.

After the first verse, I saw a shadow move over Lana's right shoulder. *Holy crap, that shadow is me.* My bow came up and tucked under the back of Lana's hat. It pushed up, and the hat vanished. Lana's hair collapsed, the lights came up, and we began playing with gusto. I watched Codie and Nessa, blown away with how professional they looked next to Lana. What the hell was I doing there with them. I blushed, and I thought I was squeezing Nessa's hand too hard. I tried to pull back, but she said, "Don't let go."

Codie looked like she was on the assault, shoulders hunched and head down as she flailed at her drums. I hadn't even noticed the cameras, but there was a close-up of me during the interlude. My eyes were open, my lips slightly parted, and the camera pulled back as I moved to the microphone and started to sing. They switched to a full shot that covered all four of us from the right. Lana was canted forward, like the figurehead of an old sailing ship. Watching her sing, I felt relief wash over me.

We would win. Who would vote no with someone like that?

Nessa said, "God, look at you."

I furrowed my brow. Me? I wasn't even on stage. Them!

The song ended suddenly. It couldn't have been that short... it had felt like hours we'd been on the stage. But Nick Young was suddenly there, shaking our hands, telling people to vote us back on the show. All my butterflies were gone and I pressed against Nessa's side. "You guys were so good."

"You were there too, you know."

I noticed Dad was texting, and then I saw other people in the room were also typing into their phones. One of Lana's friends held up her phone. "Voted yes!"

"Yes!"

The chorus went up from everyone in the room. Alia said, "How many times can we vote? I have text limits, but I'm prepared to go over."

After the initial rush of votes, the crowd began to disperse. Codie invited everyone who was interested to stick around for the episode to repeat, then put our CD in the DVD player so the sound system could really do it justice.

Dad and Ted informed me they had worn out their welcome, something that was news to me, and said I could stay out as long as I wanted. Dad said it in a way that I knew he knew I was going to do it anyway; permission was just so I wouldn't feel guilty. At Lana's urging, I danced with one of her hot friends - as gorgeous as they were, I still couldn't process that they were strippers. We made a decent-sized dent in the stack of CD's we'd gotten from Bar-E's uncle.

By the time *Settle In*'s repeat aired, the party was mostly down to the four of us and a handful of friends. I looked out on the balcony for Lana and Alia, but they were nowhere to be found.

"Codie. You seen Lana? We're about to be on again."

"She might have gone to lie down. She's had a big day." She pointed. "I told her the guest room was down that hall. She'd want to be up to see it again, though."

I agreed. "I'll go wake her up."

The guest room door was open a crack, and I pushed it open with the intention - I swear - to wake Lana gently. I didn't think about the fact Alia had disappeared at the same time, or process the sounds I heard coming from inside. I just pushed the door open, glanced inside, and immediately retreated. I pressed my shoulder against the wall next to the door and closed my eyes, like I could will myself to unsee what I'd just witnessed.

The bed was perpendicular to the door, so I'd gotten a sidelong view. Fortunately Lana's arms had kept me from seeing anything other than curves - such *nice* curves, though. They were under the blankets, and Lana seemed to be doing the lion's share of the work. I knew I should retreat, but the sound of the bed combined with the soft grunting sighs Lana was making. My hand dropped from my mouth to the curve of my breast, and I closed my eyes as I listened to her. *Put your hand on me... there. Yes, God, there.*" I must have been beet red, the heat radiating off my face as I glanced back to see if anyone was about to catch me catching Lana, but the hall was empty. Lana cried out quietly, and then a weak sob, and the protests of the bed slowed down and then stopped. The next sound I heard was a sultry chuckle - Alia, I figured - and a relieved sigh.

"God, I needed that."

"I could tell. Shit... we left the door open."

"Had other things on our mind... it's okay."

More chuckling, more kissing, and I decided it was retreat or get caught. Codie saw me leave the hall like I was being chased.

"What's going on?"

"Lana wasn't sleeping."

"She... *oh.* Well, she's been tense all day. That probably helped more than sleep."

I just smiled and took a seat on the couch. Less than five minutes later, Lana emerged. She was flushed, glowing, and her hair was mussed. She hooked her thumb on the button of her jeans and coughed quietly as she looked around to see if anyone noticed her state of disarray. She put her hand on Alia's hip to guide her to the couch. "Did we miss it?"

"No, it's going to start after this break." Nessa looked at Lana and Alia, then grinned. "Where'd you two run off to?"

Lana dropped into the armchair, her legs draping the arm, and Alia sat in front of her. She leaned back to use Lana as a cushion, and Lana put an arm around her waist. "We were napping."

"I could use a nap like that," Nessa said.

Lana looked over. "With Bar-E?"

Nessa's humor faded into shyness and she tried to lift her shoulders over her head. The show came back on, and the few remaining guests fell silent as Radiation Canary took the stage for the third time that day. The anxiety was gone, the panic and worry that it would be a horrible failure faded, and I was able to just enjoy it for what it was. It was out of our hands now.

I smiled and put my head down on Nessa's shoulder. We'd done it.

Track Five

Lana and Alia slept together in the guest room, while Karen and Nessa camped out in the living room. Codie didn't sleep. She turned the lights down low enough for sleep, but bright enough the others wouldn't stumble on their way to the bathroom. She turned on her computer and went to the site, something they'd sworn not to do until morning. But she couldn't help herself; she needed at least a peek. She held her breath and clicked on the site's stat page.

It had to be wrong.

She'd checked it the night before, and they'd only had twelve-hundred hits. Now it was saying they were up to seven thousand.

The entire album had been downloaded two hundred times in two hours. No, wait, some of them had to be from people who attended the taping. "The Importance of Your Radio" was the most popular download, but "Emerald" made a good showing as well. They had preorders for the physical album, more than they could currently fulfill. It was on back-order, but apparently people kept ordering. Codie covered her mouth to stifle her chuckle, then shut off the computer. She stood up and looked into the living room.

Karen was asleep on the couch, draped with a comforter and appearing to be fast asleep. Nessa was on the floor in front of the couch, uncovered but equally unconscious. Lana... well, considering how red Karen's face had been earlier, Codie wasn't about to go knock on the guest room door for anything less than a fire. She took her jacket off a peg, slipped outside as quietly as possible before donning her shoes in the corridor.

She went downstairs and stood on the sidewalk, hands in her pockets, and looked up and down the street. The city was quiet, but not entirely silent. It slept, but it snored. She smiled at that thought and looked at a Camry parked in front of her building.

No, Codie.

She ran her hand under her nose, brushed her hand over her mouth, and tilted her head to look through the passenger window.

Codie. No.

Codie stepped off the sidewalk, ignoring the shout in her head as she popped the lock and slipped behind the wheel. A minute later, she was three blocks away idling at a red light. She drummed her hands on the steering wheel and wet her lips. Her skin felt electric. She clenched and relaxed her fingers on the grips of the wheel and pressed her weight down on the gas pedal when the light changed.

If you get caught now, if you go to jail now, you'll ruin everything for them.

The all-night gas station was lit like an island in the dark sea. She put up her hood and made sure she kept her back to the building as much as possible. She didn't need to watch the meter because she was going to fill it up. The hose clicked off after a minute or two, Codie replaced it in the hook, and hurried inside to pay. The clerk was too bored to realize she was a person, let alone what she looked like.

None of her precautions mattered. The cops would only check out the security tape and question the clerk if charges were pressed, and who would press charges for having their gas tank filled? Prices the way they were, she might get a civic award for generosity.

As she drove back home, she imagined the same horror stories she always did when she indulged her urges. *If you get into an accident... if someone works nights and came out looking for their car... if someone saw you pop the lock and was a good Samaritan.* Only once had she returned to find someone looking for their car. She had tossed them the keys like a valet, saluted, and chirped, "Brought it around like you asked, sir. All gassed up, yes sir, of course. Have a nice drive." The man had been too confounded to respond, and she was gone before he thought that maybe a crime had occurred.

She eased the car back into its spot, nice and cozy, and headed upstairs feeling looser in the joints. She slipped back into the apartment where the rest of her band was sleeping. She took off her shoes and jacket and slumped in the spacious arm chair. She watched Karen and Nessa, smiled, and eventually drifted off to sleep.

Alia was an amazing alarm. Silent, subtle, and impossible to ignore for long. Lana pressed her shoulders into the pillows and lifted her hips in response. Her chuckle was throaty, and she reached down to run her fingers through the waves of dark hair resting between her thighs. She ran her thumb over the shell of Alia's ear as she came, her breath steady as Alia kissed up her stomach, between her breasts, and finally her lips.

"You're not the only talented tongue in the room," Alia whispered, and Lana laughed. They kissed for not a short amount of time, and finally pulled away. "You have practice with the band today?"

"Not today. We've been working nonstop the past two weeks. Show's over, so we're taking the weekend off. We've earned it."

Alia's eyes brightened. "Ahh. So, have any plans?"

"Well, I think you were onto something with your tongue a moment ago... why don't we explore that a little more after breakfast?"

Alia purred and pecked Lana's bottom lip. "Sounds like a plan."

They got out of bed and Alia pulled on her clothes from the night before. Lana searched the closet and found some of Codie's old clothes. The T-shirt was a little tight in the chest and shoulders, but the pants fit well enough to manage until she got home. "I'm going to go see what the shower situation is like." She kissed Alia's forehead as she passed and left the bedroom.

Karen and Codie were in the kitchen eating breakfast, and a pile of Nessa-shaped blankets was tucked against the front of the couch. Codie put a finger to her lips and Lana nodded as she tiptoed past. "Hey," she whispered. She gestured at her clothes. "I found these in the guest room closet–"

"That's what they're there for."

"Shower?"

"The next door down from the guest room. Towels and stuff are in there. Karen and I have already taken ours." She cleared her throat and looked pointedly down the hall. "It's, uh, big enough for two if you want to conserve water for the rest of the building."

"I'll keep that in mind." Lana pinched Karen's cheek playfully. "Early risers. Okay. We can check the website once we're all up and about."

She and Alia showered, only getting sidetracked once during the process. Alia chose to wear the clothes she'd worn to the party, since Codie's wardrobe didn't quite meet the requirements of her curves. Nessa zombie-trudged into the shower when they were done and came out livelier, but not by much. They had breakfast together, and Alia seemed to sense they had "band business" to take care of an excused herself. She would take a cab home, change, and Lana would pick her up for lunch to start off their weekend together.

Once they were alone, Codie took out her laptop. "Okay, I have to confess, I peeked last night. I couldn't sleep otherwise." She clicked onto the website as the other three gathered around her seat. She went directly to the stats.

Lana's hand closed on her shoulder. "That's gotta be a mistake."

Codie shook her head. "Nope. It jumped a bit since I saw it last."

Karen pointed. "That's downloads since the site went live, right?"

"Nope." Codie clicked a button. "That's since the site went live. The other number is how many times it's been downloaded since the show aired." She went back to the other page.

Nessa said, "Trying to be devil's advocate... even if all those people voted yes, if they're the only ones then we'd be the lowest-rated Friday Night Auditions act in the history of the show."

"That's a good point," Lana said. "But we had our best night ever, and that's because of you guys. We spent the past two weeks killing ourselves for last night, and it paid off. No practice today. We're just going to take it easy and relax. Jane said they'll let us know by Sunday night, so we'll get together then and wait for the call as a group. Sound good?"

They agreed. After finishing breakfast, they went their separate ways to enjoy the spoils of their victory before they discovered whether it was a minor win or a major one.

Saturday felt like my birthday. No one seemed to realize how special the day was, how remarkable the sun was, or how beautiful it was when the sun reflected rainbows off the puddles of rainwater from that morning's shower. Dad and Ted took me to the library, where we spent a good hour wandering the stacks. I got a few books, including a copy of *Don Quixote*, a perennial favorite of mine, and then we took a ferry to a small island for a whale watching tour. We were still en route to the island when my phone rang with a number I never expected to see. I made an excuse to get away from the Dads, walking along the railing in the cold before I answered.

"Mom?"

"Hey, Care Bear. I saw you on television last night. Thanks for sending me the email about it being on. You looked amazing. Sounded amazing, too."

It was so bizarre to hear her voice after so long. We'd let our calls get too far apart. "Thanks. We've really been working hard at it."

"I can tell. I went to your website and got a few songs. None of them seem to be about evil mothers who abandon their girls, so... are you saving that for the next album?"

I smiled sadly. "Nah, you're okay. We don't have any evil-parent songs. Besides, I owe you for making me take lessons all those years."

"We weren't exactly twisting your arm. But I'll definitely take the credit. How's your father doing?"

I looked back to where he and Ted were leaning on the ferry railing. "He's really good." I couldn't help but feel like a teenager again, caught between them like this. I'd only really stayed with Dad to finish college, and Mom understood. No one claimed a side, but the facts were that I was with him and Ted while Mom kept drifting away. "I was thinking I might come see you sometime. I mean, the band can't just tour Washington forever."

"I'd really enjoy that, Karen. I'd like to meet your friends. The lead singer of your band is so gorgeous. I imagine she's quite popular with the gentlemen."

An unwelcome flash of Lana on top of Alia was dispelled with a quick shake of my head. "She's pretty focused on the band right now."

"Well, that's good." A pause. "Well... I wanted to congratulate you on the show. I voted yes after my doorman showed me how."

I laughed. "Thanks. Did you make him vote, too?"

"I should have. I will when I get home. See you on stage, kiddo. Love you."

"Love you, too."

I was reluctant to hang up, but I did. I went back to where Dad was, but Ted was nowhere in sight. "Went down to the car," Dad explained as I sat down. He gave it a moment and said, "Your mother?"

"How'd you know?"

He shrugged. "You only walk away like that for calls from your mother or your girlfriend and... uh." He scratched his neck. "When we got home last night, there was a box of your stuff on the front porch."

"Ouch."

"Yeah, ouch. I guess you might get one no vote after all."

I shrugged and leaned back. He cupped the back of my head the way he used to when do I was small. His fingers didn't quite cover as much as my skull as they once did. We watched the little islands pass by.

That night, after we got back to the city, Dad dropped me off in front of the rehearsal space. Once the whole band was there, we piled into Codie's van and she drove us downtown. We parked in a lot in the shadow of the Space Needle, and Codie produced some of Elysian's Wise ESB beer to celebrate or drown our sorrows. At dinner time we ordered a pizza to be delivered to the van; none of us wanted to risk being away when the call came in.

Halfway through the pizza, Lana's phone rang. No one moved until the second ring, and Lana quickly wiped the grease from her fingers and answered. "Hello? This is Lana Kent." She looked out the windshield as she listened. "Yes... okay. Oh. Okay. Yeah. That's fine. Thank you."

During each pause I could hear the muffled, robotic voice of a woman coming through the speaker. My hands were cold and I flexed my fingers to get the blood moving. We were all staring at Lana as she hung up, stared at the phone, and then looked at us as if we'd materialized when she wasn't looking.

Nessa was the one to break the silence. "Well?"

"Seventeen percent."

I blinked. I had told myself to prepare for the worst, to be realistic, but that was crushing. "That... it has to be higher than *that*."

Lana shrugged. "They tallied the votes very carefully. We'll have to be satisfied with getting seventeen percent... more... yes votes... than anyone else has ever gotten."

The silence in the van was leaden. Codie shook her head. "Wait, what?"

Lana exhaled sharply and smiled. "We broke a record." She laughed, but tears rolled down her cheeks. "Our score was seventeen percent higher than any past act. We're going to be back on the show Monday. And Tuesday. Wednesday..."

Nessa launched herself at me, but I was too stunned to appropriately return her strangling embrace. Codie and Lana were laughing and crying in the front seat, and then we traded partners. I decided we could band together and kill Lana for her horrible trick later.

Preferably after we finished our week of televised shows.

Track Six

The teaser for Monday's episode of *Settle In, Seattle!* started in the dark. The light came up to reveal Nick Young leaning against the edge of his desk, his hands laced in front of him. He was staring at the floor, brow furrowed in thought, and he looked up as if the camera had intruded upon his contemplating. "Hello, friends. When last we met, I asked... no. I *implored* you to make a decision, and I begged you to make the right one. I spent this weekend hoping and praying that you would follow my advice."

He sighed heavily and pushed forward, going down the steps to the performance area. "Last night, I was informed of the results from our latest Friday Night Auditions segment." He let it hang, and then smiled. "Well done, world. Not only did you listen to me, but you broke a record!" He pointed into the camera and stepped forward, snapping his heels together as he moved closer to the lens. "Well *done*, you. You're as brilliant as you are good looking."

He turned and walked back toward the camera. "So please allow me to reintroduce you to Lana Kent... Karen Everett... Nessa Grace... Codie Renton. Otherwise known as–" The curtains swept open to reveal the band. They began playing the show's theme song as the lights came up. Nick stood among them, arms stretched wide with a gracious smile on his face. "Radiation... Canary!"

He raced forward to the camera, bending down so he stayed in frame. "You better settle in, Seattle, because this is gonna be a *good* one!"

Radiation Canary continued playing the theme song as Nick's sidekick Hank read the guests for that night's show. When he reached "And the musical guest all this week, by your votes, Radiation Canary!", the lead singer's laugh wasn't caught by the microphones. It was seen by all, though, and anyone in the audience not already smitten with Lana Kent became a little closer to being converted in that moment.

I knew the song was my own choice, but panic was starting to creep up after the monologue ended. It was one thing to hide behind Lana... I could handle that. But now I was going to sing. On television. With actual people watching. I looked out at the audience, and then down at the carpet under my feet. Someone had put it down to protect the performance floor from being scuffed up, and I brushed the toe of my boot over it. I suddenly decided that if I felt more comfortable in the space, I could settle my mind.

I bent down and took off my boots and, ignoring the crowd of people in the risers in front of me, curled my toes in the carpet. I closed my eyes and felt myself calm. I told myself that if I was barefoot, I was comfortable. And if I'm comfortable, then I'm safe. I took a deep breath and rolled my shoulders as I let the calmness take me over. The director gave Nick a ten second warning, and the panic flooded back. I had to get my boots back on before the cameras started rolling. "Wait..."

Lana said, "Leave them off." I looked at her and she nodded to reassure me it was the right thing to do. I didn't really have a choice; the time to ask for a delay was gone. The show came back, and a camera moved closer to where Nick was standing in front of his desk.

"Earlier," Nick said, "I told you folks you broke a record. Our musical guest tonight and for the next four nights received more yes votes than *any* act we've *ever* had on our stage. I begged you to bring them back, and you responded in spades. Once again, Radiation Canary! Take it away, ladies."

As we'd practiced, I stepped closer to the microphone. "Thanks, Nick." I looked at the audience, faceless shadows backlit by emergency signs. I struggled to keep my voice steady. "I know we got votes from all over, but we're from Seattle and we feel like this show is still very local, so, um, we decided to thank everyone for bringing us back by singing a special song. If your town is mentioned in the lyrics, uh, uh... no offense." I smiled. "This is called 'Emerald.'"

I sang. It was like sleepwalking; if I didn't think about what I was doing, it was easy. During the second chorus I turned toward Lana. She moved forward and we shared a microphone. The camera moved in on us both, then swept around to cover Codie and Nessa.

After the line, "Keep your Kansas, we'll take Seattle," the music faded. Lana stepped back, and I put bow to string to slowly sample the chorus of 'Defying Gravity' from *Wicked.* When it reached the end, Lana started playing again to carry us back into the chorus one last time. I heard Codie and Nessa singing harmony with me. I heard Lana's guitar. We all stopped playing, and I sang, "My city's an emerald," into silence.

The silence lasted an eternity in my head, which was later verified by video as being about one second. Then... a wave crashed against the side of the studio. Part of the ceiling collapsed. Everyone in the room began opening potato chip bags. My mind ran through the possibilities until I realized it was applause. Thunderous. I smiled and said, "Thank you," into the microphone. I wasn't even thinking. It seemed polite.

"No, thank *you.*" Nick Young was sharing the microphone with me. He put his arm around my shoulders and said his goodnights right next to my ear. I could smell his cologne and the pancake makeup on his face. He had a long, slender neck and a prominent Adam's apple. I was standing on stage with Nick Young, and every viewer of *Settle In, Seattle!* was looking at me. I thank whatever deity was listening that I made it backstage before I threw up.

That's one video we didn't really want going viral.

Lana gave me a wet washcloth and put it on my forehead, holding it in place with her fingers. My head was on her thigh and, despite my protests that I wasn't really sick, she insisted. "I know how hot those lights were. Just hush." We were in the dressing room, waiting for Nick at his request. We'd already changed back into our street clothes, but he was still in the suit from the show when he finally arrived.

"Phenomenal, ladies. I've been blown away by you four. Fairy Tale Dream added so much bullshit to their live performance that I was afraid when I saw you had changed your songs from the album versions, but my *God.* Your songs have just evolved, haven't they? Couldn't stop them if you wanted to. I haven't been this excited about an act in a very long time." He clapped his hands together and then looked at me. His face switched as easily as if putting on a mask. "What happened? Are you okay?"

"Butterflies got out."

He winced. "Oh. I'm sorry. Better backstage than on camera, eh?" His smile returned and he regarded the rest of the band again. "You have the rest of the week to look forward to, ladies. Please don't let yourselves stop here. We've had plenty of acts around for a week, and then they just disappear into the ether. Do you remember Morningside? No? I didn't think so. Use this opportunity. Get yourselves a manager, start looking around at labels, don't let it slip away. If you do I'll... I don't know. Force you to change your names, put on masks, and bring you on Friday Night Auditions every week until you hit it big." He smiled and touched his eyebrow with two fingers, tossing off a salute. "See you tomorrow, ladies."

Nessa sighed after he left. "I'd fuck him."

Nick's voice echoed from down the hall. "I'm flattered!"

Nessa tried to bury herself in the chair. But I was looking up at Lana. She looked down at me, and we knew we'd come to the same conclusion. We'd had a few other piranhas circling us, the record label equivalent of ambulance chasers basically tossing their cards at Codie's van when we pulled away from a show. Lana had turned them all down, waiting as they became more respectable and more serious in their offers.

It was time to stop playing coy. We had a decision to make.

Track Seven

I loved Naomi Marrow the second she walked into the diner. The place was designed to look like a rustic cabin without any of the downsides, giving the interior a dark and comfortable feel. Nessa and Codie had agreed that Lana and I would be the ones to handle the meeting. I didn't know if I liked being trusted to represent the whole band, but Lana once again reminded me that I was co-founder. I'd have to find a way to remember that.

Naomi was tall and lanky, with a shaggy John Lennon mop of black hair and Buddy Holly glasses that looked prescription rather than affectation. She wore a brown blazer over a faded blue concert tee and jeans, and her shoes were Chuck Taylors. Lana was the kind of beauty who could sell magazines and looked good on television; Naomi was the kind of beauty who actually existed in real life. She smiled when she saw us and folded herself into the opposite side of our booth.

She held out her hand. "Naomi Marrow, Cartography Records. Really glad you ladies decided to meet with me today." We shook and introduced ourselves. She spoke again quickly, almost too quickly for us to get anything in edgewise. "Let me tell you a little about our label. Cartography was founded five years ago by Dash Warren. She was sick of dealing with CEOs who thought of music as a business and songs as product. It is, and they are, but they can't be manufactured that way. Van Gogh never sold a painting. If he was a musician he would have been stuck doing gigs in dive bars and faded into obscurity." She spoke with her hands, waving them for emphasis and punctuation. "So she started her own label to give artists a safe place to work, but also allow them the freedom necessary to be themselves. She sees herself as a patron rather than a boss. If she likes the work you're doing, you have a home with us."

Lana said, "Cool. I'm a huge fan of–"

"Yes, it's very cool. And I'm sorry, I'm kind of steam-rolling you here. I understand, I know, and I'm sorry. I'm not usually this hyper. I've been rehearsing this whole speech all morning. I love you girls. I love your band. And I really want to make a place for you at Cartography. I'll calm down once you get to know me. Honest." She sipped her water and, in the lull, I looked at Lana. Her eyes were wide, but she shrugged.

"Let me give you an idea of how we work. You have your first album out already, and we'll remaster that, release it to a much wider audience. Do you have your second album planned yet?"

Lana realized she was being given a chance to speak. "Yeah. It'll be called *Rome Burning*. Nessa's idea. Since we have the–"

"Strings! And fiddling while Rome burns. Excellent, that's perfect. And the cover art?"

I said, "I found this really decrepit cello, so I thought we'd have that on the cover with a little fire burning on the bottom of it."

Naomi laughed. "Awesome, awesome, I love that. That's perfect. And this is a perfect example of how Cartography might be a pain in your neck. We'll ask that your third album cover have your faces on it. You two, Codie, Nessa, all four. You're beautiful girls, and sex sells. We'll raise the album sales ten, fifteen percent just from people who want to do you. It's crude, but that's the world. We're not going to tart you up or make you look like Victoria's Secret models. You'll get to choose the poses and what you're wearing. It's all in your hands. Dash had to deal with producers posing her like a Barbie doll and she's not going to do that to anyone else. I think that's a reasonable enough request?"

"Sure," Lana said. "We were thinking of doing that anyway."

She smiled. "That's what kind of record label Dash wanted. Where our suggestions mesh with your plans, or in some way point you in a direction you'd be willing to go with or without our interference. It's our job to sell you, not to make you into something that's easier for us to sell. From what I can see, you're doing a good job selling without us."

Lana looked at me, but I tilted my head. I liked her, but I didn't trust myself to seal the deal. No matter what anyone else said, Radiation Canary was Lana's band. Then Nessa and Codie. Then me. I didn't feel responsible enough to agree to anything official. Lana mulled it over and then held her hand across the table.

"I think we'll be very happy together, Ms. Marrow."

She grinned and gripped Lana's hand, then crossed her own arm to reach for my hand. I shook, and she nodded.

"We'll have a contract for you to look over in a few weeks, but for now... I think this will be a good partnership. When we have bands like you, bands who know what they are and who they want to be, it makes our job very easy. Just do what you've been doing. Just make music. Let us figure out how to make sure people hear it."

The main office of Cartography Records was on the Olympic Peninsula, so eight days later we were on a ferry to sign the contract.

We were still riding high from our week of shows on *Settle In, Seattle!* still reeling from our last appearance when Nick Young requested permission to sit in with the band and play his harmonica. He wasn't a great addition, but he wasn't bad. We chose "Survivors" for our last night so Nessa would have a chance to sing. We'd offered to let Codie sing one of Nessa's songs since she didn't have one on the album, but she declined. She was content in her kingdom of the drum set. At the end of our final show, Nick assured the home viewer we'd be back on his stage before too long as proper guests, and we tried not to look overly excited about the prospect.

Our sales continued to climb. We had to pay to make more CDs, but at that point we were making enough off the website sales that it wasn't too big of a deal. One of the biggest changes was that Lana quit her job at the club, and I could relax. Since discovering her true vocation, I'd fought the urge to put on dark sunglasses and a trenchcoat to see a show. I fantasized about it a few times, even went so far as to find out how much a lap dance cost. But I refrained, and now the temptation was gone.

I won't pretend I was happy about missing the opportunity, but I was relieved.

And now we were on our way to Port Townsend to sign the contracts that would seal us into a deal to make three albums (which included the re-release of *Action After Warnings*) in the next five years. I had no doubt we could do it. "Scene of the Crime" was finished, and I only hoped I could keep from blushing when Lana performed it. We had five other songs I felt confident about, and if I could wrangle "Say a Prayer (If You've Got One)" into a coherent form I knew we'd have a hit on our hands.

"Emerald" was shocking me with its ability to move. Every time I was certain everyone in Seattle had a copy, we got another hundred downloads. Maybe it didn't matter that we badmouthed so many cities in the song. Nessa said it was apparent the song wasn't about insulting the other towns; it was about pride in Seattle and people responded to that no matter where they were from. Apparently so.

We drove past the Cartography Records office twice before we noticed the sign. It was a Gothic red-brick building, a former school judging by the carved name on the keystone over the door. We went up the wide front steps into a cavern-cool lobby. A shining brown-black tile floor reflected the ceiling, and close to ninety percent of the light was provided by the large glass entrance. Cubbyholes lined the wall at about waist-height, and a secretary was seated at a crescent-shaped desk at the intersection of corridors directly ahead of us. Our footsteps echoed as we approached, and she smiled.

"Radiation Canary?"

"Yeah."

She stood. "I'll show you where to go."

We went down concrete steps to a floor that was eighty percent underground. Narrow windows near the ceiling let light into the former classrooms, and Nessa shuddered.

"I'd never go to school here," she whispered to me. "Too many nightmares about being buried alive."

The current owners had done its best to make the building comfortable, however, and we didn't get any premature burial feelings as we waited in Naomi's office. We had just enough time to get comfortable when she came in, still in a T-shirt and jeans with a blazer to affect the professional look without too much hassle. She greeted us all warmly, introducing herself to Nessa and Codie before she sat behind her desk.

"Okay. I'm glad to see you girls again." She sat behind the desk and smiled at me and Lana. "See? I told you I'd calm down. Now, you had someone look over the terms on the PDF of the contract we emailed over to you, yes? Were the changes okay?"

Lana nodded. "Everything looks fine."

Actually they had argued to get me a bigger chunk of the royalties, since I was the writer of the majority of our songs. I settled for letting them add a clause that I owned the rights to all Radiation Canary lyrics, since I either wrote them myself or helped polish what the others wrote. I didn't feel that was necessary but Lana insisted was important. I didn't care. I just felt weird about getting more royalties than the other three members of the band.

Naomi took the contract out, skimmed it to make sure it was the right version, said, "Yep," under her breath, and turned it around to place it on the forward edge of her desk. "Take a look over that, make sure it's all in order, initial each page, and then sign on the last page."

We took our time. The process of all four of us initialing each page seemed to take forever, but finally we reached the end. Lana signed first, then Codie, then Nessa, and then me. I dated it, and Lana handed the contract back to Naomi. She signed underneath my name, and then tapped the page with her fingertips.

"Welcome to Cartography Records, ladies. We'll put you on the map."

Later on I was ashamed that it took me so long to get the joke.

Track Eight

Call me naive, but the contract came with something I never expected: money. Naomi cut us four advance checks before we left the palatial school building, the total promised by the contract split four ways. I folded mine into my pocket, embarrassed that it was larger than the others and hoping no one would notice. Lana noticed, but she waited until we were leaving before she nudged my arm. "It's because the songs are yours alone."

"They belong to Radiation Canary."

"Right, but they're your babies." Nessa reached the bottom of the steps before Lana and I did and turned around in front of me. "We were in that rehearsal space for two and a half years before you came along. Playing music, every now and then playing a club. We were Little Cat Feet, and it was a hobby." She took out her check and held it up. "You came along, and we're Radiation Canary, and we've got a check in our hands from a record label. You don't think that deserves a little extra? I think you should get the whole check and decide how much the rest of us get out of it."

I blushed, but Codie and Lana patted my arms to let me know they agreed with her. "All right. But I'm buying you all dinner."

Nessa grinned. "Well, I assumed you would. I'm thinking lobster."

"Surf and turf," Codie offered.

Lana slipped her arm around my elbow. "You got us here, sister. Enjoy the spoils."

I let her lead me back to the van, thinking about the money in my pocket. The numbers seemed huge, but I knew it wasn't real money. Band expenditures, taxes, little bites that would make a dent in what, on the face of it, seemed like a fortune. But with my savings, there was enough for something that I'd been putting off far too long. Even though it broke my heart, I knew the first thing I had to do.

Dad loaded the last box of books into the back of Codie's van. She and Nessa were inside getting the last remnants of my clothes out of the attic, an excuse to leave me alone with Dad and Ted. I'd found an affordable apartment not far from Codie's. The neighborhood wasn't great, but it wasn't the badlands, either. Dad drove down to have a look, and donated material from the shop to mend what needed fixing. After adding a front door with brand-new locks and installing freshly painted cabinet doors they deemed it a worthy domicile.

Now leaving was all that remained. I had thought the six weeks of hunting would prepare me for the moment, but the actual departure was proving just as hard as I'd feared.

I rubbed my hands on my pants and looked at them. "I guess that's it. You have to come over for dinner sometime. A lot of times."

"Try to keep us away." Dad hugged me and whispered, "Proud of you, kid," into my hair. I closed my eyes so I wouldn't cry, then hugged Ted. Dad said, "That goes both ways, you know. If we go over to your new place for dinner, you have to come back here just as often."

"That's the plan." I saw Codie come out with the last of my clothes. "I guess that's it. I'll see you tomorrow night."

Dad nodded, and I took the clothes from Codie. I added them to the pile in the backseat, then climbed in after them so the girls could take the front. We pulled away and Codie turned on the CD player. She advanced through the tracks until she reached 'She's Leaving Home.'

I couldn't help laughing. "Nice. Keep Simon and Garfunkel handy in case I need 'Homeward Bound' on my soundtrack."

"Nah," Codie said. "It's tough now, but you won't look back. First step of the rest of your life. You're on your way."

I leaned back and closed my eyes, hoping that she was right. The maudlin runaway song transitioned into a happier circus-themed song, and I rocked my head along with the music in an attempt to stop myself from looking back.

That night, we held a housewarming party at my new place. Lana brought beer and, to my surprise, two guests. I had expected to see Alia, but the brunette behind her was only vaguely familiar to me. Alia took the beer into the kitchen, and Lana congratulated me on the apartment. "I wanted you to meet someone. Josie, Karen Everett. Karen, this is Josie Riddell. She used to work with me at Club Nightside."

"Oh," I said.

"As a... waitress." She raised an eyebrow to make sure I got it.

Josie laughed as she held out her hand. "I saw your band play live. You're so amazing."

Despite blushing, I tried to act nonchalant. "Thanks. Welcome to my home."

Lana grinned. "Big step."

Josie touched her elbow and stepped away. "I'm going to help Alia with the beer."

"Okay." Lana put her arm around my waist and led me away from the door. "So? What do you think of her?"

"I don't know. I mean, isn't Alia jealous?"

Lana furrowed her brow, then rolled her eyes. "No, for *you*, dunce. Josie asked me if you were single during the watch party, and back then I wasn't sure. But you said that you officially broke up with Penny, so..."

I looked over my shoulder. The kitchen had a pass-through that was currently open so I could see Alia and Josie loading the beer into my woefully empty fridge.

"She's interested in *me*?"

"Yeah, of course she is. She couldn't take her eyes off you the entire night. When I told her I was coming tonight, she offered to pay for the beer in order to get an invite."

I didn't know how to respond to that. "I-I don't know."

"What's not to know? She's gorgeous, she's interested..."

"She's a stripper."

Lana stopped walking. "What does that have to do with anything?"

"I can't date a stripper."

Lana frowned and dropped her arm from my waist. "Really. Ethical dilemma?"

"I didn't mean that it was... I just meant that I can't date someone who takes their clothes off in front of other people every night."

"Like I used to."

"That was different."

"How?"

I winced. "You quit...?"

Lana was irritated, but trying not to show it. I hooked my hand around her elbow and nodded toward the bedroom. She shrugged but she followed without forcing me to drag her. I held the door open for her, then shut it behind her. I hadn't quite gotten the room put together yet, so it looked more like a storage room at a second-hand store. Lana crossed her arms and waited for me to speak.

"It's nothing to do with you or what you used to do. But I am having a dilemma."

"Right. You're single. I was trying to help you out with it."

I shook my head. "We're so close to being famous. Locally, at least. Someone recognized me on the bus the other day. The girl at the supermarket knew me." I sagged against the door. "I don't want to give away my virginity to someone who just wants to fuck me because I was on TV. But my only other option is Penny, and I don't want to lose it with her, so that leaves some stranger. And that's not how I pictured losing my virginity." My eyes were burning, so I hung my head. "I waited so long because I wanted it to be special, with someone I really cared about, and now I either have to throw it away or have it be meaningless."

Lana stepped forward and hugged me. "I'm sorry, K."

"No, I'm sorry. It doesn't have anything to do with her being a stripper. If I have to throw it away, might as well do it with someone blindingly hot." Lana laughed and I pulled back.

Lana brushed her thumbs over my cheeks. "Don't throw it away. Don't sleep with anyone just because *they* want to. Wait until you find the right person and you want to do it. Then it won't matter why they want to, it'll still be special for you. That's all that matters." She kissed my cheek. "Splash some water on your face before you go back out. Take your time."

"Okay. Thank you for bringing me a stripper."

"I aim to please. And don't worry. In the future, the girls and I will keep the backstage orgies to a minimum so as not to tempt you."

I laughed. "Much obliged. I'll see you out there."

She left, and I went into the bathroom to take her advice. I splashed my eyes, checked to make sure I didn't have to redo my makeup, and ran my fingers through my hair. To be honest, I didn't have anything against strippers. I was still debating whether or not I should visit Lana's former club just to see what it was like. But really my problem was that if I had to lose my virginity to a stripper, I wanted it to be Lana.

I filled the water glass next to the sink, emptied it with one swallow, and pressed my wrist to my lips before I returned to my party.

Codie was wandering from the crowd, avoiding all the chipper, happy girls, and peered into the bedroom. The parts of Karen's bed called to her like an unlocked sports car, so she put her drink down on one of the boxes, cracked her knuckles, and went to work. She found the tools in a pile next to the wall and arranged the pieces in the center of the room so that the final product could be moved to wherever Karen preferred. She was reading the Sharpie identification on the boxes when she heard someone stop in the doorway.

She looked up from the mostly-constructed bed and saw Karen staring at her in disbelief. "Hey. Where are your sheets and pillows? I was going to make your bed for you."

"Looks like you already succeeded. Codie! This was supposed to be a party."

"A housewarming party. I think putting together furniture is more in the spirit than standing around talking to Lana's stripper friends." She turned to look for a box with a convenient "Bedding" label and gasped as Karen hugged her from behind. She tensed. "Really, really not a hugger."

"Yeah, whatever. Thank you, Codie."

Codie smiled and patted Karen's forearms where they crossed her chest. "Least I can do. Now let me go. Find the sheets, and tell me which wall you want me to move it against."

After the bed was situated, Karen insisted they return to the party. She whistled and put a hand on Codie's shoulder. "Codie Renton officially wins the housewarming."

Nessa said, "I didn't know it was a competition."

"Maybe that's why you lost." Codie winked and moved toward the refreshments table.

Lana was on the couch with Alia, half-asleep but still managing to contribute to the conversation. Karen got hijacked by Josie, who turned out to be a very cool lady. Meanwhile, Codie hung back and watched her friends flirt. Codie had known Lana since high school, a random seating assignment leading them to taking a music class together. She still remembered Lana Kent, with her frizzy hair and glasses, tenderly touching the guitars their music teacher had on display. Who knew where it would lead?

Codie had never suspected Lana was gay when they were in school, but now the thought of her being with a man was almost ridiculous. There had been boys in high school, of course... The one that she remembered most was the trumpeter with an overbite. And then there was Karen, the newest member of their little group, blushing and bowing her head bashfully as a beautiful woman touched her forearm.

Nessa came over to where Codie was brooding. "You're blocking the punch."

"Are you gay?"

Nessa backed off. "Forget it. I'm not that thirsty."

Codie grabbed her arm. "No, I mean." She nodded with her chin at Karen and her apparent date. "I just wanted to make sure I wasn't the only one."

"Don't worry. We're half and half. It's a good balance." She nudged Codie. "You're still blocking the punch."

Codie moved and let her pour herself a glass. Codie didn't mind. Hell, Lana and Karen could date each other for all she cared. She was thinking about Lana's insistence that the band didn't need an image. As she watched Alia sneak a kiss before heading back into the kitchen, she couldn't help worry that they might get an image whether they wanted one or not.

Josie was a great kisser. A really, truly amazing kisser. We'd spent the night talking and, when she said she had to head home, I offered to walk her out. We talked a little more on the sidewalk and a good night kiss turned into making out. She had a car and suggested we move into the backseat, and I was in no shape to say no. She kissed down my neck, her hands moving over my clothes and making me buck and twitch each time she reached somewhere sensitive. She nipped my earlobe and I was sure my face was glowing from the heat rising off of it. She guided my hand to her breast and I caressed the curve, heart pounding as she slid her hand from my knee, up my thigh, to–

"Wait," I gasped, twisting away and letting my hand drop to her hip. Marginally safer, but still dangerous territory. I closed my eyes and hated myself. "Wait."

"Is everything okay?" She tucked a curled hair behind my ear and then leaned in to kiss my temple.

"I don't know." I was in the backseat of a car. How many people lost their virginity in the same place, and how many would have killed to lose it to someone as knee-shaking hot as Josie? But I couldn't. As much as I wanted to, I wasn't ready. And I knew I wasn't setting myself up for a relationship. It was what I'd told Lana earlier; I had waited too long to throw it away like this. I looked at Josie. "I'm sorry, Josie. I really am. You're gorgeous, and amazing, but I ca-can't."

"It's okay. We just met." She smiled. "I don't want you to do anything you're not comfortable with. I enjoyed the kiss."

I smiled. "Me, too. We could kiss a little more if you want."

"Sounds like a nice way to end a party." She leaned in and kissed me again.

Track Nine

I don't know what happened to April. Suddenly it was late May, and we were making plans for the summer. Lana was the one who suggested we move out of the rehearsal space to somewhere more personal. We needed a place that was just ours, where we didn't have to squeeze in time with a multitude of other acts. We had a contract, so we deserved to treat ourselves like real musicians. So we said farewell to the space and started hunting for a more appropriate locale.

In the midst of our searching, Cartography contacted us. One of their acts, the Femme Reapers, was going on a tour of the Pacific Northwest. Ten summer shows in British Columbia, Washington and Oregon with two shows in Idaho. Naomi wanted us to open for them. When our cheering died down, we agreed to think about it. The label worked out all the details and we departed the first week of June.

I couldn't get over my excitement. The Femme Reapers were twins named Laura and Ella Cowan. On stage they wore outfits in subtle shades of red and blue, topping it off with long black coats. Laura wore red, Ella wore blue. They were lithe and athletic blondes, the kind of pretty that started in high school and blossomed only when they were in college. I'd once heard an actor describe a costar as "the girl next door, but that would have to be one heck of a neighborhood." It certainly fit the Cowan sisters. I was a huge fan; their debut CD had played pretty much nonstop in my bedroom from the moment it came out, so the idea of sharing a concert with them was like an early Christmas present. And they proved Naomi was right. Part of the reason I bought the CD was because of how beautiful they looked on the cover.

We met up with them at the first stop on our combined tour, and we hit it off immediately. Laura knew some of our songs and talked Lana into an impromptu collaboration backstage before the show. I was waiting for someone to usher me out so the real stars could get ready. Ella suggested a mash-up of "One in Ten" with their current hit single "Lost," asking if I minded providing the cello. I didn't, and I was blown away by how well Lana meshed with their style.

After the song, I was returning the cello to its case when Laura came over to me. Her guitar hung in front of her like an ornate necklace, swinging until she put a hand on the neck to stop its movement.

She smiled and held out her hand. "Hi. I'm Laura."

"Yeah." I couldn't help chuckling. "You guys are amazing. Hope we're not stepping on your toes or anything."

Laura shook her head and settled next to me. "We're newbies like you; we just got a bit of a head start. I've been thinking about adding some strings to a few of our songs. There's one I can't stop thinking about. Can I hear what it would sound like?"

"Sure." I got my cello out again and began to play. Laura strummed along with me, nodding her head in time to the music as she watched my hands. I felt a little self-conscious, but I pushed through it and just gave myself over to the song.

When the song ended, Laura said, "I think I got chills. We have to do that on stage. Will you stick around after your set to play with us?"

"Of course. Yes, sure, yeah."

I was grateful, but the idea of performing with them. This was the band whose CD I had bought, whose music had played while I did chores. What right did I have to ruin one of their songs? They didn't seem too worried, so I pushed aside my anxiety and joined Lana and Laura for another round. I couldn't stop smiling. We were in another country - Canada, but it still counted - playing music with an actual famous band. I was living in an apartment I'd paid for with money earned from making music.

We still had time before the show, so Codie and I took Nessa on a tour of Vancouver since she'd never been. I'd only been a few times, and Codie eventually admitted she'd only been once, but I decided half-dumb tour guides were more fun than anyone fully informed. We certainly saw more of the city than a guided tour would offer. Sure, it was because we got lost, but that's the fun of exploration.

On our way back to the club, Nessa crossed the street and waved for us to join her. A poster was hanging inside the glass wall of a bus stop, and Nessa framed the pertinent text with her hands.

At the top was a huge western-style font announcing the Femme Reapers were appearing in concert that night. The cartoonish text acted as the masthead for the image of our new friends standing in the rain dressed like gangsters. Below, in letters that were small but not humiliatingly so, was the phrase: *With Opening Act Radiation Canary.*

Nessa ran her hands over the frame, looking for a latch. "How do you get these things open? I want that."

I laughed and tried to pull her away. "I think they sell them at the concert."

"That's not the same."

Codie said, "Better than getting kicked out of a country. You want to be banned from Canada? Resist your criminal urges, girl."

"Getting arrested could give us street cred."

"Nope." Codie managed to get her away and we started walking again. "Another country, maybe. You get banned from Canada, there's no one on Earth who won't mock you. C'mon. I'll buy you one at the door. I'll even autograph it for you."

"Aw, aren't you a sweetheart," Nessa said.

We arrived in plenty of time and were surprised to find Naomi Marrow in our dressing room. She was in a charcoal blazer now, but wore suit pants and a red blouse instead of her more casual attire. I saw the tennis shoes and horn-rims had stayed, though, and I approved. She looked up as we entered and smiled. "Hey, there's my band. I was afraid Lana would have to go on alone. How do you ladies feel?"

"Fine," I said. "Is everything okay?"

"Perfect. I just wanted to make sure everything was going well for you. It's your first tour, your first performance outside of your home turf. I thought I'd show up for moral support. Just go out there and do your best. It'll be more than good enough."

We changed into our outfits for the show. Our only stipulation for wardrobe was Lana's request that her arms remain bare. I had been given a black dress that was also sleeveless, but that would be hidden by the red leather jacket. Codie wore black tuxedo pants and a red blouse, while Nessa got a white peasant blouse with the sleeves pinned above her elbows and jeans.

I took a look at us as we waited for the stage manager to give us the go-ahead to go out and I smiled. "Look at us. We look like a band or something."

Lana grinned and squeezed my arm.

We were escorted out of the green room, down a short hallway, and then into a strange small space. It was enclosed on all four sides and, for a second, I had a flash of claustrophobia. A stage hand entered behind us and opened a hatch in the ceiling. He moved a metal staircase so that we could climb up, and I realized we would be emerging from the stage floor.

"You know what would make that really cool?" Lana asked. "Fog. Pump some fog up, just enough to hide the door, and it'll look like we're coming out of the smoke."

I nodded, smiling at the image. We'd have to keep that in mind for our own shows. The stage manager motioned for us to go up, and we moved to the stairs single-file. Lana first, then Nessa, then me, and Codie last. She put her hands on my shoulders and squeezed, and I patted her hands. I caught my breath and exhaled slowly as I looked up at the hazy light filtering through the hatch. Lana was right; it needed fog.

"Ladies and gentlemen, fresh off their week of appearances on *Settle In, Seattle!*, please give a warm welcome to... Radiation Canary!"

Lana raced up the stairs with the rest of us following. We moved to the spots we'd been shown during rehearsal. Lana gripped the microphone and spoke. "Thank you, Canada! This is our first show in your country, but I get the feeling we're going to like it here."

She turned toward me and lifted her chin with an unspoken question. I nodded that I was ready, and Lana counted it out for the others as I began to play.

We started with "Carry On," then "All Clear," and onto "Duck and Cover." We were only supposed to play for thirty minutes, and we had it pretty well-timed. Rather than squeezing in more songs, we rehearsed to add in more instrumentals that would showcase Codie and Nessa. At one point Lana wandered over to me and got a drink from her water glass. She turned her back to the audience and leaned toward me. I was just close enough and she spoke just loud enough that I could hear her say, "So far, loving Canadian audiences."

I smiled and played through the chorus of "The Exclusion Zone," and we moved on to the finale of "The Importance of Your Radio." We were halfway through when the sound of a second guitar appeared out of nowhere, and Lana looked around for the source. Laura and Ella emerged from the hatch, Ella playing and Laura clutching the microphone. Laura put her arm around Lana and said, "Mind if we play through?"

"Be my guest," Lana said into the microphone.

Laura and Lana sang the chorus together and I got chills as I watched someone famous singing my words. The crowd was going crazy, of course, eating up the impromptu collaboration. I didn't need a watch to know that the Femme Reapers had taken the stage a little early, but I couldn't be annoyed. We were riding their coattails, so it was only fair that they got to share the stage with us for a while. Laura came over to me and I smiled at her, stepping aside so we could share the microphone.

When the song ended to thunderous applause - part for us, part for the surprise early arrival of the band they'd actually paid to hear - Laura took the microphone.

"It's about time for Radiation Canary to be done, but I think we want them to stick around a bit." She turned to Lana. "Do you ladies know our songs?"

I laughed at her bothering to ask such a silly question. Lana began to play "Prohibition," and Laura nodded. "Well, hell, ladies. I think we can bluff our way through this."

I was nervous, slightly panicked, as I played. I knew the majority of their songs, but under pressure feared that every note and lyric would pass out of my brain just when I needed them most. With Ella beside me, though, it was easier to relax. I couldn't help wondering if Naomi had something to do with this, if she'd known we would get more than the opening spot, but I put it out of my mind and focused on just playing.

Track Ten

The tour traveled down the I-5 out of Canada. From Vancouver Island to Richmond, then back into Washington and the good old USA. To Everett, where Lana insisted on taking a picture of me under the 'Welcome To' sign because of my surname. Olympia, Salem, Portland, then east to Moscow and Coeur d'Alene, Idaho. We traveled in a bus arranged by the label, and I spent the long hours on the road writing. We almost had the entire second album written, we just needed to find time in the studio to record it.

We were somewhere in the Cascades when I went to the back of the bus to the sleeping area, basically a large bed with a bunk on top of it. Lana was stretched out in bed with her bare feet crossed, slumped down so she could look out the back window. I sat, and she smiled sleepily at me. I handed her my journal.

"What's this?"

"It's one of the songs for *Rome Burning*. I wanted to make sure you were okay with it before I officially added it to the roster."

The song was "Scene of the Crime," and it included lines she had given to me based on Codie's description of Alia. Now that they were serious, I wanted to make sure she was comfortable with the additions I had made. I was more than willing to take out my embellishments if she thought it was awkward for me to write lyrics about how sexy her girlfriend was. She skimmed the lyrics and raised an eyebrow.

"Wow. This is kind of raunchy for us."

"Raunchy? I wasn't aiming for raunch."

She turned the journal around and read one of the lyrics. "If I didn't have her, I'd still have my hand. Not as much fun, but at least I'd know where I stand." She chuckled. "What were you going for with the masturbation reference, if not raunch?"

I have to admit, I didn't have much of an answer. "We can cut that."

"No. Like Naomi said, sex sells. We can make this work." She scratched her upper lip. "I'm more worried about the 'she' and 'her' and 'daughter' references."

"Oh... are you not out?"

"I am. But... I mean, we're doing this for a general audience. I don't want to be labeled as the gay-girl band."

"Yeah, 'cause that really held back the Indigo Girls."

She nodded like that made her point. "Yeah. I mean, they're synonymous with lesbian rock. I want to hit it mainstream before we have to deal with a label like that."

I slumped against the wall and felt the hum of the bus rattling through my bones.

"I'm not saying we have to throw the song out. Maybe just some creative editing to make it more... androgynous."

I raised an eyebrow. "Androgynous? You can't make this song androgynous." I took the journal from her and pointed to one line. "'But her heart's pounding in her breast, slide my hands under her dress, I know I'd sin again in exchange for her caress.' How do you suggest we butch that one up?"

"I don't know." She looked irritated, torn and twisted, and I felt too bad for her to be sincerely angry. "Can we just think about it before we officially stick it on the album?"

"Sure. That was the point of warning you about it." I hooked the pen on the cover of the journal and got off the bed. "We're almost back to Seattle. If you want to nap, you should probably try to fall asleep pretty soon."

She shook her head. "I'm just watching the traffic. You want to join me? It's lonely back here."

I almost made a snide comment about whether it was too gay to lie in bed with her, but I didn't feel like continuing the fight. I kicked off my shoes and got back onto the bed, leaning against the side of the bed opposite her. She reached down and squeezed the arch of my foot, and I managed a smile as I joined her in looking out the window. Cars were passing us, hovering behind us like birds flying in our vector. If I focused enough on the road, I could ignore the glass to imagine I was flying backwards through space. I grinned at the thought and fell asleep with Lana giving me a slow foot massage.

Lana wasn't sure what she expected upon their return to Seattle. A ticker-tape parade was naturally too much to hope for, but maybe there could have been an official welcoming party from the label. Instead they got off the bus, unloaded their own instruments, and went back to their cars like kids getting home from church camp. The Femme Reapers bus arrived soon after them. Laura and Ella joined the huddle between the buses, reminiscing about the tour.

Before they left, Laura touched Karen's hand. "You're a really great musician. Any time you want to crash one of our concerts, you're welcome to."

"Thank you. Uh, ditto, obviously."

"I'll take you up on that."

The bands lingered in the parking lot for nearly half an hour before Codie suggested lunch. The Cowan sisters agreed, and the whole group migrated to a nearby restaurant. Lana's head was spinning from the tour. Nowhere near enough sleep, nowhere near enough food, and way too much alcohol conspired to make her feel like the living dead.

The conversation over dinner made her feel like she was in *Rashomon*. Codie and Ella Cowan talked about a sushi restaurant they had discovered near the US/Canada border, while Laura revealed why Ella had seemed so lethargic during the Idaho leg of their tour. "Her boyfriend got sick. It's not anything serious; they both just wished she could have been there."

By the time they paid the check, Lana felt like she'd gotten a full picture of everything that had happened on the tour. They all hugged in the parking lot, still reluctant to part after spending almost three weeks getting in each other's hair. Codie left first, of course, easily separating herself from the sentimentality with a promise to see everyone later. Once she was gone, it was easier for the rest to break away. As Lana pulled out of the parking lot, she realized that was why Codie had done it. She was sly that way.

Lana parked and carried her guitar upstairs. She was bone-weary and eager to hide underneath some pillows and blankets for a few hours. How many people had stared at her over the past twenty days? Thousands? She wanted to be anonymous and completely alone. She let herself into her apartment, grateful for the familiar feel of it as she toed off her shoes and put down her guitar.

Her answering machine was flashing. Renee, who had agreed to cover Lana's dance classes for the duration of the tour, told her everything had gone fine. The building manager calling to let her know that the laundry room was being painted the first week of July. Alia, who admitted she was only calling to hear Lana's voice on the outgoing message. Lana smiled and replayed that one. That was real life. She relaxed and undressed in the living room, then carried her clothes to the bathroom.

Showering in club dressing rooms and hotels was one thing. But only her own shower could make her feel truly clean again. She held her hands under the spray and swept the water up over her head, worked her hair with clawed fingers, and let the water pelt her chest and back. She was home. She would sleep in her own bed, have food from her fridge, watch her own TV. Later on maybe she would call her girlfriend and get laid.

The tour had taught her one thing. As much fun as it was to be on the road, the main attraction of touring was that it would allow her to truly appreciate coming home.

Track Eleven

They found a new rehearsal space in July, and spent the first few days getting acclimated to the acoustics of the building. They played songs from the first album since they knew what they should sound like, then moved on to the new material.

The album exchanged the doom-and-gloom nuclear theme for a more literary approach. The first song they completed was called "Sancho Panza" after the character from *Don Quixote*. It was a ballad in which Karen swore to follow her love wherever "they" went and whatever "they" did. Lana had again vetoed mentioning gender, which Karen was amenable to.

"I'll make your windmills mine
Together we'll walk the line
Between madness and reality
We'll conquer every knight we see
We'll never wake from this impossible dream
Take me with you when you go
I'll call you Don if you call me Sancho."

Nessa contributed the idea for "There Were Badgers Here," a line from her favorite book, *The Wind in the Willows*. The sentiment of the line was that animals were around long before humans, they were here now, and they'd survive long after we were gone. Lana immediately fell in love with it, and turned it into something truly extraordinary. Karen envisioned a three minute song, but Lana orchestrated an instrumental interlude that changed it into a sweeping five and a half minute epic. Codie's drums, Nessa's piano, and during the guitar section, Karen would swap out her violin for the cello to close out the last verse.

They spent at least twenty hours a week rehearsing, carving out moments before and after real world obligations. Lana and Codie slept at the rehearsal space often enough that one room had four cots and a few blankets piled in the corner. Through it all, Karen kept writing. There were days when she would finish a song and they would start working on it minutes later. Lana saw no point in sitting around and waiting. The songs were there, so why not work on them? Finally, in August, when they had most of the tracks ready, Karen presented them with the final song for the album.

She had notations about music in the margin to either side of the verses. It started off with just Lana singing without any accompaniment, like "Radio." Then Nessa would start to play, followed in the second verse by a very subtle melody from Nessa. When she reached the chorus, Lana and Codie would start playing, building from the gentleness of the first verse to something louder, larger, and more alive.

Karen said, "I figure it starts on the ground. And the first two verses, you're pushing yourself up. When you and Codie start playing that's when you start running."

"No. That's when we start soaring." She smiled. "That's us getting up and taking off. We have to go through this. Right now."

She took the time to run off copies of the lyrics and handed them out. Five minutes after Karen wrote the last word of the song, Nessa started playing the intro. After a few false starts they found something gentle enough to work but strong enough to open the song. Karen described it in the journal as the sound of a gentle drizzle tapping on the glass in the middle of the night. Lana closed her eyes and could see it. She pictured someone broken and defeated, lying on the ground, and she took that person's voice as her own.

"I need your help tonight
Alone, I can't win this fight
I tried to call,
But I couldn't find the right words
I'm going to fall
And I'm so sick of being tired."

Karen began to play, a wail that seemed to grow out of thin air all around them, and Lana got chills as she raised her voice from the soft whisper she'd been using.

"So say a prayer, if you've got one
I'm starting to come undone
I've got demons I can't outrun
Please say a prayer if you have one."

Lana closed her eyes and felt tears on her eyelashes. Karen's playing faltered, but Lana waved her off. "Don't stop. Keep going." She took a deep breath to steady herself and then moved on to the next verse.

"I won't count the eight times I get knocked down
Just the nine times I get off the ground
I'm only so strong when I'm alone
I've done as much as I can on my own
If anyone's out there, if anyone cares
If you have one, please say a prayer."

In the silence between verse and chorus, Lana dropped her hand to the strings and began to play. Codie tapped her sticks together and, at her cue, went to work. Karen moved the bow with quick and fluid movements of her wrist, head bowed so that she could focus on the sound. Nessa's hands glided across the keys. Lana turned her back to the microphone, facing the other three. When it came time for the chorus, all four of them sang.

"If anyone is there
If anybody cares
If you hear my plea
I need you to save me
Say a prayer
Say a prayer.

Codie and Karen stopped playing and Lana sighed: "If you've got one." Nessa played the last few notes as Lana backed away from the microphone, trembling. She held the microphone with one hand to keep it steady, head down and eyes closed as she caught her breath. Finally she looked at the others, laughed incredulously, and rubbed the corner of one eye with the back of her hand.

"Okay. That was..." She sniffled. "That, Karen, was a winner."

"Are you okay?"

She chuckled. "Yeah, I'm fine. I'll be fine." She sniffled and blinked away tears. "I need some air. You guys work on 'Man of Many Wiles,' okay?" She took off her guitar and placed it on the stand, ignoring Karen saying her name as she left. She stepped outside and breathed deeply, eyes closed as she slumped against the wall outside.

Karen came outside and stood next to her, not saying anything, just providing support if necessary. Finally Lana looked at her.

"Cancer. My mom."

Karen nodded and waited. She was comfortable with the silence, willing to let the story end there.

"She was a single parent. I was fifteen. The hospital had a chapel, and I went in but I thought... it's a hospital. People die all the time in hospitals. So how many of the prayers in the chapel ever got heard?" She sniffled. "But I prayed anyway. I tried to beat the odds. I prayed every single day before I went to see her, knowing she would have thought it was a waste of time. She didn't have to know if it worked. But it didn't." She wiped her eyes. "That song, K. I don't know if I'll be able to sing it live for a while. But I know I don't want anyone else taking it from me. It's my song."

"Yeah. It is." She rubbed Lana's arm. "I wish I'd warned you about it."

"You couldn't have known." She sniffled and pushed away from the wall. "I thought I told you to work on 'Wiles.'"

"You're not the boss of me, Kent."

Lana twisted to lightly tap Karen's rear-end with her boot. "Get in there, woman. And if you make me cry again, I'll beat your ass in front of everyone."

"Do it on stage. At least we'll get box office out of it."

Nessa felt bad about kicking out her roommate, Clark. But the simple fact was they didn't have much in common, they never really spent any time together, and she could afford to live alone. The only reason they lived together in the first place was because they kept running into each other while apartment hunting. They struck up a conversation and found out they had a similar budget and agreed to pool their resources. Now that she was successful enough to afford the apartment by herself, she felt like a tool for making him leave. She gave him plenty of time to find his own place and he understood the situation. There was no rush and, as such, he was able to make leaving seem like an idea he'd had on his own.

One day she came back to the apartment to find boxes stacked on the living room floor and a stranger was examining the bookshelf. She eyed him for a moment and then cleared her throat. He turned and she gestured at the shelf. "Everything up there is mine."

"Sorry. Clark didn't really leave a list. He's out picking up a pizza."

She took off her jacket. "Okay. And you are?"

"Scott." He stepped around the tower of boxes and held out his hand. "I already know who you are. Vanessa Grace. I saw you on *Settle in, Seattle!* Your band is amazing."

"Oh. Thank you. I guess you're a friend of Clark's?"

He sighed, hands on his hips as he examined the room. "Less friend than coworker who owed him a favor. He helped get me a promotion, so I get to help him move. I'm not sure it's an equal exchange. Although I did get to meet you, which was very cool. He never told me his roommate is famous."

"Probably because I'm not." She smiled and continued into the kitchen. "I'll be out of your way in a minute. I'm just going to grab something to eat and then hunker down in my room."

"If you stay out here and have some pizza, you can make sure we don't accidentally abscond with anything that belongs to you."

Nessa grinned. "I trust you."

"Well, if you won't have pizza with me and Clark, how about a real dinner with just me sometime?"

She paused in the kitchen door, not bothering to turn around. She didn't want him to see her smile. "Are you asking me out on a date?"

"I might be."

"Well, ask again when you're certain. I might say yes." She got a salad out of the fridge, checked the date to make sure it was fresh, then kicked the door shut.

On her way back through the living room, Scott said, "I'd like it if you would agree to have dinner with me."

She stopped, looked him up and down, and shrugged. "You might as well get something out of your good deed. There's a white board on my bedroom door. Leave your number and I'll give you a call." She went on into her bedroom and leaned against the door. Scott was tall, broad-shouldered, and handsome as hell. She assumed he would lose the beard if she asked him to, if it came to that. Definitely worth a dinner.

"Hm," she said. "Hm, hm, hm..." She tapped her fork against the plastic lid of her salad bowl and considered the possibilities.

Cartography arranged for us to have the studio time to record *Rome Burning*, and we'd do 'better' versions of the songs from *Action After Warnings* at the same time. It was a strange turnaround. The first time we played those songs, we were rushing and half-awake. Now we were the scheduled artists. I kept looking around for signs some up-and-comers had shuffled out the back way before we arrived, but they must have been cleaner than we were.

Naomi was there for most of the sessions. She came into the studio after "Say a Prayer (If You've Got One)" and held up both index fingers. "Single. That's your single, ladies." There were tears in her eyes, and I saw Lana was still unable to get through without misting up a little herself. If listeners had half the reaction they did... we really would have a hit.

We were still a long way from being ready to release the second album, but in September Cartography put out a so-called Deluxe Edition of *Warnings* as advertisement. It had all the original versions, plus the revised versions of each song. We added the embellished "Radio" along with a few live tracks recorded during our tour with the Femmes. We still had eighty-four copies of the first CD, and Naomi told us to hold onto them as collector's items or just mementos.

I was ready to give up on "Scene of the Crime," but Lana surprised me. She agreed to keep all the feminine pronouns and sing it as-is. When I asked what changed her mind, she shrugged and told me that "Prayer" made our image moot. "As long as we have Prayer on the album, we're not going to be pigeonholed." I was touched, but Naomi was wary once she heard it.

"It's..." She gestured with her hands. "The song is about masturbation. The narrator is in love with herself, right?"

Lana and I looked at each other. "Right," I said.

"She's her own lover." She rubbed her thumb over her bottom lip. "It's definitely a new angle for your image. You're sure about it?"

"Yeah," Lana said. "I want it on the album."

Naomi seemed to do some mental calculations, then shrugged. "I'm the one who said sex sells, right? Okay. The song stays." She tugged on the collar of her shirt. "Might have to put a heat warning on the CD, though."

We powered through "Forgotten Lore," a five-minute instrumental that ended with Lana vocalizing. "Sancho Panza" and "There Were Badgers Here" were epics in their own right. I sang the first, and Nessa sang the second. Both of them felt like creating a movie, like we were exploring a vast landscape at high speed. During the official track of "Scene of the Crime," Lana moved closer to the microphone stand, feet braced on either side, and moved her hips against it. She slid her hands up and down the length of it, stopped just short of brushing her lips on the microphone, and tilted her head back to expose the length of her neck.

I envisioned her doing it in concert, saw the lights on her and reflecting off her sweaty skin, and I knew we'd sell out every crowd once word got out. I felt bad, selling sexuality this way, but we had the power to back it up. "Prayer" would save us from becoming just another pretty face.

After "Crime" left us all hot and bothered, "Complications" and "Mountain Time" seemed almost pastoral by comparison. We recorded vocals for "Land Among the Stars," "Icarus," and "Band of Girls" all in one session, then went back to polish up "The Man of Many Wiles."

I was weary by the time the producer finally declared it finished. I didn't want to believe it. Surely there was one more song, one more track we needed to make a little better. Just one more thing we needed to pick up. But they told us to go home and relax, and to prepare for our own tour. The thought boggled my mind; hadn't we just gotten back from a tour? What was the point of having an apartment if I never got to see it?

The *Action After Warnings* Deluxe Edition came out at the end of 2005. Naomi told us that they would hold back releasing *Rome Burning* until we were ready to tour to promote it, which would give them time to build us up in promotions.

We spent Christmas together, just the members of the band and our immediate families. Alia was there, as was Nessa's new boyfriend Scott. Naomi showed up with gifts from Cartography, and we invited her to enjoy the night with us. She tried to beg off, claiming she was Jewish, but we told her we were nondenominational in our celebrations. Try saying nondenominational after a few drinks. But somehow, she got the message and agreed to hang out for an hour or two. My drunk self was a bit too happy about that, but I tried to tame it.

We went to a bar where an Irish band was playing the typical drinking songs.

"Fairytale of New York" turned into a sing-along, and then Dad, Ted and Alia conspired to get us on-stage where the band had left their instruments. We went reluctantly, but it was really thrilling to play such a small stage after our tour with the Femme Reapers. We played "Emerald," much to the delight of the drunks, and we worked through "Mushroom Cloud" despite the lyrics being... tricky... in our state. Finally, Lana turned to us and mouthed, "Prayer." I nodded, and she moved to the microphone and sang out the first line.

The bar was silent. Christmas lights alternated in the window, and a muted Claymation special was playing on the TV. When Lana sang the last line, no one in the bar moved. She blinked, and I felt like we'd utterly misjudged the song. Maybe we were just too close to it.

One man at the back of the room said, "My God."

Then Dad began to clap. I smiled, and Lana's shoulders sagged with relief. "That's a sneak preview of our next album."

"When's it coming out?" the bartender called.

Naomi was the one who answered. "We'll let you know, pal." She caught my eye and winked.

I smiled at her, and let Lana hug me. Nessa and Codie came out from behind their instruments and joined the hug, and I looked past Lana at Codie.

"Looks like you're the hugging sort after all."

"Only on special occasions," she said with a sneer, and I laughed.

We hadn't opened our presents yet, but it didn't matter. I couldn't imagine getting anything that would make Christmas any better than it was in that moment.

Album Three
THE MIDDLE DISTANCE
(2006-2007)

Track One

January of 2006 brought Lana and Alia's one-year anniversary, which was celebrated with an impromptu ski trip to Whistler. While they were gone, *Settle In, Seattle!* contacted us through Cartography to celebrate the anniversary of appearing on the show by coming back as official guests in February. We called Lana since we didn't want to make the decision without her, but anyone could have guessed what she would say. We were loosely scheduled for one of the last Tuesdays in the month, depending on which one had a free slot. Our appearance was contingent on how the Friday Night Audition went, a situation that seemed oddly familiar. We didn't care; just being asked back was big enough to make us lightheaded.

Finally the day arrived, and the Friday Night Audition band failed (grunge rockers called Posse Come-it-at-us... it was a *huge* surprise to *everyone* that they didn't make the grade), so we made the trip back to the studios. We checked in at the guard gate, parked in pretty much the same spot, and went through the same studio doors. Codie nudged me and said, "We were just here last week, right? This is our one-week anniversary."

"Couldn't have been a whole year," I agreed. "Someone should buy Nick a calendar."

Lana grinned. "I think Nessa would be happy to. Maybe for his birthday." She put an arm around Nessa's shoulders. "I could ask him when it is if you want."

Nessa rolled her eyes and squirmed away. "I have a boyfriend."

"Everyone knows celebrities don't count."

Codie tilted her head to the side. "But *we're* kind of celebrities. Does that mean no one we have sex with counts?"

I raised my eyebrow. "Is Alia okay with that?"

Lana snorted and waved off the argument as the van rolled through the studio lot.

We felt like old pros, going through rehearsal and makeup without any confusion or delay. The first guest was Samuel L. Jackson, and Nessa seemed to shift her celebu-crush to him thus sparing Nick when he showed up on the scene. Lana wore a hat again, but we had no plans for any tricks like on our debut. I sat down to put on my boots, but Lana stopped me. "What do you think about going barefoot again?"

"That was for nerves. I don't really have them as badly when you're singing."

She shrugged. "It's up to you, but I've seen a couple message boards online that thought it was sexy. Besides, I like it when you're relaxed and comfortable."

I could have gone either way, but I'd had a pedicure. Why not show it off? I put the boots down and wiggled my toes.

We moved backstage at the appointed time, in our positions in the shadows off to one side of the stage. Nick's desk was surrounded by crew members until the last five seconds before the cameras started rolling. He straightened his shoulders and propped up our CD so that it was bracketed between his index fingers. "Welcome back. A year ago, we had a foursome of unknowns as our Friday Night Audition that received landslide, record breaking votes. They've just re-released their first album, and their second album is due out in April. Please welcome back to the show, Radiation Canary!"

The network had vetoed our first song choice, claiming "Scene of the Crime" was too provocative even for basic cable. So the lights went down, and Lana stepped forward and began "Say a Prayer (If You've Got One)." I could have heard a pin drop in that studio when she was singing, and then our music joined her voice and I had to close my eyes. I remembered being a little girl in church, how the music had seemed to grip all the hairs on my arms and neck and tug them. I felt that again, and I hoped it was hitting the crowd, too.

The song ended, and between the silence and the applause that followed, I heard a lone voice in the audience say, "Oh, wow." Nick came over again and, for the first time, I think we saw the man behind the act. He glanced back at me, Codie, and Nessa, then put his hand on Lana's shoulder. I heard him say, "That was amazing," before turning to face the cameras.

"I can't hope to follow that, so on behalf of my sidekick Hank, Mr. Jackson, Ms. Luell, and Radiation Canary, I am saying goodnight. Goodnight." He turned back to us and shook Lana's hand, then stretched his other hand out to me. "You were holding out on me, ladies."

"Wait 'til you hear what we have planned next," Codie said with a grin.

The next morning, Naomi called to tell us pre-orders were through the roof. She suggested offering up "Prayer" as a download, since *Settle In* was going to provide the live version on their website. We agreed. The site was now being operated by a minion of Cartography, freeing Codie from the maintenance, but we could still blog or add content as we saw fit. The management put up the MP3 and, within a week, it was our most downloaded song.

In March, when preparation for the album's release was finally hitting its stride, we spent twenty-three days of the month either on the road or recovering from the trip. We took to sleeping in the apartment of whoever lived closest to the part of town we happened to be in. Lana and Alia had a fight, and Lana took to sleeping on my couch. Until then, I don't think I was fully aware they'd moved in with each other.

We watched TV in the morning together before heading off to work or practice. Cartoons, eating cereal in our pajamas, like kids taking a snow day. Those were the days when I was able to pretend I was a teenager again, hanging out with the cool girl in class. One morning I was still half asleep, my bare feet on Lana's lap, and she was idly massaging them as we watched an old episode of *M*A*S*H*.

"I never thought Hot Lips was so hot," Lana said.

I smiled. "Yeah, you go for more of the sultry bartender type." She made a face. "Is everything okay with you and Alia?"

"I don't know." She stared into her bowl and stabbed her Cheerios with her spoon.

I let the subject drop and turned back to the show.

Naomi showed up at one of our Oregon shows and said she'd been called by the producers of a medical drama on NBC. They wanted to use "Prayer" in an episode. I'd never seen the show, but Nessa was a fan and said it was quality, so we agreed. I was again stunned that we got paid for their usage. It was advertising, so I felt as if we should have paid them for the privilege, but I wasn't going to argue with the check. I had rent to pay on an apartment that still had that 'new home smell.'

I was in the supermarket parking lot when a car passed me playing "My Weak Hand" on the radio. It was a big moment, but the memory I treasure was being on the monorail, half asleep, when I realized the girl across from me was humming "Emerald." I was wearing a big hat and sunglasses - because it was sunny; none of us had any illusions about actually being recognized - so I was able to watch her as she thumbed through her magazine and tapped her foot to the music in her head.

My music. My voice.

At the next stop, I stood up and leaned toward her. "My city's an emerald?"

"Yeah," she said, barely glancing up.

"It's a good song."

"It's a great song." She looked up, furrowed her brow when she looked past my glasses, and her eyes widened. "Oh, my God!"

I smiled and slipped out with the rest of the passengers who were leaving the train. I didn't look back, already feeling bad about the hit-and-run. I could have at least offered the girl an autograph. The moment was more precious than just randomly hearing a song played on someone's radio; this was someone's choice. We were in that girl's head as she went about her day. We were a part of her world. And that was absolutely enthralling.

One Saturday we got up before dawn and piled into the van Cartography rented for the day. Naomi was in the front seat with the driver. We drove out of the city to the foothills of the Cascades and, after driving around for a while, finally found what we were after. The bunker was sunken into the side of a slope of green grass, two slabs of gray stretching out as if in an embrace. Above the entrance was a metal sign with three triangles in a circle, the universal sign for radiation. Naomi jumped out and planted her feet on the grass, smiling at us with her arms extended. "Well?"

"It's a fallout shelter," Lana said without inflection. "A little on the nose, don't you think?"

Naomi was undeterred. "Yes, because subtlety wins over so many customers. Come on, you used backstage photos for both editions of *Warnings*. That was fine, but you're official now. Your album needs to reflect that. So..." She looked at the fallout shelter and shrugged. "I mean, we can arrange for a different location, but I think this will be good."

Lana scratched her neck and looked at me. I shrugged; it didn't matter to me, really. So Lana nodded and said, "How do you want us posed?"

Lana and I were instructed to sit on the top of the structure with our feet dangling. Nessa wanted to stand in the doorway, but no amount of pulling on the handle could get it open. The photographer snapped a few shots of all four of us trying to yank the door open before we gave up. Since the door was really wedged shut, at one point Lana managed to get both feet off the ground and braced against the wall while the rest of us pulled on her shoulders. Nessa was content to just lean against the door with both hands in her pockets while Codie crouched next to her. The photographer snapped a few pictures, and eventually we all loosened up enough to get some good shots. My personal favorite pose was Lana lying on her back across the top of the shelter, with the three of us standing in a row in front of the door.

Naomi supervised, instructing him to leave enough negative space above our heads for the track listing.

"Are we still going to use the burning cello for the cover?" I asked.

Naomi nodded enthusiastically from her post behind the photographer. "The management loves the idea. It's very evocative, so of course it's okayed. We just have to make sure we get it right the first time. It's not like we can burn the cello twice."

On the way home, Naomi let us look at the pictures on the back of the camera's digital display. She pointed at my favorite. "You can imagine it, right? The tracks listed above your heads in a small and unobtrusive font..."

I nodded. I could imagine it perfectly. Lana got quiet after she agreed on the image and I nudged her to see if she was okay. She nodded and, when she was sure she wouldn't be heard over the engine noise, leaned toward me and said, "I don't want to be a model. I'm starting to regret not taking Nessa's puppet idea."

I laughed and squeezed her hand.

Track Two

Codie's loft had become the band's de facto meeting grounds, so that was where we held the release party for *Rome Burning*. The usual suspects were there, save for Alia who was still "under the weather" despite the fact Lana had moved back home. Naomi and a couple of people from the label were there, music celebrities milling about Codie's apartment like they were real people. I told John Roane where he could find the bathroom, for cripes sake. The Femme Reapers were there, claiming they'd only shown up to get the CD as early as possible.

Eventually Codie was forced to guide people through the window to a fire escape that led up to the roof. "Neighbors are complaining, so out into the elements we go!"

The night was cold, but it served as a continual reminder that this was real. We were musicians and, at midnight, Naomi and a representative from Cartography arrived with the first batch of our sophomore CD. We agreed to spend at least an hour autographing them, with the people at the party getting first dibs. Naomi had dressed up for the occasion, a red checkered shirt under her ever-present blazer. I made my way over to say hello, and she greeted me with a hug before asking how everyone else was doing.

We signed CDs for the record label to take back and put on sale, and then we worked on personalized autographs for the people at the party. I felt like a machine, writing my name as quickly as I could without scribbling. Someone held out a CD to me and I searched my pockets for the blue Sharpie I'd been using. "Who do I make it out to?"

"Laura."

I looked up and saw Laura Cowan smiling at me. The moment was so surreal I got a little lightheaded, and I chuckled nervously.

"You want a CD *and* you want my name on it?"

"Well, you're the star of the band."

I looked over at Lana, who was wearing a silk blouse and a skirt with a slit high on her leg. "Oh, I'm sorry. I didn't realize you were blind."

Laura's voice softened. "I can see just fine, Karen."

I was completely unarmed by that, so I just signed the CD: "I'm honored +

humbled. Thank you!" with my name. I smiled as I handed it back to her. "I want one of yours in return, but I don't have my copy with me."

"That's okay. We'll have another chance." She winked and returned to the party, and I fiddled nervously with my Sharpie, still flustered by the exchange.

At some point *Rome* ended up in the stereo, and our music filled the night air. I recognized my playing and felt awed and small in the face of it. There was another Karen Everett at the party, and she was huge and daunting and so much better than me. Anticipating another visit from the police if the neighbors complained, I headed downstairs to brace myself with another refill.

Codie's apartment was almost completely abandoned but still brimming with the energy of a party interrupted. The only person in the room was Naomi, all by herself by the punch table. I hesitated in the windowsill before I slipped inside. "Hey. Didn't you get the invitation to ascend with the rest of us?"

She looked over her shoulder and smiled.

"Hi. I was just getting some more punch." She held up the ladle. "Want a refill?"

"Sure." I held out my cup and she took it. "Thanks. And thanks for sticking around. You didn't have to."

"I wouldn't miss this. It's a lot of fun to represent a band I actually like. Not saying it's rare, but if I wasn't working for you, I'd still want to be here. I can't wait to officially listen to the disc. You've done some great work this past year."

I smiled. "Thanks." Our fingers brushed as I took the plastic cup from her. I took a second to look at her. She wasn't beautiful like Lana, but she really was attractive. She was the exact kind of woman I would have exchanged nervous smiles with in a bookstore, or admired from afar. Now we were standing together in an empty room on the fringe of a party, and if I wanted to come onto her, I could. I was sure I was blushing as my thoughts wandered in that direction.

"I think Lana's going to blow everyone away with 'Prayer.'"

"Oh, definitely. It's going to sweep everything else up, but people who buy the album just for that song aren't going to go away disappointed."

She had no reason to linger, but neither of us made a move for the window to rejoin the party. I didn't even want to suggest moving to the couch to sit down for fear of screwing up whatever chemistry we had going. I tried to think of her relationship to the band and suddenly realized I didn't know exactly what it was.

"So are you... our boss? What are you?"

"I'm your manager, and your liaison with the record company. I let you know what they want, I let them know what you agree with, and I try to find balance. I'm like a neutral third party. I'm your Switzerland."

When she stopped speaking I kissed her. What the hell. Better to apologize than ask permission, and if I'd had to form the question I would have chickened out. She relaxed quickly and put her free hand on my shoulder, tilting her head to one side to make our kiss more comfortable. Her lips relaxed and I teased them apart with the tip of my tongue. One of us moaned, but I was too out of my head to think too hard about which one of us it was. I didn't care.

I pulled back. "Is that allowed?"

"It's probably not encouraged."

"Then we'll just not tell anyone."

"I like that plan."

We were kissing again. I'd gone this far many times, gotten right up to the point of no return, but I already knew this time it would be different. My head kept track of the distance between how long I wanted the kiss to be and how long it would be before someone came back downstairs. When they balanced, I pulled back and took the cup from her and put it down on the table with mine. I hoped she didn't notice my hand was making the punch quake.

"Codie has a guest room."

She was quiet for ten seconds. Ten whole seconds, and then she pushed her glasses up and said, "Where?"

I took her hand and led her down the hall where eons ago I had seen Lana and Alia having sex. We stepped inside and she shut the door, and then we kissed again. We tripped over each other's feet, and I had an image of people fighting in an old black-and-white movie. We were so close that we were tangled, affected by each other's gravity so we were unable to fall even though we were unbalanced. I moved her toward the bed and we fell with at least a little grace. I had my hand on her belt and pushed it up under her shirt to her stomach.

"My glasses." She took them off and twisted for the nightstand.

"Can you see?"

"I can see enough," she said, and she kissed me as she pushed herself up higher on the mattress. She moved her legs and I heard the thuds as her shoes hit the ground. I moved my head and kissed her neck, and I stroked her hip with my fingers as she hooked her knee on my hip. I felt dizzy as she tugged on my blouse to untuck it.

I lifted my head and kissed her cheek. "You should know I've never..."

She took a second to process what I was saying. "Never?"

I shook my head. A few strands of hair were caught in my eyes, and she brushed them away. "Is that okay?"

"It's fine." She kissed the corners of my mouth. "Of course it's fine. And since we're being honest, I've never–"

"Seriously?"

"No. I mean... I've slept with people I work with, but I don't make a habit of it. I don't want you to think you're just... fulfilling part of your contract." She was breathing hard, and I realized my thigh was pressed against the crotch of her pants. I thought about moving it, so I did... in a circular pattern. She arched her back and I kissed her throat again. "When I saw you play live, my first thought wasn't... wasn't 'God, I've gotta... represent that girl.'"

I laughed, and she chuckled, and we kissed as we continued undressing each other.

"I'm surprised you noticed me at all... with Lana standing there." She pushed my bra strap down and kissed my shoulder, and my breath hitched.

"Why? You noticed me in a world were Lana Kent... exists."

We held each other, skin to skin, and I kissed her slowly. I reached for something else to take off of her, but I only found smooth skin and a pebbled nipple. I rolled my thumb over it and she squirmed. "...feels good," she whispered and kissed my cheek, then my earlobe.

My hands were shaking so badly that she held the wrists and softly kissed both palms. I pressed the heels of my hands together and cupped her face, kissing her eyebrows. She looked so strangely naked without her glasses, and her dark hair was mussed and tossed over her forehead. She looked up at me and I kissed her hard, pushing her back down onto the mattress as I settled over her.

"I've always wanted to be with a violinist," she said into my ear.

"Why?"

She kissed my cheek. "I appreciate a girl who is good at fingering..."

I laughed and pressed my head against her shoulder. When I sat up, my hair was mussed again. Her hand swept the side of my head, and I figured I could get used to having her fix my hair for me. "I thought about who I wanted to be my first. And I decided I'd want her to be a lot like you. Almost exact, to be honest." I kissed her chest and moved down, my hands on her almost nonexistent hips as I took her nipple into my mouth. She arched her back and writhed against me.

"Happy to... help get it out of the way..."

I kissed down her stomach and moved her legs apart. Either she was trembling too or I was shaking so bad the entire bed was subject to a ripple effect. I rested my cheek against her stomach to feel how warm she was and, to be honest, to try catching my breath. She touched my hair and I said, "You might have to tell me what to do. I'm just winging it here."

"You're doing fine," she said. "Perfectly. Don't stop..."

I lifted my head and kissed her navel. "You know, I sing, too."

"I know," she said. I looked up and saw her eyes were closed as if she was bracing for it. I wet my lips.

"I'm just saying... I'm not just good with my fingers." I blushed, my ears burning as I closed my eyes and kissed her. She moved her hips up to meet my mouth, and my tongue pushed inside of her. I squeezed my thighs together and pressed my hand against my mound, toes curling in my socks as I realized I was close to coming. My cheeks burned red as I rode out my orgasm, my nose tickled by Naomi's pubic hair, and my gasp made her twitch away from me.

I pulled back. "Sorry... I'm sorry, I came."

"It's okay. There's something else musicians are good at."

I grinned because I knew what she was getting at.

I was great at encores.

Track Three

Lana woke on Codie's couch and, after a stop in the bathroom, slumped on the stool at the kitchen counter. Codie offered her a choice between scrambled eggs and cereal, and Lana took the cereal with as much milk as could be spared. She was halfway through the bowl before she decided she was hungover, not still drunk from the night before, and asked Codie to fry her up some greasy bacon to help with the headache.

"What time did you finally crash?" Codie asked.

"I'm not sure. There was a five in it. Where'd everyone else go?"

"Nessa went home at two. I think Karen went home even earlier than that. She disappeared right after the autograph session."

Lana yawned against the back of her hand. "I probably should have followed her out the door. But hey, at least the album is out."

"Hear-hear," Codie said.

The guest room door opened and closed, and they heard someone go into the bathroom. "Who else crashed here?" Lana asked as she was served some fresh strips of bacon.

"No clue."

A few minutes later the mystery houseguest came out of the bathroom and headed down the hall. Her footsteps paused when she realized people were in the main room, but then hurried on toward the door.

"Oh. Morning, ladies."

Lana twisted at the waist to confirm what her ears reported. "Naomi. Hey."

She was running her fingers through her hair, which was sloppier than Lana had ever seen it. The clothes she'd been wearing the night before had been draped over her body in some semblance of modesty, but it was hard to make sense of this disheveled being. Her shoes were hooked on two fingers in the hopes she could make a silent escape in her bare feet. Now that she was busted, however, she took a moment to slip them on and bent down to tighten the laces. It was like seeing a teacher outside of school. Lana felt embarrassed and shy, though she couldn't have explained why that was.

"I hope it's cool that I crashed here last night. Didn't feel like trying to make the last ferry back to Port Townsend, so–"

"No, it's cool." Codie smiled. "That's what the guest room is there for."

She adjusted her glasses and smiled. "Okay. Uh, I'll... see you." Lana had just turned around when someone else came out of the guest room. Naomi's voice was tender, soft and romantic. "Hey. I was gonna let you sleep."

"I wanted to say goodbye."

Lana froze with a strip of bacon sticking out of her mouth. She looked over her shoulder and, sure enough, there stood Karen in an undershirt and panties as she kissed Naomi goodbye. Barefoot, messy hair. She was glowing a bit, and Lana's lips curled into a smile. She looked at Codie, whose eyebrows were rising slowly but steadily.

Karen broke the kiss. "I'll walk you to your car."

"That would be sweet."

They left, and Lana finally released the chuckle-gasp that she'd been holding in. "What the hell?"

"That wasn't what it looked like, was it?"

Lana said, "Seemed pretty self-explanatory to me."

Codie laughed. "Well, go K-Pax."

Lana was finished with her bacon and had gone back to her cereal by the time Karen returned. She shut the door quietly, and Lana spun on her stool to face her fully.

"Not so fast, compadre. What the hell happened last night?"

Karen shrugged and crossed to the kitchen. "I kissed her. She liked it. We played the rest by ear. Is there any more bacon?"

"I'll make you some," Codie said. "You have to fuck the A&R girl?"

"I thought about firing her before we did it, but I thought you guys would get mad. It didn't have anything to do with the job. We like each other. So..."

Lana nudged her and, without humor, said, "You okay?"

Karen glanced at Codie's back and nodded. "Yeah. I'm okay." She hooked her finger over Lana's and squeezed. "I'm going to take a quick shower."

"The bacon'll be waiting for you," Codie said. Once Karen was gone, Codie whistled quietly. "Karen taking one for the team. Think it'll help us when we have to renegotiate our contract?"

Lana grinned. "I don't think that was her intention. But it couldn't hurt."

Karen returned, her hair slicked back and still wet as she sat next to Lana for breakfast. She chewed her bacon carefully and then looked at the clock. "What time do the buses run around here?"

"Where do you need to go?" Lana asked. "I'll drive you."

"Just back to my place. I need to crash. I didn't get a lot of sleep last night."

"Bow-chicka-wow," Codie sang, and Karen blushed deep red. Codie grinned.

"I'm just teasing. Hell, I'm jealous. I'm the only member of this damn band that hasn't gotten laid from it. Even Nessa has gotten lucky."

Lana leaned back slightly. "You mean Scott? I thought she just ran into him."

"No... She didn't tell you?"

"Unh-uh."

Codie shrugged. "One of the guys I work with came to see us play when we were still working on *Action*. He thought she was cute so I gave her his number. Two weeks later I call the guy to see if he can cover one of my shifts, and guess who I hear in the background. They aren't together anymore, but for a little while..."

Karen smiled. "I wonder why she didn't tell us."

Lana scoffed. "Would you have told us about Naomi if you hadn't been caught red-handed?" Karen admitted that with a shrug. "Don't worry, Codie. If you don't find someone, Karen and I will hire you a nice hooker."

"I'm not gay."

"They have boy hookers," Karen offered.

Codie rolled her eyes. "Yeah, that's the sort of guy I want to be with. The one who, at Career Day, decided he wanted to be a gigolo. You ladies do what you want. I'm fine as long as I have a steady supply of batteries."

Lana clapped. "Birthday shopping done!"

Karen's hair was dry by the time they finally left. Lana fished for her keys. "We can stop by McDonalds and get an orange juice if you want it."

"Sure."

They got onto the road, the radio playing quietly until Lana pushed a button to silence it completely. "So. How does it feel?"

Karen inhaled and exhaled slowly, hands folded in her lap as she looked out the window. "Fine. Strange that it's not stranger, you know?" She pushed her hands through her hair and let it fall. "I don't know what got into me. I just looked at her and suddenly it was like... if I don't pull the trigger with her, I'd regret whoever I ended up with. I had this vision of going back to Penny just to get it over with, and I did not want to have sex with Penny. If I did I would have done it while we were going out. And I know Naomi isn't gorgeous or~"

"Hey, she's plenty gorgeous. Just because I tried to set you up with a stripper doesn't mean I'm blind."

"Good." She seemed more relaxed. "I don't know why your approval means so much to me. It's not like you're my..." Her voice trailed off. "Well, it sort of is. You and Codie and Nessa are sort of like my older sisters."

"How dare you?" She snorted. "Older. I oughta kick you out of the car."

They got orange juice and hash browns at McDonalds to complete the breakfast Codie had made for them, and then Lana dropped Karen off at home. She drove back to her apartment, already dreading the idea of spending time with Alia. She wasn't sure where they'd gone off the rails, but going to Whistler for their anniversary was a bad idea. The cracks had already been present and she'd hoped getting away for a while would help smooth them over. If anything, it had stuck the wedge in deeper.

She headed upstairs and entered the apartment as quietly as possible. Alia was already up and on her laptop in the living room.

Lana hung her jacket up. "Morning. You're home early."

"I was off last night."

Lana put her keys in the dish and went to the fridge. "You could have come to Codie's, then. We had a pretty good time."

"I didn't know the address."

"Could've called." She wasn't hungry or thirsty, so she didn't know what she wanted from the fridge other than an excuse to avoid eye contact. "I didn't get much sleep on Codie's couch so I'm going to go lie down for a while."

"Okay. I'll head out soon. I don't want to disturb you."

Lana sighed. "I didn't say you disturbed me, I just--"

"No, playing guitar in your underwear is very important. Part of the artistic process."

Lana rolled her eyes and flipped Alia off as she went into the bedroom. Mature, but it was all she could muster at the moment. She undressed and crawled under the blankets, burrowing her face into the pillow. She was just about to fall asleep when Alia left, shutting the door harder than necessary and waking her up. Revenge for the one finger salute, Lana decided, and covered her head with the pillow.

Track Four

The following week was filled with countless interviews. Karen quickly forgot what network, show, or reporter she was talking to and just answered the questions presented to her. In the lull between one interview ending and while the next was being set up, she would check her phone for missed calls or messages from Naomi. She blushed whenever Lana caught her looking, but Lana just laughed and told her to live it up.

A woman in a blazer asked, "So what have you got planned next?"

"Next?" Karen tried to come up with an answer, but she just shook her head. She was desperate not to look into the camera. She made motions with her hands and then shook her head. "I'm just going to play music and hope people keep slowing down to hear it."

Later that week they discovered that *Rome Burning* debuted at the number one spot on the *Billboard* chart. Nessa couldn't wrap her head around it. "But that's... every album in the country. By everybody. We've outsold everybody? That's not possible."

Naomi grinned. "It's possible. Look, do you think it's an accident Cartography snatched you up when we did? You probably had a dozen other offers before you settled on us. We do the research, ladies. In the nineties, the atmosphere was right for boy bands. So you had eighty-two boy bands prancing around. Then the public got tired and all those bands went bye-bye-bye."

"If only their members could have done the same," Lana murmured.

"Before I started looking for new acts to sign, I looked to see what people wanted. The buying public wants female bands, and they like singer-songwriters, and they want a more classical sound." She gestured at me. "You four tapped into that just by being yourselves. Then the name, Radiation Canary... it's evocative. It draws the eye and it makes people want to know what you're about. You have the exposure of Nick Young's show, you have the Femme Reapers fans who saw you live, and you have a killer song in 'Prayer.' I'm not saying it's all math. You can put those ingredients together and then crash and burn if you don't have the talent to back it up. But you do, in spades, and that's why you won't be one-hit wonders. Enjoy your success, ladies. You've earned it. And we'll talk about renewing your contract once the furor dies down."

"Renewing?" Karen looked at Lana for an explanation, but Naomi answered.

"Your original contract was for three albums. You're working on the third now. We'll get you a new one that reflects your success."

They celebrated with champagne, courtesy of Cartography, and toasted to the similar success of future albums.

The building that housed Cartography Records' offices also had a stately theatre located dead center in the middle of the building. It was an elegant Odeon shrunk down to fit in a fraction of the space, with a hardwood stage and two sections of velvet seats that could stand to be reupholstered. We were on the stage, and a camera crew was setting up to shoot our first music video. Lana had fought for "Crime," but Naomi convinced her that could wait. If we opened with a sexual video, it would tie an albatross around our necks that would remain there for the rest of our career. Lana saw the point of that and agreed that "Prayer" would be our first foray into the world of videos.

The theatre was used for the performance segment of the video. It would be interspersed throughout the video, so we were taking care to get every part. I dutifully ignored the camera as it moved in to watch my bow cut across the strings. Nessa handled the intrusion well, simply playing without hunching her shoulders or leaning away from the lens as she'd been worried she would. Everything seemed to be in slow motion, and it felt as if we were playing to an audience who was scrutinizing our every move with a critical eye.

Once we finished in the theatre, Lana would go to a soundstage where some technical geniuses would create a rainstorm to drench her while she sang the chorus. I know she wasn't looking forward to that, but I reminded her that bare arms had been her idea. It was too late for her to start wearing a jacket now.

When the camera wasn't on me, I watched Naomi. We'd been together three times since the night in Codie's guest room, only twice for sex. The other time was just dinner and a movie, to see how we liked each other in the in-between times. We had a good working relationship and, despite my lack of experience, I imagine our sex life could be called phenomenal, but we both wanted to make sure we could just hang out and have a good time.

Unfortunately we discovered that, other than music, we didn't share a lot of interests. We liked different movies, and she was allergic to cats. I didn't have a cat, but the idea of being restricted from getting one in the future was oddly stifling. When we got back to my apartment, she saved me the trouble of admitting the truth. I remembered standing with her in front of my door, the moment of truth.

"That wasn't the best date ever, was it?"

"I don't know. The company couldn't be beat."

She smiled. "I don't think we fit together outside the bedroom."

"Yeah. I'm sorry."

"No, I'm the one who is sorry. I feel bad. I feel like I used you."

I laughed. "I'm the one who jumped you, Naomi. I wanted you. I still do. I just don't think we should fool ourselves that this is going to turn into anything serious. But I know I must like you a lot, because saying that we're not going anywhere really sucks."

"Yeah." She kissed my cheek and rubbed my arm. "But hey. You know how you can go years without having a cigarette, but then you have one and you've gotta smoke the whole pack? Sex is like that. Once a drought ends, you need a deluge. So call me if you ever want to indulge."

I opened the apartment door. "You have anywhere you need to be tonight?"

"As a matter of fact, no. I don't." She smiled and shrugged out of her coat as she went into my apartment.

I was brought back to the present by a tempo change, forced to focus on the music so I didn't look like an idiot. I caught Naomi watching me from behind the camera and I winked at her. She smiled and gave me a thumbs-up as I went on pantomiming. Lana kept forgetting to lip synch and kept ruining takes by cursing at herself for messing up. We took a break and the three of us managed to calm her down for the next run-through.

When we finished, Lana exhaled and pushed her hair out of her face. "Hard to believe the song isn't even four minutes long."

"And we still have another location to shoot," Nessa said. "I blame Karen. I say, next album, no songs longer than a minute."

I laughed. "Okay. It'll be a concept album. Eighty different songs that run thirty seconds each. I'll get on that right away."

"Eighty songs?" Naomi said as she joined us on stage.

I shook my head and grinned at her. "Nothing, just joking around. What's next?"

She pointed at Lana with both hands. "Now we take her to a studio and spray her with a hose."

"How cold will the water be?"

Naomi waved her hand in a so-so gesture. "Not cold enough to give you pneumonia, but nowhere near as warm as you'll want it to be. Sorry."

Lana grumbled, but she took off her guitar and left the stage like a good girl. I waited until Nessa and Codie had left, then descended the steps with Naomi. She lowered her voice and bumped my arm with hers. "Hey. You going back with the rest, or you want to spent the night in town with me?"

"What do you have planned?"

"Dinner, sex."

I smiled and touched the collar of my shirt. "I don't know. I'll have to check the menu."

She chuckled and held the door for me. The rest of us weren't necessary for Lana's scene, but we wanted to be there for support. If one of us had to get drenched in the name of our art, the least the rest of us could do was show up to wrap towels around her when it was over.

The bell over the door rang as I went in, and I scanned the aisles for signs of life. The door to the back room opened and Ted came down the aisle with a large box held against his chest. He spotted me and did a double-take, smiled, and then shook his head. "Well, damn. That's a disappointment."

My smile faded. "What?"

He bent to put the box down, then faced me hands on hips. "You go away to become a famous rock star and then come back… you're supposed to have a pink Mohawk, big sunglasses, cone bra… you're supposed to have like five piercings in each ear. But no, you have the number one album in the country and come back home looking like that. How are we supposed to take you seriously as a musician?"

I went around the counter and hugged him. "Don't worry. My drug scandal and stint in rehab is all set up for this summer."

"That's a relief." He pulled back and smiled at me. "Your dad just had to run to the post office. He should be back any minute."

"I can wait. How have things been without me around?"

"Quiet. I miss hearing the cello at home. It was like having our own personal Phantom. Or I guess Tevya would have been a better analogy. But now we can just pop in one of your CDs to fill the silence. And the kid we hired to take over for you here is doing a really bang-up job. We should have fired your ass years ago."

I laughed. "Gee, thanks."

"How are things with you?"

I smiled. "I'm great. Spending a lot of time with the girls." He raised an eyebrow. "Not like that." *Too busy having sex with our rep from the label for that sort of thing.* "Lana's in a relationship, and the other girls are straight."

"Ah, I see. Species has to survive somehow, I guess." He looked past me and then gestured with his head. I turned and saw Dad coming into the store. I stood up and planted myself in front of him, and he looked up in surprise and then realization.

"Oh, that's disappointing…"

"Ted already did that one."

He sighed. "He gets to have all the fun." He hugged me tighter than I expected, then kissed my temple. "What are you doing back here in the slums?"

"Well, I was sitting around, counting my money, lighting my cigars with some hundred-dollah bills, and I decided to take you and Ted out to dinner. After all, you paid for all the cello and violin lessons. Figures you should get to enjoy the spoils."

He smiled. "Well, that sounds pretty fair to me. You remember what time we close?"

I furrowed my brow. "Such plebeian information is below me now, Father."

A customer came in and I went into sales clerk mode, instantly belying my statement. Ted told Dad he'd handle it, and Dad guided me through the aisles to the back of the store. "So, have you called your mother since all this 'number one album' hullabaloo?"

"No. I'm worried she'll say it's nice, but it's not *real* music, you know?"

"She was the first one in our house to utter the word 'cello,' so you at least owe her a call. Hell, you're making enough money now you can charter a flight to New York and see her yourself."

"Sure," I said. "I think I'll start with the call. Easier."

He nodded. "So where are you taking us for dinner? You've already treated us to the Space Needle, so I think tonight I feel like Ivar's."

I laughed. "Sky's the limit, Dad."

Track Five

It wasn't until we were actually on the plane that it hit me: we were going on tour. Naomi said it was a responsibility required of having the number one album in the country. She'd mentioned it a while ago, kept bringing up dates and locations, and I listened with half an ear while Lana dealt with it. Then one day we loaded up and drove to the airport. I watched out the window at Rainier's peak rising through a solid sheet of clouds, and it became real. I had to take out the printed itinerary just to see where, exactly, we were going.

Seventeen cities in ten states. We were starting in Los Angeles, which is why Cartography splurged for the plane. Then onto a bus for two shows in San Francisco, then we'd set off across the country. Nevada, Arizona, New Mexico, all across the southwest before veering north to skirt the Great Lakes. The label dubbed it the "Trading Rainmakers for Wizards Summer Tour '06." We were crossing paths with other artists from Cartography as well as other labels. We'd share the billing, no one opening for anyone, and I envisioned more collaborations like we had with the Femme Reapers. I was sick to my stomach as I looked at the list of cities, some in states I couldn't name towns in. Kentucky... what was in Kentucky? Louisville? And... shit, what else? Fried chicken?

Naomi stayed home, which meant I would have a month without a sexual partner. She had been right; it was like smoking. I was sure I could handle it. I'd gone twenty-four years without sex, and I could go one month. Certainly it wouldn't be that hard. Right?

I kept scanning the list and froze at the next to last date. "New York."

Lana looked up from her book. "Hm?"

"We're going to be in New York."

"Yeah. June tenth."

I pressed my back against the seat. "My mother lives in New York."

"Oh." She closed her book on her thumb. "You guys have a good relationship?"

"Fair, I guess. I mean, it was a toss-up whether I'd go with her or stay with Dad and Ted when that whole thing happened. I mainly stayed because going meant new school, new friends, new state..."

Lana said, "And you wouldn't have stumbled over us. So I, for one, think you made the right decision."

I grinned weakly. "But we've drifted apart since then. I think eventually she got it in her mind that I chose Dad over her, and I decided she'd abandoned me..." I shook my head. "We're civil. I was going to call her a few weeks back after the whole *Billboard* thing, but I never got around to it. I should probably call her."

"You can get her some tickets. Backstage passes."

"Yeah. Okay, I can do that." I took a deep breath and let it out, then looked at her. "How are you? Alia decided not to come?"

Her expression hardened and she flipped her book open again. "Yeah. Basically."

"Are you guys okay?"

"Nope. Leave it alone, K."

Nothing would have made me want to pursue it more than that, but I resisted. I let her go back to her book and settled into my seat to look out the window. I'd never been on a plane before, and it was really quite a gorgeous day. My eyes drifted shut, and I dozed for a while. When I woke I had a moment of fear when the view out the window was the first thing I saw, but I settled down quickly.

"You okay?" Lana asked.

"Yeah. I just suffered from a little amnesia between sleeping and waking up."

She smiled, and I looked down to see a napkin on my thigh. It had Lana's handwriting on it and I picked it up to use the setting sun to read it.

"Put your head against the window, we'll be there before you know, trust me to get you there, take the world off your shoulder, tonight you're my passenger." At the bottom, she'd added, "A little too 'You Can Sleep While I Drive'?" I looked over and she was watching as I read it. I smiled and shook my head.

"I think it's a worthy successor to Etheridge. A Lana Kent original?"

She shrugged. "I figured we should start sharing the heavy lifting. And besides, like you said... it doesn't matter who wrote it. The song belongs to Radiation Canary."

I nodded and took her pen. I wrote "Property of RC" across the top, but then I added "by Lana Kent" along the side. She eyed me, amused, and then shrugged as she settled back into her seat. I folded the napkin and tucked it into the pocket of my shirt. Fully awake, and touched that I'd inspired Lana to write even a snippet of a song, I watched as northern California passed underneath the plane.

"You want to make an impression?" Lana asked me before we went onstage on LA. If only I'd known what she was asking, I'd have said no. Instead I shrugged and told her I would follow her lead. I did ask what to expect but she only gave me the same half-manic grin I recognized from our first shows. She then gripped the railing, leaned back and then hurled herself up onto the stage. It was our first big solo show and we had a group of local musicians backing us up. For the first time I could actually take a break from playing in order to properly sing harmony with Lana.

We went through the standard repertoire, covering most of the first album before moving to the second. We had two songs written for our third album, and we teased the crowd with a song I'd written with Nessa called "The Next Ferry." I think that was the first time I noticed the hand signs we were getting from the crowd. During "Carry On," when Lana was sharing my microphone, I whispered in her ear to see if she could make out what everyone was doing. When the song ended, she demonstrated with her own hands.

She hooked her thumbs together with the fingers extended out, then put her crossed palms over her heart. She waved her fingers like someone making a shadow puppet of a bird. It looked like a bird - a canary, of course - carrying away her heart. The audience cheered at her acknowledgement of their symbol, and soon the signal had spread across the theatre.

An hour into the show, Lana turned to me and lifted her eyebrows. I got an uneasy feeling as she took off her guitar and placed it on the stand, then turned her back on the audience as the rest of us played the opening to "Scene of the Crime." Lana ducked her head, moved her hips in time to the music, and let the backup player take care of the guitar section as she kept the rhythm by patting her flat palm against her thigh.

She turned and strutted across the stage, gripping the microphone just before her cue to start singing. She growled the lyrics, sliding her free hand down the mic stand as she pushed it forward. She bent her knees so that she appeared to be straddling the stand, and the audience went crazy as she powered through the suggestive first verse.

Lana let go of the microphone and crossed to me, she mouthed, "Keep playing," then crossed to Codie and Nessa, I assume to tell them the same thing. We had practiced stretching out most of our songs, but I was too nervous about what she had planned to feel like I did a very good job of ad-libbing. She returned to the middle of the stage and gripped the labels of her vest. She tossed her hair, threw her head back, and shed the jacket.

The crowd exploded. As did, I'm sure, the heads of the people in charge of the venue. Was there an age limit on the ticket sales? Did anyone bring their kids? Because Lana Kent was going to strip. The only question was how far she planned to go with it.

Now in her tank top, which was thin enough to see her bra underneath, she walked toward the microphone like she was moving along a runway. Her lips were parted to bare her teeth, her hair hanging down in her eyes like a veil, and she sang in a voice more seductive than aggressive. She gripped the collar of her tank top and tugged it down so far I was afraid the material would tear.

She was almost whispering now as her free hand moved to her belt. She let go of the microphone and dropped both hands, teasing the buckle before undoing it. I looked at Nessa, whose eyes were wide enough they nearly overtook the rest of her face. Codie looked like it was the funniest damn thing she'd ever seen.

Lana tugged her belt free with a hiss, then snapped it against the hard wood of the stage like a whip. Her pants sagged, revealing the lace of her underwear, and I felt beads of sweat on my lip that had nothing to do with the lights. Her bare stomach, the dimples above her ass, and the way her bra straps stood away from the curve of her breasts. My mouth was dry, but I didn't dare reach for my bottle of water. She backed away from the microphone, turned her back to the audience again, and crossed her arms in front of her.

"Lana!" I said, facing away from the mic so it wasn't picked up and broadcast. She ignored me, probably would have even if she'd heard. She took off her tank top, draped it over the end of Nessa's keyboard, then put her guitar back on. She tossed her hair back, making sure everyone got an eyeful of her plain white bra, and returned to the microphone. She played a few notes and sang the last bit of the chorus again.

"You go along every time
Then she leaves you
Standing helpless
At the scene of the crime."

The crowd roared. Lana took a bow. I had a nice view of her back, the bumps of her spine and the flare of her hips. I was turned on, but also pissed she would do this without clearing it with any of us beforehand. She squirmed back into her tank top and walked back to the microphone. "Sorry, just had to get that out. Rest of the show will be fully clothed, I swear."

There were good-natured boos at that news, and more than a few disappointed catcalls, but Lana just laughed and started playing "Mountain Time." Nessa did the vocals for that one, so Lana was able to take a step back. Halfway through the chorus she looked back at me, and I tried glaring at her subtly enough that the audience didn't notice. She noticed the look and I knew that she understood why I was mad, but she responded to it with a wink and a cheeky smile. I shook my head and focused on playing. A quick glance at Nessa during an interlude reassured me that the incident wasn't going to go by without a conversation.

Track Six

Lana expected recrimination, red-faced shouting, some sort of official reprimand from the management of the venue, but no one even gave her a cross look when they finally left the stage. The show ended after two hours and an encore, so maybe everyone was just too tired to be upset. The band filed off-stage to still-strong cheers, with Lana bringing up the rear. Despite her exhaustion, they'd agreed to sign autographs. She had just enough time to wipe off her sweat, put on something a little less revealing, and grab a drink before going out to the table.

Karen turned on her as soon as they were in the dressing room. "What the hell was that? I thought you were all about not having an image."

Lana stepped around her and got a bottle of water out of the mini-fridge. "It won't happen again. It's just... that song." She uncapped the bottle and drank half of it. She gasped and wiped her mouth, facing the wall instead of her band. "You wrote it about Alia."

"So?"

Lana sighed and sat on the fridge. "So Alia and I are done. She dumped me just before we left. She didn't think it was fair to string me along the whole time I was on the road, so she 'freed me.'" She smiled sardonically and, to her horror, felt tears in her eyes.

Karen's anger seemed to evaporate, replaced with shock and concern. Codie put her hand on Lana's shoulder, and Nessa reached out to take her hand. Lana was grateful for them and smiled so they would know. Then she looked at Karen and shrugged an apology.

"We had a blow-out. I said some nasty things, and she stormed out. She came back to get her stuff right before we left for the tour, and she told me to enjoy myself. Said that I may sell tickets now, but in five years time I would be back on stage taking my clothes off for money." Her face twitched and she dropped her chin, and Codie's hand went to the back of her head. Nessa hugged her, and Karen stepped forward to embrace them all.

"Get off me. Get off," Lana said, flailing playfully. She sniffled and slipped out of their reach, swiping at her face and then pointing toward the front of the building. "Listen to that."

They could hear the audience that remained still chanting "Ca-na-ry! Ca-na-ry!"

"We're not going to sit here and have a pity party for me while good people are spending their hard-earned money to see us. The least we can do is show up and deface some CDs with our names. Let's get out there."

Nessa said, "Right. We can have a cleansing cry on the bus tomorrow."

"Sounds like a plan." She opened the door and ushered Nessa and Codie out first. Karen hesitated, and Lana pressed her lips together. "I'm sorry. I shouldn't have done that to the band."

Karen shook her head. "You're in a bad place. And considering where the song came from, I'm not surprised you acted out a little when you had to sing it. We'll take the song off the play list for the rest of the tour."

"That would be fantastic. And don't worry," she said, slinging her arm around Karen's shoulders to walk her out of the room, "my clothes are going to stay on from here on out."

"Well, on-stage at least. Feel free to walk around the bus naked as much as you want."

Lana moved her hand down and swatted Karen's butt. "You get laid and suddenly you're Miss Innuendo."

She was relieved the band wasn't angry at her, but she still felt she'd gotten off easy. She was determined to make it up to them during the tour. She slapped her cheeks, blinked to make sure her eyes were dry, and then followed her friends out to greet their adoring public.

I didn't remember getting back on the bus. I was alarmed by that but, as I pulled the blankets up over my head and piled the pillows on top of them I decided it made some kind of sense. We hadn't gotten done with the autograph table until close to one in the morning, and I was so weary... the calluses on my fingers hated the Sharpie I was using, and the blur of album covers was so repetitive. *Warnings* and *Rome*, *Warnings* Deluxe Edition, then the original release. As Naomi predicted, the original version was apparently very sought-after. The people who had us sign those received them like we were bestowing a treasure upon them. I made a mental note to look for them on eBay in a couple weeks.

But now I was in my bunk on the bus. Across the aisle, I could see Codie's bare feet sticking out from under her blanket. Lana was strumming her guitar near the driver, but I couldn't see her. I fell back to sleep while debating whether I should go join her or stay where I was. When I woke again, the bus was silent. I sat up and listened to the sound of the tires, felt the sway of the vehicle, and slipped out of bed to use the bathroom and check the time.

We were still three hours away from San Francisco. In about sixteen hours we would take the stage again for another two hour concert. The thought made my fingers hurt, but I'd done enough marathon practicing to know I could handle it. We'd have more of a break for the next show. I stretched in the bathroom, splashed water on my face, and moved with the swaying bus back to my bunk. I was about to collapse into the bunk when I heard Lana whisper my name. I remained standing and opened the little privacy curtain on her bed.

She was in the bunk above mine, her knees curled against her chest and the blanket loosely draped over her body. I instinctively tucked her in and she smiled. "Go back to sleep."

"Alia..."

I put my hand on her cheek the way Mom used to when I'd had a bad dream. "Don't worry about Alia, okay?"

"She thought I was sleeping with you."

I was stunned. "Oh."

She smiled. "It's not why we broke up. But it was part of the argument. I thought you should know, but I didn't want to tell Codie and Nessa."

I thought about the lines she'd written on the plane, the bones of a song about someone who was taking a break while someone else took control. I bent down and kissed her forehead. "I can drive for a while if you want."

She started to smile, but her eyes teared up. "Yeah?"

"Hey, you guys keep insisting I'm co-leader. About time I took some of the slack."

"Thanks, K."

I nodded and tucked the blankets back around her shoulders. "Night, Lana."

"Goodnight."

I slid back into my bunk and pressed my pillow into the corner of the space. I rolled the lines Lana had written through my mind, thinking of the Melissa Etheridge song it was related to, and fell asleep while trying to compose the first verse.

The San Fran concert was outside, and in the distance we could see the Golden Gate Bridge as we played. I was overwhelmed by the sight, surrounded by music and such beauty. Lana told us to cut "Scene of the Crime" and we replaced it with "Band of Girls." We were nearly an hour into the show when Lana took off her guitar and stood at the microphone, waiting for the crowd to quiet a bit before she said, "Could we have it quiet, please? Just for this little bit...?"

The sound slowly tapered off, and I felt tingles in my scalp. We'd gotten this crowd to scream, but God the power it took to make this many people be quiet.

I watched Lana as she wet her lips and turned to motion to us. She faced forward and, in the eerie silence, sang the first lines of "Say a Prayer." The three of us had time to catch up; the music swelled at just the right time, and Lana held onto the microphone stand like it was a lifeline.

And then the crowd began to sing along.

My skin suddenly felt too tight, the hair on my arms standing on end as if electrified. It was hard to catch my breath, but somehow I managed.

The crowd sang softly, echoing Lana's voice, echoing my words, and I felt a tear just before it dripped into my violin. I blinked my eyes rapidly to clear them, heart pounding as I struggled to keep my mind on the vibrato of the chorus. I was sweating, trying not to cry, and feeling the strain as I tried to keep my grip on the bow just right so I wouldn't ruin the song. I couldn't ruin this song, not now, not at this sacred moment.

The song ended, and I lowered my bow as the crowd erupted. Lana backed away from the microphone and looked down at her feet, gently kicking at the corners of the carpet that had rucked up as she moved around earlier. She retrieved her guitar as the applause started to die down and she returned to the microphone.

"Thank you," she said again. "That song was written by Karen Everett, as... well, as pretty much all of our songs are." She turned toward me and held a hand out. "How about a little extra love for her?"

The cheers picked up again, and I was sure I blushed hard enough that I didn't have blood anywhere else in my body.

After the concert, we went back to the table for autographs. Lana was seated first, then me, and then Codie and Nessa alternating between taking the last seat. I'd originally thought they were just ensuring neither of them was banished to the end, but then Nessa explained that the last seat was the one they both wanted. "By the time the fans get to it, they're more relaxed because they've already fawned over you and Karen. It's a lot calmer in the last seat. I feel bad for you two, stuck up there in the front. You're like breakwaters for us."

I signed a "Rainmakers for Wizards Tour" t-shirt, smiling at the art-deco illustration of Seattle with the sun peeking out from behind clouds. A hot-air balloon was drifting over the Cascades and looked to be heading for downtown. I handed it back to the girl, and she took my hand before I could pull it back. She squeezed it, and I could see she was struggling to find the right words to say. Finally she gave up with a shake of her head and smiled at me.

"Thank you."

"You're very welcome."

She looked down at my Sharpie signature before moving on to get Codie and Nessa's names added to it. I glanced shyly at Lana.

"Thank *me*? What did I do?"

"You wrote a song," Lana said. "Sometimes people just need a song to break through to them. And the way you write, you better get used to more moments like that."

I signed the liner notes of *Rome Burning*, which had been opened to one of the pictures of me leaning against the side of the fallout shelter. It faced the lyrics of "Sancho Panza," so I was careful not to cover up any of the white type.

"That's a lot of responsibility."

"It's no responsibility at all. Hi… what's your name?" She signed and smiled as she handed the CD back. "Thanks for coming. Just keep doing what you do. Hi. Oh, thank you so much. You're beautiful, too. What's your name?"

I thought I would hate the idea of sitting at a table for an hour signing my name over and over again, smiling at strangers, mechanically writing the same twelve letters over and over again. The messages we added and the personalized messages were just to break the monotony, I thought. But the idea of people lining up for the specific purpose of having us autograph something was humbling. We also were figuring out how to have quick conversations without holding the line up too much. I would have stayed there all night, except eventually the line dwindled.

Lana loved the last fraction of people to come by. They were as weary as we were, those who had waited the longest and who hadn't given up, so she gave them extra attention. She would lean across the table for photos (some of which I'm sure also caught in frame the 'Absolutely No Photographs' sign someone from Cartography had put up on the back wall) and thanked everyone profusely for coming out and sticking around for so long.

Sometimes the longer it took, the more alive Lana seemed. I kept getting glimpses of the Lana who had collapsed after our first real show, the way she had just run out of energy in the blink of an eye. I made it my job to massage her shoulders, pat her back, make sure she was still alert for the last few stragglers.

It was a very wide country, and we had a lot of long nights ahead of us. If she burned out too early, we'd be completely screwed.

Track Seven

"Hi?"

"Is it too late to call? I woke you up."

"Karen? Hi. No, it's okay. Is everything okay? How'd the show go?" I heard her shifting in bed. I was in bed myself, wearing the hotel's robe, trying to get over the price of snack food from the honor bar even though Cartography was footing the bill. The TV was on, but I wasn't watching. We had a second show in San Francisco, so we were staying in a real hotel. It was the biggest room I'd ever had all to myself, and I was luxuriating. Of course by the time I decided to call Naomi, it was edging up on four in the morning.

"It went fine. I just missed you."

"Sweet." She still sounded drowsy. "How was the show?"

"It went well."

"No more 'incidents' like in LA?"

I winced. "Nope. We took that song out. Lana's going through some stuff right now."

"S'okay. If she'd done it in Austin, maybe it'd be a problem. But LA, LA is fine." She was drifting again.

"Hey, I'm going to let you sleep."

"No, no. I'm up."

I grinned. "No, you're not. I'm being a selfish celebrity and forcing you to keep me company. Go to bed. We'll talk in the morning."

"It is the morning. We're talking now."

"Goodnight, Naomi."

She sighed dramatically. "Goodnight."

A thought occurred to me. "Hey.. ."

"Mm?"

I softly sang a bit of Brahms' Lullaby, the parts I could remember, and she sighed again. This time it was more contented. "We could probably make millions if we sell that... 'Karen Everett sings thee to thy rest.'"

"Sweet dreams," I said. We said goodnight a few more times before we finally managed to hang up. I took off the robe and hung it on the back of the door, then turned off the overhead lights. The TV was still on and I channel surfed until I found something soothing enough to put me to sleep.

Before leaving Seattle, Nessa's boyfriend had suggested she find the time to visit Alcatraz. She woke up close to noon and spent lunch trying to convince the others to join her. Karen and Codie were up for it, but Lana begged off claiming she was still too exhausted and just wanted to go back to sleep before they had to rehearse for that night's show. Karen put off any further pestering, which garnered a brief look of immense gratitude from Lana, and the three of them left her at the hotel. Since it was Nessa's idea, she became the de facto leader of the group. She purchased the tickets, got the guide book, and proceeded to play tour guide.

"What's with all the splotches of paint?" Codie asked.

"Where?"

She pointed, and Karen grinned. "That's not paint. Watch your head."

Codie realized the birds swooping over the rocky island were targeting unsuspecting tourists and spent the rest of the tour bobbing and weaving to avoid the winged bastards.

Karen posed in the door of a cell, snarling like a hardened con for Codie's digital camera. "I think we have the cover of our next album. Now like a women-behind-bars flick. Oh, don't pretend you never watched one."

Nessa laughed, and turned to seek out the source of her feeling they were being watched. A chubby blonde woman in a visor smiled nervously when she was found out, and Nessa lifted a hand in greeting. The woman seemed to take it as an invitation to approach.

"I'm so sorry. But... are you Radiation Canary?"

Nessa furrowed her brow. "I'm not. Codie, are you Radiation Canary?"

Codie shook her head. "Nope. Karen?"

"I don't think so. If only Lana were here." She took pity on the poor lady and said, "We're a majority of Radiation Canary. Yeah. How are you?"

The woman took a deep breath and then smiled. "Oh, I knew it. I don't want to interrupt your visit. I just kept seeing you and I could have sworn I recognized you. Now I can put my mind at rest. My daughter just loves your music. She won't believe I met you."

Nessa said, "A picture would help sell the story."

"Oh, I couldn't!"

"You didn't ask, we offered." Codie motioned Karen forward and they bunched up together. "What do you think, Charlie's Angels?" They folded their hands into guns and assumed the pose made famous by Farrah and the other angels. The woman seemed a bit too nervous to take the picture, but she managed it after a few seconds of fumbling. She looked at the picture in the preview window and giggled like someone half her age. "You just made me a hero, I think. I won't take up any more of your time."

Karen insisted on signing the woman's guest book, even though afterward she felt like she was forcing her celebrity on the poor lady. Their self-imposed time limit ran up and Nessa led them back to the boat. They had enough time to get back to the hotel and have a snack before rehearsal. Nessa was thrilled with the trip, skimming through the pictures on her camera during the fifteen minute ride back to shore.

Karen and Codie went to change clothes, and Nessa knocked on Lana's door to wake her up. There was no answer, so she went to Karen to get the spare key they'd gotten just in case and let herself in. "Lana? We gotta get."

Lana was sitting in bed, knees sticking out so the arches of her bare feet could hold a beer bottle. She was in panties and a long yellow-green T-shirt with the tour name on it and a list of cities and dates running down the back. Judging from her hair, she hadn't showered yet, and her eyes were red from crying.

Nessa sat on the edge of the bed and nudged her shoulder. "Hey. You okay? Why didn't you answer?"

Lana shook her head. "Called home. I wanted to talk to Alia, but there was no answer. So I called her cell phone. She moved out. She told me not to call her anymore."

Nessa pressed against Lana and hugged her. "I'm so sorry."

"I didn't want to ruin you guys' day." She clutched Nessa's arm where it crossed her chest. "How was the island?"

"It was a prison covered in seagull poop. We got recognized by a lady."

Lana smiled, but it didn't break through her gloomy visage. "That's awesome."

Nessa tried to fix Lana's hair. "Did you get any sleep?"

"I got some quality toss-and-turn time. And then I discovered beer." She picked up the bottle and held it like a priceless artifact.

"I think someone beat you to that discovery."

"Yes." She held the bottle up to the light, squinting through the glass, "but I have perfected it."

"Come on. Get up, get dressed, shower... you'll feel like a new woman, I promise. Then we can rehearse and you can hear five hundred people screaming your name."

This time Lana's smile managed to dissipate some of the fog. "That sounds like the ideal treatment for a breakup."

"Yep." Nessa patted her thigh and kissed her temple. "You'll have the whole country paying to be in your presence over the next month. Who needs some bartender?"

"Thanks, Ness."

Nessa winked. "No problem. You spend a day walking through an inescapable prison, you can see the bright side of everything once you get back to freedom."

I tensed and took a five-count before I responded to what Lana had said. "We agreed we wouldn't do 'Crime' on the rest of the tour."

"No, we agreed I wouldn't take off my clothes anymore," Lana said. "We wrote it about Alia, sure, but that's not what the song is. Remember what Naomi called it? It's a song about masturbation. A woman loving herself. I just need to focus on that angle and I can get through the song. I know I can." She lowered her voice. "I need to perform it like that, K."

I trusted her. I looked at Nessa and Codie, saw they were leaving it up to me, and I took her hand. "All right. We'll put it back in for tonight. But if I see you take off one piece of clothing..."

She grinned. "It'll be completely PG."

"Well... PG-13." Codie gestured at Lana's outfit. "You don't see bodies like that in kids' movies."

Lana was true to her word. I admit to having a moment of anxiety when we started the song, but she kept it clean. The audience went wild, and Lana basked in their adoration. She winked at me, and I smiled back at her. We were back on track, with that song at least.

By now the others had informed me that the canary hand symbol was pretty well-known on the internet, and I started looking for it. The audience members would use it to express their approval of a current song and in lieu of cheering when they recognized a song from the first few chords. I kept a lookout for more people doing the shadow puppet, but that was nothing compared to what one group had put together. During "Icarus," three or four girls on the far left side of the amphitheater spread out and extended their arms. They had tissue paper wings attached to their wrists and belts, and flapped them like angel wings. I crossed the stage during the bridge and nudged Lana, pointing them out to her. She laughed and moved closer to the microphone.

"Looks like San Fran sent angels to watch over us."

I looked at Codie and Nessa, remembering our pose at Alcatraz, and we laughed as I went back to my position.

After the concert, the angels showed up and we agreed, as a band, to take a moment to pose with the girls so their father could take a picture. We signed along the edge of their wings, and one of the girls put me in a headlock that I later realized was the strongest hug I'd ever been given. When we returned to our seats, Lana leaned toward me and said, "Who needs bartenders?"

I smiled and turned my attention to the next person in line.

Track Eight

I had never been to Vegas. I expected sweltering heat, blinding lights, and showgirls on every corner. I was a little disappointed at how normal it all seemed as we pulled up in front of the hotel. We arrived early enough to drop off our bags and head out to enjoy the city. I went with Nessa, while Codie dragged Lana to one of her favorite off-Strip spots. We gambled a little, won a fraction more than we lost, and took our winnings to pay for lunch.

We were recognized outside the hotel and posed for pictures with a group of high school girls on a class trip. That was followed by a bizarre turnaround, an only-in-Vegas moment when Nessa spotted Jake Gyllenhaal and got his autograph. When I told her I never saw *Brokeback Mountain*, our mission became seeking out a DVD to watch on the ride to Denver.

By that point we'd settled into a rhythm. It was like a road trip sponsored by a mysterious and unseen benefactor whose only stipulation was that we spend a few hours singing to strangers in exchange for transportation, accommodations and food. It seemed like a small price to pay to hang out with my friends. I was mildly concerned with the fact I hadn't written a word since we started on the tour. No time, but also no inspiration. I told Lana about my worries, and she said it was nothing to be surprised by.

"You're cut off from your source. Your spirit is in Seattle. When we get back, it'll be waiting for you. For now, we've got enough old songs to keep the crowds at bay. Let's go give them what they want."

The Vegas theatre was more intimate than LA or San Francisco's, and it felt like we were back in the clubs playing for free beer. After "Sancho Panza," Lana started a conversation with a girl in the audience about where she was from, what her favorite songs were, if she had gambled yet... it was nothing spectacular or clever, but it felt real. It felt like a moment between two people who happened to meet each other at a concert, who cared if one of them was performing? After that the crowd seemed even more enthused.

On "Prayer," Lana asked for silence as was becoming her habit. A few wiseasses cheered as the rest of the crowd quieted, but soon you could hear a pin drop. The crowd sang along again with Lana's benediction, and I knew I'd never get used to the feeling of a room full of people singing words I'd written. I closed my eyes and thought about how many times I'd sat on the retaining wall as people I'd never seen played music, scribbling in a book I was still too shy to let anyone read. How the hell had I gotten to this place?

Afterward we didn't have an autograph session set up, but people gathered at the stage door regardless and we spent some time in the crush of people. Lana slipped off at some point and I figured it would cause the crowd to break up but they seemed just as eager without her.

When we were finally free, I whispered to Nessa that I was going to try to track Lana down. They said they'd meet us in the hotel restaurant for drinks before we went up to bed. We had to leave at seven to make it to Denver on time, and I was ready to collapse.

Backstage was eerie. Less than an hour after the show and it felt utterly abandoned, shut down and awaiting the next act to call it home for a performance. The green room light was on, so I changed direction to look for Lana there first. I heard voices and almost called out, lifting my hand to knock on the frame as I stuck my head around the door. I froze before making contact, eyes widening at what I saw within.

Lana was sitting on the couch against the back wall, one girl pressed against her side while another straddled her thigh on the opposite side. Lana was kissing the girl next to her while her hands roamed under the shirt of the girl riding her. Everyone was still fully dressed, even if Lana's jeans were undone, but it didn't look like that was going to be the situation much longer. The girl kneeling on the couch next to Lana was already tugging at her shirt, and her friend was trying to help her.

"Hold up," Lana said hoarsely, and then looked toward the door. She smiled when she saw me and lifted her chin. "K. Come on in."

I choked out a laugh. "Uh... no, I think I'll just head on..."

"Oh, please?" the girl on Lana's leg said. "It'll make everything more even."

"Yeah." Lana looked at her two new friends. "I've got my hands full here. Help me out, Karen. What happens in Vegas, right?"

I smiled bashfully and shook my head, lifting my hand in apology as I fled. I found Codie and Nessa in the bar and told them Lana was "indisposed." When she didn't show up before we called it a night, I texted her to remind her of our departure time. "Make sure your friends are gone by then." I was in the elevator before she replied.

"workin on it as we speek"

I rolled my eyes and tucked my phone into my pocket, sure I was blushing. I let myself into my room, showered, undressed, and crawled between the blankets. I thought about Lana's invitation and wondered how bad it really would have been if I'd agreed to join them. It's not like Naomi and I were really in a relationship. I assumed she'd been with other people since we slept together, and I was fine with it. Lana was single now. Would it have been the worst thing in the world if I'd let the fan adoration get a little physical.

Yes. It would. And Lana was wrong to take advantage of it. But I wasn't her mother or her guardian. Let her screw who she wanted. No skin off my nose. I drummed my fingers on my stomach knowing that if this was a movie, the couple in the next room would choose that moment to start having noisy sex. Or, no, it would be Lana's room and I'd hear her and the groupies getting down to business.

Probably good that this wasn't a movie. I didn't need that temptation. No, ma'am.

After five minutes of telling myself to just go to sleep, I rolled over and grabbed my phone off the nightstand. I had another text from Lana that I ignored, and I dialed without turning on the bedside lamp. I lay in the dark and listened to it buzz until there was a click.

"Hey. My midnight caller."

I smiled. "Hey, Naomi. Got a minute?"

"For you I have a whole half hour. More if you need. What's up?"

I wet my lips. "Are you alone?"

"Yeah..."

"I need a hand."

She was quiet, and then she chuckled. "Ahh. Well, I don't know what you expect me to do when you're all the way down south and I'm way up here in Washington. And I'm not exactly dressed to travel. All I'm wearing are some silk shorts and a button-down pajama shirt. I was just settling in for the night."

I tugged the pillow out from under my head and moved it between my thighs. I began to move my hips as I told her what I was wearing, and what I was doing. I heard her sigh and closed my eyes to picture her. We attempted more dirty talk, but it quickly devolved into a symphony of panting, moaning, and whispering each other's names. I pressed my lips against my upper arm to quiet myself, but Naomi heard anyway and told me she was coming, too.

We gasped at each other and then, finally, she said, "You going to sleep now?"

"I think so..."

"Happy to help. Maybe I'll fly out for one of your later shows and we can do that for real."

"I'd like that."

"Get some rest for now. I'm up late most nights... don't worry about waking me. Even if I'm asleep, I don't mind. 'Kay?"

"Yeah. Okay. Night."

"Night."

I hung up and, feeling greatly relieved, rearranged the pillows so I could rest. I was just drifting off as the people in the next room came back. As predicted, I could hear everything they did with crystal clarity.

I'm pretty sure it was a Tarantino marathon on Pay-Per-View.

Track Nine

After Lana's walk of shame to the bus the next morning, complete with dark sunglasses and the previous night's outfit, the band headed for Denver. I knew we were in trouble as soon as we arrived and found ourselves huffing and puffing from the walk to the elevators. It wasn't hard to breathe, but the air seemed so thin that we spent the day leading up to the concert just lying in bed and trying to catch our breath. The show was subdued, mainly because none of us wanted to move too much. We adjusted the set list so that we each had songs interspersed with Lana's just to give her a chance to catch her breath between each one.

"Scene of the Crime" was performed without any dance moves, but I think Lana's breathlessness added a sensuality to it that did the trick.

We were too tired to be excited about leaving town, but it was blissful to wake up in the morning with the ability to breathe.

The cities became a blur. I'd once heard an anecdote about a singer who praised the crowds in Boston when he was in New York. Suddenly I understood how he could have made the mistake. I tried to use the skylines as a guide, but there were so many cities I didn't recognize. They could have been Istanbul for all I could tell. I was thrilled when I spotted the St Louis Arch, just for the joy of knowing for sure where I was.

Lana either didn't repeat the Vegas incident or she got better at hiding it. We were in the middle of the Plains when she asked me to keep mum about it with Nessa and Codie, and I agreed it would stay between us. She seemed contrite, so I wasn't going to scold her. She was a grown-up, and she could make her own mistakes.

In Philadelphia, the crowd shouted for "Emerald," and Lana insisted we had to give the people what they wanted. I recalled the line in the chorus where I besmirch Philly's reputation of brotherly love and tried desperately to think of an alternate line. I took off my shoes before I took Lana's spot at the front microphone. When I got to the chorus, I adjusted the words on the fly.

"New York's an apple, that quickly gets rotten
Though Philly's love is the best I've ever gotten."

I cringed, but the crowd adored it. Later on Nessa found a review online that mentioned the moment when the "seductive Karen Everett took an erotically-charged moment to remove her boots before performing." All I remembered was thousands of eyes locked on me, and needing to feel comfortable if I was going to be able to sing. Lana told me not to worry about it; if I'd stayed shod, someone would have found something erotic in how I sat with the cello between my legs.

Like I needed something else to be self-conscious about.

I had never been to New York before, but there was no doubt when we arrived in Manhattan. The skyline was familiar from movies and television that I felt like I was coming back to somewhere I'd almost forgotten. We were booked on the *Late Show*, which I felt odd about considering it aired in the same time slot as *Settle In, Seattle!* It felt like we were cheating on Nick. But exposure was exposure, so we went. We never saw the host except for the five minutes before we went on and at the end of our set when he came over to shake Lana's hand.

The same night, we were booked at a place called Bookman's Paradise. I had no idea what to expect, but the quaint book-and-record store in the basement of a tenement building lived up to the name. There was only room for a crowd of about fifty people, and the stage was flanked with displays for the latest bestsellers. After we played we mingled with the crowd, signed records and posters, and posed for pictures. Our big show was the following night, but I knew that basement would be the high point of the tour for me.

We were booked two to a room to save on money, and I bunked with Lana. I slept fitfully and woke early the next morning, tiptoeing through my ablutions and dressing so I wouldn't wake her. I left the room and went downstairs, where the day was already starting to heat up. Summer wasn't going easy on the city, holding at almost ninety degrees before eight in the morning. I dressed light, feeling half-naked in a skirt and light T-shirt as I found a cab and gave him directions to where I needed to be.

I didn't want to think about what I'd say or what I would do when we saw each other. I had one moment planned, when I gave her the tickets and backstage passes to the show. That left me little room for disappointment, or so I hoped.

Mom's building was nothing special, but it seemed different from the others on the block as I looked up at it. Just plain white brick, windows with various detritus of residents pressed against the glass. There was a doorman positioned under a red awning, and I knew he was eyeing me as I perched on the stone wall across the street and waited for Mom to show up.

It was nearly eight-thirty when he moved to open the door and she appeared. Seeing her breeze out of the building was like looking through a window to the future. From her I got my height, hips, and hair, and that combination was hard to miss. For an instant, I had a flash of her showing me how to hold a cello, her fingers light on my wrist as she guided the bow so I could see how it was done.

I blinked it away, my breath caught in my throat as I watched her hurry north. She was already walking briskly, so I hurried to catch up as I crossed the street, taking the time to check for traffic before barreling out. The doorman was watching so I called out, "Mom? Mom!"

She didn't even slow down. I called her name instead, and she faltered and turned. Her eyes widened when she spotted me and stopped so I could catch up.

"Karen! What are you doing here?"

"The... concert. Tonight. I called and emailed–"

She gave me an exasperated look. "I know about the concert, I meant *here*."

"I thought I could take you out to breakfast. Or lunch, if you have to get to work."

"Uh." She looked at her watch. "I can't do breakfast, but lunch would be fine. You look tired."

I had to laugh. "Thanks, Mom. It's been a really long tour. I was up late last night doing a show and I woke up early to... to see you. I wanted to give you some tickets..." I reached for the back pocket of my skirt, but she was shaking her head.

"You don't have to do that."

I tensed so that my shoulders wouldn't droop. "It's fine. I want you there."

"I know, but–" She started fumbling in her purse, probably looking for her cell phone to call someone about being late to work. She'd probably call it an 'unavoidable circumstance.'

I took the tickets and passes out of my pocket and held them out to her. "Just take them in case you change your mind. Or hell, I don't know, give them away."

She took her hand out of her purse to reveal two tickets to our show. She smiled and tilted her head to the side, and I felt ridiculous.

"Oh."

"Yeah. I bought them the day you told me about the tour. I'll take the backstage passes, though. Philip will like that." I handed them over and she stacked them with her tickets, then returned them to her purse. She adjusted the purse strap on her shoulder, looking a little cowed as if she was the one who'd been acting like a twerp. "We like to think the worst of each other, don't we?"

I shrugged. "I guess so."

"How's your father?"

"He's okay. The shop is doing well. I moved out a while ago... after we got signed."

"He told me. I'm proud of you."

That came out of nowhere. "You've been talking?"

"Email. It's easier. Neither of us notices the long, awkward pauses with email." She smiled. "Come on. I'll walk you to the subway. Where are you staying?"

With the initial clusterfuck of conversation out of the way, we were able to relax. I asked her about work, but she waved me off and asked about the tour. I didn't even know where to begin. I told her about Lana, Nessa, Codie, and I hinted about Naomi. I didn't want her to get her hopes up about a future daughter-in-law, but I also wanted her to know I wasn't alone. We separated at the subway, and she promised to come backstage to say hi after the show. I decided to walk for a few blocks to clear my head, glad I'd gotten over my anxiety to come see her. We didn't hate each other; we just sometimes found it hard to be around each other.

Finally I got another cab to take me back to the hotel. My driver was a Iranian man named Ayman who spent most of the ride talking softly to his wife on a Bluetooth headset, trying to convince her he had indeed remembered her birthday. The desperation with which he cursed after hanging up told me it was a lie, but I kept quiet until he delivered me to the hotel.

I paid him the fare, and then held up the two tickets. "Does your wife like music?"

Track Ten

Lana was awake and fresh out of the shower when I got back to the room. When I came in she switched from a towel to a robe, and I was grateful I wouldn't have to avert my gaze. She went into the bathroom to brush her hair and called through the open door, "Did you see your mom?"

"Yeah. She's coming to the show." I frowned. "With someone named Philip. Huh. I guess she kind of glossed over who he was." I shrugged it off. "Codie and Nessa?"

"Downstairs getting breakfast. I'm going to join them when I get dressed."

"I'll go on down. Want me to order for you?"

By then we had the routine down pat. A few free hours, then to the theatre to rehearse, and then the show. New York was one of the cities we'd decided we couldn't do "Emerald," since we didn't want to call their city a rotten apple to their face. Philly had been all right, but New York could be a little more vocal with their displeasure. Lana turned "The Man of Many Wiles" into a duet so I wouldn't be cheated out of a song and it turned out beautifully. We did "Radio" as an encore, followed by one of Lana's most emotional renditions of "Prayer" yet.

We brought down the house. Mom was waiting in the green room with a tall white-haired man I assumed to be the mysterious Philip, and she hugged me like she hadn't seen me in years. "That was just amazing, sweetheart. Absolutely fantastic."

I bashfully thanked her, then took the focus off me by introducing the other girls. Mom was particularly taken with Codie. "How you manage for the entire show... your arms must be about to fall off right now."

Codie rolled her shoulders and slapped a bicep. "I think I'm okay. Once I get the robotic replacements, I'll be able to really jam."

Mom gushed a little more, and I found some merchandise to give her. I wasn't sure why she'd want it, and told her to feel free to give it to people she worked with, but I couldn't stop. Have a T-shirt, have a couple CDs. Here's a tour poster. It was as if by loading her with stuff, she would remember that I was really part of this. She finally released me so we could "meet our adoring public," and we went out to do the autograph table.

Lana had a headache, but she smiled her way through it. There was a corner just beyond the table that the line was wrapped around, so we could only see a small portion of it at one time. People just seemed to keep appearing, which made the stream of people seem endless. At one point, Lana held up the line to disappear backstage for a few minutes, and she came back looking green around the gills.

"You okay?"

She nodded and apologized to the next person in line.

It was three in the morning before we got to leave, and Lana was on her last legs. Codie and I carried her up to bed, and we dabbed at her head with cold washcloths.

"Maybe we should call a doctor," I suggested when I thought she was asleep.

"No," she murmured against her arm. "Shaking hands will all these people... I just caught something from one of them."

We sat up with her all night, getting her water and bringing her an ice bucket so she could throw up. At seven she was doing better enough that we could walk her down to the bus. She promised she would be better before our show in Boston, and I told her that wasn't an issue before looking questioningly at Codie. As far as I knew, we didn't have a show scheduled in Boston.

"It's okay, Lana. Just rest, okay?"

We got Lana tucked into her bunk, and the bus headed for the airport. We called the New York rep of Cartography to see if we should postpone the flight, but he suggested a quick stop at the doctor and loading her up with medicine so she could fly home without too much discomfort. We went to the address he gave us and Nessa took her inside while Codie and I waited in the bus.

Codie said, "She needs to take better care of herself."

"I think she's just susceptible to this sort of thing."

"Yeah, but she's... she pushes herself. She doesn't sleep, she only eats if someone else thinks to put food in front of her. She's so focused that once she hits the target, she shuts down. She's been shaking hands with people and getting kissed on the cheek this whole tour. Why does she get sick now, after our last show? Because she's been holding it back until now. Like how she collapsed immediately after finishing that one show, back at the beginning. The focus drops and her body collapses. It's scary."

"You don't think she's going to burn out, do you?"

Codie chewed her bottom lip. "I think she's going to do everything she can to make sure she doesn't burn out. And when she can't do it naturally, I think she'll find other ways to keep herself going. I love her to death, but she needs to think about the band before she starts down the road to artificial boosters. I'd rather be in magazines because of our music, not because our lead singer is in rehab."

I wanted to feel betrayed in Lana's stead, but there was too much truth in what she said for me to muster much. I remembered what I'd said about taking some of the pressure off her, and I decided the time to do that was now. I'd wait until we got back to Seattle and talk with her about it. Celebrities that didn't start doing drugs also never lost time to rehab, so it was best to nip it in the bud before it happened.

She left the doctor's office with a prescription of something that made her look less zombie-fied and we made it to the airport with time to spare.

When Codie and Nessa headed off to find something to eat, Lana moved to sit next to me. "I'm really sorry."

"It's not your fault you got sick."

"No, I've been off the wall this whole tour. You've been taking a lot of the weight off, and I used the freedom to have a threeway." She shook her head and pushed her hair out of her face. "I'm not playing with the band anymore."

The air seemed to be sucked away from me. "What?"

"Oh, God. No, I meant I'm not going to mess around anymore. When I get sick or distracted, it's the band that suffers. I'm not going to do that to you guys anymore." She squeezed my hand. "Thanks for being there for me and for not jumping down my throat. It means a lot."

I nodded, ashamed that I'd just been holding off my jump until we got home.

"I feel bad I made you guys stay up all last night playing nursemaid."

"It's okay. We're all due to go 'round the bend eventually. You just got there first. And considering what you were dealing with, Alia and all, you could have really gone haywire. I think a strip tease, an orgy, and a little throwing up is about as Disney as you can get when it comes to breakdowns." I rubbed her knee. "And you never know. When you get back to Seattle, maybe you and Alia can talk. Patch things up."

She grinned and twisted to see if Codie and Nessa were coming back yet. "Yeah. That probably won't happen. You mentioned that threesome in Vegas?"

I winced. "You didn't tell her about it, did you?"

"No. I was a little black-out-drunk at the end, but I know I would remember that." She paused. "There may have been cell phone pictures that found their way to her."

"Ouch."

"Yeah. So that bridge is probably pretty much burnt. How about you and Naomi?"

I shrugged. "We called each other a few times on the tour. It's not serious."

"Are you sure?"

I elbowed her gently. "Yeah, I'm sure." I slumped down and stretched. "God, I can't wait to get home and not play music for a few days. My ears are ringing."

"Thank God. I thought it was just me."

I sighed. "I need to work on the new album."

"*Rome* just came out. Relax. Take a breather. The next album will wait."

"Sure."

Codie and Nessa came back with miniature pizzas, and we gathered in a cluster of plastic chairs to eat as a group. Lana picked at hers, still feeling queasy, but she drank the 7-Up Codie offered and was able to get aboard the plane under her own power. I sank gratefully into my seat, buckled in, and prepared myself to sleep all the way across the country. It would be a nice nap to get my body used to sleep again, preparation for the two-week crash I was planning once I got home.

The last thing I heard was Codie, who was sitting next to me for this leg of the flight, humming 'Homeward Bound' under her breath, and I smiled as I drifted off.

Track Eleven

My hibernation was put off by Naomi, who called me as we were leaving the airport. We arranged to meet at my apartment, and she welcomed me home in style. When I woke up, it was the middle of the night and she was still curled against me. I kissed her, slipped away, and padded to the kitchen half-dressed. I found a can of franks and beans that were good until the end of time, warmed it up on the stove, and sat in the window to look out over the city.

I could see the Space Needle if I tilted far forward and craned my neck, but I didn't bother. The air felt right in Seattle, and it smelled like the sea. I put my bowl on my lap, held in place by my stomach and thighs, and I took out my notebook. During the tour I'd written a handful of notes and snippets of lines that occurred to me, but nothing that seemed like a real, authentic song. I turned to the first blank page and began writing.

"*The sky opens up and spills its rain on me*
Close my eyes, I breathe in and smell the sea
No matter which way the wind blows
I'm only at home here on the wet coast."

I grinned and kept writing, even after Naomi came out of the bedroom looking for me. It was almost dawn and she had to catch a ferry back to Port Townsend, so we shared a shower before she left me alone. Part of me wanted to go back to bed, but I was itching to write. I went back to the window and cracked it open so I could smell the air as I finished the song.

A week after Radiation Canary got back from New York, Lana's breasts made headlines. Technically it was the blonde woman between her breasts garnering most of the comments, but the fact Lana's face was in the frame was a talking point all over the internet.

The pictures had been published on a website from an "anonymous source." The story talked about other pictures that couldn't be published that revealed the "beautiful lead singer engaged in sexual acts with two unknown women." The identities of the other women, if known, weren't revealed. Naomi demanded to know who had leaked the pictures, but the band kept quiet. Eventually she decided that, so long as it wasn't a band member trying to roust up publicity, it was a survivable scandal.

Lana went into the bathroom of their new rehearsal space and held her head underwater until the burning in her cheeks went away. When she straightened, she saw Karen standing in the doorway behind her. She looked angry, but not irrevocably pissed. Lana patted her cheeks with water and then said, "It's not as bad as it could have been."

"Really? What other pictures did you send Alia?"

"Some of them had nudity. Like the kind they won't even show on pay cable."

Karen sighed. "Well, I guess we never really marketed ourselves as a band for all ages. Bands have survived worse, right?"

"Right." She turned and leaned against the sink. "Thanks for not ratting me out."

"We have to stick together. Even when one of us is *extraordinarily stupid*." She crossed her arms and leaned against the door. "They look hotter than I remember."

Lana winced and cringed in mock pain. "Oh, they were gorgeous. Stewardesses, K. From Scotland."

"Oh, well. None of us are to blame for our actions when Scottish stewardesses are involved." She grinned. "Come on. Codie and Nessa are waiting. We have new songs to put together."

Lana mock saluted and followed Karen out of the bathroom. The laptop was still up and showing the site with Lana's hastily-snapped picture. The well-endowed woman in the shot making the media rounds, smiling into the camera and winking a kelly green eye was Blair, and she'd had the sweetest rust-brown freckles on her chest and arms. Lana winced at the picture and shut the window, then closed the laptop.

"You guys have got to find better porn. C'mon. We've got a new album to put together."

"It's not porn," Nessa said. "That's our next album cover. We'll tease that they get to see the full picture on the inside."

Lana laughed. "I'll pose if you will."

"There's an idea for an image," Codie said. "The *real* barenaked ladies."

Lana picked up her guitar and turned to face them. "Okay, while we've got a minute to breathe, let's try and get a few of these songs finished. K, writer's choice."

"I want to get 'Wet Coast' sorted."

"All right. Uh-do-t'ree, and fo'."

Karen said, "Fi'-sis, here we go..." She drew the bow across the strings, and Lana joined in a second later.

Naomi and I ended our... no. Stopped... well. There's not really a word for what we were doing. Relationship was too heavy and tryst seemed too light. Whatever it was, we ended it in November before we were forced to give it a name. I was starting to fall for her, so we sat down a few days before Thanksgiving and I told her that we either needed a commitment or to cool it. I told her I would be happy either way but it wouldn't be long before my heart got broken. She didn't feel comfortable becoming officially involved with an artist she represented, which I understood. We slept together one more time to bookend the relationship and we parted ways as representative and artist. It was more sweet than bitter, but I'd pushed the casual as far as it would go. Ending it was the mature thing to do.

Lana dealt with the fallout of being the poster child of debauchery with aplomb. For a few days, a handful of pictures circulated on the web (including a full-frontal shot that I went to great pains to never see) until the fervor died down. Cartography issued a statement from Lana saying that she was very sorry the photos had gotten out and she would make sure it never happened again. Afterward she did a few interviews, playing contrite and repentant to anyone who was scandalized by her poor decisions. Privately she promised the three of us that she was becoming celibate, so we started a pool on how long it would last. If Lana got a girlfriend in March of '07, I was going to score big.

Lana's claim that my muse would return when I was back in Seattle proved prescient.. In the four months we'd been home, I had been writing like a machine. I went back through my old poems and scavenged some choice turns of phrase for new songs. I wrote about Seattle, the Pacific Northwest, the sea... things that I adored and that I'd been subconsciously longing for during our long bus ride through the desert.

Songs like "Away from Shore," "Simply Messing About in Boats," and "Breakwaters" poured out of me. For the first time, I wrote a song based on a riff Lana played. It was a swinging Memphis-tinged blues beat, and I turned it into a slow, contemplative song called "Neither Nor." Lana and I both gave the lyrics a try, but the song didn't come to life until Nessa tried it. We basically forced the song on her, but once it was a done deal she became protective of the song. She threw herself into it and turned the song into something really special. I decided it would be the last song on the album, a "leave them wanting more" finale.

Cartography offered us a spot in a small, charitable concert with other acts from the label and we agreed, so we spent Christmas Eve on Whidbey Island with the Femme Reapers. From their awkward reactions to seeing Lana again, I assumed they had taken a look at the full-frontal pictures I'd avoided. Lana brushed it off with grace. We were booked in a hotel on the island, even though we could have conceivably driven back home.

We gathered after the concert in front of the hotel's fireplace, dressed in red and green sweaters like refugees from some horrible Christmas special. Only Codie had eschewed the idea of a Christmas sweater for a down jacket and a knit cap, claiming the whole scene was like Norman Rockwell on anti-depressants. I noticed that she didn't leave, though, and she seemed as reluctant as anyone when we finally called it a night. Nessa made hot cocoa and we exchanged gifts at the strike of midnight.

The Cowan sisters gave each of us a necklace with a small pewter canary charm which, of course, had been colored green. I got a scarf for Lana, and Nessa got me a bottle of incredibly expensive hand lotion that I'd been eyeing for a while. It would help prevent calluses and it smelled sublime. I kept flipping up the cap to smell it as the other gifts were exchanged.

When the others finally went upstairs "to wait for Santa," and I stayed in front of the fire to finish my cocoa. I wondered how it could have possibly been an endless year, and also feel so short. The tour was the culprit, I decided. A non-stop dash from one place to another had eaten up the middle of our year, and the rest of it was occupied with recovering from the rush.

I was about to call it a night when Laura Cowan came back downstairs in surprisingly modest pink pajamas. She and her sister favored leather on stage, so to see her looking so syrupy sweet was off-putting. She caught me looking and winked. "Don't tell the tabloids. I'd rather have my sex tapes published like your girl did than let anyone know I wear pink PJs."

I mimed locking my lips. "I don't even know which one of the Reapers you are, so my gossip would be sketchy at best." I paused. "So, Laura," I stressed her name so she'd know I was kidding. "I thought you went to bed."

She laughed and sat on the edge of the table in front of me. I had to move my foot to avoid it looking awkward. "I did. But I wanted to give you this when the others weren't around." She put down a small red box on the arm of my chair.

I hooked my finger on the necklace and held up the charm. "I got mine already. It's wonderful."

"No, that was from us. This is from me, to you."

"Oh. You didn't have to get me anything."

She smiled. "Hasn't anyone ever told you how gifts work? That's not the point. Go ahead and open it."

I felt self-conscious opening a gift as she watched me, but it wasn't wrapped tightly. I got it open and lifted the lid. Inside was a small figurine made of metal nuts and bolts twisted against each other to form the shape of a person playing the cello. It fit perfectly in my palm, and I lifted it reverently.

"Wow. This is amazing. I don't know what to say."

"Say merry Christmas." She leaned forward and pecked my cheek, then the corner of my mouth. "I'm glad you liked the gift."

I nodded. "Yesh." I cleared my throat. "I mean, yes. I did."

She smiled. "Night, Karen."

I managed to say goodnight, and she went back upstairs to bed. I watched her go, then stared at the little figurine. We'd survived the year, both individually and as a band. We had a good head start on the next album, and Naomi said we'd have plenty of studio time in 7 to start recording it. I finished my cocoa, left the mug on the table as the kindly proprietor had instructed us to do, and carried my gift upstairs.

Laura and Ella were in Room B, while I was sharing Room F with Lana. I was sure that if I asked, Lana would trade with Laura and...

No, there'd be plenty of time for that. No need to rush anything. I whispered, "Goodnight," to the other girls' closed door and continued past to my room and my empty bed.

Album Four
THE INTERVENTION
(2007-2008)

Track One

In January, Lana was contacted by Curve Magazine for a profile. They'd waited until the fervor over the leaked photographs died down so it would be an open and honest article about her sexuality. When Lana hesitated to respond, I knew she was envisioning herself alone in the spotlight once again, and I offered to do the article with her. What was going to just be a profile ballooned into a cover story once I was attached, and we had to suffer through a photo shoot. They put me in a leather jacket, fussed with my hair, spent ten minutes debating how I should hold my violin, and even that was tame compared to how much time they spent on Lana.

The reporter was amazing, and the interview felt more like a conversation. Lana played an acoustic version of "Prayer," which had the loft absolutely silent and still until the last chord. When we were finished, Lana hooked her arm around my elbow and insisted on buying me lunch to thank me for supporting her.

Cartography urged us to hire someone to manage our money, but I was confused by the irony of making so much money we needed to employ someone to keep track of it all. But *Rome* really was burning up, pardon the phrase. The reporter had suggested we'd been snubbed by the Grammy Awards, but I hadn't even known the nominations were out yet. Surely we weren't eligible for an award that prestigious. We had a few more requests to use songs on television and in movies, most of which we agreed to. Nessa's favorite show asked to use "My Weak Hand" in an episode, so she was over the moon about that.

I was mostly focused on writing the new album. Lana suggested that, since we were both out now, we should capitalize on that with our music. We'd never shied away from using ambiguous pronouns or flat-out referring to women in our love songs, but she wanted to take it one step further. I wrote a song called "Kelly Green," a love letter to the Pacific Northwest that anthropomorphized it into a person (*"I'm hypnotized by the rhythm of your breathing, it rolls in and out like waves on the sea"*), and Lana countered with the song title "Diving for Pearls."

My first version of "Pearls" was so utterly filthy that I tore it out of my journal and stuck it in my nightstand, just in case I wanted to reference it later. I didn't want Lana to find it and get any ideas. I wanted something like "Scene of the Crime," which could be innocent if it was looked at a certain way. Or if, for instance, the singer wasn't tearing her clothes off during the chorus.

I went on a few dates with Laura Cowan, the last of which led to the bedroom. I was still nervous about the idea of being intimate with anyone. Naomi had been a great introduction to sex, but this was different. It was a romantic relationship with actual potential to go somewhere. Laura agreed to be gentle with me, which made me laugh, and we spent most of the night easing into it. It was mostly great, with one small snafu that went gratefully unnoticed.

Laura was between my legs, nuzzling my neck as her hand worked between my legs, and I tilted my head back and whispered, "Yes, Lana."

A slip of the tongue, whispered while Laura was otherwise occupied... it was easy to brush off as an honest mistake. I made a point to repeat Laura's name like a mantra from that point on, close to shouting it when she finally let me come. She fell asleep on top of me, and I found that I didn't mind the weight as much as I thought I would. I kissed her cheek and her temple and smiled, stroking her back as I tried to quell my excitement so I could sleep as well.

We were in the studio working on "Kelly Green" when Naomi asked if we could take a break for an important business conversation. I panicked, but Lana told me it was probably nothing bad. Still, I leaned heavily on Codie when we left the studio and met with Naomi in the small conference room at the back of the building. It was the first time we'd really interacted since ending our "personal liaisons," but she smiled sincerely and squeezed my hand when I passed her. Look at us, being all mature and grown-up.

She stood at the front of the table, arms crossed, and said, "What do you know about Greece?"

"Olivia Newton-John in painted-on leather pants," Lana said.

I made a noise of approval.

"Wrong Greece." She opened her folder and took out some papers. "The country where, apparently, people are buying your album by the bushel."

Lana raised an eyebrow. "Greece? Really?"

Naomi shrugged. "You guys are exploding over there. I talked it over with the bosses, and I made a compelling enough argument that we're sending you over there for five concerts."

"Over where?" Codie said.

"To *Greece?*" Nessa said.

Naomi held out her hands in a 'tada' gesture. "You're going in late August, early September. That should give you enough time to put the finishing touches on the album. And while you're over there, they want you to put together a music video for 'Icarus.' It seems appropriate, after all."

Lana leaned forward. "You're really sending us to Greece?"

"That's the plan, yes. Are you up for it?"

I think we might have deafened her with our acceptance.

It took them a while, but they finally found a school uniform jacket big enough for Lana. She wasn't allowed to cut the sleeves off, since she was just borrowing it, but she didn't mind. I wore a baseball jersey and had my hair in pigtails. Codie had a denim jacket and mirrored sunglasses, while Nessa was given a pair of coke-bottle glasses and a turtleneck sweater. The costume department offered to give her a fake headgear and braces, but she refused.

One wing of the Cartography offices had been transformed back into a school for the purposes of our video for "Band of Girls." We recruited a class of students from a nearby middle school and auditioned members of their Chorale and Drama clubs to play younger versions of ourselves. Our part of the video was easy; Lana and I just had to walk down the hallway pretending to play our instruments while lip-synching the song, with cuts to Ness and Codie playing in an empty classroom. The students had to do the heavy lifting.

Our teenaged stand-ins learned the song in the week leading up to the shoot, and they were able to fake their way through it even better than we did. A piano keyboard was drawn in marker on top of the desk where Young Nessa would sit, and the room was dressed as if it was an actual functioning classroom. When the girls arrived from their school, we introduced ourselves to our doppelgangers. To my surprise all four of them had merchandise for us to sign.

"We're such huge fans," the Lana stand-in said. "We couldn't believe you chose us. I hope we don't disappoint."

"You'll do great," Lana assured her. "Just relax and be yourselves."

We watched the filming, but the video didn't come together until we watched it on the monitors. Codie had come up with the idea, and Lana helped flesh it out.

A local actress played a teacher who, at the beginning of the video, was forced to separate four troublemaking girls. Young Lana was sent to sit by the window, Young Codie was moved to the opposite side of the room, while my youthful version took a seat in the front row. Young Nessa was left where she was in the middle of the room.

When the teacher's back was turned, Young Lana slid a book off her desk and held it flat against her chest. She ran her thumb over the smooth cover, which prompted the music track to begin. Young Karen looked back and smiled at her across the room, then bent down and unlaced her boot. She slid her foot out into the aisle, held the string up, and used her pencil like a bow. Young Nessa's fingers danced effortlessly across the inked keyboard, while Young Codie used two pencils to drum on the wooden surface and metal supports of her desk. When Young Lana opened her mouth, the real Lana's voice seemed to issue from her vocal chords.

"We're so nice and innocent and sweet
We always curtsey to gentlemen we meet
Yes sir, we're innocent and polite
Thank you, ma'am, never think we might
Mess up our hair, get out of sorts
Get our face dirty, tear up our skirts
If you think we might just be a band of girls
It's the nice ones you gotta watch out for."

I was impressed that the director managed to make one hallway look different with multiple angles. I had felt like a fool walking up and down the same ten feet of tile, but on the monitor it looked like we were prowling the entire school. The video ended with us opening the door while our counterparts snuck out, then waving goodbye to the teacher to run out behind them.

We had done our parts, so now it was in the hands of editing wizards. When we packed up our things to go, our costumes exchanged for street clothes, I saw Lana chatting with the woman who played the teacher. She was model-fit, her blonde hair pulled back into a bun, and horn-rimmed glasses completed the image of the perfect fantasy teacher. She wore a tweed skirt and a white dress shirt buttoned to the collar. I'd had quite a few fantasies about teachers like that when I was in school, and I hoped Lana would have a chance to live the reality.

Codie came up with the name for the third album, *The Middle Distance*. I couldn't say why I liked it so much, except that it just seemed perfect. The cover image was Lana's idea, and Naomi was eager to make it a reality. On a beautiful, cool morning in May, we arrived at an inlet off Puget Sound with Mt. Rainier in the background. The photographer had everything set up for us. A little dinghy delivered us to four platforms set up just below the surface of the water. We were delivered one at a time, our pants legs rolled up almost to the knee even though the water barely covered our feet.

We all wore black slacks and white shirts, but Lana wore a waistcoat with a pocketwatch chain hanging across her stomach. I wore a bowler hat with my hair tucked up into it, Lana wore a fedora, and Codie had found a tricorn patriot hat which made her look like Pauline Revere. Nessa chose to remain hatless, but she kept on her aviator sunglasses. We posed with Lana at the forefront, with me a foot or so behind her. Codie and Nessa were on Lana's left and, once again, they argued over who would get to be on the furthest platform. Nessa wanted to hide, but Codie was reluctant to let her. Finally Codie claimed the back position for herself, claiming it mimicked how we were situated on stage.

The photographer took pictures from the boat, having us change poses from time to time. We were all starting to get tired of standing around when I inadvertently put an end to the photo shoot. I merely moved my foot a little to the right, shifting my weight from the ball of my foot to the heel. The sole of my shoe landed on a slick spot and my foot slid forward.

I overcorrected and my right foot went entirely off the side of the platform and I fell backward with a yelp. I hit the water and went under, panicking slightly even though the water was probably less than six feet deep. After a bit of initial flailing, someone grabbed me around the waist and hauled me up. My head broke the surface and I gasped, turning to see Lana was my rescuer.

"You okay?"

"Yeah." I pushed my hair out of my face and saw Codie and Nessa were both crouching on their platforms. I looked at the photographer and Naomi, both of whom seemed like they were about to have concurrent heart attacks. "I'm fine! Just a little humiliated, that's all."

The boat was moved closer, and I climbed up before turning to help Lana into the boat with me. They picked up Codie and Nessa as well, and they hugged me to make sure I was still in one piece.

Naomi seemed to have calmed down when she saw I wasn't hurt. "Well... even if they weren't drenched, I think we can call this photo shoot complete. I think we got what we needed...?"

The photographer showed her his display screen. "Want that?"

"No. Delete that."

I was curious so I motioned for him to wait. "Want what? Let me see." One of the photographer's helpers had draped me and Lana with towels, and I felt just a touch ridiculous.

He looked at Naomi, and she shrugged. He held the camera out to me and I saw he'd captured the moment I had started to go down. The toe of one shoe was still in contact with the platform and I was falling backward with a look of utter horror. My other leg was stretched out in front of me, and my arms were angled back as if there'd been something to catch my fall. Lana was twisted at the waist, probably in reaction to my shriek, and her right hand was stretching out toward me.

"We have to use this somewhere."

"You wouldn't be embarrassed?" Naomi said.

I scoffed. "I fell into Puget Sound. I'd hate for that to be for nothing."

"If you're okay with it, then so am I. But it won't be the cover."

Lana said, “Use one of the good ones for the cover, and then Karen falling can be for the back.” She smiled. “It’ll be like the act of turning the CD over caused her to lose balance.”

I laughed. “That’s perfect.”

Naomi shrugged. “Okay. It’s up to you guys. Sounds great to me.” She looked to make sure the photographer’s people were getting the platforms out of the water and told the boat captain to head back to shore. I sat down with the rest of the band crowding around me, and I took Lana’s hand.

She said, “Sorry. The cover was my idea...”

“Hey, not your fault. Besides, it’ll look really great. Thanks for diving in after me.”

She grinned. “Of course. You’re not done writing the album. Can’t let you drown before we’re done with you.”

I laughed and squeezed her hand, slumping against her for the body warmth as the boat returned us to solid ground.

Track Two

We finished the album two weeks before our big European excursion. When all the songs were delivered, Naomi joked we could wait until we got back stateside before we started work on the fourth album. I told her we would try, but the truth was I already had two songs written. I didn't want to risk another drought like the one I'd faced while on tour, so I stayed up writing whenever Laura wasn't over. The internet had figured out we were dating, so the simple pleasure of dinner soon took on the feel of a James Bond movie. For a few weeks no one was sure which Cowan twin I was dating, a mystery that both members of the Femme Reapers took no small delight in abusing. Once I went to the movies with both of them just to make people scratch their heads.

I was worried about Naomi finding out, but she took it as a business opportunity. I was invited to play on a song from their second album as a "special guest artist." How my name was supposed to draw people to the Femme Reapers, I had no idea. It should have been the other way around. But as long as I was getting paid to play with a band I liked, I didn't really care whose album I ended up on.

Somehow I miscommunicated the situation to Dad, as he had Ted convinced we were embarking on a full European tour. I set the record straight and, even though "just Greece" seemed minor in comparison, they were still suitably impressed. Mom told me to stay away from ouzo which, I have to admit, at the time I thought was the name of a neighborhood.

The day we left, Naomi met us at the airport. Lana had led us through the parking lot, her guitar case hanging off her back like a scabbard. I had been expecting to take normal commercial flight on Grecian Air or something like that, but she guided us past security to a private hangar. I was relieved to see the others seemed equally confused by the detour.

Lana said, "Where exactly are we going?"

"Someone decided if you're going international, you should go in style. There's just going to be one other passenger, but I don't think you'll mind. You're kind of hitching a ride with her, since it's technically her jet."

Lana said, "Who would let us borrow a jet?"

"I would."

I glanced back without stopping and nearly tripped over my feet. I think I might even have cursed, but maybe that was just Lana.

Dash Warren was coming up behind us, a bag slung over her shoulder as she strolled toward the plane. *Her* plane, I realized. She was taller than I expected, with black hair like raven wings that hung on either side of her face. Her purple blouse was tucked into her jeans, showing off a thick brown belt that matched her knee-high boots. In all the time we'd been with Cartography, we'd never actually met the label's creator in person. I'd been a fan of hers since high school, and it was enough of a mind-screw to have her label's name on our CDs. But to actually see her in the flesh was something completely different.

"You're flying us to Greece?" I said.

"Eh, I was going that way anyway." She held out her hand. "I'm Dash Warren."

We all introduced ourselves, and Dash adjusted the guitar case on her back. "I know they won't leave without me, but this is getting kind of heavy. We'll have plenty of time to talk onboard."

"Right," Lana said. She looked at me, eyes wide once Dash wasn't looking, and we hurried to catch up. We boarded and tried to settle in while our musical idol casually got a drink and sat across the aisle from us. She leaned across to my seat and plucked the charm up from where it rested on my shirt, brushing it with her thumb.

"This is really cool."

"Thanks. My girlfriend had them made for us last Christmas."

"Cool. Very cool."

We took off and headed out, and I tried to decide which direction we would go. It seemed equal distance east or west; across the United States or out over the Pacific Ocean and Russia? I watched out the window and saw we were going east. Once I'd confirmed for myself, Dash made my deduction unnecessary by pointing out we'd have brief layovers in New York and Rome before finally landing in Athens.

"I wanted to talk to you guys, too, in an unofficial capacity. I'm releasing a new album in a few months, and I'd love to offer a cover of 'Say a Prayer.'"

My heart skipped. "Really?"

"Yeah. I'd want you guys to play on it. If Lana doesn't mind me taking over the vocals..."

Lana laughed. "Are you kidding? Rerecord our entire catalogue if you want." She looked at me and raised her eyebrows. "It's like Picasso asking if he can use your canvas as a starting point."

I chuckled and Dash shrugged. "I don't know about Picasso," she said, "I just think the song is amazing. I'm glad we'd already signed you when I heard it, because otherwise I'd have had to fight for you. I'm also glad you came out after we already had you. I don't think I would have handled that whole picture scandal as well as you did."

Lana shook her head. "I just did what you guys told me to do."

"Do you know who leaked the pictures?"

"Oh. Yeah." She looked at me, and I tilted my head. I'd never heard how she'd dealt with Alia, and suddenly I was curious. "I was feeling vindictive, so I sent them to my ex. She repaid cruelty with cruelty. We apologized to each other. It was civil, really."

Dash nodded. "Well, that's cool."

I left Dash and Lana talking and went to the minibar at the back of the plane. Codie met me there and tapped one of the bottles with two fingers.

"Private jet to Athens, Greece, where we're apparently very famous."

"Kind of hard to fathom, huh?"

She snorted and looked around herself. "Five years ago, I was this close to getting busted for car theft. I was inside a chop shop when the police raided it. The only reason I got out was because I knew the window in the bathroom was broken, so I slipped out and ran across a field. I thought the cops would have the place surrounded like in the movies, and I'd have stopped if I'd heard anyone yell 'freeze.' I mean, I'm brown and running from the cops, I know how that ends. But no one saw me, I guess. And now I'm on Dash Warren's plane." She put her hand on my shoulder and squeezed. "Thanks to you."

"I wish you guys would stop doing that. I didn't do anything. You were a band a long time before I came along."

"We played music before you came along. We weren't going anywhere. This plane might have all the pieces it needs, but it's not going anywhere without the pilot."

I smiled shyly. "So I'm the pilot?"

"It sounded more polite than saying you were the gas."

I laughed and followed her back to the seats. I watched Lana talk with Dash like they were old friends, and thought how bizarre it was to be in the same league as someone like her. Sure, she was at the top and we were near the bottom, but that didn't matter. I'd bought her first CD when I was freshman in high school, unwilling to admit how much of my decision to purchase it was based on how sexy she looked on the cover. I listened to her when my parents were fighting. "Flip of the Coin" was playing the first time I kissed a girl.

I settled into my seat and closed my eyes. I knew sleeping early would help with the jet lag, but I also wanted to try something.

If I could fall asleep and dream, then wake up to see Dash Warren really was having a casual conversation with my best friend, maybe I would believe it was really happening.

Track Three

The first concert was in Athens, outside, with a view of the sparkling sapphire sea. Lana wore sunglasses and a pair of shirts, both sleeveless of course, and strummed her guitar as she stepped up to the microphone. "Kalispera, Athens!" she said, having learned a few key Greek phrases for the occasion. "I'm going to speak more English than Greek, and I'm sure you'll appreciate it given my surely atrocious accent. How is everyone doing?"

The crowd replied with a cheer, and Lana cheered back.

"I apologize in advance for sweating, but we're not used to... the sun. Seattle has a different sun than Greece. It's nowhere near this effective. But we have you all to thank for our record label deciding to send us here, so we're gonna treat you really special. We're going to play some old songs." She strummed the intro to "Radio," which prompted cheers. "We're going to play some *new* songs." More cheers and applause. "Karen is going to juggle chainsaws. Codie will swallow fire while Nessa spins plates on poles. And if this heat keeps up, I may strip for completely practical purposes. So let's get right to it, what do you say?"

They started with the instrumental "Mutually Assured," to which they had added enough embellishments so to make it last nearly ten minutes. When it came to a crashing end, the music was replaced with cheers and applause. An entire section of the audience had their thumbs hooked over their hearts, flapping their fingers like bird wings. When Karen switched between the violin and cello, she returned the gesture to the delight of the audience.

Lana turned her back to the audience and mouthed a countdown to the band, then started "The Importance of Your Radio."

They played most of the first album, and snippets from the second. After an hour of playing, Lana said, "You all have been so lovely to us, how about a couple of songs from the new album? What do you think about that?"

They replied with cheers and whooping, and Lana smiled.

The first song was "The Next Ferry," which led into the Nessa-led "Neither Nor." Karen took center stage for an instrumental called "Improve the Silence."

"Those are all from, ah, *The Middle Distance*, due out early next year. And now, because you have been such a wonderful group of people, we have a special guest for you. She was going to stay in Rome, but we begged and pleaded with her to come with us. 'The Greek people need you,' we said. 'Please, please, don't let them down.' So she finally caved, and now she's here to perform some songs. Because even on vacation, musicians have to work for their supper. Please welcome the lovely... Dash Warren."

She came out in knee-high boots and a lace skirt, the guitar swinging under her arm like a purse as she hugged Lana and took the microphone. "Hello, Athens!"

They performed "Band of Girls" and "Man of Many Wiles," then Lana asked for silence. The crowd very slowly quieted down. The sun was setting, and the even the wind calmed as Lana sang the first line of "Prayer." A few people clapped, and the applause spread when Dash stepped forward and joined Lana for the next line.

The duet worked beautifully, and soon the audience was as silent as a group of people that large could be. The band could hear the sounds of the city outside the walls, but it was as if they were enclosed in a bubble of stillness. The band joined in, and Dash put her hand on Lana's hip as they came to the chorus. During the musical interlude Lana stepped back and began to dance. Dash held out her hand, Lana took it, and they swayed together in the gap between Karen and Nessa. They moved their guitars out of the way so they could press their hips together for an impromptu waltz, and Karen played a lively tune to accompany them. The interlude stretched on twice as long as the album version, but eventually Lana ended the dance to sing the final verse.

When the song ended, the crowd erupted as if releasing all the pent-up noise at once. Dash and Lana hugged, and she took the time to high-five Codie and Nessa before she hugged Karen on her way offstage.

"Dash has to go now, because the longer she's here the worse we look." Lana scuffed her foot on the stage and glanced down to check the set list to see what song was next. With the crowd making noise, the breeze coming in off the Mediterranean, and the lingering feel of Dash's hand on her hip, Lana didn't want the night to ever end. "All right, we've done nice and quiet... what do you say we pick things up a little bit...?"

Our sleep schedule was thoroughly and utterly screwed up by traveling to the other side of the world. Dash, old hand at bizarre schedules, spirited us away from the autograph sessions to appreciate the Athens nightlife. I couldn't figure out if the place we ended up was a club with a bar or a bar with a dance floor, but it didn't particularly matter to any of us. Nessa was swept up almost immediately by a man who looked like John Stamos in the eighties, and Dash corrected my mistaken idea of ouzo by getting us a bottle. Codie didn't feel like confining herself to just one partner, so she ventured onto the dance floor for what looked like an utter free-for-all.

"We have a few days worth of free time, and we've *got* to take a day trip to the isle of Lesbos."

I laughed. "Right."

Lana was game, so Dash turned to me. "You've got to go. You can't come all this way and not see Sappho's hometown. You'll love it. They even have a bay that, from the right angle, looks nice and labial." She traced an inverted teardrop shape in the air over the table and I couldn't resist a laugh.

Lana kicked my foot lightly under the table. "Come on, it's part of the tour. Plaka, the Parthenon, Pussy Island."

Dash snorted her ouzo, and I finally conceded. Who was I to say no?

After some more drinks, Lana asked me to dance with her. I was feeling lightheaded by then, detached from myself due to the alcohol and jet lag. I had no idea what day it was, let alone the time. All I knew was the sun wasn't out even though part of me felt it should have been, and I was brimming with energy, so I let her take me out onto the floor.

Lana was wearing a sleeveless button-down shirt, the tails tied to show off her stomach, and I rested my hands on the bare skin of her hips as we danced. I was in a sundress, and her hands covered the thin straps on my shoulders and warmed the sweat-damp skin. We started on a fast song, but the only difference between fast and slow was how close Lana pressed herself against me. My heart pounded, and I closed my eyes so I wouldn't be able to see her when she moved in.

I felt it, though, and braced just before her tongue began teasing my lips. I moved my hands to her back, linking my fingers over her spine, and I felt sweat bead on my forehead as I let her kiss me. Her hands moved, and she inadvertently pushed down the strap of my dress. It dropped, and I felt the material sag around my breast. My face burned and I pulled back, trying to think through the fog of pleasure and alcohol.

"Wait, wait..."

"Okay," Lana said.

I pressed my forehead against hers and breathed hard, our bodies still moving to the music. I closed my eyes and thought about Laura, waiting at home for me. I furrowed my brow and wet my bottom lip as Lana stroked my cheek. I leaned into her caress and kissed the meaty part of her palm below her thumb. I whimpered and turned my head, closing the distance between us so I could kiss her. It was just like I had imagined and yet somehow better still.

Someone touched my arm and I jerked away, breaking the kiss a fraction more sober than I'd been a moment ago. Dash smiled and said, "Sorry. Didn't mean to interrupt..."

"Do you want to cut in?" I asked.

Dash glanced at Lana. "Uh..."

"It's okay." I pulled away from Lana's embrace, which was stronger than I'd expected it to be, and smiled. "It's okay, I'm... I should go back to the room." I nodded as if trying to convince myself instead of them, stumbling slightly on my way back to the table. Remembering the adage that God protects fools and drunks, I stopped and took another shot of ouzo.

I growled as it went down, baring my teeth. "Ouzo, ouzo, such terrible booze-o..." I pressed the back of my hand against my mouth and swayed, but someone caught me.

"You're not going anywhere by yourself when you're like this." Dash slipped my arm around her neck, supporting me as Lana took my other arm. "C'mon, let's get you home."

"Bu' we're go' see Pussy Island," I muttered.

Lana laughed and helped our idol get me out of the bar or club or whatever it was. I smiled at the thought that Dash Warren was carrying me out of a bar because I was too drunk to go myself.

I really hope I didn't throw up on her shoes at any point, but I couldn't swear to it.

Track Four

The dream was really fantastic. Prompted, I assumed, by the warm body lying next to me. I pressed against her, my breasts against her back as I put my arms around her. She shifted to let me between her and the mattress and I began kissing her neck. I felt worn out, so it was obvious we'd had a good night. I was hoping to continue it with a very good morning as I kissed down the curve to her shoulder. I was about to suggest a shower when someone kissed *my* neck, and my brain did a back flip.

I pulled back and twisted my neck, my vision just clear enough to recognize Dash Warren. Her hair was a messy tangle, and she winked at me before lifting her head for a kiss. I let it happen because I didn't know how to stop it, but then why would I?

Laura.

"Wait," I groaned, pulling away from her. Next to us, Lana rolled over onto her back and stretched. The blanket was around her stomach, so I got a perfect view of her breasts. My eyes widened and a moment later my brain caught up, reminding me that I'd seen them before. But I couldn't–

I sit on the edge of the bed, Lana takes off my boots and kisses my ankle, the arch of my foot, sucks my toes and then Dash pulls me back onto the mattress and kisses me upside down, and breathlessly gasps as I look down between my spread legs to see Lana peel off her top and then her bra, and then she crawls up straddling my body

– remember when.

"Oh, God."

Lana sat up. "Hey, are you okay?"

"I-I need..." I gestured vaguely toward the bathroom and squirmed out from between them. There was a pile of clothes on the floor by the bed, but I didn't want to even try figuring out which were mine. Besides, they had already seen everything–

I press both hands against the headboard and arch up as Dash and Lana suck my breasts, then lift up to kiss each other as I watch them, and then they move down and Lana eases my legs apart as Dash bows her head

–I had anyway. I hurried to the bathroom, pushing my tangled hair out of my face as I ducked behind the door. As soon as the question of how Lana could do that to me occurred, my mind provided an answer.

"Sweetheart, stop it. You're drunk."

"No, I'm not."

"K, you're drunk and you're dating Laura, and you don't want this."

"I'm drunk and I'm dating Laura and I've wanted this so long. You're so beautiful, Lana."

And Dash, sounding like she's a million miles away, says, "I'll get out of your hair."

And someone who sounds like me saying, "No. You stay, too."

I remembered how firm Lana's lips had been against mine, opening only to say "No," her hands on my body only to push me away. I went to the sink and splashed my face with water, and there was a timid knock on the door.

"Are you okay?"

There was a robe on the back of the door and I put it on before I answered. Dash was on the bed, pulling up her jeans, and Lana had wrapped herself in the sheet. She looked horrified, traumatized, and I could almost hear her thoughts. *"I told you this would happen. I knew you'd regret it, but I did it anyway."*

I sagged against the door. "Dash?"

She cleared her throat, obviously uncomfortable with being caught in the middle of this. "Yeah?"

"Don't go." I cupped the back of Lana's head and pulled her forward. The water I'd splashed on my face had beaded on my lips, and they transferred to Lana's mouth as I kissed her. My temples were throbbing with an incipient headache, and I knew that I was basically tossing a grenade on anything I'd managed to build with Laura. I closed my eyes and felt Lana's hands shyly pushing between the two halves of my robe to touch my hips.

I knew if I let last night sit as a drunken rendezvous, it would eventually destroy the band. The truth was, I wanted Lana. I wanted Dash, too. And in an inebriated state, I'd forgotten about Laura and taken what I wanted without worrying about the consequences. I furrowed my brow as Dash joined us in the bathroom doorway and peeled the robe off my shoulders. I had to repeat it in a sober state if I wanted us to survive it.

Yeah, it was a lame excuse, but it was the one I was sticking with.

I broke the kiss and turned to kiss Dash. She put her arms around me and let me lean against her.

"We all got pretty hot and sweaty yesterday even before..." She nodded toward the bed. "Why don't we take a shower?"

I nodded and let Lana lead me into the bathroom. Dash closed the door behind us.

I was having an affair. Cheating. Being a bitch.

I'd told Laura I would call her as often as possible, but how could anyone be that two-faced? How could I act like everything was fine when I was fucking someone else? Dash, Lana and I kept our date to visit Lesbos, and I managed to enjoy it, flanked by two women I'd been sandwiched between hours earlier. Sleeping with Lana was bizarre. It was like going to bed with my cousin, and having Dash there made the whole thing easy to write off as just a fantasy.

Codie and Nessa noticed, of course. We finally came clean to them, which caused things to be a bit awkward backstage at our next show. Nessa said that she'd always assumed Lana and I had something going on the side from the start. Codie was more offended that I expected. When we were alone, I asked if she was okay.

She thought for a moment, arms crossed over her chest, and then glared at me when she spoke. "What about Laura? Your girl back home? Did you think about her?"

"Yes. I don't know what's going to happen with that."

"You should have answered that question before you fucked someone else."

I also should have thought before I said, "I didn't expect morality lessons from the car thief," but my brain failed me once again. I was lucky that all I got was a dirty look instead of a left hook, but she didn't speak to me for the rest of the night. Her playing seemed much more ferocious as well, like she was taking out her anger on the instruments. Afterward in the autograph line, I apologized, but she shook her head.

"You judged me," After a moment, she added, "And I was judging you. I know you, K, and I know you wouldn't cheat without feeling it. You're too good a person for that. But you need to take some time to think about how all this is going to play out when we get home. Are you going to keep sleeping with Laura and Lana both? Or are you gonna break that girl's heart?"

I didn't know if by 'that girl' she meant Lana or Laura, but the point stood. I shook my head and forced a smile as I signed another autograph.

The flight home was quiet, awkward. Dash spent most of it sleeping or playing on her phone. Lana sat away from the rest of us, probably more to sit away from me. I wanted to apologize, to just shout it and have it be done with, but I stayed in my seat and brooded like a coward. I didn't know what I wanted. Until I did, everything I came up with to say to Lana sounded like a lie.

When we arrived home at long last, Dash stayed on the plane while we marched across the tarmac to the hangar. Naomi was waiting for us. It felt like we were coming back to a familiar world, back to reality after a sojourn in some other dimension. She grinned and held her arms out as if to hug us all.

"Well? How was the... trip?" Her smiled wavered when she saw our expressions. "What's wrong? What happened?"

"Don't drink ouzo," I said as I passed her. She frowned and fell into step next to us, escorting us back through the airport.

I looked out the window for the entire drive. Athens and Crete were like postcards, but they had never seemed real to me. Seattle had a pristine, glassine glow that screamed home to me. The real world after a dream. I rested my head against the glass and, as if sensing we were home, the skies opened up with a gentle downpour.

We were taken to our cars and I drove myself home. Once again, I had no idea what time it was and only a vague notion of the day. I felt like there was a rubber band around the top of my head, squeezing it, forcing the concentration out of me. I trudged upstairs and let myself into the apartment, shutting the door before I realized there were lit candles on the coffee table and mantle.

Laura came out of the bedroom in the pink pajamas I'd seen at Christmas, but the top was unbuttoned and she was naked underneath. My eyes watered at the sight of the bare skin, but Laura didn't notice. She stretched her arm up, pressed against the bedroom door, and batted her eyelashes at me. "Welcome home, stranger."

I put down my bags slowly, turning my back to her as I took off my jacket. Anything to delay the only words I felt capable of saying at that moment. Finally I blinked back my tears and faced her. "Laura, we have to talk."

Track Five

Naomi shut the door to the conference room, paused with her back to the table, and then faced the women sitting across from each other. "Okay, let's talk. Something happened in Greece, and you two haven't been the same since it happened."

Karen glanced at Lana. "Have we been playing badly?"

"No. But Codie and Nessa both asked me to talk to you. It's been tense, and I can tell something's up. So spill. What happened?"

Karen shifted in her seat. "I really don't want to talk about this with someone I used to sleep with."

"That Naomi isn't here," Naomi said. "I'm just your rep, and I'm worried about you guys. Bands have broken up over reasons smaller than hurt feelings. We need to sort this out before it becomes something huge. If you don't think you owe it to me or yourselves, then you owe it to Nessa and Codie."

Lana sighed heavily. "Karen and I got drunk and had sex with Dash Warren."

Naomi winced and leaned back. "Oh. Oh, I see. God damn it. Okay. Don't let that get between you, okay? Dash has a habit of using the label as her personal harem. She never lets it get to the point of harassment... everyone's a willing participant. But if you're jealous or you think one of you stole her from the other, it's--"

"No," Karen said. "We, um. The three of us went out to drink, and when we got back to the hotel, *we* had sex with Dash."

Naomi's eyes widened. "Oh. That's different, I guess. So you two--"

Lana cleared her throat. "Yeah."

"I can see how that might be awkward." Naomi looked at Karen. "I thought you were dating one of the Reapers."

"I was." Something caught in Karen's throat, but she forced it down before it could become a sob. "She left me."

"What?" Lana said. It was obviously news to her.

Karen shrugged. "I confessed everything when we got home, and she... took it well, I guess. She said we hadn't been together that long, and I obviously had complicated feelings for you. She said once I figured them out, if I still wanted her, then she might be waiting." Karen shook her head. "She handled it a lot better than I would have."

Naomi sighed and steepled her fingers. "So I guess what we have left is the lingering awkwardness that comes from you two having sex. Have you repeated it since getting back?"

The denials came almost simultaneously.

"Maybe you should." She held up a hand before they could argue. "Hear me out. You two are closer than best friends, sisters, maybe even closer than some married couples. Lana, you rely on Karen to put words in your mouth, and Karen, you rely on her to give life to your songs. The two of you on stage, by God, it's like watching molecules under a microscope. You give and take from each other so beautifully. You need each other deeply. And out of that has grown a bond that isn't familial or sexual. You can't make yourselves sisters, so you did the next best thing. The problem comes with the way it happened. There was a third party, alcohol, you were away from your home... that all makes things off-center. You need to put it right."

Lana put her hands flat on the table. "Are you ordering us to have sex?"

"I would never do that. Besides, I think it would be illegal. I'm not a psychiatrist, and I'm just going from my personal experience here. But you two need to figure out how to relate to one another. If that's a romantic relationship, fine. If it's occasional and casual sex, then so be it. If it's just continuing as if Greece never happened, then also good. You'll know, and you'll be able to relax around each other again. And that's all anyone wants."

Lana looked at Karen and shrugged. Karen said, "Okay. We'll figure it out."

"Good."

She stood up, and a thought occurred to Karen. "You said Dash did this a lot. Did you–"

"Yeah." She adjusted her glasses and sighed, leaning against the chair. "She falls in love so easily, and she's..." She pressed her lips together. "She has a primal sexuality. Sex with Dash is fun, and it's a perk of employment. Like I said, she doesn't force it on anyone. Everything is consensual, and anyone can say no. But... she's Dash Warren. Who is going to say no? I wish I had warned you guys about her before you headed out."

"No, I'm glad you didn't." Lana looked at Karen. "I think it needed to happen. Dash just helped us get it out of the way."

Naomi nodded. "Okay. I'll let you two work things out on your own. If I'm involved beyond this point I'll just feel too much like a pimp." She smiled. "Let me walk you out."

I started to wonder if there was anyone at Cartography I wouldn't end up in bed with. Dash and Lana, Laura, Naomi. There were a few acts I hadn't spread my legs for. The receptionist at the front desk was sort of cute. On the ferry back to Seattle, I had a lot of time to think. Lana wandered toward the stern of the ship, and I stayed in the bow where I could watch where we were going. It was comforting to see the progress, to know there was a path to follow in at least one aspect of my life.

Three years ago, I'd been a virgin. Now I had my first lover counseling me on how to handle a misguided threesome I'd engaged in while in a committed relationship with someone else. At least I had avoided the drugs part of the rock-and-roll cliche. Lana found me just before we arrived at the docks and sat on the bench beside me.

"Want to have dinner?"

"Sure."

She nodded and walked off the boat with me. We had dinner at a casual dining restaurant, and the waitress recognized us from the Curve Magazine article. We signed her apron, and she brought us complimentary cocktails when we were done eating. The alcohol was enough to take the edge off, but not enough to even approach the blackout stupor of the ouzo. We walked for a while and then I asked Lana back to my place. She was quiet for so long I started to get worried, but then she agreed.

We took it slow. Kissing, just because kissing Lana was still odd despite the things I'd done to her in our Greek hotel room. When we were comfortable with that, Lana whispered that she wanted to take my clothes off. I nodded and she began undoing buttons. I kissed her cheeks, her chin, her jaw and her ear, and she bent down to kiss my chest above the cup of my bra. I hissed through my teeth and curled my hand in her hair, squirming on the couch as her hand moved under the hem of my skirt.

My face was hot, and I bent down to kiss her temple. "I wanted to see you strip. When I first found out about your day job, I had to fight the urge to go see you."

"You should have. I'd have given you a lap dance gratis, gotten this out of the way early." She smiled and kissed my lips. She pulled at my hip, arranging me on the couch so that she could lie on top of me. I cupped her face as she moved her hand between my legs, and I closed my eyes as she began to move her hand in slow circles against my underwear. I closed my eyes, kissing her bottom lip and rocking against her.

"I love you, K," she whispered, her lips moving against mine, and I could only nod. I closed my eyes and shifted my hips, and her fingers moved my panties aside. I bit my lip and Lana made a quiet choking noise of pleasure, then moved to press her hips against her hand. She thrust forward and I groaned. I tightened my legs around her, looking up into her eyes as she moved into me, and I said her name just before she made me come.

When I could move, I kissed her and took her into the bedroom. I undressed her, sat her on the edge of my bed, and knelt between her thighs. Her quick breathing soon became ragged, then eager panting. Her hand moved through my hair, over the shell of my ear, and held on. As she moved, I felt the heel of her left foot banging against my shoulder, a rhythmic tap that I used to count the minutes. I did my best to tease her, to make it last as long as possible, but her foot had barely tapped me sixty times before she began saying my name in a desperate whimper.

"Karen... oh, K..."

I kissed her thighs and the curve of her belly, then her navel. She fell back onto my bed and I climbed up to join her, sadly giving up my position in the diamond made by her crossed ankles. I lay on my side next to her, touching her stomach. For some reason, despite having the girl of my dreams naked beside me, I focused on her toes. She was curling and flexing them like she was waving to someone, an obviously unconscious twitch that made me smile.

"What?"

"Your toes are saying goodbye."

She looked down and her calves tensed, and the toes became still. I put my head on the pillow next to hers, and she rolled over to face me.

"So what do you think?"

She shrugged. "I think we can finish the album. After that, who knows?"

I nodded and we cuddled against each other, keeping ourselves warm since I didn't want to bother tugging the blankets out from under us. After a few minutes, I whispered that it was okay if she spent the night. When she didn't answer, I opened my eyes to see she'd already fallen asleep. I smiled and stroked my hand over her hip as I once again followed her lead.

Track Six

The release of *The Middle Distance* was set for January of 2008, and we were sent out to do promotional concerts and television appearances. Lana and I both took the time to apologize to Codie and Nessa for everything that happened in Greece and afterward. Lana came to Thanksgiving with me and the Dads, and Dad managed to deduce we were more than just band mates within five minutes of our arrival. We'd tried to hide it, but the same internet goons who found out about me and Laura were quick on the draw. Pictures of us on dates began to surface.

We took control of the story during a live performance on a sketch comedy show that was no stranger to controversial musical guests. In the middle of her most sensual performance of "Scene of the Crime" since Los Angeles, Lana stalked over to where I was playing the cello. I was wearing a necktie and she grabbed it, using it like a leash to pull me forward. We kissed, long enough to make sure we got the point across but not long enough that the song faltered, and Lana went straight into the next verse after pulling away from me.

The next day, we were all over the internet. Dash Warren sent us an email of congratulations, claiming we had simultaneously gotten publicity and taken the wind from the sails of every tabloid sludge artist at the same time. Suddenly no one wanted to follow us on dates to "prove" we were together, and we managed to get through a handful of dinners without photographers crowding us.

We celebrated Christmas with Nessa and Codie in Nessa's new house. She was still seeing Scott, and I finally got to meet the behemoth of a man. He was shy at first, but once he got to know us he relaxed enough for us to see why Nessa was holding onto him.

Naomi came by with a gift that she said she wanted to give us personally. From the size and shape, I figured it was artwork and I was basically right. Lana opened hers first and gave such an uncharacteristic scream that I thought she'd been cut. She turned it around so we could see what she'd unwrapped.

The gold record was positioned so it looked as if it was emerging from the sleeve of *Rome Burning*. The plaque at the bottom identified the album and its release date.

"I swear, I've only been sitting on this for ten days. I thought it would be appropriate to make this your Christmas gift. Congratulations, ladies."

That night, Lana and I went to bed at her place. Our gold records were propped up together in a chair where we could see them from bed.

"It's going to put a lot of pressure on the next album."

"You're going to burn yourself out," Lana warned, kissing my neck.

I closed my eyes and stroked her hip. "You heard what Naomi said. We're capitalizing on the atmosphere or whatever. The Beach Boys hit it big because people in the sixties really wanted surfing songs for some reason."

"Beach Boys were fifties, weren't they?"

"I don't know. That's not the point. Eventually people are going to move on to the next thing, and I don't want us to be left behind. There aren't really any epic bands anymore. The Beatles and the Rolling Stones have carried on for decades, but these days..." I shrugged. "These days we burn through our celebrities until we use them up."

"That's what I'm saying. You're wearing yourself ragged."

"I'm just trying to beat the clock. If we manage to get out five or six albums while we're still riding this wave, we can have enough money to survive for the rest of our lives on concerts and media and whatever." I kissed her cheeks just under her eyes. "I know you're all counting on me for this. I'm not going to let you down."

"As long as you know you don't have to do it alone."

I smiled. "Remember what I told you on the Rainmaker tour?"

"Well, maybe we can both be driver. Balance." She rolled over on top of me and we kissed for a while. "You know, I bought you a couple of presents that I didn't want to bring out when Nessa and Codie were here."

I raised an eyebrow. The idea made me feel flushed and out of breath. "Oh?"

"Want me to get them?"

"Wait." I tightened my hands on her arms. "I know that I've had... god, four lovers in the past two years, but I'm still... not very used to this. So if you got anything too far out there, keep in mind that I'm still pretty much a newbie."

"I'll take care of you, K." She kissed the corners of my mouth before she carefully lifted herself off of me to go get the toys. I watched her go, eager to see what kind of gift she'd given me. I saw movement from the corner of my eye and, half-expecting a paparazzo, pulled the sheet up over my breasts as I turned toward it. The movement was just the first meager flakes of snow, drifting down to melt against the glass.

"Lana. It's snowing."

Her footsteps were soft when she returned. "Huh. Look at that."

I looked away from the window to see she'd put on a red robe that just barely reached her thighs. Her hands were on her hips, and for a moment I thought she'd forgotten to bring my gift.

Then I noticed the bulge at the front of her robe and, more importantly, I realized what it meant. My breath caught in my throat and I curled my fingers in the sheets.

"Lana, I've never... had anything like that."

"Do you want to?"

I wet my lips and, after a moment of true consideration, I nodded.

Lana undid the belt as she walked toward the bed. "I was hoping you'd say that."

Codie found a Chinese restaurant and ate dinner in a huge room that was occupied by only three other diners. She felt like a queen fallen out of favor, forced to wander the halls of her palace alone. She considered the metaphor as she ate her sweet and sour chicken, then took out a pen and wrote it down. She didn't know if Karen could use it, but she treated her rare inspirations like diamonds. She had to keep them safe or she feared they would stop coming.

They were playing Christmas music over the speakers in the ceilings. She didn't understand why. Weren't the sort of people who sought out solitary dining on Christmas, by definition, trying to escape the Bing Crosby and Rudolphs of the world? When the waiter came back to top off her drink, she said, "Could you maybe find some different music to put on? Even for just a few tracks. Have mercy, man."

He smiled and bowed in the manner known to all Chinese waiters, one that always made her wonder if he'd actually understood the request. But by the time she was on her second trip to the buffet, the music had switched to something less appropriate for the day. She noticed her fellow diners relax slightly and the royal feeling returned.

She cracked open her fortune cookie after the meal. "You are surrounded by love and friendship," she murmured aloud. "Huh. Yeah. Sometimes at the same time." She took out her wallet and was counting out bills when "Sancho Panza" began to play overhead.

Codie straightened and looked toward the ceiling, hearing her own drums and her best friends' voices. The waiter came back to pick up the check, and she smiled at him.

"That's me." She pointed at the ceiling. "The music that's playing right now, Radiation Canary. I'm the drummer for that band."

"Oh!" he said. He smiled and nodded his head rapidly.

She decided to drop it. She paid for her food and tucked the slip of paper from the fortune cookie in her pocket. The actual printed fortune may have been trite, but there had to be something special about their song coming on right after she opened it. She left the restaurant to discover it had started snowing while she was eating. She looked at the cars parked nearby, slowly being shrouded in white, and found she wasn't even tempted to take one of them to get herself home.

Codie turned up her collar and headed home on foot, smiling as she let the snow accumulate on her shoulders.

Nessa tried to think of what she'd left out. She was cold, and she wanted to go back inside, but tradition was tradition. She hunched her shoulders and said, "Oh, our lead singer is now having sex with our cellist. It's a lot better now than it was at the beginning. Just so awkward and weird. But they seem to have a handle on it. They seem happy now, too. We're getting ready for the release of our third album. Kind of hard to believe, but we've been busy. We've earned it."

She wet her lips and tasted moisture, looking up to see jewel-like flakes drifting down from the sky.

"Oh, hey. It's a white Christmas after all." She stuck her tongue out to catch some flakes, then pushed her hat down further over her eyebrows. "I'm going to leave before I get frozen. I know what you'd have to say about me standing out here freezing to death just to talk to myself, so... I'll say goodbye again."

She took the small folded flower out of her pocket. It was made of laminated paper, because it "lasted longer and took more care to make. Any fool can just snip a plant. This takes time and concentration, and all that thought goes into the folds and gets released slowly. It's a love capsule." At least that was what her grandmother had told her while teaching her how to make bouquets for her parents' graves.

She twisted the stem and placed it in the small cup on the front of the headstone. She touched two fingers to her lips and then pressed them to the spot just above the carved name.

"Love you, Gran'ma. Merry Christmas."

As she walked back to where she had parked by the cemetery gates, she hummed the bridge of "Land Among the Stars" under her breath.

Track Seven

The midnight release of *The Middle Distance* was held at a massive bookstore that dedicated the second of its three levels to music. Our stage was set up on the first floor, and Cartography had provided a surprisingly massive cardboard display that showed the cover art. Our life-sized shapes had been cut out of it so that every time I glanced at it I got vertigo thinking Lana was flanking me.

We started our performance of the full album at 11:13pm, which took us right up to midnight of the "official" release date. The store brought out a box full of our albums and, since the purchase had been included in the price of a ticket, we were allowed to distribute them to everyone without worrying over pesky details like money.

Lana stepped back onstage. "Ladies and gentlemen, can I ask you one thing? Be careful when you turn your cases over. Karen has terrible balance and I think even a picture of her might turn out to be a little clumsy."

I saw people turning the CD over and laughing in surprise when they saw the picture of my tumble but, rather than feeling self-conscious, I felt it had turned out perfectly.

Lana smiled. "Okay, folks, if you're not sick of us yet, we'll be right over there-" She pointed with both hands like a flight attendant. "-signing autographs. Come one, come all."

The reporters who had videotaped portions of the concert for their programs left by that point, but I noticed a handful of people were filming us on their cell phones. Codie noticed too and forced a smile, but I heard her sigh in irritation.

"Fucking hate seeing myself on YouTube," Codie muttered.

"Just call it free advertising," Nessa said.

We had cookies provided by the store staff, and I tried to time my eating with asking people how they were and who they'd like the autograph made out to. A few people asked me about the album art. "Nope, not planned. Yeah, a little embarrassed but I think it turned out fine. Cold, cold, very cold. Yes, I was completely fine. Thanks. She actually dove in after me. My hero. No, I don't think we got any pictures of me in a wet T-shirt. Sorry, ma'am."

After half an hour, a girl in a T-shirt with the sleeves cut off and hair styled like Lana's moved up to the table, and Lana laughed. "Wow, I have my very own stunt double."

The girl lunged across the table and surprised Lana with an assault of a kiss. Her arms went around Lana's neck, preventing her from pulling away, but Lana tried regardless. She knocked her chair over and dragged the girl up onto the table in her escape attempt, and a burly man wearing the shirt of a store employee managed to peel the girl off. The girl was sobbing as she was guided back through the crowd to the exit. "I love you, Lana! I love you!"

Lana's eyes were wide spots of color in her otherwise ashen face. She wiped her lips and, when I put my hand on her shoulder, I felt she was trembling. "You okay?"

"Ye-ah." She coughed and shook her arms as if to limber up. "What's that I said about a stunt double?"

The woman from the store who had been directing the night said, "Ms. Kent, I am so sorry. She's going to be held by store security until we can get the police down here to take a statement. And we'll get everyone out of here right now. You can go into–"

"No, hey." Lana shook her head. "Only kick out the people who physically assault the band. No reason everyone else should suffer. I'm okay. I want to keep going."

"Are you sure?" I asked.

"Positive."

I nodded to the woman, and Codie stood Lana's chair back up. Lana rearranged her area, the poster and pens that had been disrupted by the overenthusiastic girl, and smiled. "Okay, uh... who is next?"

After we'd finished, the police asked us for statements. Lana didn't want to press charges. "The girl just got overexcited. I'm embarrassed she had to sit in that little room all this time. We'll just chalk it up to nerves, okay?"

The police were agreeable; no charges probably meant they didn't have to deal with paperwork. I drove Lana home to her place, waking her when we arrived. She sat up and stretched, and I nodded at the building. "You okay staying alone tonight? I could stay with you."

"No. I need sleep. But thank you." She kissed me, letting her lips linger.

"Mm," I said. "I'd jump a table and get dragged away by security for a kiss like that any day."

Lana chuckled. "Lucky for you, I give them out free to some people. Night."

I wished her goodnight and waited until I saw her light come on. As I waited, I opened the copy of *Middle Distance* I'd gotten from the store. The label gave us copies, of course, but there was something about taking it off the shelf and paying for it that made the album feel official. I'd give this one to Dad's store, so he could play it over the speakers. Lana's light came on just as "Away from Shore" was starting, and I pulled away from the curb as we filled the car with our music.

My mind was already on the next CD. I didn't want a concept album, but I was leaning toward a theme. I wanted the songs to have something that connected them so that, while individual songs stood alone, the album as a whole would tell a complete story. I drummed my fingers on the steering wheel as I traveled the mostly empty streets, tired but buzzed, and I sang under my breath along with Lana's recorded voice.

I parked in a place where I could see the Space Needle and the harbor, then took my notebook out the glove compartment. It was never far away from me these days, and I'd started keeping backup copies just to be sure there was one available no matter what. But this was the first one, my original leather notepad, the one that had led to meeting Lana and the girls in the first place. It had a sort of power, and I wanted at least one song per album taken from its pages.

"Can't take this give and take
I know tonight I'll just lie awake
And play it all over again in my mind
God, why can't we just be kind?"

I couldn't help flashing back to the moment I'd written those words. Hiding in my bedroom my left arm curled against the side of my head to drown out Mom and Dad as I scribbled the words at the top of the page, huffing and puffing rather than sobbing, fingers hurting from holding the pencil so hard.

I chewed her bottom lip and considered the page, then lifting my head to look at the city as I thought about where it might fit in a concept album. It all depended on the story. Once we had that, the rest of the songs would fall into place like dominos.

Track Eight

Naomi inadvertently provided the subject of our concept album. The phone was on speaker, sitting in the middle of the bed where Lana was lounging in a pair of pink short shorts and a top that was much too thin for November. She had her guitar in her lap like a sleeping child, occasionally adjusting the tabs and strumming a little as we listened to Naomi brainstorm about our next promotional stops.

"–and we can't do anything in April until after the fourteenth."

"What's the fourteenth?" I was lying across the bottom of the bed, Lana's feet close enough to my head that I could have kissed her toes.

"Oh, it's a label-wide retreat of sorts. Keep it on the down-low, but we're having an intervention for Derrick Lao."

Lana said, "Why are we intervening?"

"You're not, unless you want to. He was an original member of Dash's band who went solo. He was one of the first acts signed to the new label, and now he's deep into all kinds of bad stuff. He insists he doesn't have a problem, but if Dash is concerned... it's like Donald Trump telling someone to lay off the hubris a little."

I snickered and gave in to the urge to turn my head and kiss Lana's toes.

They continued talking, but my mind kept running circles around the idea of an intervention. I thought about the emotions involved, sitting in a room while everyone you care about talks about your bad habits... how would it feel to be the subject of one? What would it be like to participate in one? How could you properly express your feelings of hurt and disappointment without attacking the person?

I sat up and rolled out of bed, walking away without considering the conference call. I heard Lana say, "Whoops, it's just me now. K has fled the room." I waved over my shoulder and spent the next hour at the kitchen table creating a frame for the album. Instead of individual songs, I would focus on the story and write songs to fit what I wanted to say.

Lana came out of the bedroom and gave me a brief shoulder massage as she entered the kitchen. "Canadian tour."

"I love Canadia," I joked half-heartedly.

"What are you working on?"

I smiled without looking up. "Our next album."

Naomi wasn't entirely sold on the idea of a concept album until we played "The Long Night." I swore to her that the songs would stand-alone, and we'd have singles and music videos to spare. I sat down and explained my plan to her. The songs would serve as letters to the subject of the intervention, different narrators telling different stories of pain and love gone bad. In that respect, it was pretty much the same as a dozen other albums. But it would start and finish with songs that tied everything together.

Lana came up with the idea of overlapping scenarios. "One song could be from the subject's point of view, about a happy excursion to the beach. The next song could be from his ex-girlfriend, showing what really happened that day."

Naomi rubbed her chin, staring down at my notes. She was quiet for a very long time before she nodded. "You can have this out next year?"

"Yeah," Lana said.

"Okay. I'll run it up to management and see what they think about it. All they really care about are singles and videos, but I think we can work that out. I'll let you know, okay?"

We agreed and went back to rehearsing the three songs I'd already written. Our early insistence on sharing vocal duties would serve us well on this album. Each of us could play a different person at the intervention and if the idea was accepted, we would see about getting other artists from the label to fill out the 'cast.'

A week later Naomi called to give us the thumbs-up. "Dash also wants to do something more than the typical music video this time. Think the Michael Jackson 'Thriller' video. We could get a couple of other artists from the label to play along–" I looked at Lana and smiled. "–and we could turn it into a mini-movie. Fifteen minutes of plot leading into four minutes of the first song of the album. And the music to that point can be an overture of the album... I'm talking with our directors, seeing what's possible. I'll keep in touch with more info when we have it."

We went back to work, now with a more focused approach now that we knew it would officially be an album.

Nessa wrote the basic story. A twenty-seven year old man has been drinking since his high school years, getting by on good looks and charm. But after a nearly fatal accident doesn't provide a wake-up call, his friends and family decide the time has come to take matters into their own hands.

I wrote the first and last songs - "Without a Fight," "The Long Night," and

"Thank Me Later" - and Lana provided the majority of a song called "Letting Go." Codie surprised me with a snippet about a queen dining in an empty banquet hall after her royal subjects have fled. I worked on it a little and turned it into the mother's song, and we conspired musically to make it a near-dirge called "Save Yourself."

Our momentum was broken when we had to leave for our Canadian tour. We started in Vancouver, and then traveled by train and charter bus to Edmonton, Saskatoon, Winnipeg, Thunder Bay, Toronto, Quebec... We were a huge hit in the Maritimes, and Halifax treated us like the Second Coming. I had no idea so many people even lived in those places, but we signed autographs until one in the morning and collapsed exhausted in our beds when we were finally done. Our last stops were Yellowknife and Whitehorse, farther north than any of us had ever traveled, and colder than any of us imagined it would be in April. In every stop, we saw girls with paper wings to use during "Icarus," but the canary symbol was becoming more and more prevalent. We adopted it ourselves, using it to say goodnight to the crowd before we left the stage.

I took the travel time to work on the album. It felt like I was in a relay... as soon as one album was out, I had to jump forward to the next one so I wouldn't stagnate or get complacent. Lana was worried about burning me out, but I knew that the real threat was shutting down. I had to work my brain or it would atrophy and I would end up at a loss for words when we would really need them.

"All our endless conversations were never heard
I can't believe you have me at a loss for words
We only want to open your eyes and make you see
No one here is your enemy."

In Saskatoon, a woman in the audience was holding up a poster that said "Lana + Karen = Heartbreakers! We Luv U N-E-WAY!" I pointed the sign out to Lana, and she laughed and said, "We love you, too." The girls shrieked, of course, and I caught their eye during "Monstrous Regiment" and blew them a kiss. I thought one of them was going to faint, while the other held her up and sang along with the chorus.

Afterward, we had a twenty minute lull between the end of the concert and the start of the autograph session. Lana pulled me into a tiny maintenance closet, shutting the door and casting us into darkness. Her lips covered mine before I could protest, not that I would have if given the option. When she broke for air, she slid her hand down my leg and pulled up my skirt as she moved back toward my hip.

"Those girls in the audience... think they'll be in the autograph line?"

"Probably," I whispered. Lana was standing between my legs, pressing her hips against mine, and we were both moving in a sort of unconscious serpentine sway.

"What do you think they'd do if they knew I was shaking their hand with fingers that had just been inside of you?"

I blushed as she pressed her lips to mine again, turning her head so they fit perfectly together. Our tongues swirled and, as promised, she pushed two fingers into me. I moaned and broke the kiss by rocking my head back against the wall, riding her hand. Her breath was hot against my neck, and I cupped her breast through her thin shirt. I knew the moment wasn't about romance, so I angled my hip to brush my clit against her palm. She made a sound of approval, and I moaned as I felt my climax building.

"Make me come," I whispered, biting her earlobe. She hissed and did as I asked.

Afterward, she straightened my clothes and kissed me soundly. "One of these days, we have to find a way to do that during the show. You and me, backstage, fucking while a crowd screams our names." She growled and wrinkled her nose. "Trust me, it wouldn't take long to finish."

I laughed and kissed her, made sure my underwear wasn't riding up, and followed her out to the autograph table.

The girls with the sign showed up during the second half-hour. Lana took one girl's hand in hers, covering it with her other hand. "Thank you so much for coming out tonight. It really means a lot to us that you were here." She squeezed one more time for good measure, then released her.

I almost couldn't sign my name from fighting off my fit of laughter, apologizing profusely to the girls for my lack of composure. I signed their copy of *Action After Warnings* with "Love+Peace+Happiness, Karen Everett. A big hand for the little ladies!!" I saw Codie read it when the CD was passed to her, and she looked at me with her head tilted. I shook my head, had another giggle-fit, and tried to compose myself before the next fan came along.

Track Nine

We got back from Canada as summer was ending. "Passenger" was released as a single, so we were required to make a music video for it. We chose the director with the simplest pitch. The video for "Prayer" had ended with the camera panning through an open door as rain fell. The idea for "Passenger" was to pick up where that video had left off, panning away from the ground to a passing car. We would be inside the car, and that would be where the new video started.

Nessa and Codie would fake being asleep in the backseat, and I'd be seated beside Lana. She would lip synch while pretending to drive through the manufactured rain. Later on we would film performance shots to tie the whole thing together. The window on my side was rolled down so the pretty-up people (as Codie called them) could make sure I looked right. I glanced over and saw a woman reaching through Lana's window to adjust the collar of her jacket.

"This is so weird," I said. "It's like a car wash for people."

Lana laughed. "Just don't ask for the hot wax at this one."

Codie nudged the back of Lana's chair with her knee. "Thanks for choosing this pitch. We get to fake sleep while you do the work."

"You're going to fake it?" Nessa said. "I'm a method actor, baby. I'm going to nap and get paid for it."

Lana said, "Hey, as long as I'm not outside in the rain this time, I'm a happy camper."

We ran through the video twice, our car towed down a stretch of abandoned road, then turned around to go the other way. The song was playing on the car stereo, and it was harder than I expected to just slump against the window and pretend I was asleep. If I wasn't fighting a smile, my nose would itch or I would try to start singing along at the appropriate parts. I kept my hands between my knees so even if I inadvertently played along then at least no one would notice.

When we finished for the day, Lana treated us to a late lunch. Nessa said, "As much as I hate just miming for the camera, it's going to be a bitch when we have to do the mini-movie for *Intervention*. Maybe we can hire an actress to play my part."

"Like who?"

"I was thinking Halle Berry. She's not doing much these days."

Codie laughed. "Got a pretty high opinion of yourself, don't ya? See, I'm realistic about who'd play me. Sarah Shahi, naturally."

I frowned. "The chick from *The L Word*? She's not Indian, is she?"

"When she looks like that, who cares?"

"You're not even gay," Lana laughed.

Codie held up her hands. "Like I said, when she looks like that... I'd be Shahi-sexual."

A woman from another table who had been orbiting us finally got the courage to step up. "I'm so sorry to bother you, but my daughter just loves your music."

"Our music?" Lana said. "We work at H&R Block."

The woman blinked.

"Be nice," I whispered. To the woman, I said, "She's teasing you. Would you like an autograph?"

We signed her napkin and squeezed together on one side of the table for a picture. The woman's bravery prompted a few other people in the diner to approach us as well, and we dutifully signed autographs. After the crowd dispersed, the waitress offered to give us the meal on the house in exchange for a picture to hang behind the cash register. There were a few other celebrity pictures up, so we agreed. Lana scanned the wall and requested that they hang us next to Bono and the Edge.

"So maybe there is such a thing as a free lunch," Lana said as we left.

Codie rolled her hand in exaggerated pain, massaging the wrist. "You call that free?"

"Aw, poor baby." She kissed Codie's temple. "We'll get Sarah Shahi to bring you an ice pack and make you feel all better."

Codie needed to pick up her dry-cleaning, which included the shirt she wanted to wear for tomorrow's video shoot, and Nessa offered to drive her. Once they were gone, I slipped my arm around Lana's and took her hand.

"Got plans?" I said.

"Most of them involve you, and less clothing."

"I think that can be arranged," I said. "Your place or mine?"

We chose my place. Afterward, Lana slept and I went into the living room to work on songs for *Intervention*. Lana had written part of a song called "Fist-Shaped Windows" while we were on tour, and I knew Nessa and Codie were collaborating on at least one song. It thrilled me to think of how wide we were casting the net on this one. Hopefully by teaming up and spreading the duties around, we would succeed in making it sound like a multitude of people rather than just a single voice.

Lana came out of the bedroom in one of my old T-shirts, her hair getting further mussed as she ran her fingers through it on the way to the kitchen.

"I wrote another song."

"Oh, yeah?"

"You may hate it." She opened the fridge and took out a soda. She slid onto a stool at the counter, twisting to face the couch. "It's called 'Funeral Clown.'"

I winced and put down my pen. "It's called *what*?"

She smiled. "At funerals in ancient Rome, they had someone who dressed up like the deceased, put on a mask of their face, and dance around to–" She waved her hand in the air. "I don't know, to appease the spirits of the dead and to help the loved one move on to the next realm. They were called funeral clowns."

"You're just making that up. Right now, on the spot."

Lana pointed at my computer. "Look it up."

I put down my pad and called her bluff. As I was loading the page, she said, "If I'm right, then you owe me."

"What do I owe you?"

"If funeral clowns exist, then I get carte blanche in the bedroom."

I raised an eyebrow. "What exactly does that entail?"

"You don't know all my kinks." She winked at me, and I let Google settle the argument. I found a few websites offering actual clown services for funerals, which I thought was creepy. Near the bottom of the first page there was a link.

"Oh, you've got to be kidding me."

Lana laughed in victory. She leaned back, resting her elbow on the kitchen counter. She crossed her legs and shrugged. "Funeral clown."

"Okay, genius. What does ancient Rome have to do with an intervention?"

"The guy getting the intervention feels like he's being ganged up on. All his friends have gotten together and they're discussing his faults. It's like a roast without any jokes."

I was already writing "Funeral Clown" in my book. "Okay. You win, you sexy genius."

She rubbed her hands together. "I'm going to have some fun cashing this one in."

I rolled my eyes and blushed, trying not to think of what she had in store for me. I closed the Google page and slid back on the couch with my journal. I settled against the side of the couch and Lana got up and wandered toward the bedroom. "Want some music?"

"Sure."

I expected her to turn on the stereo, but instead she returned with the same purple and black Telecaster she'd used since the day we met. It had become iconic, showing up in magazine pictures and album art. I paused as she settled across from me, practically naked with her legs tossed casually over the arm of the chair. She nestled the instrument into the V shaped by her stomach and thighs, then began to play softly.

I rested my chin on my hand and watched her, smiling until she looked over and nodded at the notebook. "Work. I don't want to have to spank you."

"Ooh, spanking. Is that what your wild card is going to be?"

"We'll see."

I grinned and started writing.

Track Ten

We finished recording *Intervention* in December, just in time to take a Christmas vacation. Codie went to Alaska with her boyfriend-of-the-week, while Nessa stayed in Seattle to volunteer at a soup kitchen. Naomi offered to publicize it, but Nessa refused. I went shopping with her to find an appropriate disguise so her good deed wouldn't become about "celebrities giving back." When we were done, she had thick black-rim glasses and cornrows in her hair.

"Gotta say, the hipster nerd look works for you."

"I'll try it next time we have a photo shoot. You, Lana and Codie all Glamour-Shots. Me looking like Jamaican Steve Urkel..."

The media did end up finding out about it, but only after the fact. One of the other workers had snapped a picture with their cell phone and put it up on the web. Naomi asked permission to capitalize on it, claiming that we'd already dealt with the bad scandal so we deserved to enjoy some heartwarming publicity.

A week before Christmas, Lana surprised me with plane tickets to Baja. She wrapped her arms around me from behind as I looked over the information.

"Sun, surf, scuba..."

"I don't know how to swim."

She kissed my earlobe. "I'll teach you. I've already taught you so much already, what's one more thing."

I chuckled. "What have you taught me?"

She moved her hands to my waist, pulled my hips against hers, and began to thrust. "Oh, all *kinds* of things, I've taught you. It's just this one won't involve you ripping my sheets."

"But it'll still involve getting wet."

Lana laughed. "And I taught you to have a filthy mouth, apparently."

I turned in her arms and kissed her. "Thank you, baby. So since you gave me my gift early, does that mean I get to give you yours?"

She started walking me toward the bedroom. "Well, it doesn't have to be the big gift. You could just give me a little something to whet my appetite."

Three days later we were sweltering in the Baja sun while Seattle was forecasting temperatures in the single digits. Despite a very forgiving and patient instructor, when the time came to actually scuba I elected to remain on the boat with my feet in the water while Lana explored underwater. If I'd gone with her, I would have missed out on the opportunity to see the tiny slip of her white bikini bottoms as she kicked her feet like miniature flippers. I can't think of anything in the ocean I would have traded that view for.

When she resurfaced, her skin glistening with saltwater, I bent down and kissed her. She stroked my thighs, resting over the place on my hips where my bikini bottoms were tied. Against her lips, I said, "Watch it. Don't want to give anyone any good photo ops."

"Not even me? I brought a camera."

I laughed. "You get the special shots." I kissed her again, then helped her up onto the boat. She sat beside me, head on my shoulder, and we let our feet dangle in the water.

"I almost quit."

"Hm?"

"The band."

"When?"

"Not Radiation Canary. Little Cat Feet. Before you. I felt like we were just clinging to some high school hobby. I was thinking about giving it up, splitting my time between teaching dance classes and working at the club. I had three things to focus on but none of them were getting my full attention. The band seemed like a lost cause. Then one day I find a journal on the ground and..." She waved her hand, shrugged, and kissed my neck. "Thank you."

"I was just out for a walk. We really should thank Codie for smoking, otherwise I'd have never spoken to any of you."

"And Nessa was the one who found the rehearsal space. So I guess we all had a hand in this. Maybe we were just meant to be a band."

"Maybe so." I put my finger under her chin and lifted her head, kissing her gently. "Maybe a couple of us were meant to be more than a band."

She grinned. "Yeah. Let's go inside."

When we were in the cramped cabin, she showed me pictures she had taken and I allowed her to take a couple of me. "Just make sure these don't end up in the tabloids," I said as I posed, standing with a foot on either side of her hips as she pressed back into the mattress to get a good angle. "Not that any tabloids would want them."

"Are you kidding? I could sell these to *Playboy* and make a mint."

Afterward she convinced me to dive in and tread water, although I resisted her urges to take me deeper.

"Coward," she said. "Come on. I've seen your face when you sing harmony on 'Diving for Pearls.' Where's that passion?"

"You wrote that song, and you know it has nothing to do with the ocean," I said.

She held me against the side of the boat and kissed me, and we both scanned for other boats and people loitering on the beach before she wrapped her legs around me. She held onto my shoulder with one hand and the boat with the other, letting the waves crash her against me before she made her movements more fluid.

"Then what's it about?"

"Pearls." My hand slipped under the surface of the water and found the crotch of her swimsuit. I pressed against it and rolled my fingers until I found her clit. "This pearl." Soon we were both breathing heavily, and I rested my head against her chest as she came.

"I love you."

I kissed the earlobe and said, "I love you, too."

She cupped my face and I slid my hands over her thighs, holding her against me as she pinned me to the boat. Her hair was in her face, and I kissed her through it like it was a veil.

We eventually went back to dry land, to our hotel, and I celebrated Christmas by paying up on our bet to do whatever Lana wanted in the bedroom. She took it easy on me, but I discovered a few surprising kinks that I decided to take advantage of the next time we were fooling around. She cradled my foot to her face and kissed the slope, then licked down to take my two of my toes into her mouth. I suddenly realized something.

"Hey... is this why you're always suggesting I should perform barefoot?"

She kissed my big toe and winked at me. "Maybe partially. It was definitely a turn-on."

"Pervert."

I left Mexico without ever actually scuba diving, but I still felt like I'd gotten the most out of our getaway. On the plane Lana fell asleep with my hand in hers, and I smiled every time her fingers tightened in her sleep.

Codie slipped through the door, then held it open so Nessa and Lana could follow her inside. "It's okay. These buildings hardly ever collapse without warning."

"Well, I'm comforted," Nessa said. "How about you?"

Lana looked at the concrete supports in the middle of the room and then at the ceiling. She had her camera hanging against her chest, as requested, but so far she hadn't seen anything worth photographing. "Codie, I'm getting a very 'snuff film' feeling from this. If you want out of the band, you can just tell us.

You don't have to lure us to the middle of nowhere and kill us."

"Yeah, right. Come on." She crossed the wide main floor, Nessa followed, and Lana reluctantly brought up the rear. "The stairs are a lot sturdier than they look."

Lana pointed at the ceiling. "Uh, most of the second floor doesn't officially have a floor. I'm not going up any stairs, sturdy or not."

"Don't be a chicken."

"What is this, grade school?" But she followed, staying close to the walls. She idly wondered if floors gave warnings like thin ice did. Would it crack? Would stress fissures stretch across the length of it before giving way? Or would it just collapse underneath her feet with a thundering crash? She felt sweat in the small of her back as she inched across the floor. Finally Codie stopped in front of a slanted window and held her hands out.

"Voila."

"You found dirty glass!" Lana said. "It's amazing. Can we go now?"

Codie glared at her and took off her backpack. She unzipped it and took out a pillow and blanket.

"Is this a housewarming?" Lana asked.

She ignored Lana and spread the blanket out, then kicked it around a little to make it look tousled. Then she took out a pillow and dropped it onto the tangled blanket. "What do you think?"

"About *what*?"

"The cover of the album! *The Intervention*. I thought we should have something sort of bleak, considering the content of the album, but with some bit of hopefulness. That's why we had to come today even though Karen is busy writing. Look." She gestured at the window again. The day was typical winter, gray and somber, but there was a little sunlight breaking through the glass. Lana stepped forward, tilting her head to look at it more objectively.

"Can we afford to have a bleak album cover?"

Nessa said, "People know who we are now. They've seen us on TV or in magazines, so it's not vital that we show up on the artwork."

"Did Cartography agree to that?"

Codie shrugged. "I haven't talked to Cartography. But look, this light is perfect. We can take the picture and hope they'll sign off on it, or we can wait. And if we wait, we might not get this kind of perfect lighting again. I'd rather take the picture and have the label say no than miss the chance."

Lana sighed. "Me too. Okay, back up." She lifted the camera and took a few shots, then said, "Codie, Nessa, get in there."

Nessa shook her head. "I still think the whole idea is bleak."

"But the album is hopeful. It's not about someone's downward spiral, it's about someone..." She tried to remember how Karen had described it. "It's about someone who is collapsing, and the people who care about him trying to pull him up. So, uh, Nessa. Get close to the blanket. Maybe hold up one corner of it... yeah. Codie, stand closer so you'll be a little out of focus. Face away from the bed, like you're turning your back."

Codie did, and Lana took the picture. "That's perfect. Awesome." She lowered the camera and looked at the screen. "Okay, Codie. Thank you for dragging me down here to do this. Now can we please get out of here before the roof caves in?"

"I told you that almost never happens." She bent down and stuffed the blanket and pillow back into her bag. "When was the last time you heard about a building collapsing?"

"That just means it's due to happen sooner rather than later. Come on. Hurry, hurry."

Lana took the rear again, this time to make sure Nessa and Codie hurried up.

Track Eleven

We ended up releasing four singles from *The Middle Distance*. "Passenger," "Breakwaters," "Away from Shore," and "Neither Nor" all did admirably in the charts, and Naomi was happy to report that the latter two songs, with vocals by me and Nessa respectively, did as well as the Lana-fronted singles. A lesbian romantic comedy filming in Vancouver took its title from *Diving for Pearls* and asked if they could use the song over the end credits. We filmed a few low-budget music videos for the new singles, releasing them onto an official YouTube channel. I swore I wouldn't look at the hit counter, and I finally stopped once we topped six digits. It took a lot less time than I expected.

In early January Nick Young asked us back to *Settle In, Seattle!* and asked if Lana and I would be interested in doing an interview segment before we performed. Our February was mostly booked up with performances, but he still wanted us to appear even if it was a little earlier than the last two times. He said it would cement the tradition of appearing on his show at the beginning of each year, and he wanted to make sure he "got credit for his insight and genius in discovering us." How could we say no to that? We were booked for the second week of January 2008.

Nessa and Codie refused the offer to be interviewed, claiming that the audience only wanted to talk to me and Lana. We tried to change their minds but eventually we gave in and went out by ourselves.

I thought I'd gotten used to the surreal aspect of being on TV, but singing was different than talking. I watched the video later and cringed at how much I squirmed, fidgeted, shifted, and how nervous my laughter sounded. Lana carried the interview well, and once again I was grateful for her buffering me.

"Now, you two are dating, is that right?" Nick asked.

Lana looked at me for confirmation. "Yeah. Only a few months. What is it, six? It was summer, so..." She looked at me for confirmation and smiled. "It just sort of happened, so I'm not sure what the official start date is."

I said, "Well, Greece was–"

"Well, that wasn't the *start*. That was just the first time it happened."

The audience hooted, and Nick tugged at his collar. "I think that's enough information, ladies. We're on late, but not *that* late." He winked at us and moved the conversation to safer territory. We discussed the upcoming release of *The Intervention*, and I think I calmed down a bit when I explained the story we were trying to tell with the album.

They told us the interview would only be four to five minutes, but it seemed like I spent forever sweating under the lights. Finally someone in Nick's line of sight held up a piece of paper with a large number "1" written on it, and he quickly wrapped up his line of questioning. He thanked us, and then turned to the camera.

"When we get back these lovely ladies have graciously agreed to perform a song off their hit album *The Middle Distance*. Stick around." When the music stopped, he gestured for us to wait before we went over to the performance area. " We're doing a prime-time live show in a few days to urge the whippersnappers to get out and register to vote. It's going to be two hours, all kinds of political bullshit, but I'd love to have you ladies as a special musical guest. Please do it. I need something to look forward to or else I'll go nuts."

"We'll have to talk it over with Nessa and Codie. But I think it should be fine."

He pressed his hands together as if in prayer, and we went over to get ready for our performance. He had specifically asked if we would perform "Monstrous Regiment," so we donned our sunglasses (Codie's idea) and Lana shrugged into an old infantryman's jacket with its sleeves cut off. The glasses were large, like the kind movie stars used to wear in the seventies, but she definitely pulled off the look. One of the elves who always swarmed around us just before the cameras started filming pulled our hair back into ponytails and made sure they were secure.

Nick came over to join us, holding an LP-sized copy of the album. "Welcome back, ladies and gentlemen. Our old friends are back with us once again tonight, so please give a big welcome to Radiation Canary."

When the lights came up, all four of us began whistling. Codie tapped out a near-military beat, and Nessa joined in. When Lana began to play, her guitar joined the piano so seamlessly it was as if the sounds were coming from a single source. My cello was the signal for Lana to begin singing, so I plucked the strings with my middle finger and then began to saw. Her voice was a low growl.

"The clouds cleared out and took with them the light
And the points of the crescent moon look wickedly sharp tonight
You sent back the letters I sent, you didn't care what I meant
I'm on my way to make you listen, you don't want to know what happens when
You're face to face with a monstrous regiment... of women."

Codie abandoned the staccato military beat while Nessa and I worked to keep up with Lana. I tore my gaze away from her and focused on the studio audience. They were faceless silhouettes backlit by the emergency exits, but I could see they were moving to the music. Lana stopped playing and moved to the microphone again. Nessa and Codie also stopped, and I was the only music for the bridge.

"No, a lemur." Lana shut the car door, holding the phone against her shoulder as she spelled it. "Ring-tailed lemur. It's like a... marsupial. It has a long tail, lives in Africa. I want the biggest stuffed version you can find. Just get it here on Valentine morning. I want her to think I forgot and then reveal the big surprise. You realize if I don't have the surprise I just look like a moron, right? Good. Remember, *lemur.*" She hung up and sighed as she headed upstairs. "Why couldn't her favorite animal be a wolf or a whale?"

Karen was out with Codie, getting a few candid pictures for *Intervention*'s liner notes, so Lana was taking the opportunity to plan their Valentine's Day. She wasn't going to screw it up like... well, to be honest, every other Valentine's Day in her life. The day would start, hopefully, with a rose and a little sex. Then the lemur delivery, more sex. Band practice, dinner, a movie. Sex.

She chuckled as she let herself into the apartment, tossing her keys into the bowl next to the door. She might have a one-track mind, but it served her well. And she could put sex aside to focus on important things, like making sure Karen felt loved and appreciated. She was almost to the kitchen when the woman stepped out of the hallway that led to the bathroom.

Lana's heart skipped, and she felt like her body was two beats out of synch with the rest of the world. "Holy shit. What the hell?"

The woman wore a 'Rainmakers for Wizards' tour shirt under an unbuttoned sweater. Her hair was short and straight, honey blonde, and Lana couldn't shake the feeling that she was familiar somehow. The woman pressed her lips together and shrugged, keeping her shoulders up as she spoke.

"I'm sorry. I didn't know you lived here, too. I wasn't waiting for you."

"That doesn't really make me feel better. Why *are* you here?" She glanced at the kitchen counter, but it was clear of anything that could be used as a weapon. The spice rack wouldn't hurt, but maybe some of the little jars would burst open and blind the bitch.

"I just... hate what they're doing to you, Lana."

"They? They who?"

She lifted her arm and Lana went cold. She was holding a very, very nasty-looking knife. "Them!" She gestured, pressing the blade of the knife against the band's logo on her chest. "Your leeches. They don't have any of your talent, or your raw sexuality. But they keep singing on songs you could make so beautiful.

Why do you keep letting them sing on your songs, Lana?"

"Those aren't... my songs... they're Karen's songs. And we..."

"No, no. They're yours." She stepped forward and Lana retreated a step. Her mouth was dry, but her eyes were starting to water. The woman came a little closer and Lana realized where she knew her from.

"You were at the release party. You... jumped onto the table and kissed me."

She tilted her head to the side and narrowed her eyes. "I'm sorry if I scared you. I lost my head a little. I thought I could control myself better, I didn't know how powerful it would be to stand in your presence." She took a shaky breath. "But I'm stronger now. I screwed up my courage, and I'm going to do it. I don't care what happens to me. The world needs you. We just... we just want to hear you sing, Lana. No one cares about those other bitches."

Lana shook her head. "No. People love them. Without them, there's no band–"

"There doesn't need to be a band! We just need you, Lana. That's all we want. That's why I came here."

Realization dawned. "You were waiting for Karen."

The woman nodded. "Yeah. She's going to ruin you, you know. You could be so much bigger. You could be timeless. But they're dragging you down. They're holding you down. You need to go on without them. The next ferry is waiting at the dock, it's not going to wait forever, and baby you gotta be on it."

Lana recognized the lyrics, words she might never again be able to sing in concert after this, and she got angry. "Look... Karen wrote that song. Without her, I'm... I'm a goddamn stripper and a dance instructor. Okay? I'm nothing without Karen, professionally or personally."

The woman was tearing up now. "She makes you believe that. That's why she has to *go*, don't you see? She's brainwashing you into needing her. I'll show you. I'll show you how big you can be."

Lana swallowed hard and steadied herself. Finally, she nodded. "Okay. Okay, what's your name?"

"Marcia."

"Marcia. I like that name. I think you're right. And I think... you obviously went to a lot of trouble for this. It would be rude of me to just kick you out, right? So why don't I repay you? Give you something special for your trouble?" She pointed carefully at her guitar. "Why don't I play you a song? Just me alone, without them."

The woman's eyes widened, and she parted her lips in delight. "Really? You would do that?"

"Of course. You've earned it."

The knife wavered.

"Can I get my guitar? I'll play your favorite song."

She smiled, and Lana gave her and the knife a wide margin as she moved across the room. "So what's your favorite song?"

Marcia moved closer. "I love 'Away from Shore.'"

Lana couldn't stop herself. "That's *Karen's* song."

"But you would do it so much better. Prove it."

Lana gripped the neck of her guitar, held tight, and twisted at the waist. She threw her weight behind the spin, her foot slipping on the floor as she brought it up like the axe it was often compared to. Marcia shrieked as the black-and-purple body of the instrument came at her, ducking so that the curve of it hit her shoulder instead of her head. Lana didn't try for a second attempt. She shoved Marcia over, tripped over the coffee table, and ran for the door. Marcia caught her halfway and dragged her down, slamming her into the floor.

"You bitch!" Marcia shrieked.

Lana cried out as she was stabbed. She grappled for the fallen guitar, ignoring the blows raining down on her. Something sliced through her upper arm and she cursed. She managed to grab the guitar by the neck and pulled it close. It was her shield, her sword. She felt warm blood all along her side as she rolled over underneath the crazy woman, moving her hands up to grip the body of the instrument.

The knife tore along her hip as she rolled onto her back, snagging on her shirt even as it ripped the material. Marcia loomed over her, the bloody knife poised over Lana's chest. Lana shouted in rage and fright as she drove the end of the guitar up into Marcia's face. Something cracked, blood splattered, and Marcia's arms jerked like someone had cut her strings as she fell backward. Lana tossed her off and managed to get up to open the apartment door. She held her right arm against her side, the blood pouring down her arm and dripping off her fingers as she left the apartment. She took the time to pull the apartment door shut behind her, unsure of why she bothered as she sank down to her knees.

She rolled onto her uninjured side, refusing to look to see how bad the damage was. She pulled her phone out of her pocket and very carefully dialed 911. She swallowed hard, trying to work up enough saliva to speak. She closed her eyes as she listened to the operator, and then her voice broke when she responded to the question. She had to fight for each word, trembling and staring at water stains on the ceiling as if holding them in her sight would keep her vision from fading.

"I'm... Lana. Kent. I just. Got stabbed..."

Album Five
AMNESIA BETWEEN SLEEPING & WAKING
(2009-2010)

Track One

We were in the hospital when all the media shit happened, so we didn't hear the "harrowing 911 call" or the false reports that Lana died from her injuries. One news outlet apparently reported that her hands had been cut so badly the doctors didn't think she would ever play guitar again. I assume that particular rumor came from the cell phone pictures of Lana being loaded into the ambulance with her bloody hands visible. It seemed like the street outside my building was full of cell phone cameras that day, everyone eager to memorialize the moment.

In reality, the madwoman ended up stabbing the floor more than she stabbed Lana. The actual damage done was, thank God, mostly superficial. Lana had a few deep cuts on the inside of her right arm, and three gashes of varying depth on her side between her breast and the bottom of her ribs. Once she was stitched and bandaged, and after the doctors confirmed nothing major had been hit, they allowed me in for a very strictly regulated two-minute visit.

Lana looked pale, her eyelids heavy as she turned toward the door and smiled at me. "Hey. In elementary school they always said the ribs protect the vital organs. I never thought it would be practical in my life."

I cupped her face and kissed her, finally letting myself cry. "Are you okay?"

She stroked my arm. "I'm fine. Just a few cuts and bruises. I'm more upset about my guitar. It's broken, isn't it?"

"I have no idea," I said. "What happened? Was she robbing the place or–?"

Lana shook her head. "I don't know. She was wearing the T-shirt from our first big tour. Did they arrest her?"

I didn't know whether I should tell her, but I couldn't lie. "No, honey. She's dead. They think when you hit her with the guitar–"

"Good."

I stroked her hair. "Do you need anything? I could get you some magazines or books or something."

"No." She took my hand and kissed the knuckles. "Don't stay here all night, okay? I won't be able to sleep if I know you're out there squeezed into a chair."

"Where am I gonna go? Back to the apartment? It's still a crime scene."

"Go home with Nessa or Codie. I'll be fine. You can think good thoughts just as easily from a comfortable bed. Maybe you'll dream of me. And they've given me enough drugs that I know I'm going to be sleeping. So maybe we can find each other in our dreams."

Codie and Nessa both offered to put me up for the night, and I went with Codie just because her place was closer. Nessa stayed with us for moral support, and the two of them doted on me as if I was the one who'd gotten stabbed. The Dads called to make sure everything was okay, and I ended up calming them down with a report on Lana's progress. I resisted their insistence I come home with a promise I would call them again in the morning, then hung up and lay on the couch while Nessa and Codie filtered the internet for me.

Naomi arrived around midnight, apologizing for the hour even though it was obvious none of us had been asleep. She wanted to make sure we knew what was going on without resorting to watching the media circus.

Police searched the home of Marcia Rayburn, currently between employment opportunities, and found a veritable shrine to Lana. Not Radiation Canary; any group shots had been cropped or defaced until the three of us weren't in them. She posted online in several of our online fan club sites, becoming more and more vocal in her wishes and hopes that Lana would "cut the dead weight and go solo."

Her last post said that Lana would be a solo act by the end of the month "one way or another." It was only then that I realized the truth about the attack. Rayburn had been hiding in my apartment with a knife. Even though Lana spent eighty percent of her time at my place, we didn't officially live together. Rayburn had been there to stab me, to kill me.

It took me a moment to realize Naomi was still talking. "~of course we're going to postpone the release of *Intervention*."

That got my attention. "What? No. It's up to Lana, but I really don't think she would want that."

Nessa said, "Definitely not. We won't be able to promote it like we did with the others, but we should go ahead with the release as planned. We're not going to let this bitch deprive any of the other fans."

Codie nodded, so Naomi said, "Okay. It's up to you guys, so as long as you're all on the same page we'll keep the release date. There's one other thing before I leave you alone." She opened her bag and took out her laptop. "This was posted earlier tonight. It was recorded at the Space Needle. I'm going to show it to Lana at the hospital tomorrow, but I wanted to be the one who showed you." She turned the computer around so we could see the screen.

Judging by the sky, the video had been taken at dusk. A group of girls in red and green clothes were holding candles, underneath the Space Needle. I glanced at the title of the clip just as the girls started singing. Naomi said, "It's the 'Say a Prayer Vigil.' They organized it on the official website. One of the comments said there were about two hundred people there before it broke up around ten."

Codie leaned against me, and I stroked her arm. Nessa wiped her eyes on the sleeve of her shirt. She sniffled. "Well, I guess Lana's in pretty good shape. The Needle is like a satellite dish to Heaven."

I laughed and squeezed her hand. I walked Naomi to the door and hugged her. "Thanks for being here."

"Of course. You four are more than clients to me." She nodded toward the living room. "Let them take care of you, okay? You might want to play it strong, but believe me... you want to let them help you through this."

"I will."

"Okay. Goodnight."

I went back into the living room, where Nessa was using her own computer to search YouTube for other videos. "Lots of Lana Kent vigils tonight, it looks like. Some of them were organized when the news was still saying she'd died, so there's a lot of... a lot of stuff you probably shouldn't read. But lots of support."

I curled up on the couch and tucked my hand under my bent knees. "Will you ferret out all the good stuff for me?"

"Of course."

I thanked her quietly and closed my eyes, just for a minute. As I drifted off, I heard Nessa start another video with a group of girls singing "All Clear."

Track Two

The hallway is incomplete, as if the only part that's real is what she can see at that moment. She reaches the apartment door and fumbles with the key, slips it into the lock, stepping inside. The floor is red, sticky, and she looks at the coffee table to see Karen slumped against it with her throat slit, her chest cut open, blood everywhere...

Lana swallowed a scream as she woke up. The stitches in her side pulled as she aborted her attempt to sit up. She touched the bandages and gingerly lowered herself back to the pillows. The hospital was quiet, visiting hours long over, and she closed her eyes to enjoy the sounds drifting down from the nurses' station. There were cards on the tabletop, and she decided if she couldn't sleep then she could at least read a few of them.

After the tenth card referencing the lyrics of "Prayer," she decided she could stop reading every single missive. She settled for looking at the artwork on the front and then glancing inside to see if someone had bothered to write anything longer than a sentence. If they did, she took the time to read it.

She didn't want to go back to sleep and risk the nightmare again, but she didn't know the rules of the hospital. Was it lights out after a certain time, or could she watch television? Did she *want* to watch television was the real question. The news was probably nothing worth watching. She had to admit she was a decent height-level of celebrity, and news of her stabbing was probably filling up a good amount of the twenty-four hour news cycle. She didn't even consider going online, although Naomi had called to tell her about some videos that were popping up that were worth a look.

She rubbed her face. The bitch had been waiting for Karen. Lana didn't want to think about how stupidly easy it would have been for things to have turned out differently. Hence the nightmares.

The nurse had left a pen, so she turned over one of the cards and began writing.

"I don't want to go to sleep
'Cause I know what's waiting for me
The difference is so easy to make
I don't want to watch that scene
I want the amnesia between
Being asleep and being awake."

There was a knock on the door and Lana glanced up to see the person she least expected to ever see again. She put down her pen and straightened. "Alia. How'd you get in here?"

Alia stepped cautiously into the room but stayed against the wall, leaving as much room between her and the bed as possible. "I slipped a hundred bucks to the nurse on duty and explained what I wanted. Don't worry. I know what happened the last time someone surprised you, so I'm not going to make any, uh, sudden moves." She held up her hands to show they were empty, then looked down at her boots.

"So what did you tell the nurse you wanted? And which one should I ask be reassigned to another floor?"

"Please don't take it out on her. I just wanted to apologize for everything. I knew you wouldn't take a call from me, and I knew you probably wouldn't open any card or letter I tried to send, so I figured this was the only way it could happen." She cleared her throat. "I shouldn't have released those pictures. On top of being just a standard shit-move, it outed you as gay. And that's just unacceptable. I was just so hurt and angry that I acted without... well, that's not true." She looked toward the window. "As soon as the pictures went public, I wished I could take it back. And since I can't do that, then the least I can do is offer you a heartfelt apology and hope you can forgive me."

Lana smoothed her hands over the blankets. For a long time, the only sound in the room was the beep of monitors and Alia sniffling. Finally Lana sighed.

"It really hurt to see those pictures go public. Probably as much as it hurt to see them pop up unexpectedly on your phone. Hell of a way to confirm we're broken up, huh?"

Alia laughed softly and shrugged. "Yeah. Well."

"We both acted badly. But I started it. I'm adult enough to admit it. I'm sorry, Alia. I'm sorry I hurt you badly enough that you... did what you did."

"Can I come closer to the bed?"

"Yeah."

Alia moved closer and gently hugged Lana. "The first report I saw online was that you had died. I couldn't stop crying. I thought I would never get a chance to say I was sorry."

"It's okay." She kissed Alia's cheek and then, chastely, her lips. "I'll reimburse you for the bribe to get in here."

Alia laughed. "Forget it. It's penance."

"Well, I needed penance, too. I'll send you a check for fifty bucks."

"All right." She wiped her cheeks when she pulled away. "I'm going to get out of here before the nurse thinks better of it and calls security. I'll see you on stage sometime."

Lana nodded. "Yeah. See you around." She watched Alia leave the room and took a deep, cleansing breath. She picked up the pen, tapped the end of it against the card, and went back to writing.

We canceled our appearances for the month after Lana got out of the hospital. We wanted to cancel more, and Naomi was willing despite the fact we had an album to promote, but Lana insisted we get back to normal as soon as possible. I hadn't been back to my apartment since the attack. Codie and Nessa volunteered to be my gofers, dropping everything to go over and pack a bag, pick up mail, get whatever I needed so I didn't have to cross the threshold. On Valentine's Day they brought back a stuffed lemur that was almost as big as I was. Lana paled when she saw it, but then she smiled ruefully.

"I bought that for you right before... right before." She didn't have to complete the sentence.

I stayed with Lana. The first few nights, we just held each other on top of the blankets. We watched a few YouTube tributes people had made wishing her well; montages of fans doing our canary symbol, holding up written messages of support and love, videos spliced together from live performances and videos. A week after she got out of the hospital she put aside the laptop and pulled me to her.

"Are you sure?"

"Yeah," she whispered.

Our lovemaking was slow and tender, both of us remaining quiet until I made a quiet sound of release during my climax. Lana kissed my throat and held me to calm my trembling. I nuzzled her neck, kissing the shell of her ear as I trailed my hand down to her right arm.

"Don't touch them." She pressed her lips against my hair. "The scars. Don't touch them."

"I'm sorry." I pulled back and brushed my mouth against her cheek. "I know what really happened."

She lifted up to stare down at me, her brow furrowed.

"You told the story to the press, and you wrote about it on the website, but I know what really happened. She was there for me."

Lana pulled away from me and rolled onto her back. "I don't want to talk about it."

I sat up. "Lana, it's okay. I want you to know that you don't have to lie to me." I ran my hand down her back, tracing the bumps of her spine.

"Can we just forget it happened? It's bad enough it's going to be coming up in every interview we do from now on, does it have to be pillow talk, too?" She threw back the blankets and put her feet on the floor. She pulled on her jeans without underwear and swept her hair out of her face as she looked for a bra.

"I'm sorry, Lana. Come back to bed."

"No, I have to go. I need some fresh air."

"Can I come with you?"

"Probably better if you don't." She pulled her hair out of the collar of her shirt and turned back to face me. "I'm sorry, K. I'm not mad. I just need to get out for a little while."

I nodded. "Okay. Do you want me to stay up?"

"No." She leaned down on the bed, stretching to kiss me. I cupped the back of her head, and she sighed softly when she pulled back. "I love you."

"I love you, too. I won't wake you when I come back, promise."

"No, wake me."

She nodded, kissed me between the eyebrows, and picked up her jacket as she headed out. I bent my legs and wrapped my arms around them, head on my knees, and decided I could wait up for just a little while in case she decided to come right back.

The lights came on in a staggered pattern, first directly over the door, then the rehearsal space, and finally the back of the room. Lana shut the door and walked to where their instruments were usually stored, but her guitar wasn't among them. It was wrapped in plastic in some evidence room, Exhibit A or F or some bullshit label for a trial that would never happen. There was no doubt that Marcia Rayburn had broken into Karen's apartment illegally with the intent to do bodily harm. Lana's response was deemed self-defense, and the book was closed. But her guitar was still being held hostage.

Lana had a spare guitar donated by Dash Warren herself, delivered to the hospital on the last day of Lana's confinement. "For when you feel like playing it again," the note had said. Lana didn't know what would keep her from it. Without the guitar, she would have been defenseless. She didn't want to think of what would have happened if she was still just a dance teacher. She strummed a few chords and hummed "Someone Saved My Life Tonight," settling the guitar on her thigh. She was careful not to upset her injuries, angling to the right so her side wouldn't be stretched or overextended.

When she finished playing the Elton John song, she moved on to the one she'd written in the hospital. Naomi was being great, the perfect manager, giving them as much time as they needed to get back into the groove. But Lana could only think about Karen, Codie and Nessa being forced to sit around doing nothing while she recovered.

She vowed to get back to work as soon as humanly possible.

Track Three

Nick Young paced around his mark as he waited for the audience response to the last joke to die down. He lifted his head as if something had just occurred to him. "Oh, have you heard this? A month ago, one of the best musicians out there - and a very dear friend of the show - Lana Kent. Lana Kent of Radiation Canary~" The audience applauded. "Sure, sure, well deserved. Lana Kent was attacked in her home, stabbed seven times in the back, and managed to fight off her assailant with her guitar. With her *guitar*, ladies and gentlemen. Woody Guthrie used to have stickers on his guitar that said 'This Machine Kills Fascists,' but I guess Lana really does have to register hers as a lethal weapon.

"Well, now the band has a new CD out, and sales are... well, sales are naturally going sky-high. And this blowhard talk radio putz~" he spit the word, "~Russ Peck." He spit off to the side. "He has the absolute gall to suggest that the situation was staged. He's positing... sorry, Mr. Peck, if you're watching, that's a smart person word for pulling crap out of thin air... he's positing that maybe Lana wasn't as badly hurt as the press suggested. I mean, the woman could have died. And this asshole, sorry censors, is saying it was all a publicity stunt."

He put his hands in his pockets and smirked into the camera. "Well. Here with a very special message for Mr. Russ Peck is Lana Kent. Lana?"

The curtains parted and Lana walked out. The crowd, of course, went crazy. She stood on her mark, hands clasped behind her back and feet crossed at the ankle, smiling sheepishly as she waited for her cue. She lifted her arm to wave and the cheers grew, and only afterward did she realize that waving had exposed her scars. After the show, commentators would suggest that the simple act of waving was her way of making a statement, but Lana just wanted to acknowledge the love she was getting. Finally, the applause stopped, and Nick spoke from across the stage.

"Well, Lana, I hear you have a message for Mr. Peck."

"I do, Nick." She looked into the camera. "Fuck you, asshole."

The crowd erupted again. Nick crossed the stage and kissed her cheek, squeezed her elbow, and Lana waved to the crowd as she turned and walked back behind the closing curtains.

We got together for a rehearsal of the first songs from the next album, starting with what Lana was calling her "Hospital Song." The lyrics took up two full pages of my journal after I transferred them from the cards and envelopes on which she had originally written them. It was hard to read them without tearing up, so I wasn't looking forward to actually trying to perform it.

"The house shakes with thunder like a shotgun
I know I said 'say a prayer,' but right now I don't have one
I take a second and let myself forget
Pretending it hasn't happened yet
Lightning flashes when the thunder is still shaking
And I'm clinging to the amnesia I get just after waking."

I tried, as always, to ignore the verse that mentions being alone in the night, the big empty bed. She wrote it in the hospital, so naturally she was alone. But she wasn't alone now. Was she? I watched as she talked to Codie about the beat of the song and pushed aside my self-centeredness. The song was mostly for me and her, a duet between her voice and my strings. I asked for a quick run-through just so we could see what we were working with, and we took our places.

Halfway through the first verse, Lana turned to Nessa. "Lightly... like a whisper. I want it light enough to wind around my voice, if that makes sense."

Nessa nodded and demonstrated, and Lana nodded along with it before she went back to her part. The guitar was barely noticeable, so we decided it was unnecessary. Lana could focus on her singing for this one. Once the little touches had been settled on, we ran through it from start to finish. Lana inserted a brief musical interlude in the middle where Nessa and I could carry the rhythm before going on to the sixth verse.

When the last note faded, I stopped the clock. "Eleven minutes and eighteen seconds. Bands have gotten away with longer."

"And it's not indulgent," Codie said. "People are going to expect something like this after everything that happened. It would be wrong to just continue on like nothing happened. You need this song, Lana."

Lana nodded slowly. "Okay. But I still want to try to get it down. Can we cut some of the interlude, K?"

"Sure. I think if we get it down to as close to ten minutes as possible, it'll be good enough."

"I agree," Nessa said. "Let's try it again."

After the third go-round, Lana suggested calling the song "Hypermnesia," a heightened state of memory. "All I want to do is forget, but everyone keeps reminding me of what happened. Hell, I can't shower without remembering. The word won't be in the song so we won't have to worry about pronouncing it on stage, but I think it's a fitting title."

I agreed, and we booked some studio time to record it. Lana wanted to release the song early as a download from the website, a little something for the fans who had taken the time to hold vigils. Naomi was a little surprised we were already working on the new CD, but she wasn't going to complain. We were scheduled to record it in two days, so we got together often to make sure we were ready to put together the final product. During the interlude, Lana turned toward me and smiled. I watched her as I played, using her reactions to gauge how I was doing. She winked at me and turned back to the microphone to sing the next part.

Codie and I went to get dinner and take it back to the studio. Working on a ten minute song ate up big chunks of the day, so we were having more and more meals on the shaky folding table in the rehearsal space. Codie waited until we were on the main road before she said, "So how are things going with you and your girl?"

I shrugged. "Fine. She's still a little traumatized, I think."

"Well, hell. Who wouldn't be?"

We rode in silence for a while. "If you need anything, Nessa and I are here. I mean, we heard the same song you did. It's kind of harsh in regards to... you know. Feeling alone, being lonely. It's rough."

I furrowed my brow. "No, it's not. She wrote it in the hospital. She was alone in the hospital, so it's nothing to do with us."

Codie tensed her hands on the steering wheel and shrugged. "I don't know. But Nessa felt the same way I did. No matter what Lana says, the song says that she feels like she's in this alone. I don't think Nessa and I can help her."

"I'm doing what I can."

"As her girlfriend, yeah. But maybe that's part of the problem. You two were fighting against the current from the get-go when you started sleeping together. I think now it's even worse. You need to figure out how to get balanced or you'll get knocked over."

I watched the city going by outside the car, my hands smoothing and re-smoothing my skirt over my thighs. At the next red light, Codie sighed.

"Look, K, I'm sorry. Maybe I'm speaking out of turn–"

"No." I rubbed her arm. "Tough love. It's what I needed to hear. I just don't know what I'm going to do about it. Even if I broke up with her, it wouldn't do any good. It would just pile more badness on top of her at a time when she's most overwhelmed."

"I'm not saying break up with her. But you need to find a way to just be her friend without being her girlfriend. I don't know how you'll do that, but Nessa and I will help you if we can."

"Thanks, Codie." I looked out the window as we pulled into the restaurant's parking lot. The hard part wouldn't be figuring out how to help; it would be getting Lana to accept the help when it came.

Track Four

The finished product of "Hypermnesia" was ten minutes and forty-seven seconds. Lana was glad the song didn't need her guitar; her Telecaster was returned by the police, but it had been damaged in saving her life. It was currently being repaired, but she didn't have high hopes for a resurrection. Still, she was fine if it had to be sacrificed. It had given her life and saved her life, and it deserved to retire in quiet dignity in a display in her apartment. She stood in the studio in front of the microphone and waited for the cue to start playing. Suddenly she looked down, staring at her palms, and looked around.

"I don't know what to do with my hands."

We were signaled, and Lana settled her hands on the microphone stand. I played her in, she wet her lips, and she started to sing. Nessa played softly as instructed, the music just barely rising above the volume of Lana's voice. Codie provided the sound of a beating heart skipping every few beats, and I threaded it all together with my cello. Lana's fingers twitched on the microphone stand, like blind creatures that knew that they should be playing when there was music but unable to find the strings.

When we finished, Naomi came into the room and applauded us. "It's going to be off the charts. Lana, it's beautiful. It's strong, but it accepts that you need help to get through it. It's going to be epic." She made a face like she was preparing for a blow. "I don't suppose you would be open to creating a shorter, radio-friendly version--"

"No," Lana said. "It's as short as it can be."

Naomi nodded. "I concur. We have a bit of leeway releasing it through the website, so that shouldn't be a problem. Is it going to be on your next album?"

Lana looked at me, and I said, "I don't know why it wouldn't be."

"Okay. With the coverage we've been getting, we probably won't need it as a single." She rubbed her chin. "Lana? Can I speak with you privately?"

Lana slid off her stool. "K, come on."

Naomi stopped at the door. "Um, privately as in just you."

"If we're going to talk about anything to do with the band, I want Karen to be there."

Naomi hesitated again, then nodded and motioned me forward. We stepped out into the hall and she turned to face us.

"Nothing's wrong, and it's not really a band issue. It's about you, Lana. The boss wanted me to ask if you were up for doing the mini-movie for the 'Without a Fight' video. It's going to be a lot more labor-intensive than your previous videos, and even though you're already in the studio and writing amazing music, I don't want to push you into anything you won't be ready for. I wanted to give you a chance to say no without losing face, but..."

Lana shrugged. "I'm fine. We can do it whenever you guys are ready for us."

Naomi nodded. "Okay, well. That brings up another issue. Your trademark of being sleeveless means that... in the video..." She eyed Lana's right arm. "It will be close to impossible to shoot around those scars. If you'd rather wear a jacket for the video, we'd all understand."

Lana self-consciously curled her fingers around her bicep, her fingers stretching to touch the long pink remnants of Marcia Rayburn's attack.

"No. I'm not letting that bitch change anything. Not our release schedule, not our music videos... she doesn't get to change Radiation Canary." She nodded as if confirming it to herself. "I'll be sleeveless. Like always."

Naomi smiled. "Good for you. I'll let them know. We're going to start prepping for the video next week, probably Thursday or Friday. We've had a writer working on the story, so we should have some lines emailed to you before that. Get ready, girls. You may start getting offered movie roles if this video pans out." She winked and left us to consider the horror of becoming actresses.

Lana stopped going to bed at the same time as Karen so it would be less noticeable that they weren't having sex anymore. Karen occasionally moved her hand down the back of Lana's arm, an innocent and inadvertent touch that caused her to touch the scars. Lana always recoiled, and Karen's apologies were always sincere, but she couldn't bring herself to let it go. So she wore pajama tops with long sleeves and lingered in the living room until Karen went into the bedroom, then she followed twenty or thirty minutes later when Karen was already asleep.

The plan backfired the night before they were supposed to start on the video. Laura Cowan had agreed to play a role, as had two of the label's male artists. The story focused on Sarah, who would be played by Karen. She decides to gather a group of friends and family for an intervention for her brother, Mark. Mark had gotten into a car accident that left his girlfriend in a coma. Nessa would play the girlfriend's sister, and Codie was a friend who wanted nothing to do with the intervention. Lana was cast as a social worker who was helping set up the intervention.

An argument between Codie and Karen's characters would lead into the song:

"Why are you doing this for him? Why are you trying to save someone who doesn't want to be saved?"

"Because I love him, and I'm not letting him go without a fight."

Karen was sitting in bed reading her lines, mouthing them to herself in an attempt to memorize them. She looked up when Lana came into the room, smiled weakly, and held up the script. "I don't know about this. Who thought we could be actresses, huh?"

"You'll be great." She leaned against the wall next to the door.

"Are you coming to bed?"

"Yeah."

Karen noticed the hesitation. "You okay?"

Lana nodded and slid under the blankets. "I'm just nervous about tomorrow. Not really sure how to play a social worker."

"You'll be great." She rubbed Lana's arm and bent down to kiss her shoulder. "Maybe we can help each other relax. It's been a while."

"Yeah, ah... I'm tired. And we have an early day tomorrow. We should probably just focus on resting."

Karen's hand stilled. "Right. Lana, we should talk about this."

"No, we don't have to. I'll get over it." She rolled onto her side, hoping Karen would let it drop. She pressed her face into the pillow, closed her eyes, and sighed when Karen spoke again.

"Please don't take this the wrong way, but I don't think you need to be in a relationship right now."

That got her attention. Lana sat up and turned to face her. "What are you talking about?"

"I love you, sweetie. But a relationship has a lot of give and take, and right now you need to take more than you can give. You need a friend. You need someone to take care of you, and it's not fair for me to expect you to take care of me, too. So just for now, why don't we just go back to being friends until you're ready to be more again?"

Lana shook her head. "You're breaking up with me?"

"We're taking a break. Come on, Lana. We were best friends before we slept together. You need a best friend more than you need a lover. I'll make the sacrifice to be what you need."

Lana's face was hot, and she pressed her palm against her cheek. "This is unbelievable."

Karen was silent for a minute, then said, "You're the one who wrote 'Hypermnesia.' Come on, Lana. You said it clear as day. You're getting through this alone. You're weighed down by it. And it's not because I'm not here. I know you appreciate me being here, but you don't expect me to take any of the weight because we're too close. When we were friends, we were more equal than we are now. You need equals. Me, Codie, Nessa..." She tucked Lana's hair behind her ear, and Lana turned away from the touch. "Sweetie, I love you. That's not going to change. If I have to choose between being your friend and lover, right now, I think you need the friend more."

"You can't be my friend and my lover?"

"I've been trying." Karen's eyes were wet. "I've been trying, but you've been pushing me away. We haven't had sex in weeks. You barely look at me when we have dinner. So if I have to sacrifice us for a little bit, then I can do that."

Lana leaned against the headboard and let Karen stroke her hair, then threw the blankets back. "Fine..."

"Where are you going?"

"Friends don't sleep together." She put on her shoes, not bothering to dress before putting her jacket over her pajamas. "I'm going out."

"Again? God, you're getting good at running away." She stopped at the doorway and Karen closed her eyes. "I didn't mean that, Lana. Sweetie, I didn't... I just meant you've been avoiding instead of talking. And maybe you'd be more willing to talk if I was your friend and not your girlfriend."

She kept her back to the bed. "What do I have to talk about?"

"You killed someone, Lana. You can't just wash that off in the shower."

She turned. "I killed someone who was *stabbing* me. With a knife that she had brought with her so she could kill you. You think I have any lingering doubts? My only regret is that doing it broke my guitar. All I needed to do was write my song, and I did that, and now–"

Karen threw back the blankets. "Then come here and fuck me."

Lana scoffed and rubbed her forehead. "I don't... it's... I'm not horny."

"It's not about being horny, Lana. It's about a connection. It's about feeling comfortable and safe with someone. And I don't think you feel that with me anymore." Her eyes were wet. "I just want to help you, and I don't know how to do that."

"You don't have to do anything," Lana said quietly. "I'm fine."

Karen said, "Okay. Fine. Just... come back to bed. We can forget I said anything."

Lana shook her head. "No. I'll see you at the shoot tomorrow. Goodnight, K."

She left the bedroom and a few seconds later Karen heard the front door slam. She sank down in bed, dropping her head against the pillow and staring at the ceiling. She was angry at Lana, annoyed at herself, frustrated that a full week of debating with herself had proven useless... She should have just kept her big mouth shut.

Track Five

In the dark, the stairs were so much like her nightmare that she almost didn't go through with her plan. She summoned her courage and headed up, her hand sliding over the banister as she approached the landing. The police tape was long gone, and some crime scene cleanup crew had removed the blood from the floor. Still, she felt like she could see the pool under her feet as she pushed the door open.

She had been sprawled on the floor in front of the closed apartment for seven minutes before the ambulance and the police arrived. It was all a blur to her, but she remembered people standing nearby and watching in horror as she was patched up and loaded onto a gurney. She remembered giving a thumbs-up like athletes when they're carted off the field after an injury, and she could almost hear the EMT guys in the truck talking when they thought she was unconscious.

"~kid loves their stuff. I think the CD is in my car right now."

There were gouges in the floor, and she rubbed them with her toe. The deeper ones, the ones that hadn't been slowed by cutting through her skin, were strikes that had missed. Each of those jabs was an organ spared. Her spleen, her lung, her heart. She crouched and sat in the doorway, running her fingers over the marks. Her own lyrics appeared unbidden in her mind, almost as if they had been written in the wood and she was receiving them through touch.

"Here's where I bled for you,
Where I would have died for you
Here's where I put it all on the line
And traded for your life with mine."

She stood up and wiped her sleeve across her lips. She thought about the video shoot in the morning, the people who were counting on her. She pictured Karen, alone in Lana's bed trying to take back what she'd said. But words couldn't be unsaid. She left the apartment and went downstairs, typing a text message as she returned to her car. Once the text was sent, she turned off her phone and tossed it into the backseat. Her car had a GPS, and she had a few spare outfits in the trunk just in case of another incident like the *Middle Distance* cover shoot.

The best part about living in Washington was that there were very few options when it came to running away. She aimed the car south and just drove, knowing she could wait until later to make any further decisions about her final destination.

I motioned for Naomi to show me her phone again, as if re-reading the text message would make it make sense. She handed it over and slumped back in her seat, fist pressed against her cheek. The message was simple, to the point, and infuriatingly vague. "Can't make the video shoot. Need that time off we talked about. Talk to you soon. Sorry." I handed it back. She raised her eyebrows, and I shrugged. We'd run out of words a while ago.

The director was an excitable guy from Vancouver named Woody. He did more television than music videos, but given the story and nature of the video, we were comfortable he'd do it justice. He came into the trailer where we were brooding like Achilles in his tent, eyed us, and shrugged at Naomi.

"Still no sign?"

"None. She's obviously not going to make it today." Naomi stood up and sighed, hands on hips. "Okay, this isn't the end of the world. Dash is nearby. We can get the shots that didn't include Lana's character and, when Dash gets here, she can fill in." She ran a hand through her short hair, clutching at the nape of her neck like a wolf with a cub. "This is going to make the video seem awkward. We'll have to get a lot of her in the performance section so it won't feel lopsided. Is that okay with everyone?"

Codie and Nessa nodded. I shrugged. I didn't know how I felt. Guilt, anger, concern, and annoyance all vied for the top spot. Part of me wanted to kill Lana, the other part wanted to know where she was just so I could beg forgiveness. We were all working on the assumption she was okay and off on her own somewhere because we couldn't let ourselves imagine her hurt or injured. It was bad enough knowing that she was emotionally hurt, and not just because that had been my fault.

We'd spent the morning calling around to any place Lana might have gone, stopping short of issuing a missing persons report. The last thing we needed was someone leaking the information and turning Lana's walkabout into the lead story on the news. She'd gotten enough of that already. If she wanted to be alone, we had to respect that.

And it would be so much easier if you would just text already. I stared at my phone and willed it to ring, but it remained silent.

Woody said, "I don't want to rush anybody, but if we're going to take advantage of this light, we really need to get started."

I started to put my phone in my pocket, but then changed my mind. I turned it off and tossed it onto the couch in the corner of the trailer. I could be just as silent as she was.

Lana drove through the night, not stopping to sleep. Brandi Carlile and Sara Bareilles playing full-blast helped keep her awake. She kept telling herself she was overreacting, that there was still time to turn around and go home and fix things. But then she saw the battered floor, she felt the phantom pull of stitches that had been taken out long ago, and she pressed her foot down harder on the accelerator.

She skipped breakfast the next morning, stopping only for a quick lunch at a truck stop. She napped in her car and was back on the road within an hour. By then she'd decided on a destination. The GPS gave her a map that showed she was only slightly off-course, so she adjusted and headed southwest like she'd been shot from a gun.

At every state border she crossed, she stopped to check her phone. Her inbox was stuffed full of messages varying from confused to frightened to flat-out angry. Naomi had sent a few, as had Codie and Nessa, but the majority were from Karen. Lana shut off the phone without answering any of them, looking up into the sky and wondering how satellite tracking worked. On TV it seemed so easy, but she doubted Naomi and the others would involve the police. Even if they did, she doubted the real law enforcement agencies had anything half as cool as the people on TV. No one could really track a cell phone with that kind of precision. Regardless, she kept it turned off just for her own peace of mind.

She stopped again for dinner and another quick nap to refresh herself for the final leg of her trip. Finally, close to twenty-three hours after storming out and leaving Karen alone in her apartment, Lana Kent arrived in Las Vegas.

Track Six

They shot through most of the afternoon, doing take after take due to Codie screwing up her lines. She got endlessly frustrated, calming only when Karen hugged her and told her they could postpone the shoot if she needed. Codie refused a delay and, on the next take, managed to nail her part. Her anxiety had nothing to do with Lana, not really. She was just in no way an actress, and being on camera spouting lines someone else had written made her feel peculiar.

Not that she was unaffected by Lana's disappearance. It was still hard believing Lana had just flipped out and left, but if anyone deserved an unscheduled vacation, she did. It was still a bitchy thing to leave them in the lurch. Dash did a good job in Lana's stead, and the video was going to be amazing regardless. Codie sent Lana a text saying the "movie" was going well, even if she hated referring to it as such, and asked where the hell she was. She didn't expect an answer, but she wanted the yelling to be waiting when Lana deigned to check in.

Her real concern was for Karen. She obviously blamed herself for Lana's disappearance. Whether the guilt was merited or not, Codie knew she was being too hard on herself. She and Dash spent a lot of time talking in the trailer they all shared, and Codie hoped she had some sage advice that would help Karen through this awkward period.

She was sitting on a couch in Dash's house, which was being used as the video's set. Dash had given everyone permission to smoke if they wanted, so she was enjoying a rare indoor cigarette while the production elves set up the next scene. Nessa came and sat next to her and gripped Codie's knee, shaking it as she sank back against the seat. She sighed heavily and pushed her hair out of her face.

"What do you think?"

"About Lana?" Codie shrugged. "I don't know. When we were in school, she used to talk about just picking up and lighting off to wherever. But all kids do that. Even though she has the means now, I don't think she's really in Australia or Paris. She just needed some breathing space. Los Angeles, Vegas, New York. Your guess is as good as mine." She took a drag off her cigarette and offered it to Nessa, who declined.

"Do you think she'll come back?"

Codie was shocked by the question. "Of course she's coming back. She just needs some time to deal with everything that happened. I'm surprised it took her this long to freak out. I'd have disappeared from the damn hospital. She'll be back."

Karen and Dash came back into the house, and Nessa nodded at Karen. "But things aren't going to be the same when she gets back."

"No." Codie had to admit that. "Things aren't going to be the same at all."

"Beertender," Lana said. She held up a finger and the man in his black vest and bowtie made his way back over to refill her drink. That was what she liked about Vegas. No judgment. They encouraged people to plunk coin after coin into machines that rarely paid out. They turned a blind eye to anyone pulling the last bill out of their wallet for "one more shot." The only thing they really cared about was if someone tried to take some of the money away. God forbid a thief try to take the casino's ill-gotten gains.

Lana wasn't there for the gambling. People could call New York or London the capital of the world, but Las Vegas was the true king. Everyone claimed it was the city of hope, but hope never paid off. No one ever went home millionaires from a week in Vegas. The best they could expect was to leave with a little more than they came with. Lana tapped the bar, and the bartender refilled the glass again.

"Danke," she murmured as she took another drink.

Someone took the stool a few spaces away from Lana and quietly ordered a drink. Lana glanced over and vaguely recognized the Amazon currently resting her elbows on the bar. She wore a sparkling silver halter top tied at the neck, leaving her back bare from the shoulders down to the dimples above her black bell-bottom slacks. Lana eyed the curve of the woman's rear end, the long, long legs, and then moved back up to the front of her top. Her eyes lingered on the woman's breasts before returning to her face, trying to figure out how she knew her.

The woman felt the scrutiny and looked at her. She smiled. "How are you doing?"

British accent. That narrowed it down a little. She was very blonde, waves of curly hair falling on either side of her face from a center part. She had soft blue eyes and a bright smile, the face of a fairy tale cherub on the body of an Olympic athlete.

"Hi." Lana smiled and pointed with her pinkie finger. "I think I know you."

The woman's eyes widened slightly. "Oh, I think I know you, too. Lana Kent, am I correct? Radiation Canary."

Lana smiled at her pronunciation. "Rad-yay-shun." She nodded and touched her tongue to her top lip, tasting the liquor that was left behind on it.

"I love your music. We play it on our program occasionally, even though sometimes it can be very difficult to dance to."

Lana snapped her fingers. "Catherine Diehl from *Dance Star*."

"I thought that might tip the scales. Call me Kitty. It's great to meet you." She took her drink and moved to sit next to Lana as she extended her free hand. Lana took it and kissed the knuckles. "Oh, aren't you debonair? Are you having a show here? I hate to think I've missed out on getting tickets."

"No, it's just me. The others are still up in Seattle. I just had to get away."

"Right. I heard you'd had a tough time of it. How have you been?"

Lana sighed. "Trying to figure that out right now. Tried going back to work, but I think it was too much too soon."

"I'm sorry to hear that."

"Yeah." She motioned to the bartender. When he came over, Lana gestured at Kitty's glass. "And another for her. Put it on my tab."

Kitty said, "Oh, you don't have to do that."

"Please. I've probably got a dozen people cursing me out up in Seattle so I could use the karma."

"Well, thank you. Lana Kent buying me drinks. I knew there was an upside to becoming famous."

"What are you doing in Vegas?" Lana asked. "Some kind of live results show?"

"God, no. The season is over. I'm just trying to relax and enjoy myself before the next round of live shows and, God, the endless auditions." She sighed and rubbed her face with one hand, then rested her chin in her hand. She drummed her fingers against her cheek and looked back at Lana. "As long as we're both without obligation, perhaps we could find something to do together to pass the time."

"Hm." Lana dropped her eyes to the front of Kitty's top, the shapes of her breasts moving enticingly under the thin material with the movement of her breathing.

"Oy. My eyes are up here."

Lana didn't avert her gaze. "I know where your eyes are."

Kitty laughed and hunched her shoulder. "Oh. Hmm." She crossed wrists and flattened her hands on the bar. She eyed the bartender and then looked at Lana again, her shoulder raised so that she was almost hiding behind it. "Do you have a room here?"

"As a matter of fact, I do." Lana finished her latest beer and turned to face Kitty. "Would you like to see it?"

Track Seven

"I found her. Well. I didn't find her, but I know where she is."

I sat up and twisted as Nessa came hurrying into the apartment. I had been lying on the couch watching TV, my journal open on the floor in front of me as I tried to think of a bridge for a song called "Falling Up." She was holding up her phone like it was a torch, waving it as she dropped onto the couch. Codie came out of the kitchen and sat on the other side of her while I scooted close to read the small screen.

"Twitter?" I said.

"Yeah. I decided to do a search on Lana's name, and someone actually tweeted about her. Three hours ago, someone named gallerychik saw her at the Luxor."

There was one tweet on the screen. "omg! Just saw lana freaking kent at luxor!! #radiationcanaryrules"

"God bless social media, I guess," Codie said. "Can you ask her anything else? Details?"

"I didn't know if I should. If we tweet someone from the official account asking for how to find a member of the band, we might be opening up a can of worms. We're still trying to cover up the fact that she ran away, so–"

"Right," I said. "So just be subtle about it. May I?" She handed me the phone. She was already signed in to the official account, so I composed a new tweet.

"@gallerychick Hope she was having a good time!"

"How long does it usually take to get a reply?"

Nessa shrugged. "I'm not on here a lot. But it could be hours." I was about to tell her to keep us posted when her eyebrows shot up. "Whoa. She must get text notifications or something. We've got a reply. Says she was... oh." She glanced at me and angled the phone so I couldn't read it.

"What?"

"Ah, it's nothing."

I turned the phone and read the screen. "That Amazon chick she was hanging off seemed to be having more fun." Something inside my chest clenched.

Codie snorted. "At least she added a smiley face. Otherwise that would have been a shitty thing to read."

My voice was flat. "No, it's fine. Lana and I are broken up." Officially now, I guess.

Nessa said, "We can all have a nice talk about it when we go drag her ass out of there and bring her back."

I shook my head. "No."

"What do you mean?"

I stood up and hugged myself as I faced them. "Naomi and Cartography offered her time off, but instead she dived right back into work. I knew she needed time off, but I just–" I pushed my hair out of my face and shook my head. "No. We'll tell Naomi that we know where she is, and we'll put the album on hold until she's ready to work on it. We don't have to stop completely. We can still write the songs, and we can work on the tracks until she gets back to do her part. She needs time, and we can afford to give it to her. It's up to you guys."

Codie nodded. "Yeah. Better than forcing her to come back before she's ready. We can wait a week or two."

Nessa agreed as well. I sat down and rested my head on Nessa's shoulder. Putting the album on hold for a week or two was nothing; I just hoped it wouldn't be any longer than that.

Kitty was so much taller than Lana. Five inches, at least. Not just tall for a woman, but tall period. She'd felt odd walking through the casino with such an Amazon, but the effect was minimized when they got upstairs and took off their shoes. Kitty sat on the edge of the bed while Lana opened the mini-bar. She brought the bottles back and handed one to Kitty, standing in front of her to look down at her bare toes curling in the carpet.

"You know, the band was originally called Little Cat Feet."

"Is that so?" Kitty said. She lifted one foot and rested it on Lana's hip. "Hm. My feet aren't so little, though."

Lana cupped the back of Kitty's ankle and lifted it. The cuff of Kitty's pants slid down her calf, and Lana delicately kissed the big toe. "No. I think they're just the right size for what I have in mind."

Kitty bit her bottom lip and leaned back on her elbows. "And what do you have in mind, Miss Canary?"

"Oh, lots of things..."

Lana undressed her slowly, then fell back onto skills picked up at Club Nightside to make a show of taking off her clothes. She gave Kitty a lap dance, twisting around to share their first kiss as Kitty stroked the inside of Lana's thighs.

"I thought the rules were not to touch the dancer."

Lana smiled. "Maybe on your show."

Kitty chuckled, the tip of her tongue pinched between her teeth, and Lana kissed her again. She was grinding against Kitty's lap, and one of Kitty's hands was firmly between Lana's legs, but her other went roaming. She pinched Lana's nipple, stroked the backs of her fingers over Lana's stomach, and then idly touched one of her scars.

Lana hissed and pulled back. "Don't."

"I'm sorry. Is it still tender?"

Lana didn't know how to answer. "Just don't touch them, okay? That's out of bounds."

Kitty ran her eyes down Lana's body. "Hm. Okay. I think I can find other areas to occupy my interests." She kissed the slope of Lana's shoulder and pulled her backward. Height wasn't an issue when they were horizontal, and they spent a few minutes figuring out what the other liked. Whispered assurances, stifled moans, and eager gasps filled the room. Finally Lana rolled Kitty onto her back and kissed between her breasts, curling her tongue over the smooth skin.

"What's your favorite song?"

"Ha-what?" Kitty gasped. "I don't know."

Lana swirled her tongue in Kitty's navel, and Kitty writhed underneath her. "Stop... this is torture." She whimpered, and Lana decided the British accent made moaning so much sexier. She nipped at the tight skin of Kitty's hips, then kissed the soft, barely-there patch of blonde between her legs. Kitty swallowed hard, her hands balled into fists on either side of her head.

"I want an answer, Catherine."

Another desperate whimper. "'Scene of the Crime.'"

"Yeah?"

"Mm. It's so sensual." She grunted. "The growl in your voice, the lyrical seduction. It's perfect for fucking. And I should know... I've done it several times." She sat up enough to wink down at Lana, cheeks flushed with pink.

Lana grinned and lifted Kitty's legs onto her shoulders. Knowing that she'd been the soundtrack for Kitty Diehl's sexual escapades only urged her onward. She wet her lips and bowed, gently stroking Lana with her tongue. She wet her fingers and began using them on her. Kitty gasped, "Please," and Lana obliged. She brought her tongue up, curled it gently around Kitty's clit, and began humming the song.

Kitty cried out and arched her back, feet pressing down on Lana's back as she thrashed against the pillows. Kitty came before the song ended, and she put her fingers on Lana's forehead to push her back. Panting, pink as the inside of a shell, slick with sweat, Kitty gasped, "C'm'up'ere." Lana translated and slid up Kitty's body, accepting the hungry kiss and letting Kitty roll them so that she was on top.

Kitty was breathless when she finally spoke, slipping her leg between Lana's thighs. "That song... is now utterly... ruined for everyone who uses it on my show..."

"But now you'll get wet every time you hear it."

Kitty groaned. "Oh, you're bad... show me that talented tongue."

Lana stuck out her tongue, and Kitty wrapped her lips around it. She sucked it into her mouth and rocked her hips, thrusting gently against Lana. She broke the kiss and lifted her head, and Lana kissed her throat.

"You know what this makes you?" Lana whispered against Kitty's ear. "The cat who got the canary."

Kitty growled. "Actually, the saying is the cat that *ate* the canary, isn't it?"

"Well, the night's young."

"Mmm, yes it is. But first, I'm gonna make you sing, birdie..."

Track Eight

April in Seattle wasn't as wet as normal, and people tried to adjust to long periods of sunshine before the summer. Once the album was put on hold, Nessa went on a road trip with her boyfriend. Codie took the opportunity to take flight lessons, something she'd always wanted to do. In May, I was loaned out to the Femme Reapers for a series of shows across Washington State to provide back-up on a couple of their songs.

I showed up backstage at the first show and waited until Laura was alone before I approached her. "Hey. I just wanted to make sure you're okay with this. With me being here."

She turned. "Of course. Strictly professional. You're an amazing musician, and you'll help draw a crowd. We're lucky to have you here." She paused and stood up. "On a personal level, I'm happy to see you. I've missed you. How have you been?"

I had been expecting anger, or coldness. I didn't expect kindness. I teared up and shrugged, trying to speak without sobbing. Laura crossed the room and embraced me, holding me until I calmed down. It took long enough that she eventually guided me to the dressing room's couch and sat me down, resting my head on her shoulder. I made a few unattractive noises, wiped my eyes, and kissed her on the cheek.

"Thanks."

"You looked like you needed it. Lana's missing, isn't she?"

"No. Not technically. We know she's in Las Vegas." I rubbed my face. "At least that's where she was two weeks ago. She hasn't been in contact, but people keep spotting her on Twitter. She's apparently staying put there for the time being."

Laura nodded and tucked my hair behind my ears. "How's the rest of the band dealing with it?"

I shrugged. "Lana and I have been pushing them pretty hard. We've been working hard, so we can afford to take a break. I just worry that if Lana stays away much longer, it's going to be hard to pull us back together when she does resurface."

"You'll do it. You're strong. And you're the best band on the label, us included." I scoffed, but she tapped her fingers against my cheek in a mock slap. "Hey. I'm not the kind of person who will badmouth myself just to make you feel better. You're good. And you'll still be good even if Lana never comes back. You'll just have to sing more of the songs."

"Right." I looked down and saw we were holding hands. Fresh tears brewed, but this time for a different reason. "I'm so sorry, Laura. I love you, but I treated you so badly."

"Hey. You had to explore your options. You and Lana have had a bond from the very beginning... you had to see if there was something there, or you'd always wonder." She smiled. "And you're worth waiting for. So are things done with you and Lana?"

I slumped back against the couch. "I don't know. Rumor has it that when she arrived in Vegas, she spent a lot of time getting room service for two. And the reason she ran in the first place is because I suggested we put a pin in the whole thing. So yeah, I'd say we're pretty much finished. But until I know for sure, I don't want to... I don't want to lead you on."

Laura smiled. "I appreciate that. But if she's sharing a room with someone, do you think it would be okay if I were to kiss you right now?"

"I think it would be very okay. And very necessary."

We kissed. It was nearly chaste, and it made my heart soar. I touched her cheek and made a soft noise in my throat. When we parted, she kissed my closed eyes and put her hands in my hair to keep me from pulling away.

"I'm glad you agreed to do these concerts."

"So am I. And I've missed you, too."

Ella, Laura's twin and the other half of the Femme Reapers, joined us for a pre-show dinner. Halfway through the meal, Ella pointed a fork at me. "If this whole thing with Lana causes you guys to go on hiatus, there's a spot for you in the Reapers. We could always be a trio instead of just us. You obviously don't have to make a decision now. It's a standing offer."

"Thanks. I appreciate it."

The crowd proved the Cowan girls weren't just being polite. The show was divided into three acts, and I was introduced during the second. The response was deafening, and I sheepishly accepted it as I took my position beside Laura and began to play their song "Trellis Climber." I stayed on stage as planned for the rest of the show, although Laura and Ella pretended to make it the crowd's decision. They prompted cheers with shouts like "What do you say we make her stick around?" and "Think we can keep her busy for one more song?"

For the encore, Laura performed "Prayer" with my blessing. The crowd ate it up. Laura invited me to the autograph table, but I demurred. I was just a special guest, and I had no right taking up space at their table. Laura walked me to the dressing room before I left and gave me a gentle kiss. It was a little more passionate than the one we'd shared earlier, and I relaxed into it before I realized what I was doing.

"We should–"

"Yeah." She touched her lips and backed away, looking at her shoes. "We need to talk about doing a bigger tour together. I mean, if Lana's gone long enough–"

"Even if she's not. I want to go on the road with you guys. If we can swing it. Maybe a national tour... the Radiation Reaper road trip."

"Or Femme Canary."

"Either way," I said with a smile. I kissed her again. "Thank you."

"De nada." She ran her hand down the front of my shirt, fingers curling under the placket. "I really want to fuck you again. But I won't."

I blushed. "Well. It's... good information to have."

She smiled. "I love you, Karen."

This time the blush spread to my ears.

"I'm not just saying it to hear you say it back." She chuckled, and I knew she was quoting one of our earliest songs. God, it seemed so long ago. "I just wanted you to know. It's awkward because I fell in love with you after you'd cheated on me. But I guess that makes it harder to deny, huh?"

"Maybe so. I'm sorry if I hurt you."

She shrugged and looked around the room, searching for something safe to focus on. "Better to have it happen when it did and not... you know, three years down the road when we would have been living together."

"Right. I should go. Your adoring public awaits." I kissed the corner of her mouth. "I love you, too, Laura."

She squeezed my arm and walked away, and I finished gathering my things before I left the dressing room.

"I'm not saying never again, I'm just saying later. A lot, lot later."

"You're just a chicken."

"Unwary chickens get their heads cut off," I said. Codie was making an unsuccessful attempt to get me back in the air. She'd spent a month getting her private pilot license, and now she was shopping for a plane. She had convinced me and Nessa to go up with her and an instructor, and now both of us were refusing to ever fly anywhere ever again. Following through on that oath would make touring a little difficult, but so would plummeting to earth in a fiery plane crash.

She spent the entire ferry ride from Seattle to Port Townsend convincing us how much easier it would have been to just fly out whenever we had to visit the Cartography offices. The ferry was enough of a risk. Planes crashed all the time, but it was national news when a ferry capsized. Hell, ferry accidents were *international* news. So we placed our bets on that and swore we'd never let Codie take us into the air.

"You guys are missing out," Codie said as she held the front door for us. "The freedom is without compare."

"Sure, sure," I said, smiling at Nessa. My smile faltered when I saw how concerned she looked. "What's wrong?"

Nessa gestured with her chin. "The receptionist. No one's there."

Sure enough, the desk was empty. I tried to remember past visits when it had been empty, but I couldn't come up with any. It looked eerie, abandoned. I put aside my unease and shrugged. "Well, it's a Tuesday afternoon. They're not expecting anyone to just drop by with potential album art in the middle of the week."

"Told you we should have called ahead," Codie said.

Nessa didn't look appeased. We were familiar enough with the building that we didn't need an escort. Naomi would probably be surprised when we showed up out of nowhere in her office, but it would be a happy surprise. Phones were ringing in every office we passed, and I started to share Nessa's uneasy feeling.

Naomi's office door was open, and she was on her phone. Her glasses were off, her jacket was off, and the top button of her blouse was undone. She looked up when we blocked the light coming through the door and she muttered a curse, then waved us in. "Shut the door. Colin, I have to go. Yeah. They just walked in the door. Yes, I'll call you when I know anything."

I spoke as soon as she returned the handset to the cradle. "What happened? Is it Lana?"

"No. Uh." She pinched the bridge of her nose and I realized she'd been crying. "Dash Warren died last night."

The words didn't make sense to me, so I looked at Codie. She looked ashen, and Nessa was already tearing up. I looked back at Naomi and saw how pale and drawn she was. I went around the desk and put my hands on her shoulders to guide her into the chair. She pressed her lips together and nodded at me, as close to gratitude as she could manage at the moment. I knelt in front of her and took her hands in mine.

"How did it happen?"

"Her heart. She had a... a..." She sniffled and closed her eyes. "She was born with a heart defect. She took medication since she was a teenager, and she had surgery on it a few years ago. We thought it was..." She choked on the word. I stroked her knuckles and whispered that she was okay, and she squeezed my hands.

Nessa said, “So what’s going to happen now?”

“Nothing, as far as you guys are concerned. The label will go on and all your contracts are…” She sliced her hand sideways. “Dash took care of all of that when she set up Cartography, so you don’t have to worry.” She sniffled. “Right now we’re just trying to deal with the fallout. It hasn’t hit the news yet, by the grace of God, but it’s only a matter of time.”

I looked across the desk at Codie, who was still standing in the doorway, and I knew instantly she had come to the same conclusion I had. She nodded once, but it was Nessa who gave voice to what we were all thinking.

“It’s time to bring Lana back.”

Track Nine

I had already forgotten my ban on all winged modes of travel, eagerly accepting Naomi's offer to use the company jet to go down to Vegas. Codie and Nessa insisted that I should go alone and eventually I had to agree. If we all showed up, Lana might think we were ganging up on her. So I boarded the plane alone, feeling awkward and tiny as I sat in the vast and empty cabin and watched the country roll by underneath me. I imagined the plane was sitting still and we were just hovering as the planet rotated, slowly bringing Lana back to me. Then I realized that the world would have to be rotating the wrong way for that to be true, so eventually I just closed my eyes and tried to think of what I was going to say.

Nessa had written down all the clues we'd gathered during Lana's sabbatical. She had been seen three weeks ago at the Luxor in the company of a mysterious tall blonde, which someone else hinted may also have been a celebrity. A blog post revealed that Lana, alone, had been seen at a restaurant off the Strip where she happily posed for pictures. To a fan, she would have looked happy, but all three of us could see the bags under her eyes and the strain in her smile and the pain in her eyes.

We used a phony account to start a new thread on our website's bulletin board, pretending we'd also seen her in Vegas and encouraging others to post information about Lana's Vegas getaway. Naomi warned us that we were potentially opening ourselves up to a situation where our own future vacations would become scrutinized in the same way, but keeping tabs on Lana was too important. We all agreed we were willing to risk it.

There were enough reports of her at the Luxor that we felt confident she was staying there. I just hoped that the front desk was willing to give out her room information.

When I arrived in town, I used the airport bathroom to make myself look a little more presentable. I hadn't slept since hearing the news about Dash the day before; I doubted any of us had. Before I left I tasked Nessa and Codie with taking care of Naomi. I could see that she was almost burnt out with the stress of holding back the media hounds. Enough rumors were swirling that everyone knew *something* had happened. Most of the speculation involved Lana leaving the band, but it was only a matter of time before the truth was revealed.

At the Luxor, the sheer size of everything didn't help my feeling of inadequacy. I approached the front desk where a black man in an immaculate suit straightened almost imperceptibly and smiled. I cut off his standard greeting and said, "I'm sorry. But I'm in a bit of a hurry."

"Of course, ma'am. How can I help you?"

"I'm Karen Everett. I'm in a band called–"

He nodded and his smile widened. "Of course. I know who you are."

"Oh. Um, our lead singer is staying here, but I'm not sure which room. I was hoping you might be able to help me out."

He winked and began typing. "I totally understand. You want to surprise her."

I tried to remember what people were saying online. Despite the tall blonde celebrity, did people still assume Lana and I were still together? That thought prompted another... *were* we still together? Despite everything, was this just a speed bump? I didn't want to think about that right now. There were so many more important things to stress over.

The clerk handed me a key card. "It's room 402." He pointed me to the appropriate elevator and gave me another not-quite-professional smile that told me exactly what he thought was happening. I didn't care, so long as it got me to Lana without any fuss.

I thanked him and headed up. When I found the room, I paused for a moment in front of the door. I still didn't know what I was going to say, but I knew it wouldn't be pretty. And didn't people say the first casualty in any fight was the battle plan? I steadied myself, preparing myself for anything, and knocked.

"Just be alone," I muttered, looking up toward the ceiling. "I know you've been fucking around, but for right now, please, just be alone..."

The door opened. Lana was wearing a white T-shirt over boxer shorts, her hair arranged in a braid that took five years off her face. She looked like she had when I first saw her and my breath caught in my throat. She smiled without rancor or humor and tilted her head to the side.

"So you guys found me. Took you long enough."

"We've known where you were the whole time." A lie, but a small one. "We just thought you needed to get away for a while, so we didn't come after you."

Her smiled wavered. "Well... thanks. What changed?"

"Can I come in?"

She narrowed her eyes at me. "Something happened."

"Lana. Please."

She stepped aside and I went into the room. The sheets were tangled, and I counted four empty wine bottles placed strategically around the room. A pair of

French cut panties had been abandoned at the foot of the bed and I gestured at them as Lana passed me.

"Not exactly your style. The Amazon?"

"Wow. You guys have been keeping track of me." She took the panties and, after a moment of indecision, tossed them into the bathroom. "No, Kitty had to go back to LA for work." She sat on the edge of the bed and looked up at me. "Tell me what happened. Was it Codie or Nessa?"

You were fucking someone named Kitty? I pushed that thought away. "No, they're both fine. Worried about you, but fine. It's Dash."

Lana sighed. "Is she mad about postponing our next album? I mean, I assume you postponed it."

"Yeah, we did, but Dash didn't mind. She... she had a heart attack the other night, Lana. She didn't make it."

Lana blinked. "What do you mean she didn't make it? She died?"

I nodded, fresh tears brewing behind my eyes. "Yeah."

She stood up and moved toward the window, then walked back to me. "She's only... she's in her forties."

"She had a heart defect. The funeral is going to be Saturday. There will probably be a public memorial service sometime around then." A thought occurred to me, the perfect angle to take. It was risky, but if one couldn't gamble in Las Vegas, what was the point of visiting? I ran my hands through my hair and started for the door. "So... that's what I came to tell you. I guess I'll see you when I see you. Good-bye."

Lana turned. "What?"

"I didn't want you to hear about it on TV or from someone in the elevator. I wanted you to hear it from me, and not over the phone. So I told you, and now I'm going home."

"You didn't come to drag me back?"

I scoffed. "So you could just run away again the next time we turned our backs?" I crossed the room and cupped her face, kissing her forehead. "I love you, Lana. We all love you. And we'll be waiting when you're ready to come back. But I'm not going to force you to do anything. Take as long as you need."

I let my hands linger for a moment, then let her go and walked to the door.

"Karen."

I closed my eyes and hoped.

"Give me a second to pack, okay?"

"Sure." I kept my back turned until I was sure my victorious smile was under control. "I'll help you."

Track Ten

I had never been to a funeral where the deceased had already been eulogized countless times in the media. When Dash's death was formally announced, it was hard to turn on the news without hearing someone talk about it, and it was near impossible to listen to the radio without hearing one of her songs. The first time I heard "Ship in a Bottle" on the radio after her death, I thought I would never stop crying. I felt the tears starting up again as I listened to the reverend at the graveside, and Codie slipped her hand into mine. I squeezed it and glanced over to see Lana had her arm around Nessa, who was rapidly blinking through a downpour of tears.

The mood had been less friendly when we got back from Vegas. Codie was pissed and Nessa was irritated but glad to see Lana was okay. She apologized, threw herself on our mercy for forgiveness, and promised she would never do it again. Codie finally broke the silence by saying, "There can be exceptions. We'll let it slide if you get stabbed again."

With the ice broken, we were able to help Naomi through the hardest part of the news cycle. Dash didn't have any family, so it fell to those she was closest with to be the face of tragedy. Suddenly Naomi's life of hiding in the wings was over, and she was the one putting on makeup and facing the cameras.

We learned all sorts of things about Dash's life in the days leading up to her funeral. Her birth name was Dashiel, and she was initially raised as a boy. When her parents died and she was taken in by her grandmother, she was dressed and treated as a girl. After hearing that story, I dug out my CDs and found Dash's first three albums, all of which included liner notes where Dash was dressed as a man. All I knew was that Dash identified as a female, and was - as far as I knew - definitely a woman. I hadn't been *that* drunk in Greece.

The funeral was meager, and would have been heartbreaking if there wasn't a second, public ceremony a few miles away. Dash's fans were currently crowding a church to say goodbye, while a dozen of us who knew her best froze under a drizzling rain to pay our own final respects. The reverend stood under the hastily-erected awning, his shoulders hunched due to the occasional droplets that made it under the collar of his mackintosh. He closed his Bible and lowered it, then gestured to someone who was sitting in a nearby folding chair with a tape player on his lap.

"As requested in Ms. Warren's will, we will conclude the ceremony by playing one of her most popular songs." He nodded to the radio holder, who pressed a button. We were prompted to proceed past the casket to say our final goodbyes as a soft acoustic guitar melody began playing.

"We know this can't last forever,
It ends for all of us, rich or poor, dumb or clever
Sooner or later we'll all be put to rights
If you're the last one out, turn off the lights."

I slipped my arm around Naomi's elbow, supporting her as she touched the back of her hand to Dash's cheek, whispered a goodbye, and then let me and Lana half-carry her away from the grave. We sat on the bumper of the company car, rainwater soaking through the seat of our pants, and Naomi took off her glasses to pinch the bridge of her nose. The rain had soaked her enough that she didn't bother trying to wipe away her tears.

"We met in college," Naomi said. "I was so in love with her, but she never felt the same way about me. I settled for managing her career, because it was enough to just be around her."

"So that's why she was famous," Lana said. Naomi looked at her, and Lana shrugged. "You showed people what you saw. How could they not fall in love with her just like you did?"

She chuckled softly. "I guess. When she started Cartography, she put me in charge of the talent. I was supposed to assign you guys to a manager, but I didn't. I couldn't let you go. History repeated itself. I was selfish, and I channeled my desire into making you famous."

I shivered from the cold, but my cheeks were burning. "Naomi..."

"Hey, we both agreed it was casual. At least I got to be with you for a little while." She looked at me, eyes red. "It's okay, Karen. I'm okay with being the one who loves, rather than the one who is loved in return." She leaned in and kissed me. When she broke the kiss, she brushed her thumb over my bottom lip. "Thanks for helping me this past week."

I nodded, and Codie and Nessa joined us. "Everything okay?"

"Yeah." Naomi put her glasses on. "Come on. Let's get out of this rain and into something alcoholic."

We drove back to Cartography's main offices, where a private memorial in Dash's honor was being held in the studio theatre where we'd shot our first video. A refreshment table was set up on stage and everyone took their drinks and snacks down to sit in the chairs as if waiting for the show to begin. There was a show, in fact, and it started an hour after everyone had arrived. Naomi brought out a projector screen and showed us home movies of Dash at college, recording her first album, and "hidden camera" footage of Dash in disguise convincing people in stores to buy copies of it.

I remembered being with Dash on Lesbos, the night after Lana and I slept with her. The day had been so surreal, so unusually ordinary, that I'd never fully processed it. The whole day was like a dream that was only now coming back to me in full color. I was sitting with Laura, our fingers linked, and she was my anchor to the present as my mind cast back to that day.

Dash leans against the rail, naked except for extremely sheer white pants riding low on her hips and two small blue triangles of cloth over her breasts. Her body is long, lean, tan, and I've been hypnotized more than once by the movement of her muscles or the flat line of her stomach. The same body I fantasized about so many times as a teenager, and now I know how it tastes. I know how it feels on top of me. The wind makes her hair look as if it was dancing. Some of it tickles my arm and I move closer to feel the brush of it. Dash reaches over and covers my hand with her own. She strokes my knuckles.

"Are you okay?"

"Yeah." I nod. "Yeah, I'm good."

"Good. You and Lana were so beautiful together. I couldn't help inviting myself. And it's not like you were kicking me out."

I could only blush. "Well, we'd have to have been extremely drunk to say no to Dash Warren." I take a risk and kiss her shoulder. It feels natural, so I move up to her lips. I'm kissing Dash Warren, and I can hear Lana behind us. I turn, and Dash's hair whips across my face to obscure my vision.

"Beautiful shot," Lana says. "That's going in the scrapbook."

After the home movies ended, Naomi asked us if we wanted to play a few of Dash's song. Radiation Canary took the stage in our funeral clothes, and suddenly all I could think of were funeral clowns. I swallowed the lump in my throat and ignored the lyrics floating through my head (*"You make a lot of noise and you dance all around, but for all your sound and fury you're just my funeral clown."*) and began playing the first Dash Warren song I could think of. Lana invited Laura and Ella to join us, and soon the other acts in the room joined us on stage.

I can't imagine we sounded good, but we were certainly loud enough that I know Dash heard us.

Track Eleven

Lana's return to the group felt like an unofficial reunion, and they spent a few days getting used to each other again. It took a while to get over the hurt feelings, seeking out and falling back into their old rhythms. After a week or so, Lana realized they weren't just trying to get back to what they had been before her injury; they were trying to get back to who they'd been before she and Karen started sleeping together. It was a new age for Radiation Canary, one in which the leads were once again just very good friends.

By the end of summer, they only had a handful of songs written for the new album and only "Hypermnesia" was officially recorded. Rather than rush through it just to get something out "on schedule," they decided to relax and take a few months to put out something they could be proud of. Considering the year started with one member of the band being brutally attacked, the fans couldn't be too upset at having to wait.

Lana suggested a Dash Warren tribute album, and Naomi jumped on the idea. Radiation Canary was tapped to cover two of Dash's songs, "Last One Out Turns off the Lights" and "Blinked and Missed It." Lana was asked to do a multitude of talk shows to discuss the aftermath of her attack, and talk-shrink Dr. Dee tried to get her on a special about celebrity stalkers. Lana declined most of the offers, but took the ones from shows she actually watched.

In September, seven months after her attack, Radiation Canary contacted *Settle In, Seattle!* and offered their first live performance after the attack. The show agreed and arranged a full hour to the band, with a brief interview of all four band members followed by two aired performances and another specifically for the website.

The Radiation Canary special aired three days before Lana's birthday. They doubled up on their interviews; Lana went out with Codie, and Nessa went with Karen.

Lana was grateful for the sensitive, understanding way Nick handled the interview. He obviously discussed the stabbing and what followed, but he quickly shifted to more comfortable topics like music and future albums. They talked about Dash, which Lana and Codie both had a hard time getting through, but

Nick didn't push them. He made it clear that they could control when the show went to commercial with just a hand signal.

Once they were off what Nick called the "Oprah-brand tear jerker stuff," Lana regretfully announced their sixth album would be delayed a bit, and Nick feigned irritation.

"Boy, you get stabbed seven times and suddenly you get lazy."

Lana shrugged. "If only she'd stopped after six."

"Another reason to hate the bitch." Nick leaned forward, angling his body toward them like a conspirator. "Now, Lana, I hate to do this to you, but I ran it by your band mate and she cleared it for you. You can thank her later."

Lana looked at Codie, who already had a 'don't kill me' expression on her face. "Uh-oh. You know last time I was surprised with photographs, it wasn't exactly family-friendly television."

Nick laughed. "Don't worry, we have no incriminating photos. No photos at all, I swear. What we *do* have is a videotape from Codie Renton's personal collection." He looked past the camera. "Pete, do we have that all cued up? Good." He put his hand on Lana's wrist. "I fought to keep this off the air, trust me."

Lana gulped loud enough to be sure it was picked up on the microphone. "I'm scared." She looked at the monitor he pointed to and a video started playing. At first she couldn't tell what it was, but then she recognized the backdrop. She clapped both hands over her mouth and her eyes widened. "Oh, my God."

On screen was Lana Kent, in torn blue jeans and a baggy T-shirt, rocking out to a Spice Girls song. Her hair was much shorter, and a wide wave of bangs obscured her forehead and eyebrows. She sank down in her chair, laughing so she wouldn't scream with mock horror, watching as her seventeen year old version writhed and strutted through a godawful version of a song she was embarrassed to admit she even knew how to play.

When the tape ended, Lana was almost completely slumped in her chair, hands over her eyes with her fingers spread. "Is it over? Is it over?"

Nick tapped his temple. "Oh, it'll never be over in here."

Lana pushed herself up. "They were so popular back then. That's my excuse, and I'm sticking with it. And it was so much fun to perform. You could not sing that song and feel bad."

"That is true." Nick adjusted his tie. "Not that I, uh, ever tried singing it in front of my mirror with a hairbrush. That's slander, and I'll sue whoever said I did." He looked around furtively and then cleared his throat. "In all seriousness, that was a..."

"It was a talent show for our high school. It was, ah..." She snapped her fingers and looked at Codie to fill in the blanks.

"Unique Night. Everyone signed up to show what made them unique. Juggling or acting or, if you were two girls with access to musical instruments, you showed that you could make up a band. We were called Little Cat Feet back then."

Nick laughed. "Excellent name for a band."

Lana was still blushing. "I had completely forgotten about that."

"That's called a mental block," Nick said. "And it was a very... passable performance." The audience tittered.

"Hey, you laugh, but that got us a solid eighth place finish," Lana said.

Nick's voice suddenly got serious. "Well, you're number one with all of us. I want to say from the bottom of our hearts, everyone here at *Settle In, Seattle!* is thrilled that you're okay. You really had us worried."

Lana blinked back tears. "Yeah, I was kind of worried there too, for a second." She felt the mood becoming maudlin, so she tapped the desk with two fingers. "Oh. I do have one bit of band information that I forgot to share with you, Nick. Radiation Canary is currently looking for a new drummer. Preferably one who threw out her VHS tapes years ago." She turned and shook her fist at Codie. "I mean, seriously! It's the twenty-first century!"

Nick slapped his desk. "No! Play nice, ladies. We'll get these two into counseling, and we'll be right back with the heart of Radiation Canary, Karen Everett and Nessa Grace. Stay tuned. Ladies, no fighting."

When the cameras and microphones were turned off, Codie said, "Okay, seriously, how mad are you?"

"I'm pissed I didn't think of it first." She grinned. "What was that, senior year?"

Codie shook her head. "Junior year. Senior year, you dressed in drag and did a song from *Newsies*."

Lana shushed her. "Not in front of the TV man. He'll get ideas."

Nick cupped a hand over his ear and leaned closer.

After Karen and Nessa's interview, the band moved to the performance area. Despite tickets to the show being free and first-come first-serve, their appearance had been promoted so heavily that the room was packed with Radiation Canary fans. Karen made her way over and nudged Lana's arm.

"You okay?"

"Yeah. Just stay behind me, all right?"

Karen smiled. "Where else would we be?"

Nick moved to stand between them and the camera, holding up a copy of *Rome Burning*. When the show came back, he held it up next to his face. "And now, first performing a song from their now-certified platinum second album, I give you Seattle's own... Radiation Canary."

In accordance with Dash's will, the chairman of Cartography's board of directors was to take over the company. A few days before Thanksgiving, a letter was issued to all artists associated with the label. Lana stood in front of the band to read the pertinent parts out loud. "Cartography will be considered as much Dash's legacy as her music. Dash's dream was to create music that people loved, and she did that by herself for many years. With this label, she created the means by which a great many other artists can follow in her footsteps. I won't say that things will remain exactly the same because I'll never be Dash Warren. But I will do my best to ensure that what she started will continue on without her at the helm."

Nessa exhaled. "So no cleaning house, no new regime. That's good."

I nodded. I didn't want to admit how worried I had been that the label would switch gears. It seemed like Dash had known what she was doing when she named her successor.

Lana put the letter on top of a speaker and put on her guitar. "You heard the man. Business as usual. I held you guys up too much already. Now we're going to go double-time to get this album out. You ready?"

"Hell yeah," Codie said.

Lana played the first chords of "The Blackout's Lullaby" and smiled at me. "Then what are we waiting for? We have an album to make."

Album Six

VANCOUVER TO MOSCOW LIVE WITH THE WASHINGTON STATE ORCHESTRA

(2010-2011)

Pre-Show

2010 became the year of Radiation Canary coming out of the shadows. We'd spent so much of our ascent hunkered down, moving from one concert to the next, and ducking in and out of studios to keep up with my desire to release a new album every year that when we finally stopped to take a breath, we were shocked to discover how many people wanted to see us whether we were singing or not.

Lana spearheaded our appearances by going on *Dance Stars*. She appeared in a tuxedo and fedora and performed an incredibly sensual tango with the host, Kitty Diehl. Kitty's costume was basically several silver streamers sewn together in a strategic pattern, leaving most of her tall and slender body on display as she and Lana danced to a pre-recorded version of "Scene of the Crime."

I sat in with the house band on *The Late Joe Waverly*, a talk show that aired at one in the morning. Waverly ad-libbed several conversations with me, and according to the internet response, I was refreshing and funny. I was just glad the microphone hadn't picked up my heart pounding every time I had to speak on camera. Nessa pointed out that for the first three episodes, every time I was on-screen, I had my violin balanced on my knee with my hand choking the neck as if I was using it like a shield. On the fourth and fifth nights, I had dropped the shield and seemed more relaxed.

Lana secretly started seeing a therapist to deal with the aftermath of her attack. She did a public service announcement for survivors of domestic assault.

I was still living in Codie's guest room. She never expressly told me to get out, but familiarity bred contempt. We started bickering like sisters, arguing over inconsequential things, and basically getting in each other's way. I finally realized I had to get out if I wanted to preserve my friendship with her, and I could sense her relief when I told her.

"I'm not saying you have to leave right away," she said, "but thank God I don't have to kill you in your sleep."

I hugged her. "Thanks for looking out for me all this time. I needed it."

"You're not the only one who loves her, you know," she said softly. "I was lucky I had you here to lean on."

Laura was also looking for a place to live, so I suggested combining our efforts. I found one gorgeous place in downtown Seattle that I lusted after from the moment the door opened. My brain wouldn't let me accept I could afford a place so extravagant, but my money manager assured me it was well within my range. The living area was huge, with the hallway to the bedrooms blocked by a freestanding wall. The kitchen was mostly open but blocked off by three counters so anyone cooking would still be able to enjoy the view.

The view. My God. The west wall of the living room was glass, providing an absolutely gorgeous view of the Sound. We toured the space and I found myself wandering back to the raised floor in front of the windows time and again. That was where Laura finally found me.

"You obviously love it," she whispered. She stepped up behind me and linked her hands in front of my waist. She kissed my neck and I shivered happily. "You should get it."

"It's so expensive." I looked out at the water, covetous that I could have this view all to myself. No one else in Seattle would have this exact view. "I can't justify spending that much on myself."

"So justify half."

"How could I get away with paying half?"

"Get someone to share the rent."

I smiled. "Have you spoken to Codie? I'm not exactly the world's best roommate. Who would want to move in here with me?"

"Are you going to make me ask?" Laura said. She kissed down to my collar, and I surrendered. Leaving the apartment and letting someone live there would have broken my heart. I couldn't imagine any other place capturing me the way this one did. I turned around in her arms and kissed her properly for the first time since Greece.

"I'll take it if you do."

It was the first time either of us had admitted we were looking for a place to live together. The pretense had been that we were just sharing the burden of house-hunting. But she smiled and nodded, and we went to find the property manager to let him know we'd made a decision.

After spending so much time trying to talk myself out of it, I was sure that something would go wrong with the offer and I'd lose it after all. But the deal went through and we were allowed to move in. Just like that.

My old apartment was a bitch to get rid of. We had to find someone who didn't mind that an assault had taken place just inside the front door. On top of that, we had to find someone who wasn't a fan just looking to live in my apartment. Naomi told me that I couldn't discount that chance, as bizarre as it seemed to me. But we finally found a retired couple, and I gave them a phenomenal deal on it since I could afford it, and because... well, I didn't need another reason.

Ted had a heart... episode. He refused to let anyone call it a heart attack. "Pearl Harbor was an attack. This was just a skirmish."

I sat up with Dad in the hospital. I was shocked when his cell phone rang at midnight and the display revealed it was Mom calling from New York. They talked for almost an hour, and when they hung up, Dad wasn't furious or despondent. Progress. Dear lord, after all these years, progress. Ted got out of the hospital and they went back to the hardware store. Dad said it was business as usual, just with a stricter diet.

Nessa surprised us all in the summer. She and her boyfriend Scott disappeared to Whistler for a week. When she came back, she was brandishing a new piece of jewelry on her left hand. She couldn't stop smiling as she showed us the ring. "November. We're not sure exactly when in November, but that's the ballpark."

Afterward, she took me aside and asked if I would be her bridesmaid. I was stunned, certain she would choose Lana since they'd known each other longer. "You don't measure how much someone means to you with time. I've only known Scott two and a half years, and we're getting married. I've known you for six years, and I want you to be my bridesmaid."

I accepted and, when Lana found out, she was legitimately relieved. "You do not want me responsible for anything that big. I'll definitely be there to celebrate, though."

We held the bachelorette party in Vegas. Lana finally introduced us to Kitty, who was walking on eggshells around me until I took her aside and thanked her. She had been there for Lana when I couldn't, and she'd gotten Lana through an incredibly tough time. Whatever the circumstances of their hooking up, I was grateful to her for that. She relaxed after our little talk, and by the end of the night the whole band had deemed her appropriate girlfriend material if Lana should choose to keep seeing her. The relationship was long-distance, with Kitty located in Los Angeles due to her television job. Once a year she also spent three months trekking across the country doing the live audition shows. The end result was that she and Lana barely spent a quarter of the year in each other's presence, and they took full advantage of the time they were together.

2010 was also what I soon dubbed the year of my insensate nightmares. One night not long after I moved in with Laura, I dreamed that I had lost my voice. Not laryngitis or a sore throat; my voice was actually gone and never coming back. I felt a hole in my throat where it had originally sat, and I remembered trying to scream for help. But no one came, and there was no door in the apartment. I woke crying, and spent a few minutes listening to myself breathe before I risked whispering. Laura stirred next to me but didn't wake, so I just held her until my alarm went off.

After that I was partially blind. I could see people and objects, but I couldn't read music. The pages of my notebook were horrifyingly blank. I tried playing by ear, but the resulting cat yowl was atrocious.

I suffered dreams where I couldn't hear, and others where I couldn't *feel.* I could play every song mechanically, but there was no heart behind it. I heard the crowd go from an eager roar to disappointed silence, and then I heard their departure as they stood up and walked from the theatre. I dropped my violin and shouted to ask where they were going, then turned to see Lana, Codie and Nessa walking off-stage.

"Where are you going?"

Laura kissed my eyelids, waking me. "Nowhere, baby..."

The worst dream by far was the one where I woke to find my arms ended at the wrist. No blood, no gore, just smooth and slightly flattened stumps where hands had never grown. I could function, but my violin and cello were useless to me. I woke crying silently, and Laura was holding me without a word. I sniffled and kissed her neck to let her know I was awake.

"Nightmare?"

I nodded. "Bad one."

"It's okay now."

I smoothed my hands over her back, spreading my fingers before rolling onto my back. I pulled her onto me, and she straddled my waist before sitting up. I moved my hands up, then dragged my fingers down her face. "I dreamt I didn't have any hands."

"I would have cried, too. I love these hands." She kissed one palm, then the other.

"Really? The fingers are so rough and callused."

"I love your fingers." She kissed the tips of them, and I dragged them down to her breasts. She was wearing a white pajama shirt with a wide collar, and I squeezed her breasts through the material. She arched her back and I moved my hands even lower.

"You love the music I make with them?" I turned my wrist over and slipped my left hand between our bodies. "Or the other stuff?"

"I like the other stuff," she whispered. She put her hands on the headboard, lifted herself, and gasped as two of my fingers pushed inside of her. "I like the other stuff a lot."

She rocked against me, and I used my hips to guide my hand against her. After a few seconds she released the headboard with one hand and reached back, tossing the blankets aside to cup my mound and press against me with her fingers. I grunted and closed my eyes, admitting in broken English that I liked her hands, too.

Afterward we held each other and kissed, and I ran my fingers over her skin just to prove the dream wasn't true. We finally moved to the shower, and I went out in my robe to find something to eat for breakfast. On my way I stopped, as I often did, and walked to the window. There was a small dream-catcher hanging next to the balcony doorway and Laura had threaded it with a small satin banner on which she'd written "This city is an emerald and it's yours." It still made me tear up when I saw it.

I watched the boats and ships of various sizes moving into the harbor, the cars speeding along the streets below me, and I curled my toes in the carpet.

Laura came out of the bedroom wearing a Femme Reapers concert shirt and nothing else. "What do you have to do today?"

"We're rehearsing for that big show at the Claremont. You?"

"El and I have to go up to Cartography for some contract hoo-hah. Three more albums."

"Congratulations! You deserve it." I kissed her and stroked her hair. "I can drive you to the ferry if you want."

"Oh, you don't have to."

I turned away from the window and smiled. "I know. That way you'll owe me a favor at some point."

"Devious." She held up the bread and raised an eyebrow, and I shook my head. I felt like bagels. Strawberry. I sat on one side of the kitchen counter while she worked in the kitchen. I rested my chin in my hand and watched her. She hummed one of her songs as she made eggs, and I smiled and closed my eyes, swaying to the melody.

"You guys are so amazing. I was a fan of the Femme Reapers before we ever met, you know."

"So you're a star-fucker?"

I chuckled. "Guess so."

"Good. Me too." She leaned across the counter and kissed me. "Besides, you couldn't have been that big of a fan. We only had one album out when you guys hit it big."

"Sometimes one is enough."

"So we've been all downhill from there?"

I shrugged. "I've been meaning to say something."

She finished her breakfast and sat across the counter from me. We ate in silence until I noticed she was staring at me. I smiled self-consciously. "What?"

"You're a good musician. You earned this apartment, your fame, and me." She took my hand and squeezed. "You've been dreaming about losing it all, right?"

Tears appeared in my eyes and I fought hard to keep them from falling. I shook my head and a few drops fell free.

"You work hard, Karen. And you're taking a little time to enjoy that. Just because this album is going to be a little late doesn't mean it's all going to crash down. Other bands take years off between releases. Hell, it's been eighteen months since our last album, and we're not even booked for studio time until January. Acts like Radiation Canary don't just implode, and they don't just disappear. Talent like yours doesn't go out of style. Ever."

I brought her hand to my lips and kissed the backs of her fingers. "I love you."

She curled her hand against my cheek. "I love you, too. Now eat up. You guys have a big show tonight."

I nodded and let go of her hand.

"Will you marry me?"

Laura stopped. "Today's pretty busy."

"So tomorrow, then?"

She smiled. "Are you serious?"

I shrugged. "I don't know. It's not an official proposal. I want at least one of us to be wearing underwear when that happens." She laughed. "But I see marriage in our future. I just want to make sure that's as... not-scary to you as it's not to me."

She narrowed her eyes a little, tilted her head, and took a bite of her breakfast. "You know I can always tell how movies end early on?"

"Yeah, you ruined *Inception* for me."

"I apologized for that. But the point is... this movie ends with some kind of bliss. Wedded or domestic partnership or common-law. Trust me."

I smiled. "Good. That's good to know."

Showtime

Lana wore sleeves. She kept feeling the cuffs on her wrists and glancing down to see what it was, then shaking her arms to feel the material against her forearms and elbows. Codie noticed it and said, "I saw a pair of scissors. If it's going to mess you up out on stage, let me know, and I'll cut 'em off right now."

Lana shook her head. "No. I'm getting used to them."

She wanted to show a bit of respect considering the venue. The Claremont was a fifty-year-old theatre, and the auditorium looked like the kind they showed on television all the time. Box seats with velvet curtains, rows and rows of seats stretching back into the darkness. The stage was five times as large as the first one they'd ever performed on. And then there was the orchestra itself.

The Washington State Orchestra, an august body of thirty classical musicians, filled the back portion of the stage. She got cold when she looked and saw them preparing, sitting behind stands with the music for Radiation Canary's body of work displayed in front of them. A symphony orchestra! Suddenly none of their music seemed worthy of the honor.

Codie and Nessa calmed her. When Karen arrived, they huddled together in the middle of the dressing room, joined hands, and bowed their heads.

"You guys ready?"

"Yeah."

Lana closed her eyes and said a quiet prayer. The concert was going to be recorded, and it would be released as a live album after *Amnesia*. It was peculiar to spend almost two full years on one album and then have another completed in a single night. Lana squeezed Karen's hand on one side, Nessa's on the other and, when they broke, stepped forward and hugged Codie. She moved her lips next to Codie's ear.

"Remember? Ms. Clinton's homeroom class. First thing you ever said to me. You asked to borrow my pencil so you could drum on your desk."

Codie laughed. "I wasn't going to give it back. You were the pretty princess. I knew I'd hate you, so I decided I might as well get a drumstick out of sitting next to you."

Lana laughed and cupped the back of Codie's head. "Who knew, huh?"

"Oh, I knew. As soon as I heard you play, I knew." She kissed Lana's cheek. "Let's go knock 'em dead, princess."

Lana took a deep breath and tugged on her skinny tie. She was wearing a white smoking jacket with black piping, deciding that if she had to dress up she would do it Rat Pack-style. Karen, ironically, was sleeveless. She wore a white tunic top that tied behind the neck, leaving her shoulders bare. She also wore a flowing black skirt and ballet shoes. They hugged, and Lana said, "If you play as incredible as you look, it'll be a hit."

Karen laughed. "That's a big if."

"No. You always play this well, if not better." She brushed Karen's arms. "You're always amazing. Every single time we go on stage or into the studio. If I'd auditioned band members, I could have searched for years before I found someone half as good as you. You're Radiation Canary, Karen. We're just your backup musicians, and I'm your voice."

"Oh, thanks a lot. I'd just managed to stop crying."

She kissed Karen's cheeks. "I love you, K. You're my sister... which is weird, because of all the stuff we did to each other when we were dating." Karen laughed, and Lana stepped back. "Nessa, Codie. Come back in. Group hug, I don't care how corny it is." The four of them embraced, heads together and arms linking on each other's backs.

"Say a prayer," Nessa said.

"If you've got one," the other three echoed.

Lana said, "Everyone ready? Then let's give them a show."

They left the brightness of backstage and moved through dark corridors to the backstage area. Lana could hear the orchestra playing the overture and felt like she was the troublemaker out to ruin the concert for everyone else. There was a man waiting in the wings, backlit so she couldn't see his face, but he held them back until the last moment.

Karen slipped her hand into Lana's and squeezed. "Just like every other concert."

"Yeah, right." Lana squeezed back. "Thanks."

The music swelled, the faceless shadow man motioned them forward, and they stepped out on stage. Lana had a brief flashback to a poorly-lit bar, a garish light shining into her eyes, and the sound of beer mugs being dropped back to the table between every song. The memory was wiped away by the cheers coming from the crowd, and Lana's breath caught in her throat.

She put on her guitar and walked to her microphone. "Hi." She looked down at her guitar to make sure it was ready for her. It was new, but painted to look like the one that saved her life. She swallowed hard and looked back at the crowd. "Thanks for coming out tonight, and for always coming out to support us. It means a lot that you keep... coming back."

The set-list was printed on a laminated sheet of paper posted where the audience couldn't see it. She started an instrumental called "Improve the Silence" from their third album and Karen joined in on the cello. The music swelled, and the string section behind them turned Karen's quiet wave into a tidal swell. Lana closed her eyes and felt the music physically wash over her as it gathered on the stage and poured out to the audience.

The orchestra added a depth to the song almost immediately. Lana had heard digital recordings of the orchestra playing their music when the band first agreed to this concert. She was blown away by the fakes, knocked flat by the rehearsals, and now with the crowd in place, she braced herself for a complete mental breakdown.

After the first song, Lana and I took advantage of the applause to switch places. I paused to take off my slippers. When I looked up, Lana was smiling at me. I nudged her with my elbow as I walked to center stage, holding the violin by my side as Lana took position behind me. I waited for the applause to die down and then began to sing "Emerald" a cappella. There were a few cheers and shouts that erupted like sparks in the darkness, but I tuned them out and sang.

By the third line, the audience was singing along with me. When we reached the chorus, the string section behind me picked up. The music swelled and joined the crowd's singing, combining to cover me like a wave. I had tears in my eyes when I stepped back and began to play, Nessa's piano sounding like rain on the rooftops.

How many people were in the room at that moment? How many were singing words I'd written so damn long ago? How many pairs of hands were making birds because I'd decided to put a bird in our band name? My eyes were burning as I moved the bow along the strings, lips pressed together as I paid attention to my fingering. The music felt alive, and I closed my eyes so I could feel it flow. I was worried about the strength of my voice, so I ad-libbed when the interlude was over. I turned, curled my fingers at Lana, and she joined me at the microphone.

We sang the last verses together, turning the song into a duet. I put my arm around her for support, and we added our voices to the hundreds of people singing along. When we finally reached the end, Lana backed away and forced me to... allowed me to... sing the last line by myself as it had always been.

"My city's an emerald..."

The crowd applauded themselves, and I couldn't help but laugh. I pointed out at them and said, "The city may be an emerald, but you guys are golden."

Someone called, "We love you, Karen!" and I blew them a kiss as I moved back to position. Nessa winked at me and I smiled at her as Lana resumed her rightful place at the forefront. The spotlight cut around her body, making her look like a cardboard silhouette of herself. I took a sip of water, then picked up my cell phone and quickly snapped a picture. Her head was bowed, the guitar hanging loose in front of her, and I had the feeling it would end up in the liner notes somewhere.

"Thank you all," she said when the applause died down. "God, thank you so much. Seattle has been so good to us. So amazing to us from the minute we became a band, it's just amazing. We consider it an honor being from here, and we'll always consider ourselves Seattleites no matter where we go. This next song is, uh, dedicated to someone else who was always there for us from the beginning. And even though she's not with us, she'll always be a part of us. We miss you, Dash. This one is for you."

We played Dash's song "Ship in a Bottle," and the crowd fell reverently silent. Nessa, Codie and I didn't play, letting the orchestra provide Lana's backup. When the song finished, the crowd applauded. Lana bowed her head for a moment before she thanked them, turning to face Nessa. We went straight into "There Were Badgers Here," which Lana followed with some banter.

"The title of that song came from a line in the book *Wind in the Willows*. Hopefully you can tell we're a pretty literate band. K spends a lot of time in the library... we've decided to find it quirky and stop making fun of her for it. Mostly." A few laughs.

I said, "Not all of us can get by on our looks, Lana."

She turned to me, acting shocked as if the comeback hadn't been planned. When she faced forward again, she said, "Give the girl a couple gold and platinum records, she gets teeth. All right. No more teasing. And to show her there's nothing but love, we're going to sing one of the songs she wrote earlier this year. It's called 'Seven Hours to Moscow.' Hope you like it."

I put aside my violin and took up the cello. Lana and Nessa started us off, and I joined in as Lana started to sing.

"You say you'll never speak to me again, except I'm your ride
So you settle like a martyr on my car's passenger side
You stare out your window at Oregon on the other side of the river
We've got seven hours to get to Moscow from Vancouver
And I've got seven hours to change your mind
Three hundred sixty miles to Idaho
You don't like the shit on my radio
The Cascades are looking oh, so pretty
But you'd have to look past me to see
And I've still got seven hours to let you know

To tell you I'm sorry, to tell you I'm trying to change
To tell you I'm a fool, I'll stop acting strange
You're all I want, the only thing I need
And I've got seven hours to make you see."

Lana's voice was created to be backed by the orchestra. We'd been holding her back, keeping the band to a foursome. She needed thirty strings just to carry her strength. I was overwhelmed and I'd been prepared for it in rehearsals. I could only imagine what the poor audience felt like. I focused on my part of the song, playing when I was supposed to and adding my voice to harmony. It was odd to stop playing only to hear more strings taking over, but it was comforting to know they had my back.

"You laugh at my joke when we stop in Kennewick
At that diner that reminds you of the place we both got sick
Our history is stronger than your hurt
And stronger than my stupid words
I still have three hours to make that stick."

When the song ended (with the characters arriving in Moscow, Idaho, and deciding to give themselves another chance), the crowd roared. I looked back at Codie and Nessa, just to confirm I wasn't the only one having an out of body experience. Nessa winked at me and I smiled back at her. It was that moment I knew my insensate nightmares were over.

The four of us built something that was special to so many people. No matter what happened from this point on, no one would ever be able to take that away from us.

Nessa sipped her water and glanced at the set-list to confirm "Radio" was next. Her hair was braided tonight, the twin twists starting above her ears and then curling down to meet at the base of her neck. She felt like a rock star, like a bona fide celebrity, but she knew she wasn't. Not really. She watched Lana and Karen and knew who the real stars of the show were. She and Codie had accepted it a long time ago, and they were fine with their supporting role in the band. They got the accolades, they got to play along with the interviews and the music videos, but Karen and Lana earned their top spot by doing all the hard work, including the boring stuff. Karen was their voice, Lana was their face. She and Codie were the body. Heart, lungs, nervous system.

She caught Karen looking at her again and winked. Karen smiled and sipped her water as Lana bantered to the audience. From the outside it would look like Lana was randomly putting the music on hold to hold a conversation, and what was said was truly improvised. Lana chose some unsuspecting audience member and struck up a conversation about whatever was on her mind while the rest of them took a second to catch their breath.

Nessa looked down at her left hand, the ring shining on her finger. They were four weeks from the wedding date, four weeks before she became Mrs. Scott Wayland. She had worried about putting the band on hold, but it seemed her fears were unfounded. *Amnesia* and the live album were set to be released in 2011, and that would give them a little leeway to work on their seventh album. Plenty of time for her to go on a honeymoon and get settled in with her hubby before getting back to work.

She waited the rehearsed number of seconds and then leaned in to her microphone.

"Lana, are we going to finish the concert tonight, or...?"

The audience laughed, and Lana shrugged. "I don't know. I'm having a pretty good time with my new friends." The audience cheered, and Lana sighed. "But since this is going to be for sale as a CD, we might as well play an album's worth of music. So we might as well play something between getting acquainted. Karen and I wrote this next song while skydiving with some special-effects guys down in Hollywood. We kept pulling the cords trying to get the chutes out, but nothing happened, so K finally shouted over to one of the guys and asked where the parachutes were."

Karen said, "They said they would add them in post."

"Is that really when you wrote this song?"

"No, I think I wrote this one at lunch."

Lana sighed. "See, folks, this is why we lie. The truth is so boring. This song is from our first album, hope you still like it."

After "Radio," Lana performed a watered-down version of "Scene of the Crime." The lyrics were the same, but there was no corresponding dance due to the venue and the respectability of having the orchestra back them up. In rehearsal Lana also said it wouldn't be fair to the people who bought the CD. The audience was still thrilled, and applauded until well into the beginning of "Icarus."

From Codie's perch, she saw the flashing wings of people in the audience. Despite the much easier and less labor-intensive canary symbol, "Icarus" was still a big crowd-participation song. Groups of girls attached the wings to their wrists and the backs of their shirts and, when the song started, would stand up and sweep their arms back and forth in wide arcs. Tonight Lana said, "Fly for me, babies," before going into her chorus.

Codie finished the song with a flourish, and settled back on her stool. Her foot was hooked in a steel ring around the base of the seat, and she tensed and relaxed her muscles to keep them warm until the next song. She glanced toward the orchestra and spotted a man with a cello watching her. He had been watching her during rehearsal, too, and she offered him a wink. He smiled and drummed his fingers on the body of his instrument, and Codie chuckled.

Nice to see a man without a problem putting a big bulky instrument between his legs. No issues with size. She watched for Lana's signal to start the next song and, when it came, she counted them in by tapping her sticks together four times before she led them into the body of the song.

They premiered another new song, "More Rain in Rainier," and finally premiered Codie's tongue-in-cheek "wuv song" called "My Walla Walla Sweetheart." Codie sang it because none of the others could make it through without laughing. When the song ended, she twirled her drum stick, hit the cymbal, and said, "And that's why Karen writes the majority of our songs!"

Karen shrugged. "I don't know, Codie, I abso-woot-ley *wuv* it."

For their encore, they did a cover of Coldplay's song "Viva la Vida" which sounded as epic as the first time Karen heard it. They let it transition into "Say a Prayer," and they let the string section take over as Lana put down her guitar and took the microphone off the stand. "Ladies and gentlemen," she said, "you have been amazing and beautiful and not just tonight. You've given us a career in music, and that is a sweet gift indeed. You've made our dreams come true. From the bottom of our hearts, we thank you. Take a second to look to your left and my right… on vocals, violin, cello, and good looks we have Karen Everett." She crossed the stage. "Over here trying to hide behind the set decorations, number three in your programs but number one in your hearts, on keyboards we have the soon-to-be Mrs. Vanessa Grace Wayland. And back here, keeping us all in order, watching our backs on stage and off, we have the one and only Codie Renton." She returned to her position. "And I am the figurehead of this ship, the singer and guitar-player, the one with the least amount of talent but still takes all the credit, I am Lana Kent. And by our powers combined, we are Radiation Canary…. wishing you goodnight, Seattle! Goodnight!"

They left the stage, clutching one another as they followed the stagehand back to their green room. Lana was hanging off Karen down the corridor and stumbled a bit when they reached the green room. Once the door was closed, Karen half-dumped Lana onto the couch and crouched next to her so she could check her pulse. Codie lifted Lana's feet up onto the couch so she would be less twisted.

"Well, she hasn't done that in a while." Nessa felt Lana's forehead and cheeks with the back of her hand. Lana was unconscious, breathing steadily. "She pushed herself a little too hard tonight, I guess."

"Yeah."

Lana's eyelids fluttered and she looked at Karen, then Codie and Nessa beyond her.

"Oh, God. Tell me I made it off the stage."

"You did," Codie said. "Barely."

Lana sat up carefully and rubbed her face. "Good. That's good." She leaned back and smiled. "Well. That's another CD we have out of the way."

Karen laughed. She got a bottle of water from the cooler next to the table and opened it, handing it to Lana. "At this rate we'll be sitting on a half-dozen of them before *Amnesia* gets released."

Lana grinned and put her feet up. "Good. Maybe then we can have a real vacation."

We could hear the crowd shouting for a second encore, and Nessa sighed. "I wouldn't count on it, sweetie."

Karen shrugged and sat next to Lana on the couch. "I suppose it could be worse. They could have been begging for us to leave the stage."

"True. Very true. Blessing and a curse. Let's give them a few minutes. If they're still chanting, we can go out there and give them some instrumentals."

Nessa sat on Lana's other side and slapped her knee. "Sounds good to me."

Codie draped herself across their laps.

The photo taken five minutes later of the entire band slumped against each other, fast asleep, was taken by an anonymous employee of the theatre and later served as the back cover of the *Vancouver to Moscow* live album.

Post-show

"It sounds dirty."

"Doesn't it?" Lana looked at the computer again. "Vasovagal syncope. Sounds like a 'lady problem.'" She made the air-quotes. "But the doctor says it's nothing to get too concerned about. I just need to be more careful about my blood pressure before concerts. Sports drinks, salts, lots of fluids. Hopefully it'll keep me from fainting after shows so you guys don't have to keep catching me."

I was relieved to hear it was something so simple, and I knew Lana felt the same. She'd avoided going to the doctor about her fainting spells for years because she was afraid of what the diagnosis would be. This time I wouldn't let her chicken out and used Dash's situation to prompt her to action. I didn't want to just hope for the best and wait for her to collapse during the middle of a concert. Syncope was manageable. Plus, despite how it sounded, it really was fun to say.

"I don't care what you think of me, you give me vasovagal syncope..."

"Not a song," Lana said.

I had to agree with her, choosing not to write it down.

We were in my apartment in the chairs I had set up in front of the windows. Who needed a TV when Seattle was laid out in front of you like a life-sized postcard? Nessa was on her honeymoon, having survived being the center of attention for the entire length of her wedding. Codie was out in her plane and promised to fly over the harbor so we could see her from my living room. Laura was with her sister, writing songs for their new album.

It was really the first time I'd been totally alone with Lana since we broke up. There was no awkwardness, no uneasy shifting or making sure we didn't touch each other. My cello was standing beside my chair, and my notebook was open on my lap. We were bouncing ideas off each other for a new album, but Lana kept going back to the diagnosis.

"This says it can also be triggered by sex. So I have excuses for all those times I passed out right after we did it."

I snorted and doodled on my blank page. "Then Laura has the same condition. Maybe I just wear my girls out."

She closed the internet window and stood up to join me in front of the windows. "Speaking of… uh." She looked toward the door as she sat down, resting her guitar across her lap. "Are you sure Laura's okay with us being here alone? We could postpone brainstorming until Codie's here."

"Why? Do we need a babysitter? You're with Kitty and I have Laura. I checked the fridge and we don't have any ouzo, so we should be okay."

Lana chuckled. "Right. How are things going with you and Laura?"

I almost gave the standard answer, but the fact we were alone made me brave. "We're talking about commitment. Not marriage, per se. But something of the sort."

"Wow. That's really amazing. Good for you."

"How about you and Kitty?"

"Catherine," she said. "I've started calling her Catherine."

I raised an eyebrow. "That's new. Why the change?"

She shrugged and focused on her tabs. "Kitty was a one-night stand for a week in Vegas. Kitty was the host I liked flying down to Los Angeles to have sex with every once in a while. Catherine is… more serious."

I smiled. "So I guess that answers my question. And I guess Kitty Kent just sounds like a comic book character."

"Oh, shut up," she said, but she was smiling. "We're not to that point yet. We're not even living in the same state."

"But one day?"

She strummed a tune and shrugged. I didn't press; with Lana, shrugging was as good as confirmation. I made a mental note to keep my bridesmaid dress handy, just in case. We were in the middle of a discussion about whether or not to include "Seven Hours to Moscow" and "More Rain in Rainier" on our new album when Lana saw something out the window. She smiled and put down her guitar.

"Looks like Codie kept her promise."

We stood up and went to the window. Codie's little blue and white Cessna was following the shoreline, too far away to even hear the buzz of its engine. She had grown so much as a pilot that Nessa and I were no longer terrified of flying with her, although we did make sure we had a good supply of air-sickness pills in our pockets before we boarded. Codie was a fan of pulling stomach-dropping pranks on unsuspecting passengers now that she was skilled enough to make them work.

Lana waved and smiled, even though Codie was much too far away to see. She chuckled. "Amelia Earhart would have been proud."

"Actually, Harriet Quimby would be proud."

"Hm?"

I shrugged and almost let it drop. It wasn't really important, but I explained anyway. "Harriet Quimby was the real pioneer of women in flight. She flew across the English Channel, but it got overshadowed by the *Titanic*. She was a reporter, she drove cars, she did all this stuff that women weren't supposed to do in the 1910s, and she never apologized for any of it. She was a superhero."

Lana sat down. "Why haven't I ever heard of her?"

"She wasn't a pilot for very long before she crashed." I shrugged and went back to my chair. "But she wore this beautiful purple flight suit... she knew how to make people take notice. If she'd lived a little longer, she would be the icon and Amelia would be the footnote. History is full of people like her. Just left behind and ignored in favor of other icons. Amelia didn't crash and die, she disappeared. She was a mystery, which made her very attractive, so that's why we remember her. Marketing made her a star. Harriet just faded away."

Lana was resting her chin in her hand, one finger curled over her lips. "That's like Nikola Tesla. He invented all this shit that we still use today, and Edison was a conniving CEO who paid smarter people for their ideas and then took the credit."

"I adore Tesla." I shook my head. "He's the reason we have electricity right now, and he revolutionized the twentieth century, but he never got the credit he deserved. We should have been building statues of him, but he died alone and broke in a hotel room tending to doves because he couldn't stand people anymore. That's so tragic."

Lana was looking out the window so intently that I turned to see if Codie was about to buzz the building. Finally she broke her trance. "We should do a song about Tesla on the next album."

I tilted my head to the side. "Huh. That's not a bad idea. But..."

"But?"

"Well, it's just... history is full of people like Tesla and Harriet Quimby. They weren't flashy and they weren't celebrities, they just wanted to press the limits because the limits were there. They just cared about making that step so it would be easier for the person who came after them. We shouldn't just focus on one person, we should focus on as many as possible." I tried to think and wrote the names on a blank page. "Tesla, Harriet Quimby..."

"Alan Turing. He worked on the Enigma machine in World War II. He may have single-handedly helped us win the war against the Nazis, but he was gay. His reward for saving the world was chemical castration."

I wrote his name down. "Dorothy Parker."

"Oh, God, the Algonquin Round Table. Yes."

"So what are we thinking?" I asked. "An album dedicated to the waifs and strays of history?"

Lana smiled. "That's exactly what we're thinking. You can take Tesla, if you want."

"I want." I smiled and wrote "Minding Doves" across the top of a blank page. We'd had enough of a vacation. It was time to get back to work.

Album Seven
VAGABONDS & RAGAMUFFINS
(2011-2012)

Track One

Nessa woke before her alarm but didn't make any attempt to go back to sleep. She stayed where she was, feeling her husband against her back, listening to the silence of the house. She knew that in about fifteen minutes the alarm would chirp, Scott would roll over and silence it, and their day would begin. Right now she just wanted to hear his breathing. She moved her hand on top of her pillow and tilted it until the meager morning light caught the ring she wore. She smiled at it and then let her eyes wander through the room.

She had three platinum records on the wall - *Action After Warnings*, *Rome Burning* and *The Middle Distance* - and one gold, for *The Intervention*. Naomi assured them that it would go platinum soon enough, as would their latest offering. She couldn't imagine it. To be lucky enough to make money off music was one thing, but to actually be big? To be popular, famous... that was something else entirely.

Nessa closed her eyes and remembered the first time she met Lana. She'd been self-conscious about playing her piano in the foster home, so she saved money from her part-time job and rented a small room that local bands used to rehearse. She just wanted a private place to play, something of her own. Her first instinct had been to lie when Lana showed up and asked to share the space. She hesitated and Lana persisted.

"I wouldn't be such a bitch about it, but rehearsal spaces like this aren't easy to find. There are a dozen bands in this neighborhood alone." Lana stepped into the room. "I've heard you playing. You're really good, and we could use someone who knew their way around a piano."

Nessa gave in, and she discovered that playing with a band was much more gratifying than just playing solo. She never expected anything to come from the band, never really considered it anything more than a hobby. She smiled, eyes closed, and remembered Codie walking back in from one of her smoke breaks.

"She's out there again."

"Who?" Lana was sitting on a speak to tune her guitar, barely paying attention.

"The girl on the wall," Codie said. "You've seen her. Those long dresses, the jacket with the fringe on the sleeves..."

Lana looked up to search her memory, then nodded. "Oh, yeah. Blonde and cute?"

Codie grinned. "I wouldn't know from cute, but yeah. She's blonde."

Who knew what that anonymous girl would mean to them? A new name, a new direction, and a new life. Karen would deny it until her dying day, but she was the thing that made Radiation Canary happen. Without her, they would probably still be in the rehearsal room, playing covers of Adele and working mindless jobs.

Or... no. It had been seven years. Without Karen, they probably would have drifted apart by now. One day Scott would go through some old photos and ask her about the girls in a picture she'd used as a bookmark. "*Oh, those were just some girls I used to play music with. I wonder what ever happened to them.*" That is if she even met Scott in the other course of events. The thought frightened her, but not as much as the alarm did when it finally sounded.

She slapped it until it fell silent, surprised she had fallen back to sleep after all. Scott rolled over and kissed her shoulder, then her neck. She smiled and pressed back against him as she remembered the dream. "Morning, dear."

"Morning," he murmured, stroking her arm.

She rolled over to embrace her husband and greet him properly.

Codie stepped out of the tent and breathed deeply. Evergreens surrounded her, but the ground dropped so steeply in the cup between two hills that she could still see the diamond of a lake cupped between the two rises. The sky was so blue it was almost purple, and mountains rising up all around her. It was easy to forget that civilization was so nearby. Her plane and campsite were the only manmade objects in view, unless she looked too hard into the sky or scanned the distance too hard. There were always planes and distant boats. But for now, she could pretend. She started breakfast, then set up her small plastic folding chair so she could get to work.

They each had an assignment for the next album. Karen wanted them all to contribute at least one song about a hero that either didn't get their due or had been forgotten by history. Codie was fortunate that she'd just recently found an internet story about a woman who fit the bill.

A month earlier she read a *Seattle Times* article about a woman named Barbara Hillary who had visited the North and South Poles, being the first African-American woman to visit both ends of the Earth. An impressive feat on its own, made even more so by the fact she was seventy-five when she visited the first and seventy-nine when she visited the second. And all of that wasn't even taking into account the fact she was a cancer survivor.

Codie wanted to honor the woman, but she had no idea how to start. She opened the spiral notebook she'd bought and looked at the notes she had taken from the article. *You survived cancer, you journeyed to the most unforgiving corner of the planet, then you went to another desolate place just to prove you could do it, and now I'm writing a song about you. Who the hell do I think I am?*

She sighed and looked around, hoping for inspiration. She didn't know how Karen did it. During lulls in rehearsal, or while Lana was in the control room trying to perfect the track, Karen would pull out her little book and just start scribbling. Maybe that was the key. Maybe it didn't matter what she wrote so long as she wrote something. She chewed her bottom lip and started writing. "The woman from had never been on skis, went to the North Pole because someone said no one like her had ever done it before. She was special because she wasn't special, an ordinary person doing extraordinary things. She set foot where no one else had because she wanted to blaze the trail for whoever was next."

She sighed. "It doesn't have a beat and you can't dance to it." She scratched her temple and rested her chin in her hand, staring out over the treetops. She still had a few hours before she needed to be back in Seattle. She could take some time and work on it through breakfast. She looked down at the paper and, after a moment of consideration, wrote a tentative title at the top of the page.

"Ends of the Earth."

Lana never thought she would get used to the beach, to warmth in the morning and sunshine all day long. It was surprising what someone could get used to with a little motivation. She looked across the deck to where Catherine lounged in cut-off jean shorts and a white dress shirt with the sleeves rolled up. Her hair was undone, and she wasn't wearing any makeup. It was a photo the tabloids would kill for and every woman in America would hate, because it proved Kitty Diehl was so much prettier plain than she was slathered in makeup.

Catherine looked up, smiled, and then went back to her magazine. "You're looking at me again." She said it in an accusatory, British way that made the words come out sing-song. Lana loved that accent.

"I am." Lana turned and rested her elbows on the railing. "What are you going to do about it?"

"You forget I'm a television actress." She put down her magazine and settled back against the canvas of her chaise lounge, letting her hands hand to either side. "I adore being stared at."

Lana settled in for a long game, but Catherine quickly caved. She laughed and sat up, placing her feet on either side of the chair. "So what time does your flight leave for home?"

"In about three hours. But I can be a little late. What did you have in mind?"

Catherine stood up and motioned toward the door. "I'm going to teach the mountain girl how to surf. I have a wetsuit you can borrow."

Lana pushed away from the railing and followed Catherine into the house. "To be honest, I'm a little more excited about you helping me into the wetsuit."

The rehearsal space was cavernous and empty without the others there, but I wanted to focus on my Tesla song without any interruptions. It was probably the hardest song I'd written to date; I wanted to do the man justice but it was nearly impossible to say everything I wanted to say. How could I express his humanity without minimizing how amazing he was?

"The old man in room 3327, an odd quiet recluse
They can't take more from him, he's got nothing left to lose
Everything he made to advance human-kind
It made them millions, now he's left with doves to mind."

I didn't particularly love it, but I didn't hate it. I put down my pen, folded over the page, and picked up my violin. Maybe if I got the melody first, the lyrics would follow. I closed my eyes and began to play, filling my mind with everything I knew about Tesla. His story was tragic, filled with disappointment and heartache. The only real love he ever had was a potentially polyamorous relationship with Robert and Katharine Johnson.

I stopped playing and looked down at the notebook. I crouched and flipped through to a new page.

What if I've already written every song I have?

I chewed on my lip and stared at the words, letting them sink in. I'd been thinking them for a while. I felt so relieved when the others agreed to write songs for the album. Was I getting burnt out? How many songs did I have left? Did I really have a finite number of words in me? I flipped back to the Tesla song and stood up, lifted my violin, and went back to playing.

It was ridiculous. If there was a well for talent, then it wasn't finite. I just had to work harder to find the reserve. I closed my eyes and went back to playing.

Track Two

"So is that surfing?"

"Cheeky. I didn't even get you into the wet suit." Catherine kissed Lana's chest. "Next time you're down here, though, first thing. I'm getting you onto a surfboard."

"Mm." She kissed the top of Catherine's head. "It can't be as fun as what we just did."

Catherine chuckled. "No. But it's worth the effort to learn."

They cuddled a bit, kissing and letting their hands roam until the watch resting on the nightstand began to beep. Lana groaned, and Catherine whimpered, moving her lips to Lana's neck. She nuzzled as Lana reached out and grabbed the watch. She shut off the alarm and closed her eyes as Catherine's tongue moved over the soft skin behind her ear.

"That was the absolute last alarm. I have to go in ten minutes or I'll miss the plane."

"Can't your friend Codie swing down and pick you up?"

Lana smiled. "She's busy. I'm sorry, Kitty." She pulled back to kiss Catherine's cheeks and lips. "Who has the next trip? Are you going up or am I coming down?"

"You'll have to come down. The show has me shackled here for the next four months. And I'm not going that long without seeing you."

"Okay. We'll set it up." She kissed Catherine and reluctantly pulled away from her. She dressed on the edge of the bed, grabbed her carry-on out of the closet, and bent over the bed. "And I have two minutes to spare. Start the clock." She kissed Catherine and, a hundred and twenty-two seconds later, pulled back. "So I'll be a little late. Bye, sweetie."

"Bye-bye," Catherine sighed sadly. "I'll finish without you."

"Oh, you tease... have fun."

Lana slung the strap of her bag over her head, letting it bang against her side as she left the beach house.

The video for our latest single "Falling Up" was directed by a filmmaker known for his epic science-fiction fantasies. His first pitch apparently involved a scene in which all four of us are naked, but Naomi vetoed that before it ever got to us even though Lana said she would be willing to show a little skin if the video called for it. We spent two days in front of green screens, acting like children playing pretend, and then the set was closed so Lana could film her nude scene.

In the finished product, I watched myself being lifted off the ground and floating past the Space Needle. Codie loved her scenes, wide-eyed as she watched herself tumble through space without the benefit of a plane. We met over Puget Sound and mimed playing our instruments. I had never imagined a scenario where I'd be asked to pretend I was playing a cello while hanging from wires over what looked like an elementary school's gym equipment.

Colors swirled around us, then coalesced into a human form floating in the center of the triangle we made. A bare foot, a long stretch of bare leg, a curved hip. Lana's face filled in last, and she hung suspended in the middle of the rest of us with her arms strategically placed to avoid full nudity. Her hair whipped around her in the wind, and there were close-ups of her hands as she mimed playing, an excuse to show off her abs.

A shot of her from behind showed her scars, but I assumed most people would focus on the dimples above her ass. When the song faded, all four of us began plummeting to the ground. The real fall had only been about four feet and it ended on a foot-thick pad, but the director made it look like we were falling four stories.

We crashed into the water. As the song finally faded completely, Lana's head broke the water and she turned to face the camera. She blinked the water out of her eyes, smoothed her hair back with both hands, and smiled as the image faded to black.

Naomi swiveled her chair away from the TV to face us. "It's probably going to get censored. Some blurring here and there just in case something appears to be too... exposed. But that's the official version. What do you think?"

We knew the question was mainly to Lana. She was going to be the one with the side of one breast and the top of her ass plastered all over TV.

"I love it. I think it's beautiful." She shrugged. "And if people focus on the nudity, then let 'em. We'll get more hits on YouTube that way."

Naomi nodded. "Okay. And how is the new album coming along?"

"Good," I said. It wasn't technically a lie. "We should have enough to need the studio in January, maybe February. Then we should be ready to release it–"

"Next summer?" Naomi said. "I have that slot reserved for you guys."

"Next summer," I said. It was nice to have a deadline. Lana and Codie had both turned in their songs to me for fine-tuning, and I was amazed at the results.

Codie's song was about the first African-American woman to visit the North and South Poles, and Lana had written about Dorothy Parker. I loved the Parker song, and envisioned Lana singing it like a torch song. A smoky nightclub, a femme fatale in a black evening dress, making love to the microphone with ruby red lips as she moved her body to the slow, sensual beat. Codie's song was just as powerful, with an almost revolutionary sound to it. I wanted it to be loud, aggressive, and I knew it was perfect for her to sing.

My Tesla song was coming along well. My initial misgivings faded, and I focused on his final days. No inventions, no death rays, just a few doves he nursed back to health. The shift came when I realized Tesla's only real goal was peace. He wanted to give electricity away to whoever needed it, he wanted to create a weapon only to ensure the end of war... I'm sure people on the Manhattan Project would have had a few things to say to him on that, but his intentions were just. Tesla ended his life caring for doves because, in a very real way, he was one.

After the meeting, I lagged behind in the conference room to speak privately with Naomi. She smiled when she realized what I was doing and busied herself with organizing her things until the others were gone.

"Hi, Karen."

I smiled. "Hi. How have you been?"

She tilted her head to the side. "I've been okay. The new CEO is different from Dash, but he's keen on maintaining her legacy. He doesn't want to upset the boat, so we're all good so far."

"And personally?"

"Single," she said, "and I don't want that pathetic pitying look from you. I know how well you and Laura, and Lana and her Kitty Cat are doing. I'm happy for you both. I'm happy to wait for the right woman to come along." She raised an eyebrow. "Now, is that what you really wanted to talk to me about, or is there something else?"

I cleared my throat and looked to make sure we were alone. "How has *Amnesia* been doing, sales-wise?"

"Excellent." She opened her binder to find the information. "It's not quite on track with your previous albums, but it's trending the same way. The orchestra album is selling incredibly well, especially for that sort of release. Live albums tend not to do as well, but we don't have any complaints. Lots of individual song downloads. People already had 'Hypermnesia' from its original non-album release, but I don't think that's hurting the actual sales. Why do you ask?"

"You said that we were so successful because of market conditions and the atmosphere being right for us when we started out. People wanted to hear a band like us, so we filled a niche."

"Well, that and you're immensely talented."

I nodded. “Right, but you can’t drop a hat on any street corner without a busker showing up to perform behind it. There’s no shortage of talent. We got lucky.”

Naomi conceded that with a quick nod. “Yes, you did.”

“What I’m wondering is when our luck will run out. The conditions won’t stay the same forever, and people are going to move on from us.”

“That might not happen for years.”

“You’re right. But I’d rather be prepared for the possibility of it happening sooner than that. If we hold onto this until it starts the downward trend, we’ll be has-beens when we try to move on. We’ll ride the coattails into the ground and then spend the next twenty years doing county fairs playing all our old hits.”

Naomi frowned. “What are you saying?”

I wet my lips and hunched my shoulders. “I think we need to start thinking about how we want Radiation Canary to end.”

Track Three

We had pizza at my apartment, eating picnic-style on the floor in front of the windows. *Action After Warnings* was playing on the radio, one of the original pressings that was now selling for hundreds of dollars on eBay. I couldn't get over how young we sounded, and I kept turning my head so I could hear it better. I had told Lana about my conversation with Naomi during the ferry ride back to Seattle, and she was surprisingly calm about the idea and promised to help me bring it up with Codie and Nessa when we got back to Seattle.

Now she was taking over the meeting, something I was entirely happy to let her do. "We're not saying the band is going to break up immediately. We'll release *Vagabonds* and then get to work on our next album. But we need to decide if we want that to be our last album, and we should probably figure that out now. If it is going to be our last album, we should make it something special."

I looked at Codie and Nessa. "What do you guys think?"

Codie was sitting cross-legged, her elbows on her knees and her fingers folded in front of her lips. She dropped her hands and said, "Most bands get four, maybe five albums in a decade before they start to fizzle. This is our seventh album coming out, and we've been together seven years. It's about right. We even got above the trend, and we didn't have to release a Greatest Hits album to do it."

Nessa wiped her hands on a napkin and said, "We can look at it this way... we've hit amazingly big. We're famous all over the country, and we're at least known in other parts of the world. Greece still loves us, even though they're having troubles now."

Lana said, "I saw a rioter on the news wearing one of our T-shirts. I had mixed feelings."

Nessa smiled ruefully. "The point is, do we really have anywhere to go but down at this point? As a band, we're looking at either coasting or descending. And... selfishly... I'm tempted to agree because of Scott. I don't want to be doing concerts until three in the morning, recording for hours at a time, touring across the country... I want to start a family."

I said, "Why didn't you say something? We would have understood if you wanted to bow out."

She smiled at me. "That's not what would have happened. If I'd told you guys, it would have been the end of the band. We've always said that the four of us are Radiation Canary, and anything less is something else. If I wanted out, it would have ended the band. And I did not want to be the one who ended everything."

Lana cleared her throat. "I've kind of been thinking along the same lines." She looked at me and smiled. "I'm thinking of, ah, relocating."

I smiled at her. "To Los Angeles?"

She shrugged and looked down at her pizza. "It's not too bad down there, if you get past the sunshine and the heat. Besides, there are perks to living in California."

"British blondes?" Codie guessed.

Lana laughed. "Yeah. British blondes." She looked at me. "But I didn't want to abandon you guys."

Codie said, "I've spent my whole life trying to get away, move faster, thrill myself. This band got me my plane. I have what I need. I'll do session work and fill in for other bands to pay for my gas, but if Radiation Canary breaks up... hell, it'll give me all the time I need to really fly."

I laughed and a tear slipped free. "This was my idea, but you guys *could* act a little more upset about losing the band."

Lana put an arm around my neck and pulled me close, kissing the top of my head. "Look at it this way, K-bar... everything else about this band has been left up to fate. Codie asking to borrow my pencil, the two of us meeting Nessa, you finding the rehearsal space, me finding your book. Why should the end of the band be up to us? All we can do is recognize the end is nigh and figure out the best way to end things gracefully."

I kissed the back of her hand. "So what do you guys think? *Vagabonds*, and then one more album?"

"One last hurrah," Nessa said.

Codie nodded. "A goodbye to the fans."

"And a thank you," Lana added. "I wouldn't have chosen to end it, but all good things have to come to an end, right?"

I shook my head. "Not all things." I squeezed Lana's hand and looked at the others. "No matter what we're doing, or what we're called as a group, we're not going to end. We're going to stick together even if Codie flies to New Zealand and Lana emigrates to London... the four of us are going to be a family no matter what. Deal?"

"That, you don't have to convince me about." Codie held out her hand and sighed when no one followed her lead. "Come on, it's corny as hell, but we did the group hug thing before the orchestra performance. Hands in, bitches."

We laughed and piled out hands on top of hers.

Codie said, "Radiation Canary is one thing. The four of us are something else. The end of one doesn't mean the end of the other."

Nessa cleared her throat. "My grandma was the last real family I had. I grew up with foster families after she died, so I didn't really know what a real family felt like. Until now. I love all of you."

We echoed her statement, and Lana broke the handhold. "Okay, now that the important stuff is out of the way, I want parmesan on my pizza. Where do you keep it, K?"

"I'll show you." I unfolded my legs and she helped me stand up, following me into the kitchen. She glanced back to make sure Codie and Nessa were occupied before she put her hand on my arm to stop me. "What?"

"We talked about what we would do if Radiation Canary ended. What about you? You have plans?"

I shrugged. "Marry Laura."

Lana smiled. "Yeah?"

"It's what I want. We've talked about it, and the more we talk about it..." I hunched my shoulders. "Yeah."

"But what about professionally?"

I laughed quietly. "I talked to the managers Cartography got for us. They said we can live pretty comfortably for a long time on the money I already have, and the residuals that will come in from using our music in TV, movies... you guys set me up for life by giving me the sole rights to the lyrics."

"They were yours," Lana said quietly. "But that's not what..." She ran her teeth over her bottom lip. "I've been thinking about moving to Los Angeles for a while. My justification before all this was that we've been holding you back. Karen, you're so talented. Your music, and the words you write... I mean, my God, you saw the vigils after I got stabbed. 'Prayer' was basically a hymn to those people. Whatever happens to Radiation Canary, you can't stop writing. Sell your songs to other artists if you have to. Give them to Cartography, or give them to Laura for the Reapers. Whatever you do, don't stop filling those journals."

I blinked back my tears and turned away from her. "Wow. If anyone was holding anyone back, it was us with you. You're going to be a star, Lana. You don't need us."

"I've always needed you, K. All three of you. I'm scared about what'll happen without you."

"Well, like Codie said... we're not really going away. We're just going to spread out a little. I'll still be here if you need me." I nudged her arm. "And if you go solo and need some songs, I'll be happy to write a couple for you."

"Good."

From the other room, Codie shouted, “How long does it take to find parmesan cheese?”

Lana shouted back, “We’re still looking at the directory map. This apartment is fucking huge!” She kissed me on the cheek and I got the parmesan out of the cupboard before Codie came looking for us.

The thought of only having one and a half album left was terrifying, but it was also freeing in a strange sort of way. Knowing it would be the end gave us a chance to put our all into it. We didn’t have to wait and see how our sales did, and we didn’t have to rush to get it in before our fans drifted off. We weren’t going to be has-beens waiting ten years to announce the band was breaking up. I had a vision of us from the “Falling Up” video, plummeting to the water when the music came to a stop.

We were always going to hit the water, but now we had a chance to come up smiling.

Track Four

I fought back a smile as Laura applied my mustache. There was a picture taped to the mirror so she could get it right, and she kept referring to it as she ran a tiny brush over the hairs. I was wearing makeup so my cheeks would appear gaunt, and my eyebrows were darkened. Laura stepped back and declared my mustache appropriately masculine. She ran her hands down my chest, her fingers curling under the lapels of my jacket.

"My, my. You look so handsome, Mr. Tesla."

I arched a black eyebrow and stepped closer to her. "Be careful, my dear. If you stand too close, you may feel an electric shock."

"Oh, I felt that a long time ago," she admitted. She leaned into me and I captured her lips with mine. She pulled back almost immediately and rubbed her nose. "Kissing someone with a mustache is not exactly my thing. It feels like..." She dropped her eyes below the belt, shrugged, and I laughed as I smoothed my fingers over the facial hair.

"Well, it's not permanent."

She stepped behind me and adjusted the jacket's collar. "You do make a very handsome man, Karen."

I looked at her reflection. "Yeah? Maybe I can rent the suit for another day and bring it home."

Her hands slid over my waist. "Hm. Kinky. I like it."

I ran my hands up her arms and leaned back against her. I turned and kissed her, pulling her against me. I moved my lips to her ear and whispered all the things I wanted to do to her in Nikola Tesla's suit, how I would make her hair stand on end without electricity. She was beginning to press insistently against me when there was a knock on the door and we had to pull apart.

Lana, her dark hair styled into a 1920s bob, stuck her head into the room. "We... oops. Do you need a minute?"

"No. Uh, are they ready for us?"

"Yeah." She touched her top lip. "Your mustache."

"What about it?" I touched my lip and felt only skin.

Lana pointed. "It's on Laura's cheek. See you in a minute."

Lana looked as if she had stepped directly out of a sepia-toned photograph, donning the elbow-length gloves and pearl necklace as if she wore them every day. She was Dorothy Parker, and she was front and center for the album cover photograph. She would be kneeling with the three of us behind her. We were all dressed as someone we'd honored in one of the album's songs; Nessa chose Nellie Bly, ace reporter, and Codie was Harriet Quimby.

Naomi had found a photographer who specialized in simulating antique photos, and the costumes were only part of his preparation. His camera was older than any I'd ever seen, and he warned us that the exposure might take a minute or two. I made sure my mustache was smooth so the whiskers wouldn't tickle my nose and make me itch, then let the costumer put on my bowler so my hair was obscured. The portrait of Tesla we were copying had him hatless, but there was no way I'd ever make my hair look like he did. So we compromised.

We got into position, and the photographer adjusted us minutely until we were in the perfect position. As soon as he told us we couldn't move, I felt the need to adjust my collar, to scratch my cheek, to shift my weight to my other foot. I didn't know if we were allowed to blink, so I tried to do it as sparingly as possible.

To my left, Nessa spoke without moving her lips. "Anyone else's ear itch?"

"Now it does," Lana murmured. "Thanks for that, Ness."

I pressed my lips together to keep from laughing.

We ended up with ten songs for the album. Buckminster Fuller, Sojourner Truth, and Alan Turing all got their turn in our spotlight, as well as Sally Ride. We'd debated about whether or not she was really an unsung hero, but we decided to include her since she was unquestionably awesome and no one had really talked about her since the eighties. The album was rounded off with a song about unsung heroes in every day life, the people we met but didn't recognize. Teachers, of course, but also single parents and social workers. People, whoever they might be, that sacrificed themselves and their own needs to help others were our honorees in that song.

When we were finally allowed to move, Lana stretched while Nessa, Codie and I rubbed our ears and shook out the pent-up energy that had been urging us to move. We had gotten so accustomed to seeing the results on a digital camera that we were a little miffed that we couldn't at least check the finished product. He assured us we would be happy with the final picture, and we took him at his word. We had a backup plan for a worst-case scenario. Laura had been taking pictures during our stock-still moment. If the professional didn't come up with something we could agree on, we would just use one of those and digitally age it with... I don't know graphics, but I'm assuming magic would be involved.

"You know, we could keep this stuff for the concerts. Perform in the costume of each person we're singing about."

I peeled off the mustache. "The person who has to wear the facial hair gets to veto that idea, thank you very much."

Lana grinned. "Oh, come on. You'd look so cute up there with your little three-piece suit and bowler hat."

"Nope. I'm putting my foot down."

Codie said, "You really want to do nine costume changes in a single concert?"

Lana's smile widened. "Nah. I'm just busting Karen's chops."

I swung my foot up and booted her ass with one of my pointy-toed loafers. She yelped and spun on me, speaking in a thick New York accent. "Well! I've been kicked out of worse places by better people. Hrmph." She lifted her chin and stalked away, swinging her hips like a vamp from a silent movie.

Codie undid the buttons on her collar and stretched her neck as she watched Lana stalk away. "Good thing this wasn't our first album. She'd have glommed onto this image and never let it go. There'd have been no living with her."

Nessa chuckled. "She is right about one thing, though. You do look pretty cute in your little mustache."

I rolled my eyes and mashed my hat down so that it bent the tops of my ears.

My hands were flat on the mattress on either side of Laura's hips, supporting my weight so my knees could guide my body. My ankles were crossed, and I was still wearing the shirt, vest, and underwear that had come with my costume. Laura had added something extra special which was currently threaded through the open fly. I pushed into her, and she arched her back, moaning as I tried to figure out the right rhythm without collapsing on top of her.

"What do you think?" I asked. "Do I look cute?"

She chuckled and moved her body in time with mine. "Just... forget the mustache... and we'll be fine."

I grinned and began moving faster. I only had the rental for another three hours, and I intended to make the most of it.

Track Five

"This sucks."

We were onstage, and Lana had twisted so that her comment wouldn't be picked up by my microphone. I looked at her like she'd just told me she was engaged to a man, certain I'd misheard. "What exactly sucks here?"

"Look around us," she said, almost growling as she tossed her head toward the crowd behind her.

I looked, and I saw nothing to complain about. We were playing a benefit concert for breast cancer research and, as a lark, the organizer declared any woman who donated an extra twenty dollars was allowed to take off her shirt and enjoy the concert in just a bra. Bras were, of course, required. Apparently there were a lot of women willing to give, because as far as the eye could see were bras in every size and color (although white was predominant). A few of them had "Save the Boobies" written across their upper-chests in the same body-paint guys used to write on their chests for football games.

I raised my eyebrow at Lana. "And what do you have to complain about?"

"We didn't have this idea before you and I were in committed relationships. The wasted opportunities make me weep."

I laughed and kicked at her, but she moved away from me before my foot could make contact. Codie and Lana had both donated and were playing in their bras, but Nessa and I were being a bit more modest. The show was set up in three short acts broken up by half-hour performances by new acts recently signed by Cartography. We were smack dab in the middle of the second block of music; we had just finished "Monstrous Regiment" when Lana came over to talk to me. We went into "Band of Girls," and we would finish with "Complications" and "Survivors."

The tickets had sold out, which was good, and judging by the amount of underwear on display, quite a few people had splurged for the deluxe ticket. So the night was a success no matter what. I just wanted to be sure we got as much as possible without resorting to blatantly begging for it.

I looked at a well-endowed girl swaying to the music and wondered if we'd already passed the point of blatant begging.

At the end of "Band of Girls," Lana went to the microphone and said, "Ladies, I talked it over with Karen. And she said that if we get another hundred dollars before the next song ends, she'll take off her blouse."

My eyes widened. The crowd cheered. Codie clapped her drumsticks together and pointed one of them at me.

Lana turned and mouthed, "It's just one song!"

I bared my teeth at her, and she turned back to face the crowd.

"We're going to have a representative of Cartography Records going around during the song... there she is, wave so they know who you are, Irina. She's the one wearing the Cartography hat. If Irina gathers a hundred bucks before we finish 'Complications', Karen will take it off." She looked at me, eyebrows raised. "For charity, K. For charity."

I stepped forward and said, "Hundred and fifty."

"Hundred and... hundred and fifty, folks! You heard her, she's not cheap. Get those wallets out." She began playing, and I began plotting ways to get her back as Irina began moving through the crowd to gather the money people were holding out. I struggled to keep my mind on the notes and tried not to keep track of the money Irina was gathering up.

"It's the complications that make life interesting
The little moments that delight and the moments that sting
When the dark clouds roll in and block out your sun
Remember the world's not ending; it's just a complication."

We were nearing the end of the last verse when I caught movement off to the side of the stage. Laura, who had also paid the extra money to flaunt bra, was approaching with Irina. Irina was holding up a handful of bills, and I realized Lana's fundraising attempt had been successful. Laura faced the audience and lifted her hands, both index fingers extended to point at them before she spun on her heel and walked toward me.

"You are so dead," I half-laughed as she circled around behind me.

She leaned in, her lips brushing my ear, and put her arms around me. "Give the people what they want. Can I?"

I nodded, and she slid her hands up to the top button of my blouse. The crowd whooped and hooted, but I kept playing. I felt a little like that multi-armed goddess, lifting my elbows to keep playing as Laura skillfully undid the buttons of my blouse. I glanced over at Lana to see she was watching intently, a lascivious grin on her face. She winked at me, and I stuck my tongue out at her. Laura pulled the blouse off my shoulders, and I stopped playing long enough to get my hands free of the sleeves.

Lana cheered. "God, I love charity."

Laura kissed my neck and twirled my blouse over her head as she and Irina went backstage. I placed my violin back against my shoulder, the cool, smooth curve of the instrument on my bare flesh, and decided I liked the way it felt. I'd never felt so open and exposed on stage, and it was a thrilling sensation. I played the last note of the song, lowered the violin, and smiled at Lana.

"How's it feel?" she asked.

"Uh, to be half-naked on stage or get stripped by my girlfriend in front of a crowd of people?"

"Either!"

"*Fan*-tastic," I said. Lana laughed, and I looked over at Nessa. "The question is, how much money do we have to raise to get Nessa to take it off?"

Nessa didn't hesitate. "Don't get too excited, ladies. It would be six-digits. I know what a peek at my girls is worth." She winked at us, and I couldn't help but laugh. We had one more song in this set, and then I would spend our half-hour backstage negotiating with Laura to get my blouse back. Or maybe not. When else would I get a chance to perform so near to topless?

I just had to remember not to take a bow. Better safe than nip-slip.

When we left the stage, Lana put her arm around my waist and leaned close. "Too far?"

"No, it was fine. I just hope I didn't blush too much."

When we went offstage, we'd be replaced by a band called the Mean Wells. Then we would come back and finish out the set and press people for more donations. As we left the stage, the lead singer from the Mean Wells held out her hand to me and I slapped her palm. She had pink highlights in her brown hair, a mesh shirt over her tank top. My initial thought was how young she was, but then I realized she was around the same age I'd been when I first met Lana and the girls. How time flew. I chuckled and shook my head. Laura was waiting and handed my shirt back to me, leaning in for a kiss. I pecked her lips so she'd know I wasn't mad and dragged her along with us to the dressing room.

We were nearly there when a large brown dog trotted past us. I stopped and stared, then laughed and squeezed Lana's shoulder. "There's a dog back here."

"That's not nice," Lana said. "I'm sure she was perfectly attractive, just not your type."

I kicked at her, but she was too fast for me. Naomi was sitting on the couch, but she stood up when we arrived. She raised her eyebrows and nodded at my exposed skin.

"So you changed your mind, huh?"

"Under duress and in the name of charitable donations. Did you know there's a dog wandering around backstage?"

Naomi raised an eyebrow and looked toward the door. "I didn't see it. There was a fan wandering around earlier, but I got rid of her."

Lana dropped into a chair and wiped the sweat from her face and chest with a towel before squirming into a Save the Boobies T shirt. "Got rid of her? Why?"

"You have to ask why?" Naomi raised an eyebrow.

Lana rolled her eyes. "Oh, please. I'm not scared of fans backstage. I'm scared of them in my apartment. You should have let her stay. We could have signed her bra or something."

Naomi shrugged. "Well, regardless. It's better to not encourage them to sneak back here."

I had my shirt on, but was leaving it unbuttoned. I was by no means an exhibitionist, but I kind of liked the way it felt to not care who saw what. When I sat down, Laura draped herself across my lap and I held her in place.

Nessa handed out water bottles. "So how much did we raise?"

"We won't know that for a while, but a quick head-count of people waiting outside said we had about four hundred revelers. Add to that the two hundred, two hundred and fifty women who paid for the opportunity to let their tatas hang out, it's a roaring success. Congratulations, ladies." She smiled at us and hooked her thumb over her shoulder. "I'm going to see if I can track down the dog, see if it's wearing a collar."

She left, and Lana flicked on the intercom that hooked into the speaker system. The Mean Wells sounded phenomenal, and I closed my eyes so I could focus on the music. Laura pressed against me, and I listened to Codie and Nessa talking across the room as I dozed off. We'd raised a lot of money for a great cause, we had seen a lot of women in their underwear, and my girlfriend had undressed me in front of a couple hundred screaming women.

I could think of worse ways to spend a night.

Track Six

"Get to the old rehearsal space. Now."

I sat up, disturbing Laura's sleep but calming her with a soft touch to her hip. "Lana? What's wrong?"

"It's... just come here. Please."

I tossed back the blankets and walked through the darkness to my closet. Laura rolled onto her back to watch me, inhaling sharply as she rubbed her eyes with the heel of her hand. I mouthed Lana's name and she nodded her understanding.

I tried to dress one handed. "Are you okay? Did something happen?"

"It's fine. Everything's fine, I just need you to get here. Nessa and Codie are already on the way. Just please hurry."

"Okay. I'll be there as quick as I can." I hung up and quickly pulled jeans on over my pajamas. My top was acceptable, so I threw a jacket over it and brought my shoes to the bed so I could sit while I put them on.

Laura rolled over. "Is everything all right?"

"I don't know. Lana's in a panic." I realized how it looked and turned to face her. "Honey, I know it's awkward that Lana calls and I run off without–"

"Hey." She pushed herself up and leaned toward me. She kissed me and said, "Lana's not your lover. You know it, she knows it, and I know it. You came back to me." She touched my hair. "I'm not concerned. You and Lana have a bond, yes, but so do we. If she's calling you in the middle of the night, you need to go."

I kissed her softly. "I love you."

"I know."

"I'm going to marry you someday."

She grinned. "You keep threatening me with that, one day I'll take you seriously."

"Just give me enough lead time to let Mom know." I kissed her again. "I'll be back soon as I can. Go back to sleep."

I left the apartment and drove through the pre-dawn light to the old neighborhood. I passed the Dads' house and saw a light on downstairs; it was the first week of the month, so I knew Dad was doing the books. I thought about honking as I went by, but I didn't want to alarm him. If Lana's terror proved minor enough, I might invite the girls back for a big family breakfast.

I saw Lana and Codie's cars parked at the curb when I turned the corner, and they were standing near the stone retaining wall wrapped in shadows. I parked behind Codie's car and, as I got out, saw Nessa's car about a quarter of a mile away. I waved at her and then turned around. It took me a moment to process what I was seeing and, once I did, I understood Lana's dismay.

The building was gone.

"What the hell?" I squeezed Codie's arm, but I could tell Lana needed a hug. I pulled her close and held her tight as I looked over her shoulder at the large empty space. "What happened?"

Codie said, "I called the old landlord. He said Dowager's lead singer kept trying to spit flames. He finally succeeded and set the wall on fire. They all got out, but by the time the firemen arrived it was a lost cause. They kept it from spreading to the other buildings, but that was all they could do."

I remembered storing our instruments in a closet and hugged myself against a sudden chill. Nessa joined us in the parking lot and gestured mutely at the empty air. Codie explained everything again, and Nessa hugged Lana. "Oh, babe."

"I wanted to rehearse for our last album here. I came by to see if they had any free times, and this..." She turned and looked at it. "We kept our instruments here."

"When did it happen?" I asked.

"About a year after we left."

Lana said, "That would have been the end. If we lost this space and our instruments, we would have been–" Her voice caught and she looked at me.

"No," I whispered. "No, it's not... I didn't save you."

Nessa said, "It all happened at the right time." She looked at us and shrugged. "The building was here as long as it needed to be. It brought Codie and Lana to me, and it brought Karen to all three of us, and once we left... it had served its purpose."

I realized she was right. I hugged her, and Lana stepped onto the foundation. She walked to the approximate spot where the rehearsal space had been and looked around. She looked at the retaining wall and smiled sadly.

"Where were you walking? All those days when you were sitting here. Were you going somewhere?"

I smiled and walked over to join her. "No. I was just out for a walk. Getting out of the house when Mom and Dad fought, then trying to get space, getting some exercise. I just sat here because the wall was convenient, and it was a good part of the walk to let myself rest. I liked letting my feet dangle." I rubbed her shoulder. "You gonna be okay?"

"Yeah. Nessa's right. The building served its purpose."

"Come on," I said. "My Dad is up, and he makes a mean Denver omelet. He'll be happy for the distraction."

We went back to our cars to caravan back to my old home, but I noticed Lana was the last of us to pull away from the curb.

"There are rumors about a break-up."

"Hiatus," Karen corrected.

Lana frowned. "Right. And how can there be rumors? The only people who know about the group going on hiatus are in this room."

Naomi held up a finger. "And your significant others, people who work here that might have overheard me talking to one of you on the phone, Karen's Dads, anyone backstage at any concert where any of you might have said the words 'final album.' Remember the fan I sent away at the breast cancer benefit? Who knows how many there have been that weren't caught? Right now it's not important how it got out. We just have to worry about how to deal with it. Because right now it's all anyone online is talking about."

Karen said, "Is that a bad thing? Any publicity is good publicity."

Naomi shook her head. "People will start thinking of the band as defunct. Your last album will be a footnote rather than a send-off. You want the band to be strong until the end. That's the point of this 'hiatus' anyway, right?"

Lana nodded, her mind racing. "We just have to show people that we're still committed to each other. No matter what happens to the group, the four of us are as strong as ever. A strong enough show will buy us enough time to get out ahead of any breakup rumors and set the story straight."

"I'm open to suggestions," Naomi said.

"What I'm thinking doesn't need you to do anything." She swiveled in her chair to look at the other girls. "It'll require something big from us, though. We'd all have to sign off on it before anyone made a move."

Nessa said, "You're making me nervous."

Lana grinned.

Lana squeezed my hand and leaned in close so only I would hear her. "You're absolutely certain you're okay with this? You can still back out."

I took a deep breath and nodded. I was the last hold-out, but finally I'd decided it was the right thing to do. Lana was right; it would show the fans we were still committed to each other and that we weren't going to abandon them or Radiation Canary any time soon. I blinked and squeezed Lana's hand again.

"I'm just worried it'll hurt."

"I'll be right here with you the whole time."

The man sitting on my other side was missing his neck, the bald dome of his head growing directly into his shoulders. He looked like the sort of guy Dad watched carefully in the hardware store. Not because he would steal, but in case he bought what Dad referred to as "kidnap and torture tools." The effect was somewhat tempered by the bifocals he wore, and his soft voice further destroyed the badass image.

"I'll be as gentle as I can," he said.

I whimpered. "I don't suppose they offer anesthetic here."

Lana grinned. I was going first because, if I chickened out, I didn't want the others to be stuck with an incomplete set. I finally nodded at the artist and exhaled. "Okay. But don't tell the tabloids if I cry."

He smiled. "I never do. You're sure?"

I nodded. "Yeah. Let's do this."

He had already traced the design onto my upper right arm, and he lifted the small black gun that would burn it into my flesh. I squeezed Lana's hand hard enough that twice she whispered for me to lighten up, and I whispered an apology. After an entire day - or a few minutes; who could be objective? - he told me it was finished and let me look at the resulting inked image of a green canary inside a circle.

Our logo, serving as a symbol that we weren't going to leave Radiation Canary behind any time soon, no matter where our lives went in the next few years.

I exhaled, thanked the artist, and then smiled at Lana. "Thanks for holding my hand."

"No problem."

I stood up and took a second to make sure my knees would hold before I stepped away from the chair. Codie and Nessa came in, alerted by the sound of the needle stopping. Nessa bent forward to get a closer look at my new artwork and I looked at the three of them.

Codie snorted and said, "Oh, my God. I can't believe she fell for it."

My eyes widened, and I felt a moment of sheer terror. Then she let me off the hook with a grin, and I exhaled sharply. "Oh, you bitch. Lana, Nessa, hold her down. We'll have him put a dragon on her face."

Codie shrieked as they grabbed her and manhandled her toward the chair.

I looked at the artist, who seemed to be taking it all in his stride. He shrugged at me, and I shrugged back.

Celebrities. What are you gonna do?

Track Seven

We were on the cover of Lyric Monthly, lined up front to back with Lana at the front, then me, then Nessa, then Codie. Lana was sleeveless, as always, but the rest of us had rolled up our sleeves to show off our matching tattoos. We each had a segment of the band's name written underneath the tattoo in black marker: RADI on Codie, ATIO on Nessa, NCAN on me, and Lana had ARY. Our arms were curled in a Rosie the Riveter flex, and we'd tried for badass expressions. I thought I'd ruined it by laughing just as the photo was taken, but the others agreed it was the perfect shot.

In the interview, Lana broke the news of our upcoming hiatus using the strength of the cover to keep anyone from panicking and taking her words the wrong way.

"The band has been amazingly good for all of us. So good that we need to take some time away from it to appreciate that goodness. We have people we love who deserve to see us, who don't need us running around from one concert to the next or always leaving on tour. So we're going to let the canary rest for a little while. The band will always be a part of us, and the four of us won't be able to stay away from each other for very long no matter what happens."

The phone calls started almost immediately after the magazine hit stands. Was the so-called hiatus effective immediately? What could fans expect on the final album? Was there a possibility of the band continuing on with a revised lineup? That last question was met with a resounding no from all involved; the four of us were Radiation Canary. Accept no substitutions.

People started going through all of our albums looking for evidence of internal strife, something that could have led to the band calling it quits. Apparently there was a moment during our live CD where the microphone picked me up snorting at something Lana said and people assumed it had been sincere derision. Laura's favorite story was something she found online that hinted the breakup was *her* fault. Uncomfortable with the idea of me performing with Lana, she had insisted either the band break up or we would.

Lana dispelled those rumors by performing with the Femme Reapers at a handful of appearances from Idaho down to California. When they reached LA, she stayed behind for a week to catch up with Catherine. She made another appearance on *Dance Stars*, this time as a guest judge. Laura repaid the gesture by joining us on-stage at a few concerts, sharing the microphone with Lana to show there weren't any hard feelings.

On one of my rare weekends free, no touring or promotions on my schedule, I went back home and finally cleaned the last of my belongings out of the attic room. Ted was helping me carry boxes out to the car, despite Dad's admonition that he should take it easy "because of your heart." From Ted's reaction, it was a familiar refrain.

We took a break for iced tea on the porch. "So your Dad heard about this hiatus of yours."

"Yeah? What does he think?"

"Well, he thinks you definitely deserve a break, if that's what you're doing. Have you given any thought about what you're going to do with your 'free time'?" He actually made the air quotes, and I laughed.

"Not really. I'm going to leave it open so I can roll with the punches depending on what Laura's doing. It'll be nice to follow someone else for a little while and not worry about the next album, the next song, getting into the studio..." I shrugged and sipped my tea.

"So you and Laura are getting pretty serious? I mean, making life plans based on each other's schedule, living together in that de-luxe apartment in the sky."

I grinned. "We're going to end up together."

"So what are you waiting for?"

I started to answer, but there really wasn't a good one to give. "I don't know. Radiation Canary is still working. We have the last album to put together. I haven't even started writing anything for it. I want that to be done before I do anything big like propose to her."

Ted sucked on an ice cube and looked out at the street. "Don't rush into anything."

I looked over at him. "What? Aren't you supposed to tell me to wise up, grow up, and make an honest woman out of her?"

"I'd like to think I'm less trite than that. You want to marry her, that much is obvious. But if you're happy with the way things are now, you don't have to have a marriage certificate just so you can say you have one. There are certain perks to being married, but there are advantages to living in sin, too." He winked at me. "I'm just saying don't let anyone, me or your Dad or Lana, force you into something you don't want."

I narrowed my eyes at him. "I can't tell if this is a soft sell or reverse psychology. Either way, I don't trust you."

He grinned. "Take my words to heart, young one. You have plenty of time to settle down and do the marriage thing. There's a certain magic to just enjoying your life and being with the person you love more than anything."

I smiled at him. "Like you and Dad?"

He pretended to consider it. "Very similar to us, now that you mention it." He shrugged. "I support the people fighting for gay marriage, and I hope they get what they want. But me? I think it takes more strength and courage to stay with someone when you could walk away at any time. No divorce, no dividing of everything... it would be easy to call it quits and no messy legal fees."

I nudged his foot with mine. "Thanks, Ted."

"No problem kiddo. Come on. We have a few more tons of sheet music to haul downstairs before we call it a day."

I followed him back upstairs and began going through the binders of sheet music in my closet. I flashed back to sitting on the floor at the foot of my bed, the violin resting on my lap, looking at the miles and miles of staves I had to memorize for my lessons. I remember wanting to cry, wondering how I would ever hold all the music in my head, and how it would ever be a worthwhile talent to have. Soon music became a refuge for a sad little girl who needed a place without words where she could hide while her family split apart at the seams.

I wanted to go back in time and tuck that girl's wild blonde hair behind her ear, dry those cheeks that were perpetually wet in the months after the divorce, and let her know it would be all right. *Look at me now, kid,* I wanted to say. *Look what it gets you. Don't stop.*

That little girl had wanted to be a police officer and a ballerina. She wanted to be an astronaut, for about ten minutes, and then a scientist. The violin and cello were just bargaining chips gathered to look good on a college transcript, ways to get into a good college so she could study what I really wanted.

Odd how the school never had a "Celebrity" booth on Career Day. Of course if it did, the kids would line up around the block for that one and ignore more vital careers.

I found love poems I had written to Penny tucked in the back of a desk drawer. She had gotten the finished copies, and I kept the first- second- and third-drafts for myself. I sat down on the floor in front of the desk to read them. It quickly became apparent that they'd been written by a lonely girl desperate to lose her virginity but unsure if she wanted to give it to the person she was with. Lust letters was a more appropriate name, and I flushed a little at how filthy I had gotten in a few of them. Good thing I hadn't just let Dad and Ted go through the stuff on their own. I thought about the girl who had written the letters, almost a stranger to me after everything I'd been through. I reached up and rubbed my tattoo through the thin material of my sleeve, smiling at how much had changed.

I wanted to tap into the old me for the album. I wanted to sing to that girl who was sitting in her room, unsure of what she wanted to be but ready to become something... anything.

Ted came back upstairs for another box and saw me writing on the back of the letters. He sighed and shook his head in mock exasperation.

"So much for taking some time off."

I grinned and went back to writing.

Track Eight

The idea of wearing our unsung hero costumes in concert evolved into wearing them for the "Waifs and Strays" music video. I performed as Tesla in a recreation of his room in the Hotel New Yorker with trained doves swooping all around me. Lana sang standing on a round table in a hotel conference room, with a group of paid actors dressed to look like the 1920s gathering of writers and critics sitting around smoking and drinking. Nessa was Sally Ride in a space capsule, since none of us could figure out how to portray Nellie Bly in a dynamic way, and Codie performed as Harriet Quimby in front of her own plane.

The doves they rented for my segment weren't entirely thrilled with my portrayal, or else they were just winged bastards, because they caused the filming to stretch until the wee hours of the night. Since it was for a video and not a single shoot, I had to wear a dark wig so I actually looked the part. We each got a whole day for our part of the video, and then we had to dress up again to gather in an old warehouse for the main performance scenes.

As we were setting up, Lana glanced over while a hairdresser fixed her bangs. "Hey. Is that the same suit you rented for the cover shoot?"

"Yeah. I had to buy it."

"Why?"

"There were... reasons. It was a little ripped."

Lana snorted and said, "Ah. So the girl likes it?"

"The girl thinks it's a fun twist."

Lana chuckled and rolled her shoulders. "I gotta admit, I kind of like this whole cocktail dress and pearls thing. The bangs, I could get used to. It's kind of classy. And it's more fun to be naughty when you look classy."

"So your girl...?"

"Let's just say she really likes playing dress-up too, and we'll leave it at that."

I clucked my tongue. "You should have known. She's a TV star, after all."

We went through the now-familiar pantomime of performing the song, listening to the recording of ourselves and stopping now and then so the director could get a different angle. When it was over, Lana looked at us and smiled.

"The debutante, the crossdresser, the pilot, and the space girl. What do you say we go out to lunch in these outfits? See if anyone stares?"

"Oh, they'll stare," Codie said. "Every time we go anywhere with you, they stare."

I said, "I don't care how fun it would be. I'm not eating anything with this mustache on."

Lana hissed. "Oh, there's an oral sex joke in that. I just know there is. Give me until after we're changed back into our street clothes. I'll have it, I promise."

Lana was waiting outside my dressing room when I came out, my face scrubbed and shining to get all the makeup off. My hair was slicked back, and I felt like a plucked chicken in my T-shirt and sweatpants. She stepped forward, grinned, and said, "If you won't eat anything while you have a mustache, then Laura should be the one paying to have your lip waxed."

I patted her cheek. "Keep trying, baby."

She sighed in defeat.

My apartment was festooned with red and green streamers, and sparkling silver tinsel surrounded the windows to frame the lights of the city. The Dads were there, and Mom had miraculously flown in from New York to see the apartment and meet Laura. Catherine and Lana spent Christmas in London with her family, but they would be back sometime during the party and were expected to make an appearance. We had two punch bowls, one "adult" and one not. I may have been past thirty, but old habits died hard.

Lana finally showed up with her lady at a quarter to eleven, looking sleep-deprived and overdosed on Christmas cheer. She hugged the members of her band, said hi to the Dads, and I introduced her to my mother. Mom seemed more awed to meet Catherine Diehl, which was fine since it gave us a chance to pull Lana away for a small band reunion in the kitchen.

"How was London?"

"Ah, good. It was all good. Dinner with her parents. Her mum is amazing." She looked at us and furrowed her brow. "What?"

"You have an accent."

"I do not. I was only there for a week."

I laughed, and Nessa put her arm around Lana's waist. "Babe, you've got a bloody accent."

"Sod off. I'd know if..." We laughed harder and her face reddened. I put my hand on the back of her neck and rested my forehead on hers. "Is it really noticeable?"

"Nah. I'm sure it'll fade soon. Besides, you spent a week with Kitty. I'd be shocked if her tongue hadn't rubbed off on you a little."

Codie nearly fell down.

When we returned to the party, Lana leaned close and whispered something in Catherine's ear. Catherine shrugged and said, "Yeah, li'l bit. Oh, but I think it's adorable." She looked at me and made a mean face. "Have you girls been making fun of my darling?"

I held my thumb and forefinger a millimeter apart. She chuckled and pulled Lana against her. "The hazards of foreign travel. It'll be fixed by the time you have to record your next album. Promise."

"It bloody better."

I nearly spit out my punch.

Laura came to find me at a few minutes to midnight. I took her hand and guided her out onto the balcony. We left the door open so we wouldn't miss the televised countdown, but I wanted to spend the last few minutes of the year alone with her. She pressed against me in the cold, and I kissed her temple.

"2012. This is supposed to be the year we all die, according to the Mayans."

She rested her head on my shoulder and our attempt to stay warm turned into a dance. "And they've never been wrong before. All those other Mayan predictions that came to pass."

"What else did they predict, baby?"

"They predicted Nostradamus. And the pennyfarthing."

"The what?"

"That bicycle with one really giant wheel and–"

I smiled. "Oh, right. What else?"

"What do you call that white stuff you put on sandwiches?"

I frowned. "Mayo?"

"Mm-mm. Mayan-naise."

I groaned, then laughed. "Okay. Well, in that case we're certainly doomed."

"What are you going to do with your last year?"

The album, I knew. We had to put Radiation Canary to rest before any of us officially discovered what our next steps were. But I stepped back and looked into her eyes, smiling.

"Whatever I do, I want to do it by your side. Will you marry me?"

She grinned. "Sure. Any time."

"No, Laura." I looked inside to see if anyone was watching, then pinched my dress to lift the hem above my knees so I could kneel without ruining the material. Laura's eyes widened and I took her hands in mine. I measured my words, regretting all the times we'd said them in jest. I made sure she knew I wasn't joking this time. "Will you marry me?"

"Yes." She bent down and kissed me, and I let her stand me back up. We held each other, laughing quietly, and didn't move until the door opened and

Lana stuck her head out.

"Oy, you tossers." Apparently she'd gotten over her anxiety about the accent. "Get yer bums in here right quick or you'll miss the bleedin' countdown. Bangers and mash."

I laughed and guided Laura back inside. I stopped by the door and touched Lana's hand, and she hung back. I smiled at her and said, "Engaged."

"Really?" Her accent was suddenly not as thick. "Just now?"

I nodded and my eyes brimmed with tears. She hugged me tightly, rocking me from side to side as she whispered her congratulations. "I have news, too."

"You and Catherine?"

"I don't know. We'll talk after the countdown, okay?"

I agreed, and we went into the living room. At the stroke of midnight, I kissed Laura, Lana kissed Catherine, and Nessa kissed her husband. When "Auld Lang Syne" ended, I found Codie in the kitchen. She was resting her elbows on the counter, examining a small bowl of mixed nuts for her favorites.

"Hey. I thought you brought a date."

"Nah." She shook her head. "I never understood the tradition of kissing on New Years' anyway. Start the new year with a cold?"

I chuckled and leaned on the other side of the counter from her. "Sorry if everyone's being real... couple-y. It's not really fair to you."

Codie smiled and sorted some more nuts. "I'm fine with it. I've always been the odd girl out. Hanging with Lana, it's hard not to be. Just because she doesn't care about male attention doesn't mean she didn't attract them." She furrowed her brow, smiling. "I know that's a triple negative, but–"

"I got it. It's okay. But in honor of the stupid tradition..." I leaned forward and pecked her lips. "Happy New Year, Codie."

Codie laughed and mimicked Lana's adopted accent. "Happy New Year, K. Now you just have to kiss Nessa and you'll have snogged the whole band."

"Gotta talk Scott into that."

She rolled her eyes. "Scott's a man. He'll probably pay you to do it."

I grinned and said, "I'm going to head back out. Stop fingering the nuts."

"That's what she said."

I wrinkled my nose and shook my head as I rejoined the party, slipping an arm around Laura's waist. I whispered in her ear about kissing Codie, and she tsked.

"Not even twenty minutes into our engagement and you're already kissing other women?"

"Well, she's straight."

"Oh. In that case it's hot and kinky."

I moved my hand over the curve of her hip, kissed her cheek, and held her close while we enjoyed the rest of the party in each other's arms.

Track Nine

Mom insisted on a hotel, and I couldn't really argue with her. We had a spare room, but Lana and Catherine had called it. Before she left, I took Mom and the Dads aside to let them know about my engagement, and I was treated to a rare dual hug from Mom and Dad at the same time. That alone almost made it worth the trouble of getting married.

An hour into 2012, Nessa and her husband called it a night. I saw them out, and the great escape began. Guests began to leave as if a plug had been pulled, and by that point I was happy to see them go. It was the weird gray area between early and late when I stretched out on the couch with my legs draped over Laura's lap, taking a moment to rest my eyes before I went into the bedroom. Catherine was asleep in an armchair, and Lana was waiting for her to wake on her own rather than disturbing her just to move to the bedroom.

"Congratulations to you two," Lana said quietly. "I didn't get a chance to say it officially earlier, so best wishes to you both."

"Thank you." Laura rubbed my calf through my pantyhose. I didn't want to think about having to take them off in order to sleep. Maybe I could skip that step. "You said you two had news. Did you get engaged, too?"

"No," Lana hissed, then looked to make sure Catherine was still asleep. "She got a call while we were over there. Next season will be the last one for *Dance Stars.*"

"What does that mean?"

Lana shrugged. "New job. Maybe no touring. Maybe going back to England to model, or do a show there."

"So you actually might relocate to England?"

She smiled. "Already got the accent for it, don't I, guv?"

The world seemed so much smaller than it did before we got paid to travel around it, but still... the thought of Lana that far away was daunting. I knew we would be apart. But separated by an entire ocean? And the entire continent between us.

"Nothing's set in stone yet," Lana said. "But it's on the table. We talked about it while we were over there, about how this wasn't the plan when I agreed to relocate." She looked over at Catherine, her legs tucked up under her, party dress draping her thighs. "I told her the plan wasn't to move to Los Angeles, it was to move to be with her. That hasn't changed."

"That's sweet," Laura said. She squeezed my calf and then patted the bottom of my foot. "I'm going to bed."

"I'll join you if you help me up."

She did, and I bent down to kiss the top of Lana's head as I passed her chair. She reached up and patted my cheek, then forced herself up to wake Catherine. As I followed Laura to bed, I heard Lana and Catherine murmuring to each other in the living room.

In our bedroom I kissed Laura in the dark and ran my fingers through her hair. "Is it customary to make love on New Years?"

"Maybe not. But it is customary to fuck the woman you're going to marry within twelve hours of asking her."

"Well, then I have plenty of time."

"Depends on how long I make you wait before I let you come."

I shivered and guided her to the bed. "Who said you get to be in charge?"

She laughed, and I very quickly turned it into a moan.

In the spare bedroom, Catherine sat Lana on the edge of the bed. She went to the bathroom and returned with a washcloth and a bottle of water. She undressed Lana and knelt in front of her, running the washcloth over Lana's arms, chest, and stomach. She spread Lana's thighs and moved between them, leaning in to kiss Lana's neck and tease her earlobe with her teeth.

"I heard them in their room. Making love." She pressed wet fingers against Lana's sex. "Your little songbird makes beautiful music with her darling." She brushed her tongue over Lana's neck, tasting sweat. "I bet you made her sing. I bet you made her sing so loud, my love."

"Not as loud as you make me sing." Lana ran her fingers down Catherine's arm, looped them around her wrist, and rolled her hips forward.

"Sing for me."

Lana blushed. "They're in the next room..."

"I want them to hear you. Us." She bit Lana's ear, and Lana whimpered. "You'll have to do better than that, my dear. Louder. I want them to hear you scream."

"You're devious."

"Imagine how much fun you'll have getting revenge when it's your turn."

Lana chuckled, leaned back to pull Catherine to her, and captured her lips in a hungry kiss. Catherine's fingers pushed inside of her and she pressed the heel of her hand against Lana's mound. "Come on, La-la." Lana half-groaned and half-chuckled at the nickname that had been born while they were in England. "You love an audience. Sing for them..."

We were spooning, my hand between Laura's legs, gently thrusting against her. My free hand was linked with one of hers and she was stroking my thigh with her other hand. We'd perfected the position a while back, and we knew it was perfect for a long, slow tease leading up to a mind-blowing orgasm. I nibbled her ear and began to say something deliciously dirty when I was distracted by a wailing cry from across the hall.

"Guess they weren't that sleepy," Laura chuckled breathlessly.

I grinned and kissed her temple. "Canaries or Femmes... which one is loudest?"

"Ahh," she squirmed against me and tilted her head back.

Catherine laughed at the sound of a pleasurable cry from the other room. She rearranged herself, wet her lips, and said, "*Now* it's a party." She bowed her head and Lana gripped the blankets in anticipation. When Catherine's lips made contact, Lana rolled her head back and sang for the cheap seats.

The next morning, someone was already in the shower when I woke up. I pressed against Laura, kissing her neck until she squirmed away from me. "Mercy, mercy, mercy," she murmured into the pillow. I stroked her hair until she fell back to sleep, then eased away from her so she could recover. I put on a pair of shorts, then lazily buttoned a shirt just enough to be modest, and stumbled out in search of caffeine. Catherine was in the kitchen making tea, and I did up another button out of deference for our level of friendship. She smiled at me and murmured a good morning, and I returned it. Even with both of us barefoot she was at least four inches taller than I was. I felt like a kid as I joined her.

"I hope you don't mind me stealing your tea."

"I'll forgive you if you started the coffee." I looked. "And you have. What a good Brit."

"I'm as American as I need to be." She winked at me and gestured at the fridge. "Would you like me to make you breakfast? The least I can do in exchange for hosting me last night."

"That would be great." I rubbed my hands together. "And, ah, is breakfast my prize for winning last night?"

She stopped with her back to me, tilted her head to the side, then cocked her hip and looked over her shoulder at me. "Who says you won?"

"Is Lana awake?"

"Yeah, she's in the shower."

I grinned. "Then trust me. I won."

Catherine sighed and went back to breakfast preparation. "Oh, well. I suppose you deserve it, since you got engaged last night. Lana told me... congratulations."

"Thanks. You were a worthy opponent and a graceful loser." I toasted her with my empty coffee cup.

"Of course." She filled my cup and winked at me. "There's always the rematch."

I chuckled, shook my head, and hoped I wasn't blushing too much as she went back to making my victory breakfast.

Track Ten

Lana cleared her throat and then stepped closer to the microphone. "This is very odd, so please bear with me." She adjusted the guitar strap on her shoulder, rolled her neck, and looked out over the sea of faces. "I've played in a lot of places, but I think this is the most nerve-wracking. I think it's because the lights are up enough that I can see Mrs. Miller over there by the wall with her detention slips at the ready."

Some of the members of the audience laughed, most of them probably students who had her class. The silent ones were students who knew the teacher's detention sentencing all too well.

They were onstage in the multi-purpose room of Lana and Codie's old high school, performing a concert to help raise money for the music program. They were performing three mini-concerts during the school day, for the students, and another one that evening for parents and anyone who wanted to donate. Lana wasn't feigning her discomfort; far too many of her former teachers were still working there for her to relax completely.

"Codie and I started out playing music when we were here, in school. Without the music room, we wouldn't have had a place to practice. And once we graduated, we were cast out... I know what it's like to be at a loss. To have talent, but to not have a place for it to grow. No one knows where the next Radiation Canary is coming from, but I know if we sacrifice music programs in school, it's going to make it nearly impossible to find them."

She turned to Karen and nodded, then started the opening of "The Importance of Your Radio." As she played, she glanced toward Mrs. Miller, who was leaning against the wall next to one of the entrances. She had her booklet of detention slips, which she'd had specially bound into a daunting black leather notebook, clutched in one hand. She held it up... then smiled and tucked it into the pocket of her sweater.

Lana grinned.

School ended at three, and it was a few hours before the actual charity concert. Karen and Nessa went to pick up food, while Lana and Codie got permission from the principal to wander the grounds a little to reminisce. The janitor unlocked the front door for them and said, "A lot of the teachers are still around, but most of the classrooms will be locked up. Can't let you in there without permission, sorry."

"It's all right. Thank you."

The first place Lana went was her former locker. She had conned a friend in the front office to make sure she got the same one for junior and senior years, so she knew exactly where it was. She found the number and grinned as she idly spun the combination lock and tried to peek through the slats to see what the current occupant was keeping inside. It smelled like perfume, which meant at least some boy wasn't tainting it with his dirty sneakers and hidden drugs.

Codie nodded toward the back of the building. "I'm going to check out auto shop."

"You should have told the inspirational story of how that class led you to a chop shop."

Codie grinned and put a finger to her lips. "Past lives, baby. I'll catch up with you at the gym in about twenty?"

"Try to leave everything in the auto shop where you found it."

"Yeah, yeah."

Lana chuckled and wandered down the Science Hall. She had never particularly liked science, but she had adored Miss Varney. The light was on in Room 3-S, but Lana didn't hold out any hope until she peeked through the long narrow glass of the door and saw the blonde bombshell bent over her desk to grade something. She wore a V-neck sweater over a white T-shirt, her ash-blonde hair falling over the right side of her face and caught on the frame of her glasses. Lana remembered clearly the way she used to perch on the edge of her desk, skirt riding up just so to reveal a tight thigh, and–

She looked up and Lana froze. Miss Varney smiled and motioned Lana inside. Lana hesitated, but turned the knob and stepped into the room.

"Hi, Miss Varney."

"Please. You graduated long enough ago, you can call me Allison." She stood up and Lana saw she hadn't stopped wearing the wool skirts, and her legs still made them worthwhile. She sat on the edge of the desk and took off her glasses. "I would ask how you've been, but I think everyone in the school knows the answer to that question."

Lana shrugged. Suddenly she was seventeen again. "Yeah. I heard you guys were having trouble, so I thought we'd do what we could to help."

"It's very appreciated. I know I have a lot of students who were upset about the idea of losing music. And nurturing a talent in music is so much more viable than a sports program. How many students go on to play professional football, and how many are grievously injured before they graduate." She sighed and tossed her head, her hair flying away from her face. She tilted her head to the side and smiled. "So are you stopping by to see all your teachers, or should I feel special?"

"You were always special, Miss Varney."

"Allison."

Lana tried, but the attempt ended in a sharp exhale. "I can't."

She laughed.

"And no, I'm just kind of touring the school. Seeing how much it's changed since I was here. I'm glad to see one thing has stayed the same."

"Aw. Well, it makes me very happy to see one of my former students doing so well." She wrinkled her nose and leaned forward slightly, whispering. "I mean, it's obvious you weren't aiming for a career in the sciences. I don't know why you signed up for the second year."

Lana scoffed. "Right."

"What?"

Lana realized she didn't know. "I had the biggest crush on you. I sucked at tests because I cared more about what you were wearing than the atomic weight of boron." She blushed and hunched her shoulders. "I didn't want this to be awkward. You were a great teacher, and your looks had nothing... to do with that." She shook her head. "Wow. I am talking a lot. I'll go."

"No, you don't have to." Allison chuckled. "I'm a little flabbergasted. I've never had a female student attracted to me before."

"Oh, yes you have." Lana chuckled. "I'm just the first one to commit harikari telling you. I know you're straight, and I know that nothing's going to come of it..."

"Right, and you have a girlfriend according to the press."

Lana said, "Oh, we talked about it. You're a... freebie." She let her eyes wander the room so they wouldn't have to rest on Allison. "God, why are words still coming out of my mouth?"

Allison blushed a little, and the color stretched down to the collar of her shirt. "Well. That is very flattering. And I guess you're not a student anymore, so there's no reason to feel awkward about admitting how you feel."

"Wow. I've had dreams that started like this." She closed her eyes and shook her head, silently telling herself to stuff something, anything into her mouth to silence herself.

Allison stood up and said, "Nothing quite that erotic. After all, I am straight. But you're a celebrity, and a beautiful one at that. I have a boyfriend who will be thrilled to hear that I kissed Lana Kent."

Lana's mouth was suddenly very dry. "Uh."

"I figured you shouldn't be the only one saying incriminating things." She winked. "And after all, you're not the only one with fantasies." She touched Lana's cheek. "A beautiful former student of mine becomes a superstar, and comes out as gay? Lana, you're on one of my lists, too."

Lana didn't breath as Allison's lips touched hers. A quick touch of Allison's tongue moistened Lana's lips enough that they slid easily apart as they tilted their heads to deepen the kiss. Lana felt Allison's tongue in her mouth and gripped her former teacher's upper arms to keep steady, eyes squeezed tightly shut as she cast her brain back, all the way back, to the pony-tailed girl in the ripped Dash Warren T-shirt who slouched just so she would have a better angle of Miss Varney's ass when she wrote on the board.

You did it, she told her younger self. *It took a few years, but you did it.*

Allison broke the kiss, and Lana forced herself to lean back. She tried to catch her breath, but the air was tainted by Allison's perfume. God, she even smelled the same.

"I'm a little lightheaded."

"That's understandable."

"No, I have a... condition. I need to drink something."

"Oh!" She stepped back and opened her desk drawer. Lana swayed and carefully sat in one of the chairs with a desk attached. "I have half a bottle of an energy drink."

"That's perfect."

She brought it over and Lana took a long swallow. Allison sat on the crossbar of the desk in the next aisle, one hand flat on her thigh while she used the other to feel Lana's forehead and cheeks.

"Is that better?"

"If you say you should send me to the school nurse, I'm going to run."

Allison smiled. "What was it? An allergic reaction?"

"No, it's just a condition I have where I faint." She shrugged. "It's brought on by a lot of things. Lack of sleep, dehydration, sexual arousal." She closed her eyes and chuckled. "God, I need to stop talking to you."

"Please don't. It was a very nice kiss. My first kiss with a woman."

"Still batting for the other team?"

She winced and shrugged. "Afraid so. No offense."

"None taken. But we do have other tricks to entice newcomers."

Allison laughed. "I thought you had to be born gay, that it wasn't a choice."

"It's not. But anyone can be bisexual for five minutes under the right circumstances." She winked and touched her tongue to the corner of her mouth. *I'm flirting with Miss Varney, and I can still taste her lipstick on mine. I had a stroke onstage and this is just a fantasy to make dying less painful, right?* She took another drink.

"Thanks for this. I'll pay you back."

"It's on me."

"Thank you. I should let you go back to grading... are you coming to the concert tonight? I could get you some backstage passes. Well, not backstage. That little corridor between the music room and the stage, though."

"My boyfriend and I will both be there, yes. And I'll wait until you're on stage to tell him about our little, ah, run-in today."

Lana shivered. "Whoo. Kinky."

Allison batted her eyelashes and they stood up together.

Lana went to the door and looked back. "I've had a lot of my dreams come true since the band got together. Never thought I'd fulfill that one."

"Aim for the moon, because even if you miss--"

"You'll land among stars." It was an old quote, but it was also a reference to one of the songs on their second album. "You are a fan."

"Of course. Student-teacher fantasies go both ways once the student is all grown up." She winked. "See you at the concert."

"Right. The concert." She nodded and said goodbye again before she made her escape. She found Codie waiting for her in the gym, watching the boys' basketball team practice lay-ups.

"Hey. Am I late?"

"No. The auto shop was locked up."

"And you let that stop you? You really have changed." She sat down next to her.

Codie said, "Where'd you go?"

Lana grinned. "I totally just made out with Miss Varney."

Codie twisted and stared at her. "Oh-emm-gee. I thought she was straight!"

Lana plucked at her collar and affected a bad-ass pose. "Yeah, well, she'd turn for me. Told me so herself."

Codie laughed. "As if you weren't already the envy of every boy in our graduating class... nice get, Lana."

"Thank you, thank you."

That night before the concert, she took the others aside to make sure they knew the words of a very special song. After "The Next Ferry," Lana dedicated a song to a "very special lady" in the audience who knew who she was and what she did, then performed a madcap cover of "She Blinded Me With Science." The song required a lot of effort from Nessa and Codie, and they did admirably. Lana and Karen teamed up to do the vocals and, when the song ended, Lana hugged Karen and went back to her position at the microphone to get back to the set list.

After the show, Lana found Miss Varney - she was once again unable to think of her on a first-name basis - and met her boyfriend. She signed autographs for them and, before they left, Miss Varney took her aside and said, “He enjoyed the concert. A lot.” She winked and raised an eyebrow, and Lana felt her syncope threatening again.

She found Karen at the refreshment table. “Are you okay? You look pale.”

Lana put an arm around her shoulder and pulled her close. “I’m fine. I just... really... fucking love being famous.”

Album Eight
FALLOUT
(2012-2013)

Track One

I married Laura in March in New York. We discussed waiting until November to see if Washington passed gay marriage, but I didn't see any reason to drag the engagement out as we both had albums to work on. And once she accepted my proposal for real, I couldn't take any more delay in calling her my wife. So we made the arrangements and pulled the trigger, agreeing that if Washington came through we would renew our vows in our home state. Lana threw us a joint-bachelorette party at her old strip club. At one point she bought us a dance in the private room, which Laura and I… swore we'd never speak about in mixed company. But every time David Bowie's "Let's Dance" came on, our eyes would meet and we'd have to struggle to contain ourselves.

Ella was her sister's matron of honor, while Mom insisted on calling herself my "Best Woman." Lana served as my Dads' date, holding the laptop so they could watch the wedding over Skype. Due to our respective careers, we decided to keep our own names for the public. Laura asked if she could take my name for private matters, and I emotionally and emphatically agreed.

We honeymooned in Greenland and, despite my initial misgivings, I fell in love with it. Our first morning there I went outside to watch the sun rise, shivering but not caring an iota, watching as the sun painted everything golden and lit up the mountains that surrounded the town. It was the most beautiful place I had ever seen. We hiked to Norse ruins, and spent a very long and ultimately much too-short afternoon watching icebergs drift. It was like going back to the beginning of the planet to see how things worked before people got too big for the world.

For the first time since our inaugural tour, I tried writing songs in between tourism and matrimonial fun and games. While Laura dozed, I bundled up and went back outside, shuddering despite my coat and mittens and wrote. "Clean Air" took a half hour to write, and I was mostly finished with "Escaping the Light Pollution" when I heard Laura moving around inside. I went back in, shed my coat, and did wifely things to her until she begged for a lunch break.

By the time we left, I had four songs written for our last album. "You know the downside to this trip?"

"There was a downside?" Laura asked.

"Just one." I gestured at the ice out the window with my chin. "Compared to this, Seattle is going to feel like a sauna."

She laughed and kissed me, holding my hand as the plane took off.

The number of people who wanted to talk to them increased exponentially once news of the band's impending end became common knowledge. Cartography put up a pre-order page for the yet-to-be-written final album with the tentative title *Fallout*, and the sale numbers were staggering. Naomi suggested introducing creating some kind of bonus items to include in the pre-order package when fans bought directly from the store. Codie knew someone who could make one-inch pins for lapels, hats, backpacks, and they commissioned a set with the logo on a white background. The album was also going to be released as an LP with instructions to download the whole album as MP3s.

"Wow. Digital meets vinyl." Lana grinned. "I like it."

"Does anyone actually still have record players?" Nessa asked.

Naomi nodded. "Oh, yeah. There are a lot of purists out there. I'm also considering a re-release of your whole back catalogue as LPs, because even people without record players may want to frame them as art. You guys have had some very cool album covers."

Lana gestured at Karen. "You mean the one where Karen and Dash Warren are half-naked on a boat? Yeah, I liked that one, too."

Naomi snickered. "We'll include the pins and the LP in the 'super-fan collector's edition' pre-order release. People will want an official 'final album' poster, too... If you think of anything else to include let me know before the end of the month."

Karen said, "Wait, an LP and a CD and pins... how much is this thing going to cost?"

"I was thinking we'd put a fifty-dollar price tag on it."

Karen's eyes widened. "No one is going to pay fifty bucks for a CD just because we throw some extra stuff at them."

Naomi smiled. "This is just for the super-fans. We'll have the regular ten-dollar CD-only package if that's all they want. But trust me, K. As Radiation Canary's last album for the foreseeable future, people are going to want to commemorate it."

Karen chewed her lip and looked at the others. Finally she said, "I think for fifty bucks there should at least be a T-shirt."

"I concur. A choice of T-shirts." Naomi grinned. "I think with all that combined, we will officially have a collector's set. Nice job, ladies."

Lana shrugged. "Hard part's over. All that's left now is to write the thing.

And record it." She rubbed her chin. "On second thought... can we work on any more easy stuff?"

Naomi smacked the table in front of her with a file. "Don't be lazy now. You're in the home stretch. Just go do the voodoo you all do so well."

I hung back when the others left, and found my way to Naomi's office. I knocked on the open door, and she waved me in. "What can I do for you, Karen?"

"Nothing. I wanted to apologize for not inviting you to my wedding."

She raised her eyebrows in surprise. "I would have been shocked to receive an invitation. It was in New York, by all accounts it was a tiny ceremony..." She smiled and waved me off. "It's fine. You don't have to apologize to me, Karen."

I stood in front of her desk, hands in my pockets, and shrugged. "I know, but... after Dash passed away, you said that what we had was casual. But it wasn't casual for me. You were exactly what I needed, when I needed it. You'll always be important to me. I wish I could just marry you and Lana and Laura and just be done with it."

Naomi laughed. "I'm not that good at sharing."

"Me neither. But I didn't want you to think that what we had was just casual. I gave my heart and soul to Laura, and I gave my body to Lana. And none of that would have happened without you giving me the key and opening the door. All the love I've had in the past ten years is because of you. I'll never forget that."

She was blinking rapidly behind her glasses, looking down at her desktop. "Thank you, Karen. That means a lot to me."

I stepped around the desk and hugged her, then kissed her cheek. "There's someone out there who is going to move mountains to be with you, Naomi."

"And her name is Ana."

I blinked. "That's awfully specific, unless you've been holding out on me."

Naomi put a finger under her glasses to wipe away the moisture, but she shrugged. "We've been seeing each other for a while now. We bonded over a dog, of all things. We're taking it slow, but I think there's a real future in it."

"I'm so happy for you, Naomi!" I hugged her tightly. "And I'd better be invited to that wedding."

She laughed. "If it happens, you can be my matron of honor."

I winked. "It's a deal."

"Go on. Your band is probably waiting for you." She squeezed my hand. "But thank you for... stopping by."

"Sure. I just wanted to make sure there were no hard feelings about the wedding."

"Only if you or Laura played the reception. We charge top dollar for that sort of thing with stars of your caliber."

I laughed and promised her we'd been silent, then bid her goodbye. I headed outside where the others were waiting for me as she'd predicted. What she hadn't predicted was how quickly Lana would stuff a notebook between her thigh and the passenger seat when I got into the car. I frowned and gestured at it.

"What's that?"

"Nothing."

"I see what's going on. Are you worried that once we're not a band anymore I'll steal your songs?"

"Yep, that's it exactly. Drive, Codie."

I watched her on the drive back to the ferry lanes, but I couldn't read her expression. Whatever she was hiding, I was sure she would show me when the time was right.

Track Two

We were booked to do a handful of live shows around Seattle as promotion for the upcoming album. *Vagabonds* was doing well, so well that a cable documentary about the life of Nikola Tesla wanted to use "Minding Doves" as part of their soundtrack. I agreed without hesitation and asked Naomi to waive most of the usual fees to let them use it however they wished. It was what Tesla would have wanted.

We played a club called Door 16 on the first official day of summer. When I received the hand-written set-list, I noticed there was a blank between "Icarus" and "Save Yourself."

"What are we doing here? About forty-five minutes in?"

Lana looked and shook her head. "You're not doing anything. We don't need strings on that part."

I bristled, confused by how harsh her tone was. "Is everything okay with you?"

She looked up. "Yeah. Fine. Why?"

"Because suddenly you're monosyllabic, you won't look me in the eye when we're off-stage, and you're always whispering to Nessa and Codie but you stop when I walk over. Do you have a problem with me? Is it Laura, is it–"

"Hey, shh." She cupped my face with both hands and looked me in the eye. "I'm sorry. I didn't realize I was doing that." She winced. "Well, I did. But I didn't realize you'd noticed. We can discuss it after tonight's show, okay?"

I wanted to stay angry, but she was too sincere. So I nodded, she dropped her hands, and we went out onstage. Lana was her usual boisterous self; no matter what was happening in her life, she was able to put together a live show like no one else. Her breakdown after her relationship with Alia had taught her to keep the line between her lives fully drawn. I kept up with her, watching Codie and Nessa for signs they were involved with this odd blank spot that inched closer with every song.

While Nessa and I began playing "Icarus," Lana cupped her hand over her eyes to block the spotlight. "Where are my angels at?" A group of girls moved to the center aisle and extended their arms. They waved paper wings, and Lana grinned. "I knew you were here."

Finally the song ended and we took the usual ten-count for applause, and so the girls could unfasten their wings and retake their seats.

"One of these days, you-all are going to fly one of these venues up into the air. Then we'll never be able to stop playing."

The crowd cheered, and Lana winked at them.

"I thought you'd say that. This next song, ah..." She reached out and moved a wire with the toe of her boot. "This next song is a little unusual for us. It's from our upcoming album–"

Cheers rose and fell, sounding like the Doppler effect, and Lana chuckled.

"–so it's brand-new. But it's the first Radiation Canary song to not have any strings in it. And Karen didn't write it. This is a composition by me, Nessa and Codie, so–" She turned to look at me. "–K, you can sit this one out."

I feigned indifference. "Do I get paid the same?"

Lana flashed her teeth. "Yeah, you get paid the same. Uh. I'm a little nervous. I'm not used to playing music without Karen backing me up. So I hope it's not too hard to hear. I hope you enjoy it." She began to play, and I held my violin at my side and sipped my water as I listened to the mystery song. The music was beautiful and ethereal; I could almost see Nessa forming circles in the air over her instrument, a hypnotic swirl of music that wrapped around the words when Lana began to sing in a soft, reverent voice.

"She's filling the pages of her book
With all the words she doesn't know how to say
All the times I never gave her a second look
She just sat silently and listened to us play."

I put down my violin and turned, leaving the stage before the audience could see me cry. Lana either didn't see me or didn't let it deter her. Nessa's melody softened to give over the power to Lana's voice, and I grabbed the first soft thing I could find to bury my face in it.

"I didn't have a voice until I found it in her pages
And now I'm singing to the world, standing on its stages
She gave me a voice, and let me share it with you all
I'm only standing here tonight 'cause of the girl on the wall.
There was a girl on the wall
Quiet and shy
She gave us her all
Gave us wings to fly
And we will never fall
Because we met the girl on the wall.
The girl on the wall made us canaries

And set me free so you could hear me sing
Every time the world brought me to my knees
She came down, took me under her wing
And with a word she calmed my wildest seas."

The music slowed, with Lana's guitar fading to be replaced with Nessa's keys and a steady beat from Codie. I focused on the sound so I could make it through the next verse. Lana's voice was reverent, reminding me of the opening of "Prayer," and I wiped the tears from my cheeks. A stagehand asked if I was okay and I could only nod.

"There was a girl on the wall
Until we took her down
And this song is so small
But I hope that now
She knows that we love her
And we'll never get over
How lucky we are to know
The girl on the wall."

The song faded out and, just before the crowd started cheering, I heard Lana speak. Her voice was slightly muffled, as if she had turned away from the microphone to say, "Where'd she go?"

I wiped off my face and walked back out, and the cheers got louder. Lana smiled, and I could see she was anxious about the song. I nearly knocked her over when I barreled into her, hugging her hard enough for her guitar to dig into my stomach. She kissed the side of my head.

"I'm sorry. If you'd known, I couldn't have written it," she whispered. "Every time I looked at you I wanted to cry."

"I love you so much."

She laughed and patted the back of my head, kissing my cheek as we pulled away from each other. I went back to my position, and Lana went to hers. She cleared her throat and wiped at her eyes. "Some of you may know that Karen was, um. She sat on a wall outside our rehearsal space. That's how we met, and that's how Radiation Canary got our start, so I wrote that song for her. I love her so much. She's the sister I never had."

"Some sister," I said. "She expects me to play music after listening to that? What a bitch."

Lana threw her head back and laughed, then began the intro to "Save Yourself." She turned to me, but leaned forward so her voice would be picked up by the microphone. "Just try to keep up, darlin', okay?"

I winked at her and settled my violin against my collar, bow poised until Codie whistled. I looked back at her.

"This song is for the cello, babe."

I closed my eyes and blushed. "Not my fault! I'm so flustered!"

Lana clapped at my confusion and laughed along with the crowd, giving me a moment to get settled in before she started the song over. The rest of the show went off without a hitch, but I quickly discovered I was wearing a smile I couldn't have wiped off if I'd wanted to.

Track Three

Lana was willing to leave "The Girl on the Wall" off the album, and I felt odd insisting on it considering it was basically a love letter to me. Codie and Nessa broke the standoff by sending it to Naomi, who insisted it not only needed to be on the album, it would be the first single. "It taps into the love people have for you, and it shows that you share the love for each other. It's the perfect song to represent the album. An ending, but not the end." Lana finally acquiesced, and we went into the studio to record it. The studio version would open with a quick composition of my own, then it would fade into the song the others had played in concert. I still couldn't get through it with dry eyes, and I was glad to see Naomi had much the same reaction. When we finished recording, I sniffled and ran my thumb under my eye as I glared at Lana.

"How do you ever manage to sing that without bawling your eyes out?"

"I take it one word at a time," she said. "And I sang it about a hundred times in the shower so I could inure myself to it. Catherine thinks I have very deep emotional issues involving soap bubbles."

I laughed and hugged her.

Since we had the studio, we also worked on a few of the other songs that were written and ready to go. The last song on our first album was called "The Question," so Naomi thought it would be a nice touch if we ended this album with "The Answer." Codie and Nessa also wrote songs, and I was happy to share the workload with them. Lana called my "Greenland writing" some of my best work, and I had to agree. Playing them made me remember those cold, cold mornings and the magical feel of the vibrant buildings against the backdrop of their harsh but gorgeous environment.

Our farewell tour continued, stretching on until I became convinced Naomi was trying to give every person in the Pacific Northwest a chance to see us perform one last time. And considering the line for autographs after each show, I had a feeling we were getting close. We had just finished a show at one of Seattle's most historic nightclubs, relaxing in the green room with bottles of water and complimentary snacks when a security officer knocked on the door.

"We have a guest who wants to say hello. He's not on the list, but I think you guys want to see him anyway."

Nick Young brushed past the man. "Of course they want to see me. They're my girls!" He held his arms out, smiling like he was addressing his studio audience. Instead of his standard suit, he wore a black T-shirt under a charcoal blazer, and he had a few days' growth of beard. His hair was a little unkempt, and the look very much worked for him. I smiled and stood up, sneaking a hug from him before he addressed the others.

"I hope you don't mind me dropping in like this. I fully intended to attend this as Joe Q Public and enjoy your performance like everybody else for a change, but I just couldn't do it. You girls were phenomenal. Tonight and every night, you blow me away. It breaks my heart that this will be your last album. Say it ain't so, gals."

Lana shrugged. "It's graduation day, Nick. Life isn't about getting into a comfortable rut, it's about moving on to the next thing to see how high you can go."

He chucked me on the chin with a knuckle. "And they said *you* were the wordsmith. Very well said, Ms. Kent. I shall accept your decision with a heavy heart and hope, and pray, that you will deign to appear on my piddling little television show one more time before you call it quits."

I looked at Lana, and she nodded for me to go ahead and spill the beans. "Actually, Nick... we were hoping you would host our last appearance as a band. I mean, it's only fair since you started it all. We want to use your show to say goodbye."

In that moment, I saw the real Nicholas Young. His stage persona vanished completely, and I realized just how touched he was. He slipped his arm away from me and stepped back, one hand on his hip and head bowed.

"Uh, yes." His voice was solemn. "I would like that very much, ladies."

"You gave us our break, Nick," Lana said. "It's only fair."

He blew air out threw his lips, looked at the ceiling tile, and then spoke very carefully.

"*Settle In, Seattle!* started Friday Night Auditions because we couldn't afford to book real bands five nights a week. It was a way to save money and make the show a little more interactive. That was our sole intention. I would put the MP3s on my computer and play them while we wrote the monologue. Half the time, I didn't even know the band's name. 'Book number four,' I would declare." He chuckled and shook his head. "But I didn't care. It didn't mean anything. Until I heard 'Emerald.' I stopped what I was doing and I listened to it again, because my *God*, Karen. I knew that I would hear that band again. I knew it was just a matter of time, so I snatched you up so no one else would get credit for discovering you. So... confession over... I hope you can find it in your hearts to forgive me."

Halfway through the speech, his persona had started to slip back into place, but the sincerity was still there.

"Aw, heck," Lana said. "I guess your heart was in the right place."

He grinned. "That's my girl." He rubbed his hands together. "Now... what do you have in the way of swag for a fellow celebrity?"

Track Four

Laura and Ella put out a new Femme Reapers CD, their fourth since Radiation Canary burst onto the scene. I played violin and Lana provided guest vocals on one song, "Wicked Women," and rumors began to swirl that our two bands were merging into a super-group. We entertained the possibility for a day or so - who was to say that joining forces wasn't a viable next step? - but we ultimately decided against it. I didn't want to take anything away from the Cowan sisters; they had their own fans and deserved their own successes.

Dance Stars ended, and Catherine relocated back to London. Lana was forced to remain behind due to scheduled performances and the work we had left to do on the album. We still hadn't settled on cover art. I was daunted by the idea of coming up with something a person would actually consider hanging on their wall, while Lana was afraid that it would be the image we were leaving people with. She wanted something iconic and memorable.

Nessa found a graphic artist who promised he could create something memorable. The first one he produced was a Seattle street with the Space Needle visible above the apartment buildings on the right. The entire picture was shaded red-orange, and a single person was standing in the middle of the cracked pavement of the street as a cloud raced toward him or her.

"That would be amazing," Lana said, "if we wanted to suggest the band had exploded."

I had to agree. It was just too desolate. His second choice was a profile shot of a woman wearing a leather jacket, scarf wound around her throat. She was wearing goggles, her bottom lip thrust out defiantly as the wind blew against her so hard that her hair and scarf were sticking straight out behind her. Despite the obvious strength of the wind, the girl was leaning forward into the gust. Lana approved it, and I agreed. We didn't know what was ahead of us, but we were willing to face it without flinching.

The back cover art was Codie's idea. A building near her had been gutted by a recent fire, and the foundation was dotted with piles of bricks like stone gopher holes. We got permission from the city to shoot it, waited for a safety inspector to confirm it was safe, and went in. We wore the clothes we would normally wear on stage, and someone spent a good hour coating the site with fake plaster dust.

Lana ascended to the top of the pile with the rest of us lined up behind her as if we were emerging from a crater. A copious amount of dry ice vapor wafted past us, and we were instructed to look stunned but happy to be alive. I called up the memory of the first time I walked out on stage for the proper combination of fear and joy. They snapped a few pictures of us, and then we lined up in front of one of the few standing walls.

Codie was first and held up a sign that said WE. Next, my sign said LOVE. Lana was beside me with YOU, and Nessa brought up the end with ALL. Propped against my foot and Lana's was another sign that said simply "THANK YOU."

Naomi had been watching the proceedings. When the photographer said he'd gotten what he needed, she walked over and applauded us.

"Your last album photo-shoot. For the time being, anyway. How does it feel?"

"Odd," I said. "I was starting to get used to the whole model thing." I narrowed my eyes and pursed my lips.

"Okay, easy, Zoolander," Naomi chuckled. "You've got the back cover settled. Now you just need a track listing to put on it. How many songs do you have done?"

I didn't have to think. "Seven. If we use all the songs we're working on," And I figured we should; it wasn't like we need to hold them back for another album, "it'll get us up to thirteen total."

"Your first album had thirteen official tracks, not counting 'Emerald.' Nice symmetry."

I blinked at Lana. "Did you know that?"

"I didn't even think about it."

Naomi chuckled. "Karma, then. I'm a big believer in the universe guiding things like that. Come on. Get yourselves cleaned up and I'll buy you all lunch."

A tabloid speculated that Laura's twin sister was pregnant. Not a huge deal until Laura explained the picture they used as proof - captioned as "Baby bump?" with an arrow pointing to the abdomen of a tight blue T-shirt - was actually her. She was sitting on the arm of my chair, leaning back as she stared at the offensive picture on my laptop. "I was leaving a Subway. Why do I even bother making healthy choices if they're just going to pick and poke at every unflattering angle? Next time I'm going to McDonalds. If they're going to say I'm with child, then I'm going to at least earn it."

I rubbed her hip. "I'm sorry, sweetie. But they published a retraction, right? 'Oops, sorry, wrong twin. A t'ousand apologies.'"

"Yeah, because when it's me, it couldn't *possibly* be a baby bump, right? No way the lesbian is going to have a kid." She slid off the arm of the chair and trudged barefoot into the kitchen. "I want a Pop Tart. If they're going to call me fat on the internet, I'm going to go ahead and have two."

"Butter 'em," I suggested.

She came back out with just one Pop Tart, unbuttered. She sank onto the couch and stretched so that her feet rested on the arm of it. "You know, they fell over themselves so fast to say they screwed up when they found out it was me, I want to get back at them. Make them look even more wrong. Just come out and say that I *am* pregnant."

I glanced at her without moving my head. "Is this like the thing where I proposed to you a dozen times before we got married?"

"Hm?"

"Well, just claiming to be pregnant is a great lie for about nine months, assuming you pig out a lot and gain enough weight. But around the year mark, people are going to start putting the pieces together."

She shook her head. "No, they won't. Remember that actress? You and I did the math and realized it was fourteen months between her announcement and when she actually gave birth."

"Yeah, but there was a baby at the end of that lie."

"Nah, forget it." She waved me off and munched her Pop Tart. "I'm not having this conversation about something I'm not really thinking about."

I leaned back. "What if we did? Think about it, I mean? You guys just put out a new album, Radiation Canary is about to go on hiatus so we can focus on other projects. Nessa and her husband are trying to conceive." I shrugged. "We might as well discuss it."

She laughed. "We haven't even been married for a year."

"I'm not saying we have to drop everything and start searching for a sperm donor. I don't even know which of us would carry it to term. I guess I just want to know if it's something you can see us doing."

She broke off part of the Pop Tart and stared at it, popped it into her mouth, and chewed carefully. "It's a scary world out there for adults, let alone a baby."

"Yeah."

Finally, she quietly said, "It's an option. I mean, it has to be an option."

I nodded and smiled. "Yeah. I agree."

"Yeah?"

I put down my computer and joined her on the couch. I bent down and kissed her, and she put the remaining pieces of the Pop Tart on the coffee table. After a few minutes of comforting her about her waistline, and a few more minutes of exploration, she said, "You know we can't make a baby this way."

"Mm-hmm."

She sighed. "Okay. Just checking. Carry on."

She turned out to be right, and it was impossible to have a baby that way. But we gave it the old college try just to be absolutely certain.

Track Five

Lana leaned against the wall, one thumb hooked in the pocket of her jeans as she held the other against her ear. "I hate time differences."

Catherine's chuckle was throaty, thick with sleepiness. "It's all right. I don't mind waking up to your voice no matter what country I'm in. The only downside is I can't cuddle with you until I fall back to sleep."

"Poor baby. All alone in your bed." Lana smiled. "I wish I could fly out there." She looked toward the street, stretching her legs and resting her shoulders against the wall. "I was lucky to get five minutes to call you between recording sessions. I was so eager to hear your voice I didn't even think about what time it must be there."

"S'all right," she murmured, and heat pooled in Lana's gut.

"God, your voice is sexy."

"Mm. Thank you. Yours is good, too."

Lana wet her lips and looked toward the door. "Are you wearing your normal pajamas? That long shirt that reaches your thighs?"

"Mm-hmm."

"Lift it up."

Catherine chuckled. "You're being naughty, beautiful."

"Uh-huh. Slip your pillow between your legs."

"I will not! Where are you?"

Lana looked around. "Standing outside the recording studio. There's a mostly-empty parking lot, a dumpster against a wooden fence, and there are three trees between the asphalt and the street. It's almost dark, but there's no one out." She grinned and lowered her voice. "Put your pillow between your legs, Kitty."

"Tit for tat. I want you to rub yourself."

"That's not exactly fair. Unless you're sleeping outside."

Catherine said, "You're the one who called me. Disturbed my beauty sleep."

"Trust me, baby, you can afford to miss a couple of those."

"Oh, how I love you." She heard muffled noises against the phone, Catherine grunted, and then she sighed. "Okay. I've done it. Now what, lover?"

Lana closed her eyes and pictured the scene. Catherine was in the same cottage where they stayed over Christmas, so she knew the bedroom well. There was a slanted roof, a four-paned window covered by a sheer curtain, and a little lamp on the nightstand served as a nightlight. In her head, she imagined the light was on, spilling over Catherine's face, making it glow even more than usual. "It's my leg. Pressing against your sex. Rub against it... make yourself come."

"Are you touching yourself, La-la?"

Lana looked at the door but didn't really care if anyone was coming. She bent her leg to offer a bit of privacy, flattening her foot against the wall as she unfastened her jeans with one hand. She pushed her fingers into her underwear. "Yeah. I'm touching myself. I want to hear you moan, Kitty."

"Oh, you do the best bad things to me," Catherine moaned.

Lana laughed. "God, that belongs in a song..."

"Use it. I'll think of you touching yourself... and your leg between mah-hai... mine every time I hear it. I want to hear you sing it and remember your juices are on your f-fingers."

Lana squeezed her eyes shut and grunted as she came, and Catherine's breath puffed onto the speaker of the phone with each sharp, harsh exhale. Lana slipped her hand out of her underwear and wiped them against the cotton of her shirt. Catherine gave a final, tremulous moan, and then sighed.

"Darling."

"I'm moving there."

"Hm?"

Lana blinked back the tears that were suddenly in her eyes. "I can't take being eight hours and thousands of miles away from you. As soon as the album is done and we're finished touring, I'm going to move. I can make music there as easily as I can here."

"Lana... call me tomorrow and say this all again. I don't trust myself to believe this isn't just a dream."

Lana smiled. "I'll remind you every day until I can put you to sleep properly."

"La-la."

"Go to sleep, Kitty. I love you."

"And I love you, too. I think I can sleep now."

"Sweet dreams."

They hung up, and Lana adjusted her jeans before buttoning them again. She looked at the street and both directions to make sure she hadn't been seen, then ran her fingers through her hair. She went back inside where the rest of the band was working on a song Codie wrote called "Tandem Fall." Karen glanced up and did something akin to a double-take.

"You okay? You look flushed."

Lana gestured vaguely over her shoulder. "It's fine."

Karen said, "Are you sure? If it's your syncope, we should get you something to drink."

"No, I'm fine."

"Better safe than sorry." Naomi turned to the producer. "Can we get Lana some Gatorade or--"

"I'm fine!" Lana said, a little more harshly than she expected. She smiled and picked up her guitar. "I just had phone sex with my girlfriend in a semi-public place, and now I'm telling all my friends about it, so what do you say we just ignore this little interlude and work on 'Tandem Fall'?" She looked around. "Unless you all want details."

"How does it start?" Karen said.

"G," Nessa said.

Lana nodded. "That's what I thought. One, two, three, four..."

I parked outside the Dads' house, knowing they were at the store and wouldn't have minded even if they were there. I stood at the end of the driveway and looked at the neighborhood. The people across the street had done some landscaping, and it seemed like there was a party going on a few houses away. It was close enough to familiar to recognize, but it was shockingly different. Kind of like me.

I turned and started walking south, following the trail I'd first blazed when Mom and Dad were still married and holding World War III clashes in the kitchen. I just needed to get out of the house and catch my breath, let my ears stop ringing for ten or twenty minutes before diving back in. By the time I got home, they were usually to the bitter silence part of the night, so I just hid out in my room until bedtime.

I walked the familiar sidewalks and looked at evidence the neighborhood had gone on without me. One house used to have an old RV parked next to it, but it was curiously absent. On a trip, sold, or had the owners moved? Where was the yappy little bastard dog that always tried to give me a heart attack when I passed his territory? I hated him, but I hoped nothing had happened to the beast.

My path led down the old dead-end street. I walked all the way to the end, past the property where our rehearsal space once stood, then turned around and angled myself up into the parking lot. I hoisted myself up onto the retaining wall, surprised at how easy it seemed. I wasn't any taller, but there was the possibility I was a little stronger than I used to be. All the hours of practicing and playing and hauling my instruments on and off-stage. Not to mention hoisting Lana and Laura onto... well. Onto things.

I rubbed my arms to feel if the biceps were noticeably larger, but then I looked at the blank square of concrete in front of me. I don't remember when the building became musical. There was just a day when I stopped and noticed I could hear someone playing inside, so I stopped to listen.

Of all the streets in the neighborhood, of all the places to stop and rest, I'd chosen here. The music had been soothing, and I'd desperately needed something relaxing in my life. I blinked back tears and wiped them away with the back of my hand.

"Thanks," I whispered.

I didn't know who I was speaking to. A TV show I used to watch with Dad coined the phrase 'God, Fate, Time or Whatever' as an all-encompassing deity, and I felt it was apt enough for the situation. Whatever had guided my steps and put me on this wall... Whoever had taken the vile acts of divorce and Codie's smoking and combined them to make something so wonderful occur... I felt blessed to have been guided.

I slid off the wall and walked to the spot where we had once rehearsed. I pictured myself standing in the doorway with my instruments, torn between fleeing and standing my ground as I looked at Codie and Nessa. And Lana, so reassuring, motioning me inside so they could see what I could do. The great G.F.T.W. bless her for taking a chance on a girl who had suffered through a lifetime of lessons and the odd recital for her *rock band*. What guts that must have taken. She must have really liked my music.

I took the Sharpie out of my shirt pocket, crouched, and leaned forward to write on the concrete.

"Radiation Canary, born here 2004. Thanks for my life. Karen Everett."

I stood up and brushed off my skirt, and slipped the pen back into my pocket. I sighed, wishing the building was still there so I could touch a wall or walk through it one more time, but all good things had to end. I left the property and walked back to where I'd left my car.

My wife was waiting for me. In two hours my band was scheduled to be in the studio to record one of the songs from our farewell album. But it wouldn't hurt to be a little late.

Track Six

Cartography set us up on a whirlwind tour that would begin the day of *Fallout*'s release. When I first saw the dates, I thought they had us hitting every single state over the course of four months. Eventually I noticed we did miss a few states, but not many. We would start in Georgia, moving up the eastern seaboard until we hit Maine. Then into Canada for two shows, back down to hit Wisconsin. We would barn-storm through the Plains, spiral over the desert, then shoot across to California to follow the west coast.

Our final five shows were in Washington, and our farewell concert was in Seattle the same week we were scheduled to be on *Settle In, Seattle!* I couldn't wrap my head around it, the number of hours we'd be required to fill with music and banter... my fingers ached just at the thought of it. Laura had made a ritual out of rubbing my hands with lotion, giving extra care to each of my fingers. It made me feel decadent to sit in front of the TV while my wife idly massaged my hands, decadent and adored. I had the feeling I was going to miss her desperately during the tour; the Femme Reapers had their own album to promote, so for a few months she and I were going to be ships passing in the night.

We tried to make up for it during the nights before I left, but I still feel like we could have done more.

In Atlanta, a beautiful blonde woman asked us to sign her bra. I refrained, but Lana agreed. I gave in when the woman pulled a bra out of her purse and laid it on the table. I had been expected a lifted-shirt scenario, so I was greatly relieved to just sign the cup and hand it back to her. Codie and Nessa added their signatures to the other cup ("Because otherwise your boobs will be lopsided," Codie explained).

In Arlington, a girl in line begged us not to break up, sobbing as we signed her copy of *Fallout*. I was at a loss, but Lana took her aside and spoke with her for a good five minutes until she stopped crying. We left her in the capable hands of the man she was with, apologized to the crowd for the delay, and went back to signing our names.

Lana suggested we use our free afternoon in New York to take Mom out to lunch. We had enough time afterward to attend a taping of *The Daily Show*, and

Mom watched our concert from backstage. In the green room, Mom surreptitiously pointed to one of the VIP guests and asked if it was who she thought it was. It took me a moment to place her.

"Dee-ya," I said. She was a British pop star with pink hair and a career built around cinematic music videos. She actually released them on DVD with bonus features and making-of documentaries. She was hugely famous, but had become so only after we became big. It was odd to think somebody of her caliber was joining our circle, rather than inviting us in. We were the stars and Dee-ya, as huge as she was, kept looking around to make sure someone was documenting her appearance at a Radiation Canary concert.

I decided I would never consider it normal to go to sleep in one state and wake up in another, so I gave up trying to acclimate myself. I went to bed in New York, and the bus departed without waking me. The next morning we were on a road somewhere in New England, passing between trees, and I had no idea which of the many clustered states we were in. I found it comforting.

In Boston, Lana asked me if she could perform "The Girl on the Wall." I didn't have a problem with it, but I had to leave the stage during every performance because I didn't want everyone to see me sobbing. Lana decided to take advantage of it, playing up the fact I was leaving the stage. She stepped to the microphone and intoned, "Would the owner of a lime-green Gremlin please report to the parking lot? Your lights are on, and your engine is smoking, and all of the tires are flat."

"Shit," I murmured, putting down my violin and hurrying off-stage to the sound of laughter from the audience.

When I came back after the song, Lana said, "K! Your car was smoking and the tires were all flat?"

"Yeah. That's all normal. But you didn't say anything about the fuzzy dice. I thought I'd been robbed!"

While we were in Canada, our album displaced Femme Reapers on the bestseller chart. Naomi suggested Laura and I call in to a Seattle radio show to set up a mock feud between our bands, each of us demanding that listeners go buy our CD. "And then buy their CD, just so you can throw it in the trash." I ruined the image by saying, "Love you, baby," out of habit when Laura hung up, but Naomi thought it was a masterstroke. Sales of both albums surged, and I just hoped people knew we were joking when we said to throw them in the trash.

I was shocked at the number of people who showed up in the autograph line with items from the collector's set release. Posters and T-shirts that weren't available anywhere else, meaning these people had shelled out fifty dollars just for one album. I was humbled, and tried to make it up to them with conversation and photographs. How could I refuse to take a picture when they'd gone the extra mile for our work?

Catherine flew out when we performed in Vegas, ostensibly just to spend time with Lana. But considering what past visits to Sin City had done to her relationships,, I'm sure Lana wanted her there to keep her under control. I was sleeping when Lana blundered into my room and started throwing clothes at me, whispering that I had to get up right then, immediately, no time for questions or explanations.

That was how I came to be standing in front of a minister at four in the morning wearing sweatpants, two different shoes (one of which I was positive wasn't mine), and half-asleep as Catherine and Lana exchanged vows. Lana was drunk, and Catherine was sober but brimming with energy as they kissed, and I signed a paper that said I was a witness even though my eyes had been shut for most of the ceremony.

They consummated the marriage in a rented limo as they drove me back to the hotel. Or so I'm told. Apparently I slept through the entire thing, including transport back to my bed. I didn't find out it was real until breakfast the next morning when they displayed their rings.

"We'll do the whole ceremony when we're settled. But right now she's a British citizen, I'm a US citizen, we're going back and forth from one country to the other..." She kissed Catherine's cheek. "But it felt right to do it now, while we're in the place where our romance started."

Codie playfully sneered, "Thanks a lot. Now I'm the only single woman in the group. Did you even think about how I'd feel?"

Nessa put her arm across Codie's shoulders. "Well, I'm the only one not married to a woman. I'll marry you and take care of two birds with one stone. Isn't that big of me?"

"Did you say 'bigamy'?" I asked.

Lana shook her head. "It's Vegas, so it doesn't count. Besides, she's married to a man. She can still Vegas-marry a woman without it being weird."

"I thought that was a Utah thing."

Catherine shook her head, chuckling. "Oh, you're all barking mad."

"You're the one who married into this madhouse," I said before sipping my orange juice. "You're one of us now."

On cue, Codie and Nessa both intoned, "One of us... one of us..." Lana took the opportunity to neck with Catherine, and I had a sudden flashback to the limo ride the night before. I quickly turned my mind to other subjects before I remembered too much, turning to talk to Codie about the possibility of marrying her plane so she wouldn't feel like the odd woman out.

Track Seven

Fallout stayed at the top of record sales, and the Femme Reapers' *Ozymandias* was right below it at number two. When I got home I dropped my bags, hugged her tightly and kissed her hard. I let her go and stroked her cheek and, I swear with only innocent intentions, asked about the "war" between our albums by whispering, "Who is on top?"

She smiled, kissed my nose, and pulled me to the bedroom. "Whichever of us gets to the toy box first."

It turned out that Radiation Canary was number one in the country, but the Femme Reaper was able to claim the better victory.

Afterward we lay in bed, my arms loosely wrapped around her waist, her hair in my face. I was stroking her body and listening to her breathe, trying to decide if she was asleep or awake judging by her breathing. It started to rain, and I watched it pour down the bedroom window for a long time before Laura shifted in my arms and pressed back against me.

"Welcome home," she said. "I missed you."

I smiled and kissed her neck. "For the last time. From now on, I'll be free to follow you around on tour. I'll be your mistress, hanging around making sure you have mimosas and peeled grapes in the dressing room."

She chuckled. "Right. You can't just stop working after all this time. You've released, what, eight albums in ten years? Anyone running that fast can't just stop on a dime without falling flat on their face. Answer me honestly. What are you working on right now?"

"You."

"Honestly," she chuckled, slapping my arm.

I hesitated and then said, "Well. I was thinking about a concept album set during a masquerade party."

She grinned. "I want to play on it."

"Have your people call my people."

She rolled over in my arms and kissed my cheeks, my nose, and my lips. I chuckled and kissed her forehead. "This is so bizarre."

"What?"

"I had your album. The first Femme Reapers album, I owned it before I even knew you. And now I'm in bed with you talking about having you play on my next album. I want to go back in time, get behind myself in the store, and whisper in her ear that one day she's going to marry that beautiful blonde on the back of the CD."

Laura grinned. "You thought I was beautiful?"

"Well, I was more focused on your sister..."

She pinched me under the blankets, in a bad spot, and I yelped. "Of course, I could be mistaken. Back then I couldn't tell you two apart."

"How do you tell us apart now?"

"You're the one who is always fucking me."

Laura said, "Ah," under her breath and licked my bottom lip. "Good system." She pulled me close and proceeded to reconfirm her identity.

In keeping with the tradition of the past two weeks, the Radiation Canary regained the top spot.

Laura and her sister invited the band out to dinner, and we gratefully accepted. We were dying for some kind of sit-down meal after weeks of nothing but tour cuisine. I knew something was up when we arrived to find the restaurant was nearly deserted, and my suspicions were confirmed when I saw Naomi waiting in the coat-check room. I slipped my arm around her elbow as we were led to a table.

"You're going to kill us, right? Go for that 'post-tragedy' sales bump?"

"Right. Even if you all go solo, I'll still make more off you alive than dead."

I crossed my eyes at her. "So comforting, thank you."

"Just relax. Your wife set this up for you. I just helped organize it."

We were sat in front of a large stage where instruments had been set out. Lana eyed the guitar and said, "You don't think they want us to perform, do you? I wouldn't mind, but I'm so damn beat."

I rubbed her shoulders, sure that Laura wouldn't spring a surprise performance on me. We placed our order with the bow-tied waiter and, as he scurried off, the house lights slowly faded.

"Here we go," Codie said, sounding a bit wary.

The Femme Reapers took the stage, and Laura winked at me. I held up my hand with my pinkie, thumb and forefinger extended to say 'I love you.' They were already wearing their guitars and Ella counted them into the song. I recognized it as soon as Laura began the opening chords, and I realized what was happening. They were playing "My Weak Hand," from our first album.

Ella's voice had a lower timbre than Lana's, so the tone of the song became much more aggressive. I absolutely loved it. I looked at Lana and saw she was nodding along with the music. She caught me looking, mouthed, "wow," and then sang along when Ella sang, "Talking to you is like fighting with my weak hand."

Derrick Lao was next, singing "The Man of Many Wiles." Our food came, but I'm afraid we didn't actually pay much attention to how it tasted. One by one, Cartography acts took the stage and performed songs from each of our albums. Thin Ice Walkers performed an all-male version of "Diving for Pearls" that had Lana slapping the table, her head down to stifle her laughter as the men did a nearly-burlesque rendition of our subtle ode to cunnilingus.

Yeah, I said it. We'd danced around it in interviews, but everyone knew we were full of shit. What did we have to lose now? It was a song about tonguing a woman's clitoris, and I don't care who knows it.

The Guardian Angels performed "Monstrous Regiment" in full military regalia. During dessert, Sarah Wiley and the Coyotes did a heartbreaking version of "The Long Night" that had me embarrassedly in tears. A person shouldn't cry over something they wrote, but my God. Sarah's voice was so beautiful and the anguish was so sublime that I couldn't help myself. Lana put an arm around me and held me until the song ended.

By the time Regan Duffy finished "Falling Up," we had moved on to after-dinner drinks. The last two songs - "Waifs and Strays" and "Count to 1 Million" - were performed by the Femme Reapers. We started to applaud as the last song ended, assuming the concert was over since they had done one song from every album. But then someone began to play the violin and all the acts returned to the stage.

It felt like my skin tightened around me as they began to sing "Say a Prayer." I looked at Nessa and saw tears streaking down her cheeks, and even Codie looked moved. The only other time I'd seen that look on her face was when she was in the air. When the song was over, Sarah Wiley took the microphone and smiled at us.

"We know you're just going on hiatus and not officially breaking up, but we want you to promise you won't stay away too long."

Lana wiped her eyes. "Why would we ever come back when you just proved you can play our songs better than we ever did?" She looked at me. "Early retirement?" To Codie and Nessa, "Early retirement? Early retirement? Okay, then. See you folks!"

Naomi whistled from the back of the room. "I have a boilerplate contract locking you in to ten more albums, and I'm not afraid to forge your signatures on it."

Lana turned to me and stage-whispered, "Your ex-girlfriend is such a *bitch.*" We sat back down and Naomi stepped up onto the stage.

"We just wanted to let you know how much you four have meant to Cartography. Not just your music or your record sales - although that helped - but your strength to get through the tragedy of Dash passing away and carrying us into a new era. I know when we met I promised to put you on the map, but you're the ones who helped make our name. Thank you. And whatever any of you do in the future, just know that you'll always have a home with us."

We joined them on the stage, hugging Naomi and complimenting the other bands on their renditions of our songs. I seriously wanted to hear Sarah Wiley play a full album of covers, because her sound just blew me away. I gave her my email address so we could stay in touch while I was working on the potential masquerade album.

I caught Lana's eye and she winked at me. I smiled and hugged Derrick Lao, and for the first time it didn't feel like the band was closing a door. It felt like we were stepping into a new arena. God knew how we would fare, but the important thing was taking the first step.

Track Eight

Nessa woke up nauseated the morning after the Seattle concert, staying in bed longer than normal and clutching her stomach. Scott stayed with her until he risked being late for work, and she shooed him out the door promising it was just a tour virus. They had all picked them up from time to time, and there was nothing to do but ride it out. At noon, she dragged herself to the bathroom and spent some time on the tile floor before a thought occurred to her. She searched the cabinet for the item they'd bought after the Valentine's Day 'spur of the moment attack' as they had called it and read the instructions before taking the test.

She waited the allotted amount of time, closed her eyes, and held up the test alongside the part of the manual that told her what the different displays meant. She exhaled sharply and shook her head, meeting her own tired eyes in the mirror. She smiled and rested her hands on the edge of the sink, trying to wrap her head around the fact, according to a bit of fifteen dollar plastic, she was pregnant.

"Nice timing, Vanessa. Looks like you have a future project to work on after all."

Lana marked the show's date on her calendar; three days until the end of the road. They were going back on *Settle In, Seattle!* on a Friday, displacing any Friday Night Audition band who might have taken the spot. Nick told them it was only right to end on the same night they began. For the farewell episode, the show held an online raffle for fans in the Seattle area. The audience was going to be full of fans that not only loved the band, but had fought and paid for the right to be present at the end.

Catherine was back in England, but they were able to video-chat every night before bed. That meant Lana was saying 'sweet dreams' at two in the afternoon, but it was worth the forced jet lag. One morning Lana woke to a text message at five-thirty-two in the morning. "I sent the sun to keep you warm today. Has it arrived yet?"

Lana rolled over to see the sky was tinged with gold. "Just showed up. Thank you, baby."

Catherine responded with "XOXOX," "groping-O," and "tongue-X," and Lana went back to sleep with a smile on her face. That day she broke the news to the others that she was officially moving to London to be with Catherine. Karen took it hard as Lana had expected, but Codie shocked them all. She said nothing, just stood up and walked out of the room. Lana followed her outside, standing on the grass and looking down at her boots.

"You okay? Don't tell me all this time you've been harboring feelings for me."

Codie scoffed. "Don't flatter yourself, Kent."

"So what is it?"

"Seventeen years, Lana. From that day I waited for you outside class, to the rehearsal space, to–" She gestured at the air around them. "Everyone who ever meant anything to me has left. But I didn't care. I told myself I didn't make attachments, didn't need the responsibility of meaning something to someone. But you were always there. You were the one thing I could count on not changing. You bailed me out when I got my DUI."

"Hey, did you pay me back for that?"

"Don't change the subject. I've been ignoring this because, hey, it's just LA. I got the plane. I could always fly down and have lunch or something. But now... England. That's a long way to go for a lunch. It's like another world over there, and I don't know... how to say goodbye to you." Her eyes were wet, and she was shifting her weight from foot to foot like she was boiling over with energy. "I do love you, Lana. You're my sister. And I'm going to miss you. A lot." She laughed and her tears fell free. "See? Lame, right? No wonder I never wrote any good songs."

Lana hugged her. "Don't you dare badmouth 'Walla Walla Sweetheart.'"

Codie laughed against Lana's shoulder.

"I'm serious. It's my favorite song." She kissed Codie's cheek. "I love you, too. And I'm going to miss you, too." She put her hand over Codie's tattoo. "But I'm not leaving you. Got that?"

"Yeah."

Lana wiped her thumbs over Codie's cheeks. "Good. Now, do you want me to punch you in the stomach in case the others notice you were crying?"

"Nah. I'll just say you Maced me."

Lana grinned and led Codie back inside where the others were waiting. Karen said, "Everything okay?"

"Aces."

Nessa said, "So when do you leave for the jolly ol' island?"

"The morning after the show. I have to leave the studio and go straight to the airport. I'm not eager to get away from you guys, I just... need to hold my girl."

Karen smiled. "I understand entirely." She held up her beer bottle. "Cheerio."

"Oh, don't–"

"Pip-pip, gov'nah," Nessa said. She was toasting with a bottle of water, in deference to the condition she had revealed to them earlier in the day.

Codie held up her bottle. "Uh. Some British thing."

They laughed and tapped their bottles together. Karen said, "And push comes to shove, London could always be our first stop on a big European tour. I've always wanted to see Lichtenstein."

Lana paused with the beer bottle poised at her lips. "Oh, there has to be a Sapphic joke in that somewhere. Come on. Lick-ten-stein?"

Nessa affected a Groucho Marx accent and waggled her bottle like a cigar. "Lichtenstein? I hardly *know* ten-stein."

They all agreed that it was the most solid joke they could come up with. They also agreed they could never visit that country with a straight face. Worse things had happened.

Track Nine

The day finally arrived. We thought about donning special costumes to commemorate the night, but finally decided it would be best to just wear what we would normally wear for a concert. Nessa had gotten an amazing navy blue pea coat that she wore over a khaki shirt and black pants. I wore a peasant blouse and a skirt, but I didn't wear shoes in honor of the first time I'd taken the lead to sing "Emerald." Lana wore a hat with her hair tucked under it so I could pull it off of her at a pre-determined time. Codie wore a T-shirt with a new logo on it: the circle was broken and crumpled over her abdomen, while the canary that had once been entrapped by it was flying over her left breast, the bird's widespread wings resting over her heart.

I threw up an embarrassing number of times before show time. I was more nervous now than when we did our first show. We had said our goodbyes to Lana already, throwing her a farewell party the night before so she could go to the airport without lingering hugs and well-wishes. Signing autographs for the people waiting outside the studio helped calm my nerves a little. Only then did I accept that we weren't just patting ourselves on the back for the past ten years; the show was simply a way to say thank-you to the fans. To show our gratitude for everything they had done for us, and everything they had built us into. I could handle that.

We didn't see Nick before the show, so we were as shocked as the studio audience when he walked through the curtains and revealed he wasn't wearing his normal three-piece suit. Instead, he was wearing a burnt-orange T-shirt from the Rainmakers for Wizards tour. He held his arms out and did a fashionista spin, took a bow, and then plucked at the sides of the shirt's design so the cameras would be sure to pick up the text. He reached his mark and hooked his thumbs together over his heart and flapped his fingers in the now universally-known canary symbol.

When the audience quieted, he clasped his hands behind his back. "Yes, ladies and gentlemen. The night you and I have been looking forward to and dreading in equal measure has finally arrived. Tonight, on this stage, Radiation Canary will take their final bow. Yes, it's true." The audience booed and he held up his hands. "They have promised it's not forever. It's a hiatus, not a break-up.

It's just a graduation to something bigger. *Is* there anything bigger than Radiation Canary these days, though?"

One girl in the audience shrieked, "No!"

Nick pointed at her. "Thank you, ma'am. Not the interactive portion of the show, but I like your enthusiasm. So instead of holding another Friday Night Audition and trying to find the next big band, I thought I would honor these lovely ladies by postponing the Auditions until next month."

The audience began to applaud, and I hoped my blushing wasn't apparent as I meekly approached the spot where Nick was standing. He turned, saw me, and feigned surprise as he held out his arms like a model working the boat show. "Karen Everett, ladies and gentlemen!" When the applause died down, he tugged on his shirt collar in lieu of adjusting his tie. "Ah, Karen, what are you doing out here? You're not being interviewed for another ten minutes or so."

"I just had a question. Uh, did you say this was Radiation Canary's final performance?"

"Yes, uh, yes. For a while, at least. You're... going on hiatus to work on other projects."

I blinked at the camera and then began backing away. "Um. I have to make a call."

The audience laughed as I hurried backstage, and I heard Nick say, "Well, it's a truism in this business that the talent is always the last to know..."

Once again, we were broken into two pairs and interviewed during the first and second segments of the show. I was with Codie, and Lana was with Nessa. We discussed our upcoming plans, various loved ones who were waiting for us to have some free time, and Lana talked about moving to London to be with "a certain celebrity." I had noticed that neither Lana nor Catherine referred to themselves as married, and I knew Lana wasn't wearing a ring. I had confronted her about it and she said they had the Vegas marriage annulled so it wouldn't diminish any real wedding they wanted to have in the future.

Nessa, having already broken the news to everyone close to her, revealed her pregnancy to the audience. "So you see, Nick, even without this planned hiatus, the band would have had to take some time off so I could be a mommy."

"I see!" He adjusted his tie and leaned close. "Have you considered names? Because Nick could work for a boy or a girl. Nicholas, Nicole, Nikki..."

Lana said, "Nope, the name is already spoken for. She's going to name it after the band."

Nick laughed. "Radiation Canary?"

"R.C. for short," Lana said.

"You're joking, but I think you've just given at least one of my viewers an idea."

Lana held her hands out in prayer. "Please do not name your children Radiation Canary. Or either of those words by itself. Lana's a good name, though."

Nick laughed, "Yes, it is. Okay, folks. We have to take a quick commercial break, but when we come back... Radiation Canary is going to give a very special performance. For tonight, I am not your host, I'm just the lucky S.O.B. who has the best seat in the house. Stay tuned."

The four of us stood shoulder to shoulder at the front of the performance area. It made it easier to hold hands, squeezing until the cameras came on and the lights came down on us. During the commercial break, the crowd had been chanting the band's name, but Lana and Nick requested silence when the band started. Across the stage, leaning against his desk, Nick smiled as the camera zoomed in on him.

"Welcome back to one of the darkest moments in this show's sordid history. Ladies and gentlemen, if you're a member of my audience, the band needs no introduction. With a brand-new song which will be available for *free* download off our website after tonight's show." He put his hands over his chest and I was shocked to hear his voice break when he spoke again. "With a heavy heart, I present... Radiation Canary."

We let the applause die, and then the lights came up on us. We sang in one voice.

"When our nights were darkest
And the heavy clouds hid the sun
Through the times that were hardest
You were always the one..."

Nessa broke off and walked to her piano. She took her position, rested her hand above the keys, and softly began to play.

"You made me smile in times of strife
When I was sure my words weren't worth a dime
You were the ones who provided light and gave me life
So now I want to thank you, one more last time."

We moved into position. Lana slipped the strap of her guitar over her head, I positioned my violin, and Codie trotted to get behind the drums in time. The song swelled and exploded with sound. Small colored spotlights at the back of the stage swept over us in wide arcs, occasionally illuminating Karen with blues, purples, and pinks. I smiled and thought that she was still gorgeous when bathed in blue.

I'd written "One More Last Time" as a special goodbye to the fans, and I could tell they loved it. Tears filled my eyes as Lana finished the chorus, moving from one side of the stage to the other so she stood by every member of the band for at least half of one verse.

When we reached the end, she stopped playing and took her microphone off the stand. "We're not going to be casual about this. You all have made our dreams come true, and you gave this band life. Thank you. Thank all of you who are here, who are watching, who bought our albums and came to our shows. We may go away, but we'll never be gone."

She walked to me. "The woman who gave me a voice, the girl on the wall, the final piece of the puzzle that made us who we are today, let me hear it for Karen Everett!"

A crowd of people applauded for me. My heart swelled and I smiled at Lana as she backed away to where Nessa was playing.

"You know her as the amazing, dexterous, modest and shy Nessa Grace but we know her by another name. And soon we'll all know her as an amazing mommy. Give it up for Mrs. Vanessa Wayland!"

Nessa stopped playing long enough to do a mock curtsey as Lana ascended to stand next to Codie's stool.

"And this... oh, God, I can't believe I'm blanking."

Codie turned and tapped her drumsticks off Lana's breasts. The audience cheered as Lana retreated, laughing.

"Oh, right. Ladies and gentlemen, the band's heartbeat, the woman who keeps us all on track, one *heck* of an aeroplane pilot, and my best friend for almost... half my life." Her voice broke and she covered it by patting Codie on the shoulder. "My friends, I give you Codie Maia Renton."

She bent down to kiss the top of Codie's head and moved back to her front position. In rehearsal, Lana had tried to end it there. We let her think she'd succeeded, but I nodded at Nessa and leaned closer to my microphone. "And the voice of Radiation Canary..."

Lana stopped and looked at me, but it was Nessa who spoke next.

"...and the beautiful face of the band..."

"The woman who brought us together," Codie said.

I shouted, "Miss..."

Nessa continued, "...Lana..."

And Codie was nearly loud enough that she didn't need a microphone when she said, "...Kent!"

Lana blushed bright red as the crowd roared. She returned to her microphone, eyes shining as we kept playing behind her. "Thank you all so, so much. From the bottom of our hearts. You *will* see us again, and I hope we see you. Thank you, for everything. You've been a great audience, and we've been Radiation Canary. We love you! Goodnight!"

Nick had told us he wouldn't intrude on our farewell, so the lights shut off and the show ended without him saying anything to the audience at home. The cameras were off, the music stopped, and the last performance of Radiation Canary came to an end. It was quite a while before the audience stopped cheering, however.

I can still hear them today.

CURTAIN CALL
(2014)

The airport is bustling, busy as always despite the fears heightened security would deter people from traveling. I walk past the pizza restaurant and go for the bookstore. She's standing with her back to the door, and I take a moment to appreciate the curve of her hips before I press against her. I put my face in her hair and breathe deeply. "Oh, my God, Laura Cowan. I'm such a huge fan. Can I have your autograph?"

"It's on the marriage certificate. Isn't that enough?"

"Yeah, right. Like I could sell that on eBay."

She chuckles, twists her neck and kisses me. "I thought you were waiting for me at the gate."

"There were fans. I felt awkward. They were great, though." I move my hands over her belt to span her slightly-widened hips. My fingers tease the hem of her shirt and come to rest on the bump of her lower abdomen. "How's the Bug? Giving you any trouble?"

"She's being good for now. They don't kick this early. If we were in the kicking stage, I wouldn't be able to fly."

"Oh. That would be a bad thing. I'm not flying to London without you to keep me company." I sway with her and look at the books in front of her. "Find anything good to read on the flight?"

"A couple of books, yeah. A magazine."

"Good. Come on. I bet the girls at the gate are Femme Reapers fans, too." I take her hand and lead her to the counter to pay for her books. She actually isn't showing yet, and even a tabloid would be hard-pressed to say she has a baby bump. But because I know, because I was there when we got the positive result, I think I can see it. Her body has adjusted to its new condition, and it's getting ready to nurture our baby.

I can't stop smiling when I even think those words. Our baby. I emailed Lana that I had great news for her, but I'm playing it coy. I want Lana to be the first to know. It seems right.

Nessa's son Nathaniel is beautiful, and his first pictures helped convince us to take the step ourselves. At the moment Nessa's career is on hold while she deals with a rambunctious toddler. I've convinced her to play piano for a couple of tracks on *Masquerade*, and we'll find some time to get into the studio together after we get back from London. I think my brain was protecting me, because I didn't realize how much I've missed working with the girls until Nessa and I started making plans. I can't wait to see her, to play music with her again.

Codie has played on an astounding seven different albums since the end of Radiation Canary. Sometimes I'll listen to Cartography artists and as soon as the drum beat starts, I know it's her. And on days when the weather is good, I'll hear the buzz of a Cessna engine and I'll look outside to see her plane swooping across Puget Sound. I love knowing she's keeping an eye on us. She doesn't tell us everywhere she goes, but I know she's been way up north into Canada. I've told her that if she ever makes it to the North Pole, I want pictures.

Lana and Catherine have had their hiccups, but they're still together. Lana has started doing music for television shows; she wrote the theme song of a show that Laura and I never miss. She's part of a renaissance in the theme song industry; shows that once just put up a title card and played a musical sting were now using actual compositions on their DVD releases. The right song could create a mood for the entire series, and Lana was at the forefront of the revival.

Catherine also got a new job in television, playing the down-to-Earth human on a British science-fiction show. There was the standard groundswell of irritation from fans that a leggy model was playing a "typical Earth girl," but her character quickly won over viewers. A poll held after her first six episodes listed her as one of the best compatriots in the show's long history.

As for me, I'm deliriously happy. Laura and I have fought, as couples do, but all the energy we spend fighting is equal to the energy spent making up. When we decided to have our baby - our Bug, as we say until we settle on a name or at least know the gender - we spent long hours discussing the pros and cons of which one of us should carry it. I was willing, but Laura implored me to let it be her. She didn't have to push hard; I could tell how much it meant to her. And I am completely in love with the idea of Laura giving birth to my son or daughter. It's meant that the Femme Reapers have to take a small break, but Ella isn't too concerned about that. She simply shrugged and said, "We don't have to release a CD every year, like *some* people used to."

The Dads are doing well, and the store is flourishing. A sign in the window, put up with my blessing, advertises that it's run by "the father of Radiation Canary's Karen Everett." Apparently we're still quite the draw, which shouldn't be surprising since the residuals keep rolling in. At least one television show or movie per month contacts us to use a song. Two months ago I saw a movie that used "Breakwaters" during a love scene with Olivia Childress. I may have assaulted Laura in the car after that one.

Mom and I are closer than ever, and I try to visit New York at least a few times a year. Mostly just to hear Mom's well-meaning concern. "Are you sure I can't pay for the ticket or Laura's ticket? I know-" and here her voice always drops to a whisper, "-that you're not working right now. And with a baby on the way..."

Oh, Mom.

At the gate, Michelle and Erin are still oohing and ahhing over the autograph, so they don't see us when we approach. I introduce them, and I think Michelle is going to have a heart attack on the spot. I leave them to fawn over her and go back to my seat.

I miss Radiation Canary. The long hours, the endless tours, the strain of thinking one day I'll simply lose my talent... the insensate dreams have stopped, and working on the new album keeps my songwriting muscles from atrophying. I miss seeing Lana, spotlight shining off the sweat on her face. I miss watching Nessa bend her knees and rock her head in time to the music, and God how I miss seeing Codie attack a drum set.

But I wouldn't trade what I have now just to have it back. I wouldn't ask them to give up their lives just so I could hold onto them and never let them go. But we left the fans wanting more. Every now and then there's a resurgence of Radiation Canary on Twitter, and I know that a reunion album would be a smash hit.

I reach up and massage my upper right arm through my shirt, imagining I can feel the tattoo through the cloth. I watch Laura sign autographs for Michelle and Erin, and I see the copy of *Vagabonds* with my name scrawled on it on Michelle's lap. Is there a possibility? Could Radiation Canary make a comeback? Anything's possible, but just in case...

Say a prayer. If you've got one.

END

Acknowledgements

I never wanted to write a book about a band, or even a single musician. I liked musicians just fine, but I didn't have the inspiration. Then one day one of my best friends (who is like a sister to me) introduced me to Brandi Carlile with the song "The Story." She tempted me into thinking about writing a story about a rock star. I agreed (because a writer can never turn down any inspiration, no matter how small. And let's face it, sometimes it's just easier to say yes to family) and then put the idea on a shelf in my mind palace that said "Erin's Rock Star Story." There it would have sat, unwritten and ignored and cobwebbed, except Erin frequently ended our conversations with "Hey, how's that rock star novel coming along?" I put her off, I listed all the other projects I was working on, I told her that the spirit was willing but the muse was weak. Soon, I told her. Someday. Then she did something completely unfair.

She went to Afghanistan.

I figured that if she was brave enough to do that, then the very absolute total least I could do was write a story for her. So I sat down and I began forming a band in my head. I got their name first, then I worked backwards. Who were these girls? How did they come together to form a band? What was their origin story? So I started writing and before I knew it, I not only had a novel, I had one of the biggest novels I'd ever written. When it was done, I couldn't stop touching it up and finding more stories to tell about these four women and the people in their lives. The resulting overflow will show up in an ancillary volume called "Radiation Canary: Bonus Tracks" (I'll keep you advised!)

When all was said and done, I ended up with not only a book I'm really proud of, it may be the book I'm proudest of. I hope I did justice to the characters and their stories, and I hope Erin likes it. I also hope she and Michelle enjoy their cameos in the "Overture" sections. Sure, it may be a bit presumptuous to write that they're fans before they've even read the book, but I don't think they'll mind too much.

The thank you not only goes to Erin, to whom this novel is rightfully dedicated, but it goes out to everyone who read it as it was being written. So also huge thanks to Amanda Q, Chris, Debbie, Heidi for giving me one of my favorite book covers yet, the person who wanted to be acknowledged with the phrase "Banana is a funny word" (because some of my readers are obviously insane people), KC Connor, Morning_Dew (at Archive of Our Own), Patrick... to these people I say THANK YOU! You're my cheerleaders, my eagle-eye error finders (and if any remain, the fault lies solely on me), my Greek chorus of support who got me through the rough patches and you always get me to the final page. Maybe I could have done it without you, but I don't want to test that theory any time in the future.

Another special mention goes to Jack Orman and his website AMZFX and its list of band names, which provided the name of the Cowan sisters' band, Femme Reapers. If you need a band name, if no one else can help you, and if you can find him (actually that part's easy; the site is at http://www.muzique.com/band.htm), maybe you too can choose a band name like Zombabies or Porn Queens of the Bible Belt.

RADIATION CANARY
DISCOGRAPHY & LYRICS

ACTION AFTER WARNINGS - 2005

Mutually Assured
One in Ten
Carry On
Mushroom Cloud
The Importance of Your Radio
My Weak Hand
The Exclusion Zone
Duck and Cover
Survivors
Fallout
All Clear
The Day After
The Question
Bonus track: Emerald (Seattle Song)

ROME BURNING - 2006

Forgotten Lore
Sancho Panza
There Were Badgers Here
The Man of Many Wiles
Scene of the Crime
Complications
Say a Prayer (If You've Got One)
Mountain Time
Land Among the Stars
Icarus
Band of Girls

THE MIDDLE DISTANCE - 2008

Away from Shore
Simply Messing About In Boats
Passenger
Howl at the Moon
Diving for Pearls
Kelly Green
The Next Ferry
Breakwaters
Improve the Silence (*instrumental*)
Wet Coast
Monstrous Regiment
Neither Nor

THE INTERVENTION - 2009

Without a Fight
Funeral Clown
Hand Me Down
Teary and Torn
Save Yourself
Pointless Cacophony
Your Enemy
Letting Go
Fist-Shaped Windows
The Long Night
Thank Me Later

AMNESIA BETWEEN SLEEPING AND AWAKING - 2011

(Album dedication: To Dash, who made it all possible. We miss you already)
Top of the World
Plea Bargain
No Limits but the Sky
Static
Hypermnesia
The Blackout's Lullaby
Don't Let Me Sleep Too Long
Where I Am
Falling Up
Tall Tales
Holding My Breath
Look at the Time

VANCOUVER TO MOSCOW
(Live with the Washington State Orchestra) - 2012

Overture
The Next Ferry
Emerald (Seattle Song)
Ship in a Bottle (Dash Warren cover)
There Were Badgers Here
Seven Hours to Moscow
The Importance of Your Radio
Scene of the Crime
Icarus
More Rain in Rainier
Diving for Pearls
Wet Coast
My Walla Walla Sweetheart
Hypermnesia
Top of the World
No Limits but the Sky
(encore)
Viva la Vida (Coldplay cover)
Say a Prayer (If You've Got One)
Curtain Call

VAGABONDS & RAGAMUFFINS - 2012

(Lana as Dorothy, Karen as Tesla, Codie as Harriet, Nessa as Sally)
When She Was Bad - Dorothy Parker
Minding Doves - Nikola Tesla
The Shape of the World - Buckminster Fuller
Speak Now - Sojourner Truth
Enigma - Alan Turing
Doing Everything She Shouldn't Do - Harriet Quimby
Secrets Laid Bare - Nellie Bly
Straight On 'Til Morning - Sally Ride
Ends of the Earth - Barbara Hillary
Waifs and Strays

FALLOUT - 2013

Clap if You Believe
Prodigals
Weaker Sex
Switch
Count to 1 Million
The Girl on the Wall
Clear Air
Better Half
Other Girls Aren't Like Me
Tandem Fall
Escaping the Light Pollution
Reset
The Answer
Bonus track: One More Last Time

ONE IN TEN
It's so comforting to hear 'nine times out of ten'
Nothing goes wrong and everybody wins
But it's never brought to your attention
Someone's bound to be the exception.

CARRY ON
Walking into the wind makes you strong
And I'm going to fight when I think you're wrong
I'm not going to miss you when you're gone
Baby, I'm going to carry on, carry on,
I'm going to carry on.

THE IMPORTANCE OF YOUR RADIO
Reaching out for you, trying to be heard
Gonna raise my voice, no one hears a word
I'm out here shouting into space, sound in a vacuum
Flip a switch, turn the dial, bring me into your room
Gonna make it something simple, easy to follow
I'm going to tell you the importance of your radio.
The worst things happen in silence
Quiet makes you think you're just alone
Drown out the absence
You've always known
We'll stay up with you until dawn's glow
Never forget the importance of your radio.

MY WEAK HAND
I've built up my strength like building a wall
And I get right back up every time I fall
But when I'm with you, I have no idea where I stand
Talking to you is like fighting with my weak hand.

DUCK AND COVER
I think you mean it when you end calls with 'love'
But lying in bed alone and staring at my clock
I don't think it matters to you when push comes to shove
Now I think you say it just to hear yourself talk.
I don't say I love you just to hear it back
Love is something declared like a statement of fact
But if you're only saying it to feel like a lover
Baby, I got news... you better duck and cover.

SURVIVORS
I'll rise up, I won't let you keep me down
I won't keep my face to this shattered ground
While the hot wind keeps blowing debris around
When everything else in this world gets unsure
I'll get back on my feet with the other survivors.

THE DAY AFTER
Hold onto this moment, don't let it go,
Nothing is certain, what's next I don't know.
Don't look back at the disaster
Try to see what happens the day after.

THE QUESTION
I don't have any of the answers you want
Only the same questions no one asks
We all put on a decent front
But we're wearing the same masks.

EMERALD (SEATTLE SONG)
Auntie Em said it was just a dream
Oz wasn't magic as it seemed
It wasn't really real, they all say
Well sorry, Dorothy, Auntie lied
Sit down here by my side
I'll take you to the Emerald City by the bay
There's no Tin Man in these woods
But we've got something just as good
You can see it all from the streetcar
The Space Needle's as high as you can go
The Underground shows the secrets below
And the monorail cuts through a giant smashed guitar
New York's an apple, that quickly gets rotten
Philly's Brotherly Love is too often forgotten
Chicago's got wind, Vegas is full of sin
These cities are gorgeous for a day or so
But their glory fades, and I'll always know
I only have one true home in this wide world
Because my city's an emerald
The sky may be grey but the ground is green
Most beautiful harbors I've ever seen
Cradled by mountains and touched by scaspray
Glinda, don't take my ruby slippers away
I don't want to go back to the gray
Over the rainbow is where I'm meant to stay
I want to trade rainmakers for wizards
It's not just some story I heard
Once in a lullaby your auntie used to tell
The Emerald City is real, and I call it home
It's the greatest city I've ever known
Keep your Kansas, we'll take Seattle
New York's an apple, that quickly gets rotten
Philly's Brotherly Love is too often forgotten
Chicago's got wind, Vegas is full of sin
These cities are gorgeous for a day or so
But their glory fades, and I'll always know
I only have one true home in this wide world
Because my city's an emerald

SCENE OF THE CRIME

If I didn't have her, I'd still have my hand.
Not as much fun, but at least I'd know where I stand.
But her heart's pounding in her breast,
And as I slide my hands under her dress,
I know I'd sin again in exchange for her caress.
Her curves take you by surprise, like a dangerous road
She'll make your heart beat faster, you just gotta grab hold.
Her lips shine like peppers but they burn hotter
She's slippery when wet, she's Aphrodite's daughter
You're her willing accomplice
You go along every time
Then she leaves you
Standing helpless
At the scene of the crime.

SANCHO PANZA

I'll make your windmills mine
Together we'll walk the line
Between madness and reality
We'll conquer all the knights we see
We'll never wake from this impossible dream
Take me with you when you go
I'll call you Don if you call me Sancho.

COMPLICATIONS

It's the complications that make life interesting
The little moments that delight and the moments that sting
When the dark clouds roll in and block out your sun
Remember the world's not ending; it's just a complication.

SAY A PRAYER (IF YOU'VE GOT ONE)
I need your help tonight
Alone, I can't win this fight
I tried to call
But I couldn't find the right words
I'm going to fall
And I'm so sick of being tired.
So say a prayer if you've got one
I'm starting to come undone
I've got demons I can't outrun
Please say a prayer if you have one.
I won't count the eight times I get knocked down
Just the nine times I get off the ground
I'm only so strong when I'm alone
I've done as much as I can on my own
If anyone's out there, if anyone cares
If you have one, please say a prayer.
Yes, say a prayer if you've got one
I'm starting to come undone
I've got demons I can't outrun
Please say a prayer if you have one.
If anyone is there, if anybody cares
If you hear my plea, I need you to save me
Say a prayer
Say a prayer.

BAND OF GIRLS
We're so nice and innocent and sweet
We always curtsey to gentlemen we meet
Yes sir, we're innocent and polite
Thank you, ma'am, never think we might
Mess up our hair, get out of sorts
Get our face dirty, tear up our skirts
If you think we might just be a band of girls
It's the nice ones you gotta watch out for.

PASSENGER
The city sleeps, but it snores
I need to get someplace a little more
Silent, you need to get someplace
Where you can feel the sun on your face
So put your head against the window
We'll be there before you know
Trust me to get you there
Tonight you're my passenger.

KELLY GREEN
I'm hypnotized by the rhythm of your breathing,
It rolls in and out like waves on the sea

THE NEXT FERRY
The next ferry is waiting at the dock
It's not going to wait forever
And baby you gotta be on it.

WET COAST
The sky opens up and spills its rain on me
Close my eyes, I breathe in and smell the sea
No matter which way the wind blows
I'm only at home here on the wet coast.

MONSTROUS REGIMENT
The clouds cleared out and took with them the light
And the points of the crescent moon look wickedly sharp tonight
You sent back the letters I sent, you didn't care what I meant
I'm on my way to make you listen, you don't want to know what happens when
You're face to face with a monstrous regiment... of women.

FUNERAL CLOWN
You make a lot of noise and you dance all around
But for all your sound and fury you're just my funeral clown.

YOUR ENEMY
Can't take this give and take
I know tonight I'll just lie awake
And play it all over again in my mind
God, why can't we just be kind?
All our endless conversations were never heard
I can't believe you have me at a loss for words
We only want to open your eyes and make you see
No one here is your enemy.

HYPERMNESIA
I don't want to go to sleep
'Cause I know what's waiting for me
The difference is so easy to make
I don't want to watch that scene
I want the amnesia between
Being asleep and being awake.
Here's where I bled for you,
Where I would have died for you
Here's where I put it all on the line
And traded for your life with mine.
The house shakes with thunder like a shotgun
I know I said 'say a prayer,' but right now I don't have one
I take a second and let myself forget
Pretending it hasn't happened yet
Lightning flashes when the thunder is still shaking
And I'm clinging to the amnesia I get just after waking.

SEVEN HOURS TO MOSCOW

You say you'll never speak to me again, except I'm your ride
So you settle like a martyr on my car's passenger side
You stare out your window at Oregon on the other side of the river
We've got seven hours to get to Moscow from Vancouver
And I've got seven hours to change your mind
Three hundred sixty miles to Idaho
You don't like the shit on my radio
The Cascades are looking oh, so pretty
But you'd have to look past me to see
And I've still got seven hours to let you know
To tell you I'm sorry, to tell you I'm trying to change
To tell you I'm a fool, I'll stop acting strange
You're all I want, the only thing I need
And I've got seven hours to make you see.
You laugh at my joke when we stop in Kennewick
At that diner that reminds you of the place we both got sick
Our history is stronger than your hurt
And stronger than my stupid words
I still have three hours to make that stick.

MINDING DOVES

The old man in room 3327, an odd quiet recluse
They can't take more from him, he's got nothing left to lose
Everything he made to advance human-kind
It made them millions, now he's left with doves to mind.

THE GIRL ON THE WALL

She's filling the pages of her book
With all the words she doesn't know how to say
All the times I never gave her a second look
She just sat silently and listened to us play.
I didn't have a voice until I found it in her pages
And now I'm singing to the world, standing on its stages
She gave me a voice, and let me share it with you all
I'm only standing here tonight 'cause of the girl on the wall.
There was a girl on the wall
Quiet and shy
She gave us her all
Gave us wings to fly
And we will never fall
Because we met the girl on the wall.
The girl on the wall made us canaries
And set me free so you could hear me sing
Every time the world brought me to my knees
She came down, took me under her wing
And with a word she calmed my wildest seas.
There was a girl on the wall
Until we took her down
And this song is so small
But I hope that now
She knows that we love her
And we'll never get over
How lucky we are to know
The girl on the wall.

ONE MORE LAST TIME
When our nights were darkest
And the heavy clouds hid the sun
Through the times that were hardest
You were always the one
You made me smile in times of strife
When I was sure my words weren't worth a dime
You were the ones who provided light and gave me life
So now I want to thank you, one more last time.

About the Author

Geonn Cannon was born on the fortieth anniversary of the attack on Pearl Harbor. He writes to get the ideas out of his head so he won't mumble to himself in public (which he already does a little more than is socially acceptable). He currently lives in Yukon, Oklahoma, although his mind is still stuck in Washington state. If you see it wandering around the shoreline, just make sure it's warm and comfortable and leave it be.

www.ingramcontent.com/pod-product-compliance
Lightning Source LLC
Chambersburg PA
CBHW060601310726
48982CB00008B/1191/J

* 9 7 8 1 9 3 8 1 0 8 3 0 3 *